READERS ALSO LOVE BRYAN'S DRAGONS IN OUR MIDST SERIES

As parents of boys who are avid readers, my wife and I struggled to find reading material that fed their appetite while reinforcing the virtues we value. Bryan Davis is a good man and a great storyteller. And this series is an all-time favorite my sons still speak of, even now into their college years!
MARK T. HANCOCK, HUSBAND AND FATHER, CEO OF TRAIL LIFE USA

One of the best blends of contemporary fantasy and allegory that I have read, Dragons in Our Midst will have you hurting and rooting for Billy and Bonnie. If you love fantasy, King Arthur, and hopeful adventures, this is the story for you.
SCOTT APPLETON, AUTHOR OF THE SWORD OF THE DRAGON SERIES AND THE NEVERQUEEN SAGA

It all started with a boy who could breathe fire and a girl who had wings. Dragons in Our Midst invites readers to lift up their swords and join Billy Bannister and Bonnie Silver as they battle dragon slayers, uncover ancient legends, and—of course—come face to face with dragons. Bryan Davis delivers a clean, complex series that challenges and uplifts its readers. When I was a teenager, Billy and Bonnie's story captured my own heart and imagination. And today, its poignant messages of faith, sacrifice, and courage endure and stand ready to inspire the next generation of young readers.
JESSICA SLY, AUTHOR OF *THE PROMISE OF DECEPTION*

WHAT READERS ARE SAYING

Raising Dragons is an excellent start to a thrilling, inspiring, and faith-building series. Bryan Davis's unique meshing of legends, myths, and truth is incredibly creative. Together with his strong storytelling and thought-provoking themes it makes for an unforgettable ride. Bryan Davis's books exceed any others in the genre for thematic depth and yet are just as gripping and exciting story-wise as other books of the genre (or even more so). Bryan Davis is my favorite author, and I hope he will become yours too when you dive into the fascinating world of dragons and slayers, of light and darkness, and of truth and deception in *Raising Dragons*.
JOSEPH B., AGE 17

If you love fantasy, you NEED this book! You won't be able to put it down! If you love dragons, you'll love this book! Dragons aren't just portrayed as big bad beasties, as in other books—they're actually heroes! Are you a Christian who wants a deeper relationship with God? This book models that too! Are you seeking God, but always afraid of committing? This book models what true faith looks like and shows that you can love and trust God through everything!
NICK B.

Absolutely brilliant. This is not your typical dungeons and dragons book. Even at 28 I find this book/series addicting. Mr. Davis combines faith and fantasy flawlessly. There are books about King Arthur, Merlin, and dragons aplenty, but to find one whose story line spans centuries and also teaches modern Christian values, that is rare. Mr. Davis includes many unexpected twists and turns and a story line so unique it simply cannot be rivaled. *Raising Dragons* is guaranteed to pique the interest of readers of all ages.
LORI W., AGE 28

Bryan Davis tells a terrific tale teeming with perilous predicaments, fascinating fantasy features, and likeable, charismatic characters who grow in their faith. The engaging writing style captivates the mind and the Christian themes captivate the heart. This epic novel is a superb start to a sensational series.
SHANNON, AGE 24

When I first picked up this book, I didn't know what to expect. By the time I finished the first chapter, I couldn't put it down! I love the way Bryan Davis mixes dragons and faith. It is a very touching experience.
ANNABETH, AGE 13

Bryan has a natural flow in his writing that make his characters come to life through his in-depth description of each character and the way the narrative evolves. I would heartily recommend this book to any fan of the genre regardless of age as the book has a broad appeal to all ages and all walks of life.
JOHN B., AGE 59

I recently reread the Dragons in Our Midst series and fell in love all over again, probably even more so than the first time. Bryan Davis's writing really makes the story and characters come alive. The Dragons in Our Midst series is a fresh take on the fantasy adventure genre, mixing dragons, knights, and the Arthurian legend with modern day. Even a reread makes you want to keep coming back for more.
MADI T., AGE 20

Mr. Davis's work *Raising Dragons* and the two series that follow are some of the best Christian fantasy I have ever read. They are the perfect example of an author's work that challenges his readers to learn and grow. He also has a great way of leading his readers to Christ and to become more mature Christians. The series is great fun to read, no matter your age.
JEREMY D.

Books by Bryan Davis

The Astral Alliance Series

Across Astral Realms
The First Starborn
At the Speed of Mind

Dragons in our Midst

Raising Dragons
The Candlestone
Circles of Seven
Tears of a Dragon

Oracles of Fire

Eye of the Oracle
Enoch's Ghost
Last of the Nephilim
The Bones of Makaidos

Children of the Bard

Song of the Ovulum
From the Mouth of Elijah
The Seventh Door
Omega Dragon

Dragons of Starlight

Starlighter
Warrior
Diviner
Liberator

Tales of Starlight

Masters & Slayers
Third Starlighter
Exodus Rising

The Reapers Trilogy

Reapers
Beyond the Gateway
Reaper Reborn

Time Echoes Trilogy

Time Echoes
Interfinity
Fatal Convergence

The Oculus Gate

Heaven Came Down
Invading Hell
My Soul to Take
On Earth as it is in Hell

Wanted: Superheroes

Wanted: A Superhero to Save the World
Hertz to Be a Hero
Antigravity Heroes

Standalone Novels

Let the Ghosts Speak
I Know Why the Angels Dance

**To learn more about Bryan's books, go to
www.daviscrossing.com**

BRYAN DAVIS

ASTRAL ALLIANCE

— BOOK THREE —

AT THE SPEED OF MIND

At the Speed of Mind
Volume 3 in the Astral Alliance series

Part 01

Delta Zero

Light flashed throughout our ship, the Nebula Nine. Sharp tingles buzzed through my body followed by numbness. Everything around me blurred in the radiance, and nothing moved, as if time itself had halted. Even Perdantus, perched on my shoulder, stayed perfectly motionless, not a feather out of place.

During those plodding seconds, a rush of thoughts flooded my mind. We had expected some kind of time shift when traveling from the Gamma Five Zeta station to its counterpart orbiting Delta Zero, so no surprise there. We also knew to be ready to zoom out of the arrival docking bay as soon as possible, not knowing who had control of the station, perhaps an enemy.

Then our mission came back to the forefront—learn where Omen had established glowsap mines on the jungle planet, forcing children to suffer through the dangerous slave labor. We had to set them free.

And maybe, just maybe, I could find my father. The dragon's eye ruby in my locket glowed, a sign that he was still alive, but I didn't know much else. After the Gamma Five station's transmission ray disintegrated him when he sacrificed himself to save me, I could only guess that it sent him to the Delta station, but, since he wasn't aboard a ship, I had no idea if the arrival process restored him.

After what seemed like a full minute but was probably only a few seconds, the light blinked off. The scene around us clarified. Our ship sat in a dimly lit docking bay, much like the bay we had left at Gamma Five. The reintegration gun mounted on the wall still pointed at the ship, no longer active since it had finished restoring us.

Perdantus fluffed his feathers and spoke in his chirping language. "That was a rather bizarre experience that I do not wish to repeat."

"I know exactly what you mean," I replied in Alpha One, my native language. I reached to my shoulder and ran a finger along his chest. "Let's hope it's all over."

Jillian, still seated in the copilot's chair directly to my left, looked out the front viewing window. Since she was my father's twin sister, I could always see his face in hers—the same high cheekbones and narrow chin that sketched that pensive expression, though her shoulder length auburn locks, pulled back into a ponytail, didn't match his short graying hair at all. "Far from over. The bay doors are closed. No zooming out of here until we can open them."

"How is that possible?" I asked. "Don't the doors have to be open for transport?"

"Maybe it closed while we were sitting here getting our bearings. That's the normal arrival routine. The doors close, and air fills the bay. And we should switch to speaking Humaniversal. Nobody in the Delta system speaks Alpha One."

"Good point," I said in Humaniversal. "Emerson, any sign of life in this Zeta station?"

"Negative." Emerson, the ship's computer, always switched to whichever language we were speaking. "I am picking up encrypted transmissions as well as the warmth of machinery, but there are no life forms within my sensor range."

From the weapons seat behind me, Zoë spoke up. "The lasers are ready to fire if you see any hostiles. Maybe there aren't any carbon life forms, but we've seen robotic shooters before."

I swiveled in my chair to look at the rear of the ship's bridge. "Does anyone have a reading on breathable air?"

Crystal, sitting at the navigator's station across from Zoë, stared at her console screen, twirling her blonde locks with a finger, her pale face a stark contrast to Zoë's much darker skin. "Air is spewing in from somewhere, and it's pretty good stuff. Looks like nineteen percent oxygen. Not bad at all. In about twenty seconds, the pressure will be high enough to keep a human's skull from imploding."

"Then I can go out and look for a manual way to open the bay doors."

"No, Mophead," Jillian said. "That's a job for someone who hasn't had a near-death experience lately, and I think I'm the only one on board who qualifies."

Oliver, sitting at the physician's console, raised a hand. "I haven't nearly died lately." He grinned, his cheeks no longer pale and sunken like when I first met him at the iron works factory, and his dark brown hair neatly trimmed, unlike the rat's nest he wore as a slave.

"I need you and your healing powers to stay on board in case I get my hide perforated by some kind of ..." Jillian looked at Zoë. "What did you call it?"

"Robotic shooter," Zoë said.

"Right. A robotic shooter."

I touched one of my bracelets. "But it'd be much easier and safer for me. With just a flex of my muscles, I could charge my legs and jump to the ship before the doors open enough to suck the air out. And a spark of electricity from my hands might short out the mechanism and make the doors open. Or, even better, I could use one of my Starborn powers to move the latch with my mind. I probably couldn't do it from inside the ship, but maybe I wouldn't have to step off the ramp. Almost zero danger."

"Yeah, yeah," Jillian said in a mocking tone. "I'm the super-powerful Megan Willis who should do all the dangerous stuff because

I'm Starborn, and everyone should sit back and watch because they're not needed when I'm around." She blew through flapping lips. "Well, honey, I'm your aunt, and since my brother … your father … is missing, I'm in charge of your safety. You need to avoid swimming with sharks for a change and sit this one out."

I gazed at her sincere expression. She truly was worried about me. Although I was still the best option for the job, I could stand down. It probably wasn't all that dangerous for her to do it.

Crystal tapped on her screen. "The air's perfect now, and whatever was spewing it has stopped."

"Good." Jillian pressed the button to open the front ramp and rose from her chair. As the ramp lowered, she checked her belt. "I've got a spool line, a grappling hook, a knife, and a laser blaster. I think I'm set."

"Except for a pressurized suit," I said. "The moment you open the bay doors, the vacuum will suck all the air out."

"I knew that." Jillian winked. "Just checking to see if you're on your toes."

"Sure, Aunt Jillian. Thanks for the alertness check."

She walked to a cabinet at the side wall and withdrew a suit and air tank. As she put them on over her clothes, she looked at the ceiling. "Emerson, I'm sure you've done long and short range scans by now. Give us all the data you've got."

"As expected," Emerson said, "this Zeta station is in orbit around a planet that has a considerable amount of jungle-like vegetation growing on its surface in its equatorial regions. Those regions span much farther north and south than on Alpha One. Rivers and mountains abound, providing literally thousands of suitable places for bramble bee mines."

Remembering my flight over those dense jungles a short time ago, I pressed my lips together. "That's not good. We'll have too many places to search."

"As I said earlier," Emerson continued, "I detected transmissions. Although they are encrypted, I can pinpoint their sources, which should provide places to begin your search."

"How many sources do you detect?"

"At the moment, seven."

I sighed. "Could be worse, I guess. Better than thousands."

Jillian, now wearing a helmet, spoke into the suit's microphone, making her voice come through the ceiling speakers. "I'm ready."

I pointed out the open front ramp. "If this station's design is the same as the one at Gamma Five, you should find the handle on the left side of the left door panel."

"Gotcha." Jillian plodded down the hatch's ramp. "I'm going to latch my hook onto the ship's front ring, so if something goes wrong and you have to scoot, look for me dangling from there."

"Just don't let the vacuum jerk you loose."

Jillian turned left and walked out of sight. "Trust me, honey. I don't want to join Raven in the frigid rigid club. I'll be clinging to the spool line like a python to a pig."

"Well, nothing's going to go wrong. When the pressure stabilizes out there, just detach your line from the ring and walk up the ramp to the airlock chamber. Haven't you done a spacewalk before?"

"Enough times to know that something always goes wrong."

"Don't be such a pusillanimous pessimist."

Jillian huffed. "Oh. Good one. And I say to you, don't be such a supercilious sophist. You're not the only one who's opened a dictionary around here."

As I reached for the console, I sang, "I love you, Aunt Jillian. I'm closing the airlock barrier now." I pressed the button. The interior panel lowered from the ceiling. The moment Jillian opened the bay doors, we would need the airlock to protect us from the vacuum of space. I turned the camera to put her on the front viewing screen. Jillian reached her silvery gloved hands toward a gray horizontal latch handle at her eye level. "We're watching your progress."

"Here goes." Jillian set her feet and grabbed the latch. A loud click reverberated, and a light flashed, blinding us for a moment. When it cleared, Jillian was no longer on the screen. She had probably already rushed toward the ramp.

The door panels began sliding apart. As air rushed out through the growing gap, I engaged the engine. "Aunt Jillian, let me know as soon as you're on the ramp. I'll pull out at impulse speed when the opening's wide enough." I looked at Crystal. "Work with Emerson to plot a course to the closest transmission source."

"On it." Crystal studied her screen, her eyes narrowing. "Blazes! We're up to nine sources now. But I got a lock on the closest one. Looks like it won't take long to get there."

"Keep me posted." With the doors almost fully open, the Nebula Nine would have no trouble passing through the gap. Since Jillian was still out of the camera's view, I looked at the ceiling speakers. "Jillian, are you on the ramp?"

Only light static replied.

An icy chill ran along my spine. "Aunt Jillian? Are you there?"

Again the speakers emitted only static.

"Emerson! Check for life forms outside the ship and on the ramp."

"There are none," Emerson said.

I shot to my feet, making Perdantus flutter down to my console. "What? Where did she go?"

"My sensors indicate that she disappeared thirty-two seconds ago."

"Disappeared? How could that happen?"

"I will analyze the video for possibilities, but I need to interrupt the process to tell you that we are being hailed on an unsecured frequency. Shall I allow a connection?"

The cold chill spread across the rest of my body. I looked at my shipmates. Everyone stared at me wide-eyed, Crystal with her mouth hanging open. They were scared. So was I. But I had to stay strong. "Yes," I said firmly. "Patch it through."

When a click sounded from the speakers, I cleared my throat. "This is Captain Megan Willis of the Alliance ship Nebula Nine. Who is calling?"

The speakers emitted a calm male voice. "Well, Megan, it's good to finally talk with you. My name is Omen, and I have heard many interesting tales about you. The fame of your escapades has risen to mythic proportions."

I crossed my arms in front. "State your business, Omen."

"Very well. It seems that I will have to defer pleasantries until another time. As you know by now, you are missing a crew member."

My cheeks warmed. "You took Jillian?"

"I did. Since I have control of the Zeta technology, it wasn't a difficult task. But have no fear. She is safe … for now."

I breathed a silent sigh of relief. "What do you want?"

"Simple. I want you to leave."

"Why? Are we bothering you?"

"Not yet, but I know you plan to disrupt my business."

"What makes you think that?"

Omen shifted to a sarcastic tone. "Oh, maybe it's the fact that you killed Thorne and ruined his business. You also killed Admiral Fairbanks and burned his ship. And to top it all off, you murdered Camille and Raven and buried their training camp. That's a lot of destruction for a girl your age."

I smirked. "I guess news travels fast."

"It does when I have spies who are loyal to me. Money loosens many lips. And I have plenty of money."

"Money earned from the labors of slave children."

"Spare me the morality drama, Megan. I simply don't care who gets hurt, even children. They're just beasts of burden to me."

My rage burned. Curses stormed through my mind, but I kept them in check. "If I leave, how do I get Jillian back?"

"I will send her to another bay that has a ship in port, and from there, I will transport her to the Gamma Five Zeta station. Once you are all gone, I will lock down this Zeta to keep you from returning."

I ached to ask if he knew where my father was, but it would be better to stay quiet in case he was on the planet and Omen didn't know about it. "Prove to me that Jillian is still alive."

"I will send a live video stream. Prepare to display it and send me a live feed of your bridge. That's the only way I'll let you see Jillian."

When I reached for the control that would send the bridge camera's feed to him, I paused. Why was he so insistent about seeing our bridge? Maybe if I left the outgoing video feed off to get his reaction, I could figure it out.

I switched the front screen to accept the incoming feed. A man appeared—dark hair, three-day beard growth, piercing eyes, maybe thirty years old. In any other context, I would have considered him handsome, but now he looked like a devil.

He smiled. "Ah, there you are, exactly as I pictured you—strong, self-assured to the point of cockiness, and—"

"Cut the crap!" Crystal shouted. "Show us Jillian!"

Omen chuckled. "Very well."

As the camera view shifted to one side, I squinted at the scene. How could Omen have reacted to seeing me? I didn't send our camera feed through the connection. Did he somehow have a way to get the feed without me allowing it?

The incoming feed's camera stopped panning, putting Jillian in the center. Still wearing the pressure suit, she carried the helmet under her arm, her expression looking as angry as a hundred hornets. She glared at Omen. "So, what do you want me to say, you ghastly ghoul?"

"You have said enough." The camera shifted back to Omen. "As you might imagine, Jillian would attack me if she could, but I have three armed guards watching her every move. She is helpless."

Jillian called from offscreen, "Megan, don't leave. You need to stop this madman, no matter what happens to me."

Omen nodded toward someone. "Silence her, but not permanently. I still need her." A sizzling noise buzzed through the speaker.

I winced. Poor Jillian! How could I leave knowing she was suffering like that? And how could I trust Omen to keep his word to send her back to Gamma Five? If I were to go and if he were to shut the Zeta station down, I wouldn't be able to return to check on her.

Omen furrowed his brow. "You're plotting something, Megan. I can see it in your eyes. Whatever your plan is, it won't work. I have already initiated the countdown to send your ship back to Gamma Five. Obviously, you can depart from the bay if you choose, but then I will kill Jillian myself the next moment. If your ship stays where it is, I will send it to Gamma Five and then proceed to also send Jillian back to you. You have two minutes to decide."

"Two minutes." I closed the transmission channel and looked again at my shipmates. "Thoughts? Hit me fast and hard. No holding back."

"We should leave," Crystal said, "and figure out how to come back the normal way. Emerson already pinpointed where we are in space."

"How long will that take in a wormhole?" I asked.

"Only Emerson could calculate that."

I looked at the ceiling. "Emerson?"

"It depends on a multitude of unknown factors, but I would say approximately eight weeks."

"Eight weeks! By then, the time shift could be enormous again."

"That is one of the unknown factors. After eight weeks, many years could pass by here, and I don't know where the time shift begins in the space continuum."

"So, basically, it'll be forever till we can return."

Oliver raised a hand. "We have five one-person space gliders on the ship. Plenty for the four of us."

"Good idea. Perdantus, you're with me." When he flew to my shoulder, I hurried to the cabinet and grabbed a pressurized suit, a laser blaster, a sheathed knife, and a belt for the blaster and knife. "Everyone get a suit and a weapon, then on my six."

"I don't have a suit," Perdantus said. "Only my feathers."

"That's your birthday suit. The suit you were born in. Good enough for me." As I jogged toward the ladder with the others trailing, I called out, "Emerson, how much time do we have left?"

"One minute, five seconds."

"Put a note in your permanent storage to leave behind for Lyric. Tell her what's happening here."

"Acknowledged."

"Can you transfer yourself to my glider?" I asked. "I want to take you with me."

"Affirmative, but the computer on that vessel is not as equipped as the one on board the Nebula Nine. My functionality will be more limited."

"Better to have part of you than none of you." I grabbed both sides of the ladder and slid down to the lowest level, forcing Perdantus to flutter alongside.

When my feet hit the floor, he flew ahead. "Will I have to ride in your helmet again?" he asked.

I jogged toward the glider bay. "No. The suits are a precaution. You can perch on my leg if you're more comfortable that way."

"Definitely."

When we arrived, we hurriedly put our suits on with the weapons attached to our external belts, though we left our helmets off. We climbed into the gliders, me in the command craft with Perdantus on my knee, my helmet at my side. The moment I closed the glass shield over me, I pressed the button that opened the glider bay door. "Everyone follow me."

I flew the glider from the room, then out of the arrival bay. I pivoted the glider and looked back at the Zeta station. Once the other gliders had joined mine in a row, I toggled the communications port to speak through the channel to Omen. "We decided to stay put where we are. Send the Nebula Nine back to Gamma Five."

Omen's voice came through my glider's console. "Wise choice."

In the Zeta station's arrival bay, light shot from a disintegration gun and bathed the Nebula Nine in glimmering light. Within seconds, she was gone, and the light faded.

I switched the comm link to a group channel. "Can everyone hear me?"

"Loud and clear," Oliver said.

"Yup," Crystal added.

Zoë chimed in. "Wall to wall, Sister."

"Crystal," I said, "Do you happen to remember the coordinates of the closest source?"

"I fed them to Emerson. I think he's got you covered."

"Emerson? Are you aboard?"

His voice emanated from the console speaker. "I am here, but I feel like I've lost most of my mind. Still, I do have all nine sets of coordinates. I am putting them in this glider's navigation system now."

A vector map appeared on my screen. "Got it. Everyone follow me."

I turned my glider in the direction of the planet and pushed the throttle. We zoomed single-file toward an area of green vegetation near the equator.

"We will arrive in two minutes, seven seconds," Emerson said. "Because of the inferior abilities of this craft, I don't have a way to scan the surface for detection devices. We could be discovered."

"We'll have to chance it." I glanced at Perdantus, perched on my knee, his claws embedded in the material. "Any thoughts, my friend?"

He fluttered to my shoulder and gazed behind us. "I am concerned about Jillian. In our hurry, you were not able to ask Crystal if Omen was telling the truth. In fact, you have not checked to see if you have the lie-detecting ability yourself. In theory, you should have all of the Starborn powers."

"Good point. I should've done that." I spoke toward the console's microphone. "Crystal, did you get a read on Omen? Was he telling the truth?"

"Funny you should ask. I couldn't read him at all. I was wondering if my power's on the fritz."

"Wait a second." I pulled the thin chain around my neck and set the attached locket on my palm. Unable to detect any glow, I pressed my thumb on the locket's tiny back panel. When it popped open, the ruby's light told me again that my father was still alive, but its glow was usually more vibrant than this, especially when I used my Starborn powers. Maybe they weren't working here for some reason. "Perdantus, you warned me about this possibility. I don't think I have any powers. How did you know?"

"It was merely a guess. Since Omen enslaved children who might be Starborn, he had to realize that their gifts could be his undoing. I wonder if he has some way to neutralize their powers."

"Like Raven did. She was able to radiate negative energy."

"Yes, but Omen seems to be able to do it on a larger scale. From a distance, so it seems."

"Maybe a device on the planet's surface broadcasts a disabling signal, or maybe he has a disabling device on the Zeta. Or both."

"Before you ask," Emerson said, "I am unable to scan for such a signal. The scanner on this craft has a range that spans only the usual Alliance frequencies."

"Understood, Emerson. Thank you." Now that we were closing in on the surface, I studied the treetops—green and dense with hardly any gaps in the foliage. "When I was talking to Omen, did you pick up the location where his signal was coming from?"

"Affirmative. There was an odd delay, as if the signal had been relayed from somewhere else. In any case, the source point is not the same as our current destination, but it is relatively close. This glider could arrive there in about twenty minutes."

"Maybe it's better to check out the one we're heading to first. Wherever Omen is, he's likely to have more defenses. Better to keep away from danger for the time being."

"Acknowledged."

Now gliding above the treetops, I spotted a break in the canopy and dove through it. As I descended toward the forest floor, the thrusters underneath the craft blew leafy debris all around until I settled. Soon, the other three gliders joined mine, barely fitting in the gap among the tree trunks.

"Secure your gliders," I called as I recoded my own glider's security on the console. "New codes, just to be safe. You can tell each other your codes, but no one else. And put your earbuds in."

Knowing from my previous visit that the air quality here was good, I opened my glass shield. Perdantus flew out and perched on the glider's front edge. "The odors are interesting. A blend of holly berries and …" He took a long sniff, then sneezed. "Glowsap. It almost always makes me sneeze, as do quite a number of other smells."

"Glowsap?" I climbed out of the glider and began taking my suit off, switching the weapons belt to my uniform. "Can you track it?"

"Not yet. I'll have to fly around to see where the odor is most concentrated." He flew upward and began flitting from branch to branch.

Oliver, Crystal, and Zoë joined me, all wearing only their normal Alliance uniforms with their blasters on their belts. "I saw zoa trees like we had on Delta Ninety-eight," Oliver said. "If they run the mine like we did, they'll also need a water source."

Crystal crossed her arms in front. "I don't think any stream around here will have the kind of clay we used. This place is way more tropical. They might make the containers somewhere else and transport them here."

I think I located the source of the glowsap aroma," Perdantus called from a high limb. "Follow me."

"Wait," I said, raising a hand. "Comm check. Oliver?"

He touched his ear. "Yep. I hear you."

"Zoë?"

"Coming through."

"Crystal."

"Not yet." Crystal tapped her ear bud. "Try again."

"Crystal?"

"There you are. Your voice is a little frosty, though."

"Frosty?"

She nodded. "Yeah. Frosty."

"Whatever." I waved at Perdantus. "Lead the way."

He flitted to another limb. "This direction."

I laid my suit in my glider, closed the glass dome, and followed, the others close behind. The dense forest forced us to dodge trees, duck under hanging vines, and step over protruding roots, all the while listening for Perdantus's chirps of "Over here" and "Now turn left" and "Now turn right."

After a few minutes, we arrived at a bigger clearing next to an arched cave entrance. A low buzzing noise emanated from deep within, as if the cave were whispering.

Crystal sidled close and spoke quietly. "Bramble bees."

Oliver nodded. "Definitely bramble bees."

Perdantus landed on my shoulder. "And the odor of glowsap is strong."

Human chatter blended into the buzzing noise, drawing closer. I waved for everyone to fall back. We each chose a tree to conceal ourselves as we watched.

Soon, a person walked out of the cave, short enough to be an older child or a young teen. Wearing a red armored suit and helmet, somewhat thicker than the ones we wore at Thorne's mine, he or she carried a small clay jar in gloved hands, glowsap dripping over the rim.

The worker set the jar down and removed the helmet, revealing a girl with brown locks that fell to her shoulders. About fourteen years old with copper-colored skin that dripped with sweat, she blew out a sigh. "Another day without dying," she said in Humaniversal.

A boy about the same age with shorter hair and similarly colored skin, followed, his helmet tucked under an arm and his own glowsap jar just as full. Sweat trickled down his face as well. "Yep. Call it in."

The girl snapped a radio from her belt, pressed a button on the side, and spoke into it. "This is Kattica. Scamp and I have twenty jars ready for pickup."

While she waited for a response, they stripped their armor off, revealing shorts and T-shirts. I whispered, knowing that the sensitive earbud would pick up my voice. "These two are bigger than any kids at Thorne's mine."

"Yeah," Crystal said. "I wonder how they managed to climb through the hole in the bees' netting."

"And their jars," Oliver added, "look like they're made of the clay we got from the river, but I don't see a source for that kind of clay anywhere."

A voice crackled through Kattica's radio. "Only twenty?"

Kattica rolled her eyes and pressed the button again. "This mine isn't producing like it used to. We can't get thirty in a day anymore. We barely managed twenty."

"Quota is thirty. You'll be penalized."

She let out a huff. "If you don't believe me, go in there yourself. You'll see. The hive is moving on. We need to figure out where they're going and start a new mine there."

"Duly noted. I'll see what I can do about the penalty. Pickup in ten minutes."

Kattica reattached the radio to her belt and looked at Scamp. "That moron has no clue."

"Or a brain." Scamp brushed a sleeve across his forehead. "Let's just hope Omen doesn't find out."

I whispered, "Perdantus, you're with me. Everyone else stay hidden." After withdrawing my blaster and setting it on the ground, I walked toward them with both of my hands raised. "Hello," I said in Humaniversal. "Don't be scared. I'm a friend."

Kattica and Scamp stared at me, wide eyed. "Who are you?" Scamp asked.

"Megan Willis, Captain of an Alliance star cruiser called the Nebula Nine."

Kattica grinned. "Sure. And I'm Admiral Fairbanks, head of the entire Alliance fleet."

"I'm the Astral Dragon," Scamp said. "This is a fun game."

Kattica narrowed her eyes in a skeptical way. "You're new. Which mine did they assign you to? And where did you get that ridiculous uniform?"

"And what's with the bird on your shoulder?" Scamp asked. "Is it a mechanical drone?"

"The bird is a friend of mine, and he's real." I lowered my hands. Obviously they wouldn't believe who I was, so I had to change tactics on the fly. "I don't have an assignment yet. I'm kind of lost, and I need to find headquarters."

"Headquarters?" Kattica repeated. "You mean base camp?"

"I guess so. The labels are new to me."

Kattica's skeptical stare deepened. "Are you saying the transport captain just dropped you off here and expected you to figure out where you're supposed to go? And why so late in the day? It's quitting time."

I shrugged. "I have no idea what he was thinking. I'm just trying to figure everything out."

"Don't be so mean," Scamp said to Kattica. "Look at her. She's obviously as green as a jackfruit. Clueless. Give her a break."

Kattica sighed. "You're right." Her expression softened as she looked at me again, her hand extended. "I'm Kattica. What's your real name?"

I shook her hand. "My name is Megan. Really."

"Ah. No wonder you pretended to be Megan Willis. Trying to intimidate us."

Scamp shook my hand as well. "I'm Theodore, but everyone calls me Scamp."

I smiled. "Pleased to meet you, Scamp."

Kattica spoke in a mocking tone. "Pleased to meet you, Scamp." Then she laughed. "This girl's got manners, not like the nose pickers you usually fall in love with."

Scamp rolled his eyes. "Don't mind her. She's just grouchy because we didn't make quota today."

"Yeah. I heard her talking on the radio." I lifted one of the armored suits. "This is a better design than what I had to wear in the last bee cave I harvested. Whenever I bent over, the protective plates would separate and make a gap."

"True, but with this suit, you basically can't bend at all. Tough to walk around, but pretty safe. I'll take uncomfortable over getting stung any day." He gave me a quizzical look. "So you've mined glowsap before, but how much training did you get with our methods before they sent you here?"

I nodded toward the cave. "I worked a mine on Delta Ninety-eight that looked a lot like this one, but you're both bigger than any of the kids we had. How do you fit through the hole in the netting?"

Scamp glanced at Kattica. "Can I tell her?"

She crossed her arms. "You're dying to say it. Go ahead. Tell her."

Scamp smiled. "When Kattica and I came here three years ago, we were a lot smaller, so—"

"Wait," I said. "You came here at the same time?"

Scamp nodded. "She's my sister. One year older. Anyway, we had no trouble getting through the netting the bees knit, but as we got older, it got harder, so I wanted to figure out a way we could still work the mine as we grew. I was able to cut off a piece of the netting, and I tried a bunch of mixtures from the plants around here to see if I could get it to dissolve without upsetting the bees."

"Because," Kattica added, "they would just repair whatever hole you make."

"Right. So I came up with a formula that softens the netting so we can stretch it. After we go through, it snaps back to the way it was, and the bees don't care."

"That's genius," I said. "Good job."

While Scamp smiled, Kattica shoved his shoulder. "That's what you were waiting for, right? A compliment from a pretty girl."

My cheeks warmed. It was time to change the subject. "Well … um … I guess your ride's going to be here soon."

"*Our* ride, you mean," Kattica said. "If they dropped you off here to work the mine, you should go back with us. There won't be any other shuttles to the base camp today."

"And you don't want to be out at night," Scamp added. "Not with the bats that fly around here. One bite, and you're dead."

Kattica waved a hand toward the sky. "And the thunderstorms that come just before sunset. They can be wicked. Besides, they might shut down this mine and transfer us to a more productive one. No use staying around here."

"That makes sense." I looked at the two in turn. "Can you keep a secret?"

"Of course." Kattica set her hands on her hips in a cocky stance. "We sap collectors are like family. We watch out for each other."

Scamp laid an arm over her shoulder. "And we don't rat on each other."

"Then here's the deal." I waved toward the trees where my crew hid. "Come on out everyone."

When Oliver, Crystal, and Zoë joined me, Kattica's and Scamp's eyes widened. "Who are you?" Kattica asked.

I stood as tall as I could manage. "Like I told you before, I am Megan Willis, captain of the Alliance starship Nebula Nine. I've come here to destroy the bramble bee mines and set all of the slaves free."

It felt great to state my mission in such a straightforward manner, and I was hoping these two kids would be excited, but they just looked at each other and shrugged before turning toward me again. "We're not slaves," Kattica said. "We're paid employees."

"And we're paid well." Scamp unclipped a computer pad from his belt and ran a finger along the screen for a moment before showing it to me. "This is my account balance."

I locked my gaze on the bottom line—6,544,487.02. "What's the currency?"

"Mesots."

I sucked in a breath. "You have more than six million mesots?"

"Yep." He reclipped his pad to his belt. "Pretty nice, huh?"

"Blazes!" Crystal said. "That's more than a ship's captain makes in a lifetime."

Kattica pointed at Scamp with a thumb. "He got a huge bonus because of his stretching formula. And I have over three million in my account."

A humming noise reached my ears, probably whatever ship was going to pick these kids up.

Kattica hissed. "Everyone quiet. They'll be able to hear us now."

Zoë nudged my side and whispered, "Let me go with them. I can be a spy. I doubt that Omen would recognize me. He was too focused on you."

I looked at Kattica and Scamp and raised my brow, hoping that would signal a request for their approval.

Kattica extended a hand toward Zoë. "Look what we have here, Scamp. A girl wandered to our mine."

When Zoë took her hand, Scamp frantically waved for us to leave.

With Oliver and Crystal on my six, I pivoted and jogged out of the clearing, picking up my laser blaster and holstering it along the way. Once the forest had concealed us well enough, I turned and looked back. A transport glider big enough to hold twenty people lowered to the forest floor.

The noise from its engines allowed me to speak without concern that I'd be overheard. "Zoë had better come up with a good story to cover her tracks. She's wearing an Alliance uniform and a blaster."

"She's smart," Crystal said. "Don't worry about her."

"Let's get back to the gliders and see if we can follow them without being spotted."

Perdantus flew to a branch and helped us retrace our steps. When we arrived at our gliders, we entered the security codes on the external pads to raise the hatches, jumped in, and took off, leaving Zoë's glider behind. I flew above the treetops and retreated far enough away to keep from being detected, at least that's what I hoped, and the others joined me in a slow orbit over the forest.

Soon, the big glider rose to the sky and flew in the direction it had come from. After waiting for it to get nearly out of sight, I pushed the throttle and followed, staying well back. "Emerson, got any data on that glider in front of us?"

"Affirmative. It's a transport glider, Alliance model five-seventy."

"That's an old model, right? The glider model numbers are up to the eight hundreds now."

"Correct. It's a castoff from about ten years ago. It was primarily used to transport rebel prisoners. Standard equipment, therefore, includes leg irons and other restraining devices with rudimentary weapons."

I cringed. "That's more evidence that they're really slaves instead of paid employees."

"You got that right," Crystal said through my earbud. "Those kids were chirping about all the money in their accounts, but I'll bet they've never seen a single mesot of it. Just numbers on a screen."

Oliver piped in. "I'm going to make a guess here. Omen's somehow been shipping glowsap back through the time warp. On the other side of the warp, it feels like the sap's coming in like a flood, but the process is a lot slower here. Or it *was* a lot slower before we spilled the negative energy from here to Gamma Five. So, my guess is that Omen set the mines up, built a team to manage it, and then left. He collected the money while on the other side and got super rich. Then when we busted the warp bubble, he came back to rebuild his little empire."

"Good theory, Oliver," I said. "And he'll rebuild by creating more negative energy. Then he'll leave before the time boundary warps too much. He'll rake in the cash again while his stooges run the mines."

Perdantus hopped onto my thigh and looked at me. "Interesting, but since the warp caused time to be so skewed, wouldn't he have to send replacements every hour or so? I don't see how it's possible to run such a system from outside the warp zone. Enslaved children would grow to adults, have children of their own, and die of old age in less than a Gamma Five day."

As I stroked my chin, I stared through the windshield, imagining the cauldron of negative energy somewhere on this planet. "True, unless the skewing didn't get real bad until Raven showed up. She became the source of the negative energy."

"Even then, however, the mines would have operated for decades while Raven aged here."

I lifted a finger. "But Omen could still come here during those decades to fix things up and then leave without losing much time at all on our home side of the warp."

"Stop it," Crystal said. "My brain is melting."

I nodded. "Mine, too. But one thing makes sense. Since Omen's here, he probably came to make some changes. And with the warp minimized for now, he doesn't have to worry about it."

"So we need to find out what he's up to," Oliver said.

Emerson's voice came from the console. "The ship we are pursuing is decelerating. Take precautions as necessary."

"Slowing down," I said as I eased the throttle back. "Let's find a place to land, and we'll walk from there."

"I see a clear spot at two o'clock," Crystal said. "I've been studying about analog clocks just so I could say that."

"I see it." I steered toward the clearing, dropped below the tree line, and flew in a tight circle over a river while the others joined my orbit. When we landed single file at the river's edge, we got out, secured our gliders, and looked toward the direction the transport had gone, Perdantus on my shoulder. "No use waiting. Let's march."

"Right." Crystal looked upward. "We don't want to upset any bats when night comes."

Moving at a slow jog while Perdantus flew from tree to tree, we again dodged the forest growth, glancing between the obstacles and the direction we had to go.

Soon, another clearing came into view. I signaled a halt and studied the scene. This clearing covered much more territory than the others, with log cabin buildings throughout the expanse. At the far side of the clearing, a bell rung at one of the largest buildings, a metal-framed, warehouse-like structure with three windows on the wall facing us. Smoke rose from a chimney at the far right of the roof, maybe from a cooking stove inside.

Kids poured out of the smaller buildings and walked toward the one with the bell, most of them quiet, though a few seemed to be chatting. Nearly all were dressed in warm-weather clothing like shorts and T-shirts, probably not only because of the tropical air but also because they were recovering from being in those armored suits all day.

"Base camp." A shudder ran along my body. This place was giving me the creeps for some reason. I needed to figure it out, fast. "Anyone spot Zoë or the two kids we met?"

Crystal shook her head. "Not a sign of her. I thought her Alliance uniform would strobe like a flashing beacon, but she might've already changed clothes and hid her blaster somewhere. She's had time to do that, and Kattica might be trying to hide her."

"Right," Oliver said, "and I also looked for brown skin and poofed-out hair. I saw at least six kids with brown skin but none with Zoë's hair."

Perdantus flitted down to my shoulder from a nearby low branch. "Shall I fly a scouting mission? I could search for Zoë and report on potential dangers."

I raised a pair of fingers. "Two minutes. No more. And be super alert. Something about this place is really bothering me."

"I will be careful." Perdantus lifted off my shoulder and flew toward the camp. He landed on the roof of the building the children were entering and watched the last few go in. When the final one entered, he flew inside before the door closed.

I cringed. "Perdantus is probably trapped in there. I see windows, but I don't think they're open."

"I should go after him," Oliver said. "I know how to blend in with bramble bee miners."

I grabbed his wrist. "I can't lose you, too. We're getting whittled down one by one. Besides, dressed like that, you'll be a flashing light, like Crystal said."

"Megan ..." He pulled free and began stripping off his uniform, revealing shorts and a T-shirt. "Trust me. I know what I'm doing." His uniform balled under one arm, including his laser blaster, he jogged into the clearing, heading toward the building where Perdantus disappeared.

I looked at Crystal. "I guess it's just you and me now."

"Well, I'm not going anywhere. Like I said before we left, I'm gonna be on your six, seven, eight, and nine. Someone's gotta keep you out of trouble."

"That's the problem. It looks like everyone else is getting into trouble—Jillian, Zoë, Perdantus, and now Oliver." At that moment, Oliver opened the door of the building and walked inside, leaving the door ajar after entering, maybe to give Perdantus a way of escape. "But I'm standing on the outside looking in, just guessing on their strategy instead of planning it for my crew. I feel helpless."

"That's because you're usually the one dashing into danger while the rest of us watch you be a superstar hero. Now it's time to let your crew members do some of the dirty work while you watch from the sidelines like a worrywart coach."

"I'm not a worrywart. I'm just … well … protective of my friends."

"Exactly the same thing. You're worried. Deal with it."

I spread my hands. "But we can't just stand here and do nothing."

"Why not?"

Thunder rumbled in the distance, and dark clouds rushed in, hiding the sun. I pointed at the sky. "There's one reason."

Crystal sighed. "Just when I was finally winning an argument with you, the weather takes your side." She looked up into the tree canopy. "At least there aren't any bats yet."

A hefty breeze kicked up, and big raindrops pelted our heads. "We need to find shelter."

"The gliders?"

"Yep."

We ran toward the river where we left the three gliders. When we arrived, the river had risen, and the water lifted the side of the gliders that sat closer to the current, threatening to break them loose from the surrounding soil.

"Get in your glider!" I shouted. "We'll push Oliver's away from the river. It's rising fast."

I set my feet next to my glider, entered the security code, and pressed the button to open the hatch. As I waited, my shoes sank into the mud. I looked down to pry them out and noticed other deep footprints here and there, much bigger than my own. With no time to investigate, I braced my hands against the side of the glider, pulled free from the mud, and climbed into the pilot's seat.

By the time I started the engine and closed the dome, Oliver's glider had shifted off the shore and floated downstream. "Crystal, on my six!" I called through my earbud.

"Okay, but don't be stupid about this. It's just a glider."

"It's Oliver's way off this planet. I don't want anyone to be marooned here." I zoomed downstream, following the current as it carried Oliver's glider, swishing it from one shore to the other. When

I caught up, I eased to its starboard side, hoping to push it to safety on the port side, but the river had risen so much, it sloshed against huge trunks. Even a gentle nudge might send it crashing into a tree.

I shifted my glider upward and flew directly over Oliver's, steering to follow the river's curves. "Emerson, can you fly this glider?"

"Affirmative, but I cannot—"

"Land it. I know. Just keep it over the glider below. I'm going to commandeer it. Once I'm gone, find a safe place to hover. Talk to me through my earbud."

"Acknowledged."

I opened the dome. Since it connected to the glider by a hinge at the back, the curved glass caught the wind, slowing me down. When Emerson adjusted, I climbed over the edge of the glider, grabbed the side, and dangled over Oliver's glider. Since his dome hatch was closed, I would have to slide to the front, open the dome, and crawl into the cockpit, all the while riding out the thrashing river.

Crystal's voice came through my earbud. "I can't believe you're actually doing that. Are you out of your mind?"

I grunted, "Maybe."

"Megan, you're being stupid, exactly like I told you not to be."

"Well ..." As the glider below rose and fell, my feet nearly touched the dome, probably super slick because of the rain. "It's *kind* of stupid."

Crystal moaned. "Don't you ever listen to me?"

The toes of my shoes touched the dome for a split second, but it dropped again. "Probably not as much as I should."

"Do you know Oliver's entry code to get inside? He changed it, just like you told him."

"Good point. I don't know it."

"I'm coming closer to rescue you."

"Not a bad idea."

"Blazes!" Crystal shouted. "Megan, a wall of water is hurtling downstream super fast. It'll be on us in a heartbeat. We have to get out of the way!"

I glanced upstream. Crystal's glider shifted to the side, revealing a five-meter-high wave zooming toward me. I swung my legs up to my glider and rolled into the pilot's chair, my back on the seat and my legs straight up. "Emerson! Close the dome and get us away from the river!"

"Acknowledged."

The moment the dome started closing, the wall of water crashed over my glider. The force sent the craft tumbling in forward flips. With the wave flooding the cockpit, I clutched the sides of the seat, digging my fingernails into the material. Water surged into my mouth and nose. I gasped for air to cough the water out, but more rushed in. Still tumbling, I couldn't breathe at all.

My throat clamped shut. My lungs burned. Darkness seeped into my mind. Seconds later, everything went black.

Air poured into my mouth. Pressure weighed on my chest in rhythmic pulses. A girl spoke, grunts punctuating her words. "C'mon, Megan, Breathe! ... I saw Oliver ... do this to you ... but he's a healer ... and I'm just a lie detector, ... or I was one." Something touched my lips, and air rushed in again, then the pressure returned. "If you breathe ... I promise I won't ... say I told you so ... about doing ... something stupid."

When air poured in once more, water erupted from my lungs, surged through my throat, and gushed from my mouth. I sat up and retched, then coughed over and over with painful spasms.

Something thumped me hard on the back. "Megan, it's Crystal. Just keep heaving your guts. You're going to be all right."

Still coughing, I opened my eyes. Crystal knelt at my side, her hair dripping and her clothes saturated as heavy rain fell on us. "I don't know what I'm going to do with you," she said. "You've been knocked out, what, eight times lately? One of these times, no one's going to be around to jerk you away from the gates of death."

My spasms finally eased, though my lungs still burned. I blinked at her and smiled. "I'm like a cat. I still have one life left."

As raindrops pelted her head, her expression hardened. "I'm not kidding, Megan. I know no one likes to hear 'I told you so,' and I promised not to say it, but you need to hear it blasted over a loudspeaker." She cupped her hands around her mouth and shouted into my ear. "I told you not to do anything stupid!"

She leaned back and sighed. "But you did anyway. For once, you were put on the sidelines, and you couldn't stand being out of the action. You just had to go out with guns blazing and risk your life one more time. Oliver's glider wasn't as important as your life. Not even close. And you didn't even know the code to open the dome. You're addicted to danger. Stupid danger. And it's not just your life at stake, it's all of our lives." Tears filled her eyes as her voice pitched higher. "Megan, we need to be a team to survive, and we'd be a lot less of a team without you. And if you keep doing stupid stuff, that's going to happen."

I looked into her pleading blue eyes. I had no idea what to say, so I tried to buy some time. "Are you finished?"

As thunder rumbled nearby, her expression hardened again. "I don't know. Should I repeat myself to get it through your thick skull?"

"No." I wrapped my arms around her and held her close while rubbing her wet back. "You came through loud and clear. And you're right. I have a thick skull, deaf ears, and a run-to-danger hero complex."

She rubbed my back as well. "Okay. You're getting real close to the truth. Add that you're stubborn as a mule, and I think you'll be on target."

"Okay." I pushed away and smiled. "I'm as stubborn as a mule, but I have a loving sister who isn't afraid to knock some sense into me."

"There you go!" She set a fist in front of me. "Let's seal it."

I stared at her fist as rainwater dripped to the saturated ground. "Seal it?"

"Seal what you said with a fist bump." Crystal rolled her eyes. "C'mon, Megan! Haven't you ever done a fist bump before?"

"Just teasing." I bumped my fist against hers, then gazed at her. "Thank you for saving my life. You really did have my six, seven, eight, and nine."

"Yep. And I'm staying there for now. At least until you've learned not to be so crazy courageous."

I rose, my legs wobbly as I spread my feet to keep my balance. I checked my belt. The sheath still housed the knife, and the holster held my laser blaster. A few centimeters of water surrounded us with protruding roots breaking through the surface. "Any idea what happened to my glider and Oliver's?"

"I saw them both, but I was too busy saving your life to look them over."

"Show me."

"Over here." She led me out of the clearing and into a more forested area. Shallow water covered the ground there as well. Oliver's glider lay against a tree trunk, its shell cracked. "No idea if it can still fly, but it's not leaving the atmosphere anytime soon." She pointed deeper into the forest. "Yours is over there, still hovering. Emerson refused to land it, so I had to reach up and drag you out."

"No surprise." I walked in the direction she pointed and found my glider in hover mode about a meter off the ground, its downward jets blasting the water underneath and sending a spray in all directions. Crystal's glider sat nearby on the ground, tilted by exposed tree roots.

After passing through the wall of spray, I looked inside my glider. Water half-filled the cockpit, soaking everything, including the spacesuit I had left there. "Are you all right, Emerson?"

"I am fine," he said from the console, "but I was unable to land this craft."

"I got this." Crystal climbed into the glider and flipped a switch. The jets stopped, and the glider fell to the ground in a splash. "See, Emerson, that wasn't so hard."

"It is not a matter of difficulty. My programming—"

"Save it."

While Crystal climbed out, I pulled my necklace's chain and checked the ruby in the locket. As before, it glowed, signaling my father's life force, but still weaker than usual.

I closed the locket, slid it behind my shirt, and looked inside my glider again for anything that might be broken. "Emerson, can you do a system check?"

"A rudimentary check. All systems seem to be functioning, but with water flooding the cockpit, it is only a matter of time before it leaks into the engine compartment. Some of the components there are sensitive and could be damaged."

"I'm pretty sure this glider has a bilge pump." I reached in and flipped a switch on the console. A hum emanated, and a stream of water poured from a hole in the rear panel, adding to the flood on the ground. As the water receded inside, a glimmering metallic object on the floorboard caught my eye, a small disk of some sort, like a large coin.

I picked it up and held it near my eyes. Odd markings covered both sides, like ancient runes. I had no idea if they were letters that spelled words or symbols that signified something else.

Crystal squinted. "What's that?"

"A coin, I think. Some kind of writing on both sides, but I can't read any of it."

Crystal eyed it closely. "I can't, either. Could it have been there before and the water pushed it out, like from under the seat?"

"It's too clean and shiny for that. Not a speck of dirt or tarnish."

"Then why was it there?"

"Not sure. When I got to my glider, I saw big footprints next to it. Maybe someone left this coin for one of us to find."

"Like a calling card?"

I shrugged. "Maybe, but how could someone have put it there? You have to enter a security code to get in."

"Okay. Another mystery, but we'll have to solve it later." Crystal looked around the dim forest. "Night's almost here. Deadly bats will be coming out soon."

I slid the coin into my pocket. "How about if we try to sneak into one of the cabins? Together, I mean. You on my six and the other numbers."

Crystal pointed at me. "Now that sounds like a plan I can get behind."

I walked toward the clearing where I had regained consciousness. Crystal caught up and aimed me in a different direction. "We need to go that way. I'd be the leader, but then I couldn't be on your six."

"Gotcha." I sloshed through the water until I reached higher ground and continued through the mud with Crystal close behind as we again dodged trees and roots.

After a few minutes, the area grew more familiar and my legs felt stronger, allowing me to stride quickly. Soon, wings fluttered above, far more loudly than Perdantus could produce.

"Bats," I said as I broke into a jog.

"I heard them. Good thing we're almost there."

When we reached the clearing where we had seen the buildings, I slowed to a quiet walk. With twilight fading to darkness, lights on tall poles illuminated the base camp, casting a yellowish glow on the slanted metal rooftops, making them gleam.

The fluttering noise spiked. Wings appeared in my peripheral vision. When I instinctively ducked, a bird landed on my shoulder and chirped. "I finally found you. Where have you been?"

I craned my neck and looked at Perdantus. "I was going to ask you the same thing. You were in there way longer than two minutes."

"I was delayed, but I learned a lot of valuable information during the extra time."

"Like what?"

"First, Oliver and Zoë are safe. Kattica and Scamp made sure they were accepted into 'the tribe' as they call it. They were given mine assignments and bank accounts. Second, I found a tower that is apparently transmitting some sort of signal. A box at the base emits a beeping noise, and a light at the top flashes dark violet exactly at the same time as the beeps. Third …" He tilted his head. "Why are you so wet? Did you get caught in the storm?"

"Yep. I'll explain more later. Go on. What's third?"

"Oh, yes. Third, I saw Omen sitting with the camp operators. I listened to his conversation with another man, and he seems convinced that you went back to Gamma Five, but he made no mention of your aunt or your father. I don't know if Omen is still in there, but at least we know he's at the base camp. Although they have transport ships, none have departed or arrived since my initial count."

"Good job, Perdantus," I said. "You're an excellent scout."

He bowed his head. "I am grateful for your kind words."

A bat swooped low and nearly hit Crystal's head before flitting out of sight. She shuddered. "That was close."

I looked again at Perdantus. "Think we can sneak into the cabin where Oliver and Zoë are?"

"Without a doubt. Security is rather lax here. The members of the tribe are convinced that they are sending a lot of money home to their relatives, so they have plenty of incentive to be obedient."

Crystal ducked under a swooping bat again. "Can we continue this fascinating conversation under the roof of one of those cute little log cabins? I think the bats are attracted to blonde hair."

"All right, Perdantus," I said. "Please fly to the cabin where our crewmates are."

"Right away." Perdantus fluttered off my shoulder and headed toward the cabins.

I looked at Crystal and smiled. "On my six?"

"If you don't mind bats on your six-thirty, sure. But let's run."

I took off at a quick jog, my legs still stiff. With every step, the terrible feeling I suffered earlier grew stronger—a sense of dread, oppression, and strife. A battle waged somewhere, but what kind? No one seemed to be involved in a physical battle, so maybe it was mental or spiritual.

With Perdantus standing on the roof of the second cabin, I slowed to a halt in front of the entrance, turned the knob, and pushed the door slowly open. Inside, darkness shrouded the room except for the light coming in from the poles outside.

When my eyes adjusted, I tiptoed in and looked around, my hand close to my laser blaster. Bunkbeds, much like those we used at the underground training camp, lined the cabin's interior side walls, five to the left and five to the right, most filled with kids, either lying down or sitting up with legs dangling.

One of the seated girls on a top bunk to the left waved us over, a finger to her lips. When Crystal and I tiptoed to her, her identity became clear—Kattica. She whispered, "I thought you might show up. Zoë said you wouldn't be able to resist."

Crystal nudged me with an elbow. "I'm not the only one who reads you like a book."

"Where is she?" I asked Kattica.

"Sneaking around the camp with Oliver. They think we're being bamboozled about our money and where it's going, so they're looking for proof. I'm staying awake to see their faces when they come up empty." She put on a fake sad expression. "I'll be so sorry that they're disappointed and wasted their time."

"Any idea which way they went?" I asked, ignoring her drama.

"Nope. Just outside to sneak around."

Crystal nudged me again. "Show her the coin."

"Right." I withdrew the coin from my pocket and set it on my palm. "Any idea what this is?"

"Of course." She pinched it and held it by the edges. "It's a bank account token. It lets you access your balance, make transfers, and other stuff like that. One of the miner's must've lost it. No big deal, though. You need a password that's not on the coin."

Scamp walked over from the other side of the room, apparently the boys' side. "Let me see that." He took the coin from Kattica and looked at it closely. "This is a supervisor's token. How did you get it?"

I pointed at myself. "I found it."

"Where?" He lowered his hand as if to pocket the coin.

I snatched it back. "Never mind where."

"It doesn't belong to you." He reached for it again. "I'll take it to the office."

"I don't think so." I twisted away, avoiding his hand. "I'm going to study it some more."

He grabbed my wrist. "It's not yours."

I tried to break free, but his grip was too strong. I flexed my biceps and charged my bracelets. Electricity surged into his fingers. He yelped and staggered back, letting me go. "What in blazes did you do?"

"Never mind. I'm going to find my friends." I turned and walked out of the cabin with Crystal, Perdantus flying past us as we exited.

Breaking into a quick jog, we hurried to the rear of the cabin and looked around in the dimness, the illumination from pole lights barely reaching this area at all. Occasional cloud-to-cloud lightning provided extra flashes of light now and then. When we stopped, Perdantus landed on my shoulder.

"Can you lead us to the tower you told me about?" I asked him.

"Quite easily, but from here, you can see the top of it yourself." He tilted his head upward at an angle and pointed with a wing. "There."

I looked that way. A purple light pulsed above the tree line, barely visible against the dark sky. "Let's check it out."

Crystal and I jogged again, Perdantus flying ahead. When we reached the base of the tower, we found Oliver and Zoë sitting with their backs against one of the tower's four concrete support columns, both with their eyes closed, apparently asleep as they breathed easily.

I glanced around at the site. Each concrete column encased a metallic leg that angled upward to meet the others near the top, probably about ten meters above my head, leaving a five-meter gap between the columns. A concrete pad lay at the center of the ground that separated the columns, the foundation for a number of metallic pieces of equipment. From the midst of that equipment, a metal rod rose to the top, probably housing wires that connected to the purple light.

I knelt in front of Oliver and Zoë and spoke with a sharp whisper. "Hey! You two all right?"

They slept on without a flinch. I set a hand on Zoë's chest. Her heart beat steadily. I patted her cheek. "Zoë, wake up." I shifted to Oliver and patted his cheek. "C'mon, sleepyheads. This is no time to snooze."

They both blinked, then stared at me. Oliver scrunched his brow. "How did I get here?"

"Crystal and I found you at this tower. Perdantus showed us."

"Right. The tower."

Zoë looked at him. "We opened that box. Then we got dizzy and closed it quick. I don't remember anything after that."

"That's the last thing I remember, too."

"What box?" Crystal asked.

"I'll show you." Oliver reached for her hand. When she pulled him up, he walked with a staggering gait toward the equipment at the center.

I hurried to follow, Crystal and Zoë trailing. Oliver knelt in front of a metallic box attached to the central rod and touched a hinged panel with a pull handle on front. "I used a stone to break a little lock on this box, then we opened it."

"Strange." I laid a palm on the exterior metal, cool and damp. The surface vibrated, like a swarm of bramble bees hovered inside, though without making a sound, certainly no beeping, like Perdantus had reported. Maybe it beeped at a frequency that humans couldn't detect.

That awful feeling spiked, my heart raced, dizziness rushed in, and it felt like my soul was draining from my body.

"That's enough." Oliver grabbed my wrist and jerked my hand away. "Looks like you're about to pass out."

I blinked hard, waiting a second for the dizziness to settle before answering. "I nearly did."

Crystal took a step back and looked up. "What if this tower's transmitting a signal that's crippling us? You know, our Starborn powers."

I pulled her back even more. "Could be. That means Omen must have Starborn kids here. Otherwise, he wouldn't need to disable them."

Oliver and Zoë stepped back as well. "But why Starborn kids?" Zoë asked. "Sap miners don't need special powers."

"Rejects." Crystal pointed over her shoulder with a thumb. "Ousted from the training camp."

"Maybe some of them are rejects," I said, "but there are too many kids here for them all to be Starborn."

Oliver glanced up for a moment, as if thinking. "Let's see, twenty to a cabin and five cabins means a hundred miners could sleep here. I did a quick count and got up to seventy, but I'm sure I missed some."

I walked back to one of the base columns and touched the concrete surface. "I wonder how hard the tower is to climb."

"Oh, no." Crystal grabbed my sleeve and pulled me away from the column. "No more stupid danger out of you."

"Stupid danger," Oliver repeated. "What're you talking about?"

"Tell you later." Crystal gazed upward again, mumbling, "She actually thought climbing slippery metal up to a bat roost with lightning flashing all around was a good idea. Honestly!"

I drew my blaster. "Maybe a laser would disable it."

Crystal shrugged. "Tough shot from here, but it's worth a try."

I took aim at the purple light and pulled the trigger, but nothing happened. I shook the gun hard. Water spilled out of the barrel. "So much for that." I pushed it back to the holster. "It's swamped. I'll have to wait for it to dry."

"Try mine," Crystal said, extending her blaster. "I'm sure you're a better shot than I am."

"Not necessarily. You've been practicing, and you didn't drown recently."

"All right. Here goes." Crystal aimed at the light and pulled the trigger. A laser bullet zipped out of the barrel and sliced into the light, smashing it.

The purple glow died away, and the awful feeling faded. Crystal holstered her gun and looked at me. "I can feel a difference. Can you?"

"Yeah. I feel a lot better."

She smiled. "And I can tell you're not lying. My power is definitely back."

A chorus of squeals cascaded from above. Perdantus zoomed to my shoulder and shouted, "Run!"

Bats swooped down by the dozens, snapping and clawing. Zoë raised her hands and blocked the bats with a mental shield that looked like a flexible bubble, making the bats bounce away. She shouted, "Go! I'll keep them off us."

As we hurried together toward the cabin, Zoë kept pushing the bats back, but her power fluctuated through the awkward effort. A few bats broke through and took swipes at us. A claw scratched my scalp, and another sliced Crystal's hand, but no deadly fangs pierced our skin.

When we reached the cabin, we rushed inside and slammed the door behind us, gasping as we leaned against it while Perdantus flew to a corner out of sight.

Kattica dropped from her bed and ran to us. "What happened?"

"Bats," Crystal said breathlessly. "Swarms of them."

As the other children rose from their beds and gathered behind Kattica, she pulled Crystal away from the door. "All of you. Get over here."

The moment we stepped forward, a sound like a machine-gun volley rattled the door. The points of claws broke through amid riotous squeals. The wood splintered here and there, but it kept the bats out.

"They'll give up soon," Kattica said. "We've been through this before."

After several more seconds, the claw points withdrew, and the squeals ebbed. I pulled my chain and looked at my locket. The red glow pulsed brightly, leaking through to the outside. I had my powers back, at least for now.

Kattica glared at me. "You're behind this attack, aren't you?"

I put the locket away and returned her glare. "Probably."

Scamp pushed between us, a hand on my shoulder and another on hers as he looked at me. "Did you notice if the tower light went out?"

I nodded. "It's out."

"There," he said to Kattica. "The bats always come when the light goes out. Probably just burned out again. Megan had nothing to do with it."

"She didn't," Crystal said as she touched her holstered blaster. "I did. I shot it out."

Several children gasped and began chatting among themselves.

Scamp frowned at her. "Why did you do that?"

I stepped in front of him, blocking his glare. "Because I told her to. The tower was emitting a signal that destroys my energy. It makes me sick. But I had no idea that it was also protecting the camp from the bats."

Kattica pushed past Scamp and stepped close to me, scowling. "Then you shouldn't've told her to shoot at it. It's not yours, and you had no idea what it's really for."

I held my ground and met her stare. "I know that this is a slave camp, and I'll do everything in my power to tear it apart, piece by piece if I have to. The light was just the first step."

Kattica pointed toward the tower. "That light keeps us safe at night. It's our only protection against those crazy bats. We don't need you or anyone else to decide what's good for us. Now pack up your posse, Miss Captain of a starship, and get out of here, or I'll call Omen and have you put in chains."

Scamp grabbed Kattica's arm and pulled her back. "You're not going to call Omen. No one wants that. He'll punish us all."

Kattica's scowl loosened. "I know. I just had to take that uppity girl down a peg or two. She's way too full of herself."

Her words shot a dagger into my heart. I hated to admit it, but she was right. I had acted too hastily, taking action when I didn't know what the results would be. Again, I was being stupid, and the stupid disease seemed to be getting worse. "Kattica," I said in a soft tone, "you're right. I don't have an excuse for what I did. It was brash, presumptuous, and stupid. And I'm sorry. I'll try to be more respectful in the future."

Kattica crossed her arms and took a long look at me. "Well, I gotta say, that's quite an apology. I wasn't expecting it." She extended a hand. "Apology accepted."

With my powers back, I could tell that she was being sincere. I shook her hand and smiled in the humblest way I could. "Thank you."

Scamp gave us both a nod. "Now that's what I like to see."

"I know, little brother. You're always the peacemaker." Kattica sighed. "But that doesn't fix the bat bulb. If they don't have a spare, Omen's going to go ballistic."

"Why?" I asked. "If the bats only come out at night, everyone can just stay inside. I mean, it's inconvenient, but at least you're safe, right?"

"It's not that simple." Scamp looked at the other kids as they all watched with wide eyes. "This isn't a theater play, people. Don't be gawkers."

Amid grumbles of "Give me a break" and "Look who's boss now" the children shuffled to their beds.

"Follow me." Scamp led us to Kattica's bunk and sat on the floor, gesturing for us to join him. When we did, I sat with my back angled toward the door, not a great position for security reasons. Kattica sat next to Scamp, directly across from me, while Oliver and Crystal sat to my right, Zoë to my left.

Scamp spoke in a low tone. "The tower doesn't just repel bats. It sends transmissions to a space station, and those get relayed to a databank where all of our accounts are stored. If the transmissions are blocked, nothing gets updated, and we can't access our funds. We all count on that system to send money to our families. That's why we're here, to support them."

In my mind, a signal shot from the tower to the Zeta station. That definitely could be true. "But if it's a temporary outage, you won't lose anything, right? When the tower signal's restored, you'll have access again."

Kattica shook her head. "You don't get it. We work hard all day, risking our lives every second, and we look forward to checking our accounts at night before going to bed. We use our communication devices to send money along with messages, telling people we love that they can count on us. If I miss contacting my mother even once, she gets worried."

"It's true," Scamp said to me. "Mom does worry. Ever since our dad died, it's been hard for her to live alone."

"Again, I'm sorry. But that raises an earlier question." I pushed a hand into my pocket, a difficult maneuver while wearing wet pants in a seated position, and pulled out the bank token. "I didn't tell you this before, but I found it in my space glider. I have no idea how it got there. Maybe if you tell me more about it, we can—"

The door opened, prompting me to glance back. Omen stepped in and looked around. Before his piercing eyes could aim in my direction, I slid the token away and angled my head so he couldn't see my face. "I assume," he said in a clear, calm voice, "that you are aware of the tower malfunction. We think that lightning struck the bulb. It has been replaced, and the bat shield has been restored. Unfortunately, we had to reboot the transactions system, so your accounts will be inaccessible for the remainder of the night. But don't worry, the data is kept offsite, so your accounts are safe."

When he left and the door closed, a chorus of disappointed moans erupted. I exhaled and looked at Kattica. "Did he act like he suspected anything?"

She shrugged. "He's hard to read. Always calm. Never angry. Even if he doles out punishment, he never raises his voice."

"Cold as an icicle," Scamp said. "Always cold."

I pulled my locket out again. The glow no longer pulsed through the edges, and the bad feeling grew once more. My powers were probably gone. I opened the back panel and looked inside. The ruby glowed more faintly than I had ever seen it. Papa was still alive, but he seemed to be dying. Somehow I had to find him, and soon.

"What's that?" Kattica asked.

"A locket. It's personal. A family heirloom." I put it away and withdrew the token. "I guess we can't see what this can do since the system's down."

"Maybe we can." Scamp took the token and set a computer pad on his lap. "Just because the account access system is down, that doesn't mean the system itself is. I want to see if the codes on this token will let me into the top level of the system without a password." As he read the token, he tapped on the pad's screen.

"What is that language?" I asked.

"Cyber X. Computer symbols that we choose from the screen." After a final tap, he widened his eyes. "Whoa! It let me into the accounting system without even asking for a password. I can see everyone's accounts."

"What?" Kattica said. "That's impossible. The system is supposed to be secure."

He shrugged. "I don't know what to tell you. I see a list of a hundred and seven account numbers. Probably everyone who has ever worked here, including Benny."

Kattica leaned toward him and pointed. "That should be mine. Tap on it."

When he did, she squinted at the screen. "Yep. That's my balance."

"That's not exactly like the usual screen we see. There are more data fields. Like this one." Scamp set a finger close to the screen. "What do you think 'AI' means?"

"Amount Invested?" Kattica offered. "Maybe how much I've sent to Mom? It should be a little under two million mesots since we got here. Tap on it and see."

When he did, he narrowed his eyes. "It came back with two prompts. 'AI to date' and 'Next AI.' I'll see if AI to date shows the two million." He tapped again. "No. It's a list of dates, probably the times you sent her money. I'll select one." He tapped once more. "It's a thank-you note from Mom."

Kattica leaned close again. "Right. That's her most recent message to me."

"I'm going back to see what 'Next AI' shows." Scamp ran a finger along the screen and read out loud. "Dear Kattica, thank you so much, pumpkin, for such a generous gift. It amazes me that you can send …" He drew his head back. "It has a blank field that says, 'Enter amount and units here.'"

"What?" Kattica took the pad and used a finger to scroll. "It reads just like she writes, but she hasn't sent it yet."

At that moment, everything clicked in my mind. "AI isn't amount invested. It's artificial intelligence. A computer is generating her responses. She's not writing them at all."

Kattica and Scamp both stared at me, their mouths partially open. Scamp swallowed hard. "Does that mean she's not getting the money?"

I gave a light shrug. "I can't be sure of that, but if they're lying to you about who's sending the messages, they could be lying about everything else."

"Then if she's not getting the money," Kattica said, "who is?"

"Maybe no one. The money might not exist at all. It could be just a number on a screen."

Kattica shook her head. "No. I don't believe it. They wouldn't make us risk our lives every day by baiting us with the idea that we're helping our families survive. That would be cruel, sadistic, evil."

"You're right. It would be."

"Scamp?" Kattica looked at him, trembling. "Tell me it's not true. Tell me Mom got all of the money we sent her."

He wrapped his arms around her shoulders and patted her back, tears gleaming in his eyes. "I don't know, Sis. I just don't know."

I extended a hand. "Mind if I have a look?"

Scamp drew back from Kattica and passed the computer pad to me. I scanned the screen, searching for a clue about why someone left that token for me to find, but every link seemed to be in code or some kind of initials. I tapped on a few, but they didn't lead anywhere.

A message popped up that said, "Alliance captain fingerprint identified. Tap here for instructions." When I did, a longer message appeared. "Captain Megan Willis, meet me at the tower at dawn. I have something to tell you that is for your ears only, so come alone. If someone comes with you, all might be lost."

I looked at my crewmates. If I were to tell them about the message, they probably wouldn't let me go alone, especially Crystal. She would say I was being stupid again. And maybe she would be right. But how could I ignore the message's warnings?

The message disappeared, and the screen cleared.

"Did you find anything interesting?" Scamp asked as he massaged Kattica's shoulder.

"Just a strange message." I passed the computer pad back to him. "I should sleep on it. I'm really tired."

"And you're still wet," Kattica said. "I'll find everyone something dry to wear that'll help you fit in." She patted her bottom bunk. "Megan, want to bunk with me tonight? This one's empty."

I glanced at Crystal and Zoë. They each offered a quick nod. "Um … sure. Thanks."

Kattica slid a small cardboard box out from under the bed. "I also have some snacks. I'm sure you and Crystal are hungry." From the box, she withdrew two muffins wrapped in plastic and gave one each to Crystal and me. "Oliver and Zoë already had a good meal."

While I ate my muffin, Oliver went to the boys' side, Crystal and Zoë were given bunks on the girls' side, and I sat on the bed under Kattica's. She gave me loose-fitting gray shorts with a drawstring, and a baggy white T-shirt, both perfect for the warm, muggy conditions.

After I changed my clothes in a curtained alcove, used the toilet there, and hung my wet things on a line that stretched across the room, I slid under the sheet and laid my head on the thin pillow, while Kattica climbed into the top bunk. When she had fully bedded down, she whispered, "Megan, can you talk for a minute?"

I whispered in return. "Sure. What's on your mind?"

"At first, I didn't believe that you're really the captain of an Alliance starship. You're just a kid, probably younger than me. I know I couldn't take charge of a ship like that. Anyway, watching you tonight, I think I figured out how you do it. Take charge, I mean. Now I believe you."

"What did I do that changed your mind?"

"You did what you thought was right, no matter what anyone else thought, and you didn't mind risking your life to do it. That's what real leaders do."

I gave her a soft laugh. "Even if it seems stupid afterward?"

"I guess so. They say hindsight has perfect vision. You can't beat yourself up over bad decisions. They're in the past."

"That makes sense. As long as we learn from them."

Kattica sighed. "Good point."

She stayed quiet for nearly a full minute, prompting me to say, "I'm guessing you had a reason for bringing this up."

Her voice pitched higher. "I did." She paused for several more seconds before continuing, her voice settling, though still a bit choked. "The last three years of my life have been one big lie. Every day, I go to the bramble bee caves, thinking I'm doing something brave for my mother." A sob squelched her voice.

I gave her a minute to cry before prompting her again. "How did your father die? And tell me about how you got here and why."

Her voice cracked as she replied. "Traffickers killed my father when they took Scamp and me."

"Were you born on Gamma Five?"

"How did you guess?"

"Traffickers look for Starborn children there."

"Starborn children?"

She seemed ready to cry again, so I took some time to explain what Starborn children are and some of the powers they have, though I didn't mention that my crewmates and I were all Starborn. I did include our theories about positive energy and negative energy, as well as how negative energy can drain a Starborn, which could be happening here because of the tower, and that was why I wanted to shut it down.

"That's really interesting," Kattica said, "and I'm glad you told me why you tried to shut down the tower, but it doesn't relate to us much at all. Scamp and I don't have any of those Starborn powers. We're pretty normal." She let out a long sigh, and her voice strengthened. "We were being auctioned on Delta Ninety-eight. Omen showed up and outbid everyone for all of the kids being sold. Then he took us on his starship and told us we could either go home or join him here to work his mines, that we'd be paid a lot of money because it's so dangerous, and we could transfer as much money as we wanted to our home. Our mother would get rich, and so would we. We just had to decide if we were brave enough to do it. His speech was so inspiring. He kept praising us for our courage to survive being kidnapped and for loving our mother enough to want the best for her, no matter what it cost us."

"Really convincing, huh?"

"Definitely. Anyway, that takes me back to why I started talking about this. When Scamp and I made the decision to go with Omen, we thought we were doing the right thing. We didn't know he was lying. So ever since you found out the truth, I've been beating myself up over it. I'm furious at myself for not checking it all out more carefully. I'm an idiot for getting fooled by the replies from my mother. I wanted it all to be true so badly, I ignored any nagging questions that it was too good to be true. I kept telling myself that it all made sense. Omen paid us a lot because of the danger, and we would all share the rewards."

"Did the money blind you?"

"No. That's not it at all. Wanting to help my mother blinded me."

"So it was love," I said. "Not greed."

"Exactly. And that's what I'm telling myself now. Don't beat yourself up. You did what you thought was right. It was all about love."

"Do you think you would make the same decision now if you had another chance?"

"Definitely not. I learned something important, not to trust anyone who tries to tell me something that's too good to be true. I won't get fooled again. So now, instead of beating myself up for being so stupid, I'm going to help everyone here." She leaned over the side of her bed, her hair dangling as she looked at me and whispered, "I'm going to wreck this place and get everyone home. Are you in?"

I smiled and raised my fist toward her. "I'm in. With all my heart."

She bumped my fist with hers. "Let's make plans in the morning."

"You got it."

When she lifted back up, the sounds of her settling into her bed drifted down, then the entire room fell silent. It seemed that she had gotten a huge weight off her chest by talking it out, and now she could finally go to sleep.

But I couldn't. My own burdens came roaring back to mind. Someone had called me to a meeting at the tower at dawn. I was supposed to come alone. But should I? Going to the tower to meet a stranger from a base camp that enslaved children by lying to them seemed like a bad idea, especially after getting scolded by Crystal for my stupid-hero antics. We needed to be a team, and going solo had nearly killed me too many times.

But how could I risk putting them in danger? Wasn't protecting my friends an act of love? If I could sacrifice myself so others could live, especially my friends, shouldn't I do it? They probably wouldn't want me to do it, but that shouldn't be their decision. It was mine alone, wasn't it?

As I lay there, the battle continued in my mind—one side shouting "Teamwork!" and the other shouting "Sacrifice!" Both sides made sense, but only one could win the battle.

I sighed. If only Papa were here. He could help me decide. Of course, he would insist on going with me, and that would be okay. It always seemed appropriate for him to be my sacrificial teammate because we had been risking our lives for each other for so long, that is, until that fateful day we were arrested for piracy.

I lifted the locket from my chest and opened the back again. The ruby still glowed weakly, adding to my worries. How could I sleep while thinking my father was dying? He needed my help, and I had no idea where to find him. Who could possibly help me search for my Papa?

The answer hit me like a lightning bolt. *Barnabas!* He was still inside the ruby. He had said I could call on him for advice but only in my darkest hour, because once he left the ruby to give me help, he wouldn't be able to enter it again. And his presence kept anyone from using the ruby to harm me or my father.

But was this my darkest hour? My crewmates and I were marooned on a planet run by slavers. We had no Starborn powers to battle against them. And, most important of all, Papa was probably dying. Since Barnabas was a prophet, he might be my only hope of finding my father alive.

I nodded. Yes, this was my darkest hour. All the other times, I could think of a way to get out of whatever mess I was in, but not this time. I needed help.

I gazed at the ruby and whispered, "Barnabas, I'm calling you. I need help. Please answer me."

I waited in silence. The ruby continued glowing with the same dimness, no hint of change. Just as I opened my mouth to call again, the ruby pulsed with brilliant scarlet hues. A white stream flowed out and collected on the floor at the side of the bunk, rising to the height and form of a man. When the flow ceased, the form clarified into a ghostly version of Barnabas, white from top to bottom, semitransparent, and pulsing with radiance.

Wearing a glimmering white robe, he folded his hands at his waist. No longer gaunt, balding, or sickly looking, he seemed far healthier, with a head of thick white hair and fuller cheeks. "Megan." His voice boomed and echoed throughout the room.

I cringed and whispered, "You'll wake everyone up."

"Don't worry about that. You're the only person who can hear or see me."

"Oh. Okay. But you're still really loud, even if it's just me hearing you."

"I will adjust my volume." He knelt at the side of my bed and set a hand on my arm. I expected not to feel it, but warmth radiated into my skin. "I assume this is your darkest hour, Megan. What can I do for you?"

I showed him the ruby. The glow had faded even further, now flickering as if static were interfering with the signal. "I think my father is dying."

He looked at the ruby. "You're right. He is in great peril, and his life force is fading. This is serious, indeed. You were right to call on me." He ran his warm hand along my cheek. "But there is more. Much more. Tell me as thoroughly as you can while being as brief as you can. We don't have any time to waste."

I took a deep breath and gave him the quickest summary possible of everything that had happened since he entered the ruby, including my dilemma about going alone to the tower or telling my crewmates about it. The last thing I wanted was to make another stupid decision.

When I finished, he nodded slowly. "Your quandary is real. I understand your difficulty. Your lack of powers weighs on each side of the balancing scales. If your crewmates had their powers, you wouldn't be worried about them joining you. On the other side, if you had your powers, you wouldn't be concerned about going alone. It wouldn't be stupid at all."

"Right," I said, "but since no one has powers, it's dangerous no matter what I decide."

"Of course. Of course. But would you rather be in danger alone or with your allies?"

"With my allies. Definitely. But the message said for me to come alone. I'm worried that bringing them along might hurt my chances of finding out what's going on around here."

"Ah. The message insisted. You skipped that part of the story."

"Sorry. I guess I told it too fast."

Barnabas stroked his ghostly chin. "Perhaps there is a way to do both."

"What do you mean? I can't be alone and with them at the same time."

"No, but you can show your trust in your allies. They would be encouraged by that."

"You mean tell them that I'm going but they should stay away?" I laughed under my breath. "They would never agree to that."

"Too loyal?"

"Well, no. You can never be too loyal."

"Too stubborn?"

"No, they're not stubborn. They're just … loyal."

"So loyal that they'd be willing to die for you?"

"Absolutely. In a heartbeat."

"As you would die for them."

"Exactly."

"Then, as the leader, you must decide if your willingness to sacrifice for them is more important than their willingness to sacrifice for you."

I furrowed my brow. "You make it sound like I'm being selfish to think that way."

"Why would it be selfish?"

"Because they want to sacrifice for me as much as I want to sacrifice for them. If I don't let them, then I'm taking something away from them. The chance to sacrifice."

"So being able to sacrifice is a good thing, and it's good to let other people do it."

"Right. I mean, I guess so. But it hurts to see anyone suffer for my sake."

"Megan ..." He held my hand. This time I felt a physical touch, not just warmth. "Here is a law of life that too many people don't understand. It is a blessing to be a blessing. If you take on all burdens yourself without the help of others, you are taking away their ability to bless you, thereby taking away their blessing. The same law holds true for sacrifice, for sacrifice is the ultimate blessing."

"So you're saying I should take my crewmates with me, even though I'm supposed to go alone?"

"Not at all. I'm saying you should invent a way to go alone with their complete support. Get them to buy in on an idea that allows everyone to share in the blessing of sacrifice."

I narrowed my eyes. "How can I come up with a way to do that?"

"I am confident that you will come up with something. You are a magnificent leader in every respect, and your cleverness is unmatched."

"I wish I had that much confidence in myself."

Barnabas chuckled. "I don't think you're lacking in the confidence department."

I smiled. "All right. Fair enough. I'll come up with something."

"I'm sure you will. You are quite the wizard with words. In fact, there is a Starborn power that perhaps you have not yet experienced.

I have heard that some Starborn children are gifted with eloquence. Words come to their minds that they did not expect, and the phrases are often poetic. Since you have every Starborn power, you should have that one as well, or you would if not for the tower's signal."

"I know I have a big vocabulary, and Perdantus taught me to be a good negotiator, but I don't think I'm particularly eloquent. Certainly not poetic."

"Ah, well, perhaps that power will manifest later. I suppose you will recognize it when it happens."

"I'll watch for it." As the ruby's glow flickered again, I frowned. "What about my father? Any idea where he might be?"

"I have some prophetic insight that is rather vague and carries no certainty. I feel that he is close, perhaps not in body but in another form. He is aware of your attempts to find him, and he is also searching for you." Barnabas let out a long sigh. "I'm afraid that's all the insight I have on that topic."

"That's all right. It's helpful to know he's alive and trying to find me. But, as long as you're here, do you have any other advice?"

"I do. I have a strong impression that difficult decisions you have made in the past will affect the future in ways you can't predict, and decisions that you are yet to make will have similar consequences. Let the following principle guide you when you face a challenging dilemma. Mercy begets mercy, and wrath begets wrath. Wrath can alter someone's behavior for a moment by physically preventing an action, but mercy plants a seed that can alter a heart forever, even if only in the heart of those who witness the mercy."

I blew out a long breath. "I'll have to let that soak in for a while."

"As you should. I suspect that you will learn what it all means as you face dilemmas along the way. And now that I have no more to tell you, it is time for me to go."

"Where will you go?"

"To be with God in heaven. And I have looked forward to that homecoming for many, many years."

"Homecoming?"

He nodded. "For those of us who live according to the law of God's love, our real home is in heaven. We will never feel fully comfortable anywhere else. Perhaps that's why you are so willing to risk your life. Subconsciously, you're longing to go to your real home."

I smiled. "Actually, I'm pretty happy to stay around here awhile longer, but I get your point."

"Understood." Barnabas rose and walked to the door. He stopped and turned, his voice thundering again. "I said many things to you that will likely be a jumble in your mind for a while, but I want to emphasize an important point. As I mentioned, you need to allow others to experience the blessing of sacrifice, but I also said that as the leader, you might have to decide that your willingness to sacrifice is more important than that of others. And you will know the time has come when you are the only one who can provide the greatest benefit." He walked through the closed door in a splash of light and disappeared.

"Wow," I said, a bit louder than a whisper.

"What?" Kattica asked sleepily. "Did something happen?"

"Just some inspiration. I think I can sleep now."

"Okay. Good night again."

"Good night, Kattica."

Perdantus flew to my bed and nestled next to my pillow. "I plan to stay here and guard you all night," he chirped softly. "I have a feeling that you need me."

"I do, my friend. More than ever." I patted his head. "Can you wake me up the moment you see first light?"

"I will. You can count on me."

"Yes, I know I can. Thank you." I closed my eyes and fell into a deep sleep.

After a few dreamless hours, I awoke to a pricking sensation on my shoulder, then a low chirp. "Megan," Perdantus said. "It is first light."

I opened my eyes to the darkness of the cabin. After taking a few seconds to get my bearings, I turned my head toward Perdantus and whispered, "Get our crewmates together. Earbuds in place. We'll meet outside the front door."

I jerked my clothes off the line, hurried to the alcove, used the toilet, changed into my uniform, and touched my earbud. "Comm check."

"Loud and clear," Crystal said. "Now quit hogging that pot. I gotta go!"

I pushed the curtain aside and rushed out of the alcove, nearly colliding with Crystal. "See you outside," I whispered as I hurried toward the exit.

When I walked out, I began pacing in front of the door. At the moment, I had no plan for how to ask my crewmates for help. Maybe an idea would come to me soon.

Oliver rushed from the cabin first, followed by Zoë, then Crystal, who held the door open until Perdantus flew out and landed on my shoulder. "You seemed hurried," Crystal said as she closed the door. "What's up?"

"Here's the deal." I touched my locket. "I called on Barnabas last night, because I'm sure my father is dying. He agreed. And someone sent me a secret message that says I'm supposed to go to the tower at dawn, but I have to go alone. The message said if I bring anyone with me, all could be lost."

"Okay," Zoë said, stretching the word. "Why are you telling us?"

Crystal nodded. "Right. I would've guessed that you'd already be there, waiting in the darkness for dawn to come. Hero Megan doing her thing."

"Not this time. I learned my lesson. I need my crewmates. I don't want to do this alone."

Crystal crossed her arms in front. "Well, I like hearing that. Tell us more. How can we help if you're supposed to go alone?"

"The tower's surrounded by trees, right? While it's still pretty dark, I want you to hide behind a nearby tree and be ready to shoot out the light if I get in trouble. Since it'll be past dawn, the bats shouldn't bother us. If you knock the light out, we should all get our powers back."

Crystal nodded. "Got it."

I touched Oliver's back. "I want you to hurry to the river and get my glider. Emerson will open the dome and let you fly it. It's farther downstream than where I left it. I want you to fly over the area in big orbits. I'll have my earbud in, so you can hear what I say, and Emerson can scan for other voices around me. If I get in trouble, you can zoom in and help us, maybe give me a ride on top."

"On my way." Oliver ran into the woods and out of sight.

"Zoë," I said, grasping her shoulder. "Do you think you can work with Kattica and Scamp to dig deeper into the accounting system? I want to know who sent me the secret message. There should be some kind of log." I withdrew the token and set it on her palm. "It happened while I was in the part of the system that the token let me into."

She closed her fist around the token. "I'll find out, one way or another."

"Great." I looked at Perdantus. "I want you to fly to a treetop near the tower and watch for anything suspicious. Let me know if anyone's coming. That'll help me prepare. I doubt if anyone in the camp will be able to understand your language, so you can talk all you want."

"I will." He took off from my shoulder and flew toward the tower.

Crystal gave me a tight hug. When she backed away, she looked at me, her jaw firm. "It's good to be on your team, Megan."

"Thanks. You really helped me—"

"Stop right there. You can tell me how right I was later. It's almost dawn." She gave me a push. "Go to the tower. I'll be close by."

"Yep. Let's get this done." I jogged toward the tower. As I passed one of the cabins, a flickering light came on inside, probably a lantern. The kids would be rising soon to get ready for the daily trip to the bramble bee mines. But maybe I would be able to do something to stop it.

When I arrived at the base of the tower, the sick feeling drilled into me again with a vengeance. Trying to ignore it, I looked around. With dawn breaking, the surroundings clarified, fairly easy to see, though Crystal had hidden herself well enough to stay out of view.

"I don't see anyone yet," Perdantus chirped from high above. "I will continue watching."

Not wanting to reveal to any stealthy onlookers that I was listening to him, I focused on the box at the center of the gap between the columns. Whatever was inside had to be the source of our power drain and the dark, horrible feeling. The growing daylight probably kept the bats away, but the box held the more important mystery. Could I possibly disable the box and keep the light on? It might be worth a try.

"I see something," Perdantus said. "I was watching for humans, but what I see doesn't appear to be human. Look behind you."

I pivoted. A radiant form stood in front of me. I stepped back, giving myself more room to look it over. Somewhat human in shape with amorphous arms and legs, it sizzled with electrical arcs. "Who … what are you?"

A sound came from where I assumed its head was. "Megan …" The rest of its words buzzed, too indistinct to understand.

"Yes, I'm Megan. Who are you?"

More words sizzled forth, again too fractured, until it spewed a clear, "Papa."

"Papa?" I took a step closer and looked at the form carefully. "Can you show me your fingers?"

A finger-like appendage rose from its hand, then another, then a third.

"Okay. You can. If you're really my father, then show me the numbers for my mother's birthdate—month, then day, then year.

The form lifted and lowered fingers, answering correctly. When he finished, tears filled my eyes. "Papa, what happened to you?"

"Crystal is aware of your father's presence," Perdantus said. "She has an idea. Since your mother knew Intergalactic Morse Code, your father surely does as well. Get him to answer your questions in that code, one finger for a dot and two fingers for a dash."

"Papa," I said, "can you answer me in IGMC? One finger for dot. Two fingers for dash."

He spelled out *yes* in IGMC.

"Great. Now tell me what happened as briefly as you can."

He spelled out his response quickly, though it seemed unbearably slow. *Gamma Five transported me here. Tower signal keeps my energy together. Almost died last night.*

I gasped. "So when we knocked out the tower, the loss of the signal almost made your energy disperse?"

He spelled out *yes.*

I swallowed hard. My decision to break the light almost killed my own father. "That means we have to keep this tower running, even though it neutralizes our Starborn powers."

He spelled *If that is your priority.*

"Of course it's our priority. Keeping you alive is more important than anything."

Perdantus called from the treetop. "Crystal knows that she is to stand down from your order to shoot the light, even in an emergency."

I tapped a finger on my chin. "This means the tower is transmitting a signal that holds you together and also takes our powers. Or it could be that there are two signals instead of one, and if we can figure out how to stop the one that's neutralizing us, we can get our powers back without hurting you."

He spelled, *Yes, but better to get gun from the Zeta.*

I nodded. A reintegration gun. "I can take the glider to the Zeta station, but I'll have to figure out how to haul a gun. They're too big to fit in a glider."

True.

"Hello, Megan."

I turned toward the voice. Omen stood a few steps away, but how could he have sneaked up on me with Perdantus watching? I stepped toward the tower, hoping his eyes would follow me and not see my father. "Yes, it's me. What do you want?"

"Crisis!" Perdantus called. "Crystal is aware of Omen's presence. I apologize for not warning you, but he appeared out of nowhere."

Omen's brow dipped down in a disapproving way. "I want to know why you're here when you promised to stay in your ship."

"I didn't promise to stay in my ship. I promised to stay where I was, and when I said it, I was in my glider."

He chuckled. "A childish appeal to semantics. Your intent was to deceive me."

"Absolutely. You're a kidnapper and a slaver." Papa slowly moved away as I continued talking. "The possible wrongness of deceiving you is about number ten million on my list of things I'm worried about. If you'd prefer a bald-faced lie, I can arrange that."

"Frankly, that would be more mature. You see, I told you a bald-faced lie. I didn't send Jillian back to Gamma Five. I killed her. A much simpler solution."

I shouted, "You killed Jillian? Why you sick, twisted—"

"Or did I? Maybe telling you I killed her was the bald-faced lie, and I did so to knock you off balance."

I stared at him, my throat tight. I needed Crystal's lie-detecting gift more than ever now. Not only that, the pain from the tower seemed to be increasing. Being exposed to it for so long had to be wearing my defenses down.

Omen frowned in mock sympathy. "Would you like to move away from the tower? I'm sure you'll feel better if you do. Being a powerful Starborn has its drawbacks, doesn't it?"

I swallowed through the pain. Just as I opened my mouth to respond, he continued. "Camille and Raven told me all about you, so I know how powerful you are, and I'm sure the influence of this tower's signal has a more painful effect on you than it does on any other Starborn who feel it. The torture must be excruciating."

A laser bullet zinged in and zapped Omen. Brilliant light filled his body, and he disappeared.

I felt my mouth drop open. A hologram?

Crystal shouted from the forest, "He wasn't really there!"

"Three men ran out of one of the cabins," Perdantus chirped, "and they're coming this way!"

I flexed my biceps and charged my leg muscles. Just as I set my feet to run, a glider zipped down from the sky and skidded along the ground, stopping at my feet. Oliver sat in the cockpit, waving at me. "Get on!" he called through my earbud. "They're almost here!"

I leaped onto the glass dome, straddled it, and looked at my father's electrical form. "I'll come back with a reintegration gun, Papa. I promise."

He flashed the IGMC signal for *I love you* with his fingers.

I returned the signal, squeezed the dome tightly with my legs, and slapped the glass. "Go!"

Oliver fired the thrusters underneath. We lifted off just as the three men ran into view. As we rose, they leaped and tried to grab my legs, but I kicked their hands. Oliver shifted forward, and we raced away, zooming high over the jungle.

I looked back at the clearing. At least twenty paces from the tower, a man lay on the ground, motionless, a pool of red under him. I touched my earbud. "Crystal. Looks like we have a corpse. Omen and his goons might be cleaning house, if you know what I mean."

"They probably offed a squealer," Crystal said. "Maybe whoever sent you that message."

Zoë piped in. "Most likely. Someone sent another message a couple of minutes ago, but it got cut off. I'll forward it to Emerson."

Oliver made a tight turn, forcing me to squeeze even harder with my legs. "Perfect. Stay where you are and keep snooping. Crystal, get your glider, and bring Perdantus. We'll meet you where Zoë left hers. We're going to the Zeta station, and I'm coming back with a reintegration gun."

"Copy that," Crystal said. "But ride to the station *inside* a glider. This is no time to be a space cowgirl. Holding your breath that long isn't an option."

With me still on the glider, Oliver flew just over the trees while Emerson gave him navigation guidance. Soon, we arrived near the site of the bramble bee cave where we first met Kattica and Scamp.

When Oliver landed the glider next to Zoë's, I slid off the dome. Oliver opened it and climbed out, his expression grim. "It sounds like we had an ally at the base camp, and now he's probably dead."

"Yeah. He looked bad." I spoke toward the glider. "Emerson, did you get a transmission from Zoë?"

"Affirmative. Shall I read it to you?"

"Yes. We have some time while we're waiting for Crystal." I touched my earbud. "Are you on your way, Crystal?"

"Yep. Just got to my glider with Perdantus, and I'm taking off. Emerson's got me connected. I'm all ears."

I nodded. "Go ahead Emerson."

"Zoë forwarded the following message."

I apologize, but I am unable to meet with you at the tower. The head of security at the base camp is suspicious of my activities, and he is watching my every move. Even now, I told him that I need to write a message to my brother in the Gamma system, and he keeps passing by my station, trying to look at my screen. Since I can't meet with you, I will tell you what I was going to say.

I am the head of technology here, and I left the system access token for you in your glider. It was a simple matter for me to hack into your security system and figure out your entry code. In any case, I can tell from access logs that you have already seen the fake AI message generator, so you know that the kids here are being scammed in a terrible way. They put their lives in danger every day, thinking they are helping a loved one back home.

Since I arrived here three months ago, nine children have died from bramble bee stings, one of them only eight years old. At the end of this message, I plan to give you a list of their names so you can report the sad news to their families.

Now back to the critical message I need to give you, Megan. The moment you arrived, your presence on a security camera triggered an alert. When I saw your image on the video feed, I recognized you immediately. You see, I was in the courtroom when Judge Mason Statler sentenced you for the crime of piracy. I knew that the charges were ridiculous and that the judge was being paid off to render his verdict. How did I know? I am Anton Statler, the judge's son, and I overheard him talking to Captain Tillman about the captain's desire to take you as his personal captive. Having no authority, I couldn't do anything about the injustice at the time, but I followed your progress from afar, and I cheered you on through every amazing feat you accomplished.

As a result of the inspiration you infused in me, I made it my goal to find the head of the child-trafficking viper and kill it. My research led me to this planet and the nefarious deeds of Omen. He has worked with the likes of Admiral Fairbanks, his horrible wife, and their equally horrible daughter, Raven, to set up this glowsap mining business, and the money he has made by taking advantage of the time shift has been astronomical.

But now that you have eliminated the time shift, his flow of glowsap revenue has slowed to a mere trickle, comparatively speaking, and he is in the process of trying to accelerate the production of negative energy here to swell the time shift gradient again.

The formula for doing that is simple. Make the children suffer more. And now that the children will soon find out that their income as well as their money transfers are phony, their motivation for working is gone. I suspect that the algorithm will change from bribery to punishment, perhaps even blackmail by threatening the lives of the miners' family members.

I fear for the children, because the surest way to control these kids will be through fear, and the surest way to instill fear is to get a significant percentage of them stung by the bees. There is nothing worse than watching a child die from a bramble bee sting.

When Emerson paused, I heaved a sigh. "That's for sure. I'll never forget what Cynda suffered."

Oliver winced. "And I've seen worse suffering than that."

"Okay, Emerson, you can keep reading."

"There is nothing else to read."

I kicked a protruding root. "Blazes! Anton probably knew someone discovered what he was doing, so he sent the message without giving us the list of names of the kids who died."

"Then we'll have to count on Zoë finding them," Oliver said. "She read the message. I'm sure she's looking into it."

"Without a doubt." I pulled my spacesuit from the glider and began putting it on over my uniform. Fortunately, the waterproof exterior kept the interior from getting wet. "I wonder what Omen's hologram is all about. Why did he come to the tower that way? And since a hologram is advanced technology, the head of technology here should know about it."

"You mean, Anton."

"Right." I rolled my eyes upward in thought. "Did you notice that Anton said the algorithm will change from bribery to punishment? Not that Omen would make a change. The *algorithm* will change."

"What's an algorithm?" Crystal asked. "Another Willis word? And, by the way, I'm thirty seconds out."

"An algorithm is a way to solve a problem, like a series of steps to take to get from one point to another. You see it a lot in computer programs."

Oliver snapped his fingers. "A computer program!"

I narrowed my eyes. "What are you thinking?"

"Could Omen be just a computer program? You know, artificial intelligence?"

I began pacing slowly in front of him. "That would explain a lot. Apparently, he's not really here, but if he were outside the time shift, the only way he could communicate would be to overcome the shift by modulating the message in real time. A computer could do that. My father programmed Nike to communicate between here and Gamma Five when the shift was at its worst."

Crystal landed her glider. The moment it stopped, she opened the dome and stood on the seat, Perdantus on her shoulder. "Wait a minute, you two. You're flying in crazy land. Are you saying Omen's not real?"

"Maybe." I smiled at her. "Crazy land is a fun place. Won't you join us?"

"I suppose so." She stepped out of the glider. "Someone's got to bring a sanity anchor to keep you two moored in reality."

"All right, Miss Sanity Anchor, do you have a theory that makes more sense?"

"Nope. I'm just going to poke holes in your theory. I mean, if Omen's not a real person, who's pulling his strings? Who's collecting the cash? Whoever's behind this has to have some serious evil going on, and a computer doesn't fit that description."

"Good point, but could Omen be a real person and the hologram is an artificial manifestation of him? The real Omen could just sit back, maybe on Delta Ninety-eight, and collect all the cash while the computer algorithm and the hologram do all the dirty work."

"But," Oliver said, "the Omen I saw in the dining hall wasn't a hologram. He sat in a chair, picked up stuff, and patted someone on the back. A hologram can't do that. Same for the Omen who came into the dorm after the bat attack. He opened the door. But when I walked close to him in the dining hall, I heard some weird noises, like clicking. I'm sure it wasn't my imagination."

"Like a robot?" I asked. "Or an android? They don't vanish like he did at the tower."

Oliver shrugged. "Maybe. I'm just telling you what I heard. Could he show up as a robot sometimes and a hologram at other times?"

"I don't know about the robot issue," Zoë said through the earbud. "But I think you're on to something about the punishment theory. The kids got a message through their access pads that all bank accounts have been closed. They don't have any money and no motivation to go to the bee caves. And we're all in lockdown in our cabins. We're trapped."

I kicked the glider. "Blazes!"

"Double blazes." Crystal lifted her spacesuit from her glider and slid a foot into the pant leg while Perdantus fluttered off her shoulder and perched on a nearby branch. "If Anton's right, they're all in danger, including Zoë. If they force her to go to a glowsap mine, she won't know how to protect herself unless someone is with her who can show her the ropes. She's never done it before."

Oliver raised a hand. "I'll stay and help Zoë. Since we both have laser blasters, we should be safe for a while. You two go to the Zeta station and get the reintegration gun."

"Sounds like a plan," I said. "Take Zoë's glider and hide it well. We'll be out of earbud range till we get back, but keep listening for us."

"Will do. Good thing Zoë told me her code." Oliver punched in the code to Zoë's glider and climbed in. The moment he closed the dome, he took off toward the base camp.

As Crystal continued putting her suit on, I refastened my suit in front and looked at her. "I can't tell if my plans are stupid or not, but I know I have to save my father's life."

She put on her second glove. "Of course you do. It's not stupid at all."

"Perdantus," I called. "You're with me."

"I am at your service." He flew to my shoulder. "As always."

"You're the best." I stepped into my glider and smiled at Crystal. "On my six?"

"Yep. And be sure to keep an eye out for Jillian. After what the Omen algorithm said about a bald-faced lie, maybe she wasn't sent back to Gamma Five."

"Good point. And I wonder if he also lied about shutting the Zeta station down. Maybe we can figure out how to go to Gamma Five and get the Nine." I sat in the pilot's seat, set the helmet in my lap, and pushed the button to close the hatch. "Emerson, plot a course for the Zeta station."

His voice came through my earbud. "Course plotted."

When the dome clicked shut, I called to Crystal as she sat in her glider with her helmet on. "Comm check."

"I'm here," she said, "but I'm wondering how you plan to haul a reintegration gun in one of these gliders. I mean, it's roomy enough for me but not for anything else, except maybe a bag of popcorn."

"Speaking of not enough room." I lifted my helmet. "Get close, Perdantus. It's a short trip, but we'll have to get out of the glider in an airless docking bay this time."

"If I must." He flitted to my neck and squeezed into the helmet as I put it on.

With his feathers tickling my cheek, I started the engine, lifted off the ground, and followed Emerson's route. "Back to the gun, Crystal, I'll think of something to get it here, and I'm guessing you're hungry. No breakfast."

"Or dinner last night," Crystal said as she flew behind me. "Besides the muffin Kattica gave me."

"Same here. We've been so busy, I forgot about eating more than that muffin."

"I would have to be dead to forget about eating, and maybe not even then. I'd be a zombie hunting for brain flakes."

I laughed. "Brain flakes. Good one."

Perdantus grunted as he moved next to my cheek. "Why is that funny?"

"Bran flakes are a cereal humans eat. Zombies supposedly eat brains. So instead of bran flakes, she said brain flakes." I sighed. "I guess it's not so funny when I have to explain it."

"It isn't funny, but thank you for the explanation."

"Maybe it wasn't very funny," Crystal said, "but that Zeta station better have something to eat, like in a break room. I'd even eat stale doughnuts, though any doughnuts there are probably years old by now. Paperweights with holes in the middle."

"Let's change the subject so you won't think about food." I looked at the route. We were about five minutes away from our destination. "Emerson, are any signals coming from the Zeta station?"

"Affirmative, but nothing worth alerting you about. The spherical station is emitting a signal on the main Alliance warning frequency, probably to alert ships to its presence."

"Like a lighthouse beacon?"

"That is an apt comparison, though this signal has an interesting aspect that makes it differ from a mere warning to avoid colliding with it. It appears to have an unusual pattern, a series of shorter and longer bursts."

"A code? Could it be IGMC?"

"I already tried decoding the signals using the IGMC protocol, but I could make no sense of it."

"Could it be a negative-energy signal?" Crystal asked. "Remember, we didn't have our powers there."

"Good theory. I didn't have the same awful feeling there, but maybe because I was always in a ship or a glider, partially shielded from it. Emerson, can you tell if the signal is coming from an internal antenna or an external one?"

"Based on the signal strength, it is most likely external."

"Then we'll disable it." When we drew close to the station, I spotted an external antenna on the metallic surface and flew straight toward it. The glider clipped the top of the antenna, breaking its support.

"The signal is no longer transmitting," Emerson said.

"Perfect." I flew to the bay where we had left the Nebula Nine and found the entry doors still open. "Might as well land in that one. We know it works."

Crystal and I settled our gliders onto the bay's floor side by side and turned off the engines. Obviously, the base's artificial gravity was working, but, as I had guessed, the doors stayed open, keeping the bay from filling with air. Lights at the high ceiling provided enough illumination to see clearly.

"Stay put, Crystal," I said as I pressurized my suit, sending fresh air from the glider cockpit into the helmet. "I'll see what I can do about getting some air in the bay so we can look for Jillian."

"Nope. Not staying put. I gotta stay on your six."

"Suit yourself."

Crystal laughed "Ha! Suit yourself. I like it."

"An unintentional pun."

"Again," Perdantus said, "I did not understand the pun, but don't bother explaining it to me."

"Okay. I won't." I opened my dome hatch, climbed out of the glider, and walked toward the control lever that Jillian had used to open the doors, Crystal hurrying to catch up. When I arrived, I reached for the lever, but something seemed wrong. I drew back. "Crystal, when Jillian touched the lever, that's when she disappeared."

"Think it triggered the disintegration gun?"

"Maybe, but if it did, it had to be following her, waiting for the right moment to shoot." I scanned the room and found the gun, definitely aiming at us. I set a hand on Crystal's shoulder. "Back away slowly."

As we crept back, I kept my stare on the gun. It stayed aimed on the lever. When we were at least a dozen steps away, I stopped. "In theory, we should have our Starborn powers now."

"Right," Crystal said. "What are you thinking?"

"I should have Zoë's power. Maybe I can move the lever from here."

"But if nothing's there for the gun to zap, will it put a hole through one of the doors?"

"Only if the doors are closed, and they're not. If I move the lever and the gun shoots, it'll probably turn off before the doors close."

"Good point. Give it a try."

I focused on the lever, staring at it as I tried to use my mind to pull it down. Warmth pulsed at my chest. My dragon's eye had to be throbbing, but I couldn't see it.

I extended an arm and aimed my palm at the lever. I closed my fist, mentally grasping the lever, and pulled down. The lever shifted with my move. The door mechanism activated. A beam shot from the gun and through the opening, knifing into the darkness. A few seconds later, it shut off, just in time for the door panels to avoid getting hit.

Soon, the door panels met at the middle, though without an audible click in the airless chamber.

"Well done, Megan," Perdantus said into my ear. This time his tickling feathers felt good.

"You called it," Crystal said. "Someone programmed a booby trap."

"And we don't know how many other traps are here."

"So we have to get out as quick as we can." Crystal nodded toward the gun. "Will that one work for reintegrating? I mean, I know it can do both, but do you know how to change what it does?"

"Probably. With the guns at the Gamma Five station, it was just the flip of a switch."

"Then that part's easy, but like I said before, it won't be easy to get it down to the planet. That ray gun is at least as big as a glider."

"And combining it with the battery that it's sitting on doubles the size."

"I didn't even know about the battery." Crystal shook her head sadly. "Then there's no way."

"We'll figure out a way, but first we need to turn on the air or find an airlock to get out of this bay."

Crystal pointed at the bay's rear wall. "That door looks promising."

I followed her line of sight. A door the size and shape of a typical interior door of a house stood closed with a green light glowing above it. "That's got to be an airlock, and the green light means it's safe to go through it."

"No zapping?"

"Probably not."

"*Probably* not?"

I shrugged. "We can't stay out here."

"Nope." She gestured toward the door with a hand. "If I'm staying on your six, you have to go first. You know, do that brave thing you do."

I rolled my eyes. "Of course. You'll be protecting me from anything that'll attack me from behind."

"Exactly."

I turned the knob slowly, opened the door, and walked into a room about two meters wide and deep with a door on the other side, a red light illuminated above it. When Crystal joined me, I closed the door, shutting out all light except for the red glow. I found the airlock button and pushed it. A digital meter on the wall, shining white, started at 0% and rose quickly.

Crystal tapped on her helmet with a finger. "I'm looking forward to getting out of this suit."

"As am I," Perdantus said.

I pointed at the meter. "It'll be safe to take our helmets off at about eighty percent. These airlocks usually give you more than you need."

When the meter rose past 70%, Crystal's brow dipped down, barely visible in the dimness. "Something's wrong."

"What do you mean?"

"You know how I can sense if someone's lying, right? Well, I can also sense if a situation is a lie. Like this airlock. I don't think it's doing what it's supposed to be doing."

"It looks like it's working." I pointed again. "The meter's still going up."

"But is it air, or something else?"

"You mean, like a poisonous gas?"

"That's exactly what I mean."

"The suits won't let any gas in, and we'll probably be safe once we leave this room." When the meter rose to 100%, the light above the exit door switched from red to green. I turned the knob, but the door wouldn't open. "Blazes!"

Crystal moaned. "Another trap. And this one is designed to lock us in here until we take our helmets off, and then the gas will kill us."

"Probably." I turned and slammed the heel of my foot against the door, but it stayed intact.

"Both at the same time," Crystal said as she turned alongside me. "On three. One … two … three!"

We slammed our heels against the door. The jamb shattered, and the door swung open. We ran out of the room and jogged along a well-lit corridor. Once we had put a good distance between us and the airlock, I slid my helmet off and took the slightest of sniffs. The air seemed fine, though I couldn't be sure it was safe since some gases were odorless.

Perdantus sidled away from my face and shook his head hard. "That was not pleasant."

"Sorry it took so long." I gave Crystal a nod. "I think we're okay."

She took her helmet off and tucked it under an arm. "But what's the *next* booby trap?"

I shrugged. "Maybe there aren't any others. Those two traps were deadly, so whoever designed them might think one of them would've gotten us."

"Don't be so sure. Bad things always come in threes."

I tilted my head. "Threes? How do you know that?"

"Because if you get past the first two, you get all cocky, and you think you're ready for anything, but then the third one comes along, more devilish and more surprising than the other two, then …" She slapped her gloved hand against her forehead. "Bam! Right between the eyes, and you're dead."

"All right. Duly noted." I continued walking along the corridor. "We'll watch out for a third trap."

"A devilish trap," Crystal said, again following me.

"Right. I heard you say that before."

"Probably using doughnuts for bait."

"Most likely." When we arrived at the end of the corridor, we found a door standing ajar. I peeked around it. An elevator stood open with an empty elevator car.

When I pulled back, Crystal peeked as well and huffed. "All it needs is a sign that says, 'This is not a trap.' Then it couldn't possibly be a more obvious trap."

I spread my hands. "But I don't see any other way out of here."

"That's the point. The third trap gets anyone who made it past the first two."

"Okay, Miss Lie Detector …" I opened the door fully. "Is this elevator lying?"

Crystal stared at the open elevator for a long moment. "I don't feel a lie, but maybe you should try. You have the same power."

"Nope. I'm trusting yours. You have a lot more experience." I walked into the car and looked at the buttons for the different floor levels, each labeled with a cryptic symbol.

When Crystal joined me, she scanned the symbols. "Good luck with that gibberish."

My own scan came across a symbol that looked like one I had seen on the access token. Since that token had security codes on it, maybe the symbol represented security and indicated the access floor for the control room. I pressed the button next to the symbol. The door closed, and the car shot upward, making us bend our knees to compensate. As we zoomed, Crystal gave me a tight-lipped smile but said nothing.

The car slowed to a stop, and the door opened to a semicircular room filled with computer monitors, keyboards, and microphones on console pedestals positioned around the perimeter, each pedestal with a wheeled chair, similar to the room in the Epsilon station where I found my father.

After looking in all directions for potential danger, I walked to one of the pedestals, put my helmet on the floor next to it, and studied the monitor, Perdantus still on my shoulder. The screen showed an empty arrival/departure bay. "We need to find a log of departures. That'll tell us where the Nebula Nine went and if Jillian was sent anywhere."

Crystal set her helmet next to mine. "And we need to find out if this station is still operational."

On the screen, I found an icon labeled History and tapped on it. A window opened filled with lines of data. The line at the top showed yesterday's date with a destination of Gamma Five and a departure bay of D-4.

I scanned the monitors on various pedestals until I found the camera feed for D-4. On that screen, our gliders sat on the floor where we had just parked them, the same bay where the Nebula Nine had been. "This log proves that the Nine got zapped over to the Gamma Five Zeta station."

Crystal drummed her fingers on her thigh. "Then Lyric's mother probably knows about its arrival with no crew, but she hasn't sent anyone to investigate."

"Proving that this station isn't operational."

"So Omen wasn't lying about sending the Nine to Gamma Five or about shutting this station down. The only other possible lie is what he said about Jillian."

"Right." I scanned the history and found no other events on that date or any after it. In fact, our arrival in the Nine and its departure without us were the only two events in the past several weeks. "I don't think Jillian went anywhere. Nothing's in the log."

"But if that gun disintegrated her into a bunch of sparkles, it had to send her somewhere. We saw her on the video feed when Omen talked to us. Maybe the system doesn't log zaps on humans. Only on ships."

Perdantus flew down to the computer console and looked at me. "If your theory is correct that Omen is a figment of computer intelligence, then how could Jillian have been with him? You have theorized the possibility of a robotic version of Omen at the base camp, but how does he get around so quickly? Have you seen his ship or a glider? How could Jillian disintegrate and appear at his location without a record of the transport? These odd circumstances lead me to believe that something is going on that we have not yet considered, though I have no answers to my own questions."

I stared at him. In my mind's eye, I saw Jillian standing next to Omen, looking at me on a projection screen, but like I wondered at the time, how could that be possible since I hadn't allowed our camera feed to go through the connection? The only option that made sense was that they were looking at the bridge from within the ship itself or maybe a data connection from the ship to the Zeta station. In that case, maybe she was still in the station somehow or in a place where a hologram like Omen could reside.

I grabbed a microphone, turned it on, and spoke into it. "Jillian? Can you hear me?"

"What in blazes are you doing?" Crystal asked.

I snapped my fingers and pointed at a monitor. "Look for a way to turn on a speaker."

"Okay, mystery girl." Crystal touched an icon on a monitor. "That should do it."

"Jillian," I said again into the microphone. "Are you there?"

Jillian's voice came through a speaker on one of the computers. "Well, it's about time you figured it out, Mophead."

I smiled. "That's her."

"How do you know it's not Omen imitating her?" Crystal asked.

"Listen, genius," Jillian said, "do you think Omen knows that I call Megan Mophead?"

"No. I guess he doesn't."

A sigh came through the speaker. "Sorry to be so blustery, but you have no idea what it's like trapped in this computer system. It's like being submerged in electrified salt water with a hundred eels nipping at your toes and fingers."

I lifted my brow. "Wow! That's really descriptive."

"Yeah. I've been working on that illustration for a while. But enough of that. Tell me what's going on."

"Not much time, but here's the short version." I gave her a super condensed summary of our activities and ended with, "So priority number one is to reintegrate my father, because he's in danger of dispersing. My guess is that you're pretty stable, so you'll drop down the priority list a bit."

"You're right. Put me last on the list. We have to rescue those kids from Omen and his slavers."

"Do you know if Omen's real?" Crystal asked. "Or is he an artificial intelligence … um … thing?"

"He's both. Sort of. Omen is a handle for whoever programmed him, so that's not the programmer's real name. Anyway, he created the computer-generated Omen and a robot version. We'll call them Omen AI one and two, and we'll call the creator Omen Real. The programming for the Omen AIs exists in a supercomputer on Delta Ninety-five."

"The volcano planet?" Crystal asked. "Sonya said Omen was on Delta Ninety-one."

"That was a guess," I said. "The planet's name was on a messy handwritten note. Sonya wasn't sure she was reading it right. I looked Ninety-one up in the database. It's a lot like Beta Four, pretty much frozen. Delta Ninety-five makes more sense."

"Right," Jillian said. "I suppose Omen Real thought no one would discover the code for Omen AI on a planet that might spew the residents with lava. Anyway, from Ninety-five, Omen Real uses the Omen AI programming to send instructions through the Zeta station down to Delta Zero where he appears as a hologram or a robot. When you heard from me earlier, I was also in a hologram form, already stuck inside this computer. I had no idea what was going on then, but I have my bearings now."

"Can you block what the Omen AI programming sends to Delta Zero?" I asked.

"No. I'm barely able to use the speaker, but I can read data. I know exactly what he's doing."

"Okay. What?"

"He's downsizing his business. Now that he can't control the kids with bribery, he has to control them with force, and he doesn't have the manpower to keep all the kids in line. So he's going to send one group of his oldest and strongest kids to the busiest bramble bee cave, escorted by his thugs. And they'll have to go into the cave without their armored suits. If they refuse, they'll get shot."

I balled my fists tightly but stayed quiet as Jillian continued. "Then, the kids who get stung will be put in a cage outside to die horrible deaths while the others watch. And the kids who get shot, their corpses will be thrown in the cage, too. One way or another, they'll learn to comply. Then, once the survivors are all in line, they'll get their armored suits back. Lower glowsap production rate, I suppose, but he's made more money on the mines than he can ever spend, so he doesn't mind trimming the business a bit, as he put it."

I shouted, "Trimming the business!" I raised my fists as I roared, "They're human beings! Children! They should be home with their parents! Playing in the fields, flying kites, building model spaceships!" I kicked a chair, sending it wheeling across the room. "Blazes to Omen and his evil minions!"

As I heaved deep breaths, Crystal crossed her arms and gave me an approving nod. "Exactly how I feel, but what are we going to do about it?"

Trying to cool off, I paced in front of her. "Let me think." An image of the kids marching through the jungle to a bee cave came to mind, men with laser blasters pointed at them. I mentally shouted at them to run into the trees. Try to survive in the jungle on your own. Raven did. My father did.

I sighed. But my father and Raven were skilled adults who had loads of experience. These scared children needed a leader. And here I was, safe in an orbiting transport station. As prideful as it might be to think this, those kids needed me.

"I know what you're thinking," Crystal said, "and I'm no mind reader like Chip or Riddle. You can't be everywhere. You have to rescue your father, and you're the only one who can do that. Besides, we have Oliver and Zoë on the planet. I'd bet you a dozen doughnuts that they'll volunteer to go to the mine. And since they're two of the oldest and strongest, they're sure to be picked anyway."

I halted and spread my arms. "And that's a good thing? Oliver and Zoë will just die with the rest of them."

"It's a good thing, Miss I'm-the-only-one-who-can-save-the-universe, because they're every bit as brave and resourceful as you are. And maybe, just maybe, they'll go to a glowsap mine that'll be far enough from the tower for them to get their powers back."

I snapped my fingers. "Right. Then Zoë can keep the bees away from the kids or even send them flying at the thugs to sting them. And Oliver can heal any kid who gets stung by a bee."

Crystal lowered her head. "Yeah, well that was a maybe. The tower's probably designed to cover all the mines."

"Now, don't go getting all pessimistic on me. It was your idea." I started pacing again as I spoke toward the microphone. "Jillian, have you been listening?"

Her voice came through the speaker. "Yep. You two are helping me keep my sanity."

"Do you have any way of knowing which glowsap mine they'll be heading to?"

"Not only can I find out, I might be able to do a lot more."

"Like what?"

"I've been studying the commands Omen sends out. I wonder if I can send one of my own that looks like his."

I halted. "If you could, that would change everything. We could stop the whole plan from happening."

"If I may interject," Perdantus said from the back of a chair, "Jillian's idea is excellent, but you should take care to use it in a way that will not raise suspicion. If Omen or any of his minions realizes what you're doing, you will not be able to continue. Therefore, I suggest minor tweaks that will benefit our cause, alterations that will not raise doubts in the hearers' minds."

"Like what?" I asked.

"Like suggesting that they go to the glowsap mine that is farthest from the base camp. The reason we invent could be that a long march will tire the kids out and make them more likely to be stung by the bees."

I grimaced. "That's awful. We could get more kids killed that way. And we don't even know if the most distant cave will help Zoë and Oliver get their powers back."

"Then perhaps we should concentrate on the tower. I know it's essential for your father's survival, but if its signal could be reduced enough to help our Starborn allies while still keeping your father intact, you wouldn't have to give the minions a questionable command."

I shook a finger at him in an approving way. "Your idea is good for the kids' sake, but I'm worried about lowering the tower's signal. I don't know how strong it has to be to keep my father alive."

Perdantus flew to my shoulder and caressed my cheek with a wing. "You should be worried, Megan, but we are all taking risks. I'm sure your father would be willing to take risks of his own, especially if his risks would help secure the safety of the children."

"You're right about that." I picked up the microphone and spoke into it. "Jillian, were you able to hear Perdantus?"

"Yes. Loud and clear. He is quite brilliant."

Now certain that she could hear us without the microphone, I set it down. "Have you seen any data about the tower's coverage?"

"I've been searching ever since I heard his idea. It looks like the consoles in your room can access diagrams, but I can't tell if you can change anything. I'm pretty new at being inside a computer. In pilot school, we didn't have classes about how to be a digitized phantom."

"Yeah. Go figure." I turned toward Crystal. "Want to see what you can find?"

"I'm on it." She tapped a computer screen. "You guys brainstorm what you're going to tell the evil minions while I look for the diagrams. We still need to tell the minions to go to the farthest mine."

"How about simulating a test?" Perdantus said. "Tell them that you want to test the tower's reach, and the only way to do that is to travel to the signal's limits. You could say that you want to reduce the tower's signal for reasons they don't need to know."

I imagined the thugs at the mine trying to carry out the orders. A big piece was missing. "How will they be able to report if the signal's reaching the glowsap mine? And if they do report it, won't Omen AI get word about the test?"

"A receiving meter." Crystal pointed at the computer screen. It showed a diagram of a square box with a digital readout—2.3. "They have a meter that reads the signal. According to this documentation, the signal has two parts, one that snuffs Starborn powers and one that shields against the bats. The meter they have detects the bat-signal part, so if we can reduce the Starborn-squelcher part, they'll never know we did it."

"Can you reduce it?" I asked.

"We should know in a minute." She tapped on the screen a few more times until a map popped up with a tower icon at the center. Red lines and blue lines radiated from the tower over images of green treetops, like ripples on a pond. White dots glowed here and there on the map.

"I think the white dots are the glowsap mines." Crystal pointed at one at the edge of the map. "And that one's the farthest from the tower. The red signals are the Starborn snuffers, and the blue ones are the bat bannishers."

"Okay, Miss Alliterative, can you change the Starborn snuffing signal?"

"That's Alliterative Ally to you, my fussy friend." She looked at the screen again. "Let's see what I can ... um ... concoct."

I tapped on the microphone. "Jillian, start thinking about how you can get a fake Omen message to the minions. You'll have to do some acting to convince them."

"Let's practice," Jillian said. "Turn on the hologram projectors in the room."

I scanned the room's walls and found a projector at each corner. At a console next to Crystal's, I tapped on a screen until I found the projector controls and turned them on. Multicolored beams of light emanated from the lenses and combined at the center of the room to paint a three-dimensional rendering of Jillian. Although her face looked perfect, her body seemed thin, almost skeletal.

"Oh, I can see myself." She ran her hands along her sides and down her scant hips. "I look emaciated, but it'll have to do."

I walked close and waved a hand through her image. "So you can make a hologram. That's great. But can you look like Omen?"

"Probably. I see his profile in the database. One minute." Jillian's image crumbled into sparkles that swirled through a column of light. After a few seconds, they congealed again into the shape of a man. Soon, the image clarified into Omen.

The image spread its arms. "How do I look?" the image asked with Jillian's voice.

"You look fine," I said, "but a woman's voice won't fool anyone."

The image frowned. "Wrong voice print." After a few more seconds, Omen set his hands on his hips and spoke again. "My name is Omen. I am the evil AI version of the evilest ratfink in the galaxy. You must do my evil bidding."

I grinned. "That's a lot of evil."

"Don't worry. I won't pour it on that thick when I talk to the minions. I just have to find where the hologram projectors are on the planet so I can use them."

"I know there's one at the tower. That's where I saw Omen earlier. But you'll have to figure out if there's some kind of alert that'll tell the minions you want to talk to them."

"That shouldn't be difficult."

"And this is even better," Crystal said, pointing at her screen. "Here's how to turn down the Starborn snuffer. According to the computer's prediction model, the signal will die just before the farthest glowsap mine. So we're good to go."

I nodded. "Perfect. But who's going to tell Oliver and Zoë to make sure they're going with the doomed group?"

Perdantus lifted a wing. "Allow me to do that. If you can get me to the base camp, I'm sure I can do what is necessary."

"Great." I furrowed my brow. "But how're we going to get you to the camp?"

"I'll take him." Crystal jabbed my ribs with a finger. "But don't you dare go off on some crazy quest without me. Just wait here until I get back, and I'll glue myself to your six again."

"All right, but if either of you sees my father, tell him I'm working on getting a reintegration gun down there, and I'm planning to go to the Gamma Five Zeta station to get the Nine. And ask him if the tower's signal change is hurting him at all."

"Will do, worrywart, but I probably won't see him. It'll be better if I drop Perdantus off far away from the camp so no one notices me. He can fly the rest of the way." She picked up her helmet. "Just remember to watch out for the third booby trap. And don't do anything stupid."

"In other words, don't do anything Crystal wouldn't do."

"I didn't say that. I do lots of stupid things." She put her helmet on, and her voice came through my earbud. "Now I have to figure out how to go through the airlock without getting poisoned and how to open the bay door without getting Zeta zapped."

"Since I'm in the control room, I'm sure I can control those now. You'll be fine. And you can cut out the alliterations. It's getting old."

"If you say so." She looked at Perdantus. "Let's go, brilliant bird."

He flew to her shoulder and gave me a nod as they left. "Allowing your allies to assist in your admirable adventure is meritorious, magnificent, and magnanimous."

I suppressed a laugh. "Crystal, look what you started."

When she entered the elevator car, she pivoted back to me and grinned without a word, then waved as the door closed.

The Omen image bowed its head. "I'm going to disappear from this room and work on sending the message to the goons on the planet. I'll report on the results as soon as I can."

"I'll see you soon." After I refamiliarized myself with the Zeta station's controls, I turned my attention to a security monitor. After a couple of minutes, a video feed, apparently motion activated, picked up Crystal walking through the corridor we had come through before getting on the elevator. Perdantus was no longer on her shoulder, probably squeezed into her helmet, but from the back, I couldn't tell.

She went through the usual airlock motions, entered the ship's bay chamber, and got into her glider without incident. "Ready to fly, Captain Willis," she said. "Can you open the bay doors from there?"

"Yep." I pushed a button on the screen that initiated the opening of the doors, revealing Delta Zero, a bright disc against a starry backdrop. The moment the doors finished opening, Crystal flew through the gap and shrank out of sight as if the planet had absorbed her.

Knowing that she would return soon, I left the bay doors open. "Any progress, Jillian?"

"I just finished delivering the message. Omen's stooges seemed to buy it. I guess they're not expecting someone to impersonate an AI slave-trafficking monster. Let's hope Perdantus has time to clue in Oliver and Zoë so they can be sure to volunteer."

I crossed my arms. "So now I wait."

"You don't have much choice, unless you want to leave without Crystal, and that would be the stupidest thing you've ever done."

I laughed under my breath. "I've done some pretty stupid things you don't know about."

"But I do know you. Doing nothing will drive you bananas. You should find something to keep your brain busy."

I lifted a finger. "I could detach one of the disintegration guns from its mooring. Then when I return with the Nebula Nine, the gun will be ready to go."

"Do you mean detach a gun in one bay and haul it to the bay you're going to use for your transport to and from Gamma Five?"

"Exactly."

"Won't it be too heavy?"

"Not if we temporarily turn the artificial gravity off. I have magnetic shoes, and the gliders automatically engage their magnets when they land, so they'll stay put. It should be easy."

"Famous last words. But go ahead and give it a try. It'll keep you from going crazy while Crystal is gone. Of course, maybe you already *are* crazy, but—"

"You can stop talking, Aunt Jillian." I found the gravity switch on the computer and turned it off, then put my helmet on, pressurized the suit, and used my toes to flip on the magnets in my shoes.

In order to take the disintegration gun with me, I would have to somehow attach it to my glider. Recalling the basic schematics for Zeta stations, I hustled to the mechanic's room, collected a coil of rope, and hurried to a bay we hadn't used yet. After going through the airlock to enter the vacuum environment, I left the rope in the corridor and walked out onto the bay's floor.

I scanned the area. This bay's doors were also open, exposing me to the bitterly cold, airless environment. Fortunately, the heating element in my suit would keep me from freezing. Still, I had to work quickly. Since I didn't have a tank, the air in the suit's auxiliary pouches wouldn't last long. And with the possibility of a third booby trap still niggling at my brain, I had to be careful. I was facing far too many horrible ways to die.

The disintegration gun stood on a five-meter-high platform in front of a wall adjacent to the bay door. With no gravity, I didn't have to charge my legs to get up there. After turning my shoe magnets off, I leaped toward the gun, turned my shoes back on as I sailed, and set my feet on top of the platform.

I touched the base of the gun and looked it over. Although I had transported a gun like this to Delta Zero in the past, I had never studied one up close. Attached to the top of a cubic battery with dimensions of about a half meter, the gun stood on a black metal tripod that made it rise about a meter above my head. A ball joint atop the tripod allowed the gun to pivot in any direction, making it able to cover an entire ship with its disintegrating ray.

Under the battery, a track of chained links ran in a recessed channel leading to an airlock compartment at the outer wall. Apparently, the chain was designed to pull the gun to the exterior of the station, maybe as a weapon against attacking ships.

With my gloved hand, I reached through the channel under the battery and felt a cog that connected the battery to a chain link. The glove made it difficult to dislodge the cog from the chain, but after a few seconds I managed to disconnect them. Then I shifted the battery and its attached gun off the track.

With the gun-and-battery assembly in my arms, I walked down the wall. At floor level, I pushed the weightless unit through the airless vacuum to the inner corridor where I collected the rope and pushed it along as well, then walked to the bay where my glider sat.

I set the gun against the back of the glider and tied it securely to the towing hook. Of course, I couldn't fly very well like this, but this bay's gun would likely disintegrate both the glider and the gun since they were attached. Then the Gamma Five station's gun would reintegrate both the glider and this gun on arrival. At that point, I could find the Nebula Nine, load the gun in the cargo hold, and return to Delta Zero with it.

I opened the glider's top hatch and used my earbud to contact Emerson. "Are you doing all right?"

"Affirmative."

"Want me to get you up to speed with what's going on?"

"There is no need. I have been listening to your chatter, and I have deduced both your problems and your plans, if you don't mind me joining in your alliterative game."

"Actually, I'd like that game to get squashed."

"The game is now squashed. But I would like to help with one of your problems. I could load Jillian into the glider's computer, and when we go to the Gamma Five Zeta station, the reintegration process there should restore her."

"How is that possible? She's just computer data, right?"

"At the present time, but the situation is more complex than that. All data is fundamentally binary, that is, on or off. Her energy was transformed into binary code, but within that code is an algorithm to transform everything back into energy. All I have to do is use the algorithm built into her data to change her into energy again. At that time, her energy would come out of the computer to be reintegrated, but our timing will have to be perfect. If she is not reintegrated quickly, she will disperse and scatter."

"That's a super critical *if*. How quickly is *quickly?*"

"Not knowing the fine details of the regenerating gun's speed, it is impossible to be precise, but I would say that after three seconds, her chances of successful regeneration would fall under fifty percent."

"Three seconds!" I heaved a sigh. "We'll have to let her decide if she's willing."

"Of course, but to be ready, you can remove me from the glider by sliding out the CPU module and plug me into the station's computer. Once there, I can analyze the situation more precisely."

"Okay. We'll talk when I get you plugged in." I reached under the console, found the module's handle, and pulled it out. With Emerson in tow, I went through the airlock procedure again and closed the inner door. Strange that it tried to kill us one time, but it had worked fine ever since.

I hurried back to the control room and found Jillian's hologram standing at the center of the room. "That didn't take too long, did it?" I asked.

Jillian shook her head. "Not long at all. While you were gone, I visited the minions again, looking like Omen. At a distance, I saw Perdantus talking to Oliver, so he got the message in time, and Crystal's probably on her way back. While I was there, I told the minions to ask for volunteers first. We wanted the most courageous kids to be the ones we make an example of. That'll strike fear into the hearts of all the others."

"Whew! That's pretty savage." I flipped the artificial gravity back on and turned the magnets off in my shoes. "Do you think it worked?"

"They loved the idea. One of them even said it was a classic Omen move."

"Then you were convincing. No surprise there."

Her hologram self rolled her eyes. "Right. Because I'm the evil twin sister who conned her way to the top rank in pilot school. Devious actress extraordinaire." She waved a hand. "I know you're not saying that. It's just me still feeling guilty. I feel like maybe I'm being punished, and deservedly so."

"Stop beating yourself up." I lifted the computer module. "I've got Emerson here. He says he should be able to put you in the glider so you can be reintegrated when we go to the Gamma Five Zeta station. I can plug this module into the computer here and he can transfer you over. The glider module has a standard interface, so it should connect without a problem."

She gave the module a skeptical stare. "Is Emerson sure about this?"

"As sure as he can be. He says he has to locate the algorithm that transformed you into data. It should be embedded. Then he just has to reverse it."

"*Just* has to. That *just* is probably a lot bigger than it sounds."

"True, but it's better than being stuck in the Zeta station's computer for the rest of your life."

"But if Emerson's wrong, the rest of my life might be minutes instead of years."

"Maybe it would be better if I plugged him in. Then you two can talk about it while I try to fire up this station so we can leave as soon as Crystal gets back."

She gave me a resigned nod. "All right. Plug him in."

After finding the interface slot in a computer cabinet and sliding the module in, I used the computer screen to open the port. A few seconds later, a man formed next to Jillian. Gray haired, trim, and wearing an Alliance space travel uniform, he smiled at me. "Greetings, Captain Megan Willis. I am Emerson. This is the form I chose to converse with you and Captain Jillian Willis. I hope it is acceptable."

I smiled in return. "Yeah. It's great. Sort of a wise-professor look. Go ahead and explain to Jillian what you want to do while I restart this station."

"Very well, and if you have trouble doing so, perhaps I can help from within the system."

"Sounds good." While Emerson and Jillian talked, I scoured the command prompts on the computer screen, but every icon for initiating a transport was dimmed. Tapping on them did nothing. Finally, I found an administrator override button and tapped it. A box appeared, asking for a password, but, of course, I didn't know what the password could be. "Emerson, can you find the administrator password?"

His hologram looked at me. "Perhaps." Two seconds later, he said, "OMENLIVES. All capital letters with no space."

As I typed it into the keyboard, I spoke the words, "Omen lives." I moved my finger over to tap the Enter key, but activity in the security camera feed caught my attention. Crystal's glider arrived in the bay and landed next to mine. I shifted over to that computer, closed the bay doors, and sent air into the chamber.

"Welcome back, Crystal. Stay put for a minute while your bay gets filled with air. That way, you can pop the hatch and take your helmet off. Then I'll set up the transport on a timer and come down there, and we'll all leave together, including Jillian. I'll give you the full scoop then."

"Okay by me. I'll just chill out. Maybe take a nap. I found banana trees in the jungle, so I ate five of them. Not five trees. Five bananas. Anyway, I'm feeling sleepy now. And, by the way, Perdantus stayed with Oliver. He wasn't too keen on riding in my helmet again."

"Sounds good. You'll have maybe ten minutes to snooze. I'll see you soon." Just as I lifted my finger again to enter the password, a sense of unease filtered in, like a shadow lurking at the back of my mind. I turned toward the hologram. "Emerson, is someone else here? I didn't see anyone on the security feed."

Emerson's image turned toward me. "Yes. The Omen AI presence has been here the entire time, but Jillian successfully locked her data area away from him. She and I are safe."

"But he knows what I'm doing. I mean, getting ready to restart the transport system."

"That is highly likely."

The thought of his phantom presence sent a chill up my spine, making me shudder. "Can he interfere?"

"When you enter the password, you will have administrator access, so he will not be able to override the restart or the transport mechanism, but he might be able to alter other conditions, such as air compression and other survival needs."

"Okay. Speaking of survival, why would the ventilation system be able to send poisonous gas into the airlock like what happened to Crystal and me?"

"Only as a way to eliminate intruders."

"And we would all be considered intruders."

"Affirmative."

"That's good to know." I again eyed the Enter icon. "When you're ready to do the transfer, I might need to zoom out of here in a hurry, so I'd better find a toilet and a bite to eat."

Jillian pointed toward the corridor. "Break room to the left has a fridge with a freezer. Maybe something's in there that isn't spoiled yet. Bathroom is across the hall from that."

"Got it." After using the toilet, I hurried to the break room and found a couple of sealed bags of trail mix. I stuffed one into a pocket under my spacesuit and tore the other one open. On my way back to the control room, I wolfed down the mix—a blend of various nuts and dried fruit. When I arrived, I found Jillian and Emerson still standing where they were before.

"I'm ready," Jillian said. "Emerson, buzz me out of this computer."

"Very well." Emerson looked at me. "We will disappear from view. At that time, allow us thirty-two seconds to enter the module. Then you can remove it from the computer."

"Got it, but if Omen AI decides to pump gas in here to stop me from restarting the station, I'd better get ready." I put my helmet on, pressurized the suit, and checked the laser blaster in the holster on my belt, most likely dry by now. Everything appeared to be ready. At another computer screen, I set a timer for 32 seconds. "Go."

The moment Emerson and Jillian vanished, I started the timer, then punched the Enter key to send the administrator password. The screen responded with "Password Accepted," and a set of control icons appeared, showing the other Zeta stations. I chose the Gamma Five station, highlighted one of its arrival bays, and selected the bay our gliders were in as the departure point.

For the Target Area prompt, I chose the entire bay floor space so the gun would send both gliders and the gun next to my glider. Finally, I set the departure countdown timer to five minutes. That would be plenty of time to get to the departure bay. When I entered the parameters, the screen responded with digits that started at 5:00 and counted down.

An alarm in the ceiling wailed. A new hologram appeared at the center of the room—Omen. He looked at me with a calm demeanor, his hands folded in front. "Megan, you should not have restarted the Zeta station. Since you were able to access the administrator password, it would do no good for me to change it. You would merely find the new one. I have no choice but to eliminate you. Since you are wearing a protective suit, gassing you won't work. I'll have to deploy other anti-intruder measures."

"You talk too much." I drew my laser blaster and zapped all four projectors, making them explode in splashes of sparks. After holstering the gun and noting that Emerson's 32 seconds had expired, I pulled the module from the computer and hurried to the elevator but halted in front of the door. Even with my protective suit, the elevator car could be a death trap if it plunged to the lowest level and slammed into the landing.

I ran back to the control room, turned the gravity off again, and engaged the magnets in my shoes. The timer showed 3:17. I could still make it. Mentally counting down, I hurried back to the elevator car and pressed the button for the floor I needed. When the door closed and the car moved down at a normal speed, I exhaled in relief. Fortunately, an elevator like this could function without gravity. It just couldn't go into a free fall.

After leaving the elevator, I jogged toward the door leading to the bay, slowed by the pressurized suit and the magnetic shoes. With about two minutes to go, I still had enough time if Omen didn't spring any other surprises on me.

As I neared the airlock, I slowed my pace. Since we had atmospheric pressure on both sides, the light glowed green above the door. I pushed the button, and the door opened. A suction jerked me through the airlock and into the bay. On the opposite side, the bay doors stood partially open. Air whooshed through the gap and sucked me toward it headfirst. Clutching the computer module with all my might, I flew by the gliders. With my free hand, I grabbed the barrel of the gun attached to my glider's towing hook, my feet pointing toward the bay doors.

With both hands occupied, I tried to close the doors with my mind, but they felt too heavy. They wouldn't budge. In seconds, I would be sucked into the void.

Crystal shouted through my earbud. "What in blazes is going on?"

My hand that held the gun began slipping. "Third booby trap!"

"Hang on, Megan!"

"Yeah. Good idea."

Her glider's engine roared to life. She whipped it around, hovered behind me, and pushed its nose under my body, but the force jerked my hand away from the gun. I flipped over backwards and flew toward the open doors.

Blinding light flashed. Something stung my body all over, like a thousand bramble bees attacking every centimeter of skin. The suction returned, and I flew again, this time into Jillian. Wearing her pressurized suit and helmet, she clutched my wrist as the bay doors closed behind her, both of her feet pressed against a door's panel.

When it finished closing, the suction ceased. She dropped to the floor and set me down, the computer module in her other hand.

I shouted, "It worked! Emerson did it!"

"He certainly did," Jillian said, "and it's a good thing I got restored wearing this suit. Otherwise, I'd be gasping for air. I guess it makes sense, though, I got zapped while wearing this."

Crystal opened her glider's dome and spoke through my earbud. "Never a dull moment with Megan around."

"Right," Jillian said. "It took two of us to make sure she didn't become scattered stardust."

"Thanks, you two." I touched my helmet. "Any idea if we have enough air pressure in here to take our helmets off?"

A girl's voice emanated from a hidden speaker. "It's high enough. Plenty high. I saw that someone was coming, so I closed the doors and turned on the air as soon as I saw you. Turned it on quick and high speed."

I blinked. "Echo?"

"Yes, yes. My bud is tuned to your frequency, so we're able to hear each other. Welcome to the Gamma Five Zeta station."

After taking my helmet off, I spotted the camera at a corner near the ceiling and waved at it. "Thanks. But we can't stay long. We have to find the Nebula Nine. Is it here?"

"Yes. Yes. Level four. Bay six."

Jillian took her helmet off, walked toward me, and extended the module. "Let's get Emerson reinstalled, load the disintegration gun in the Nine's cargo hold, and hustle back to Delta Zero."

I took the module and lifted it so Echo could see it. "Want a fun project?"

"You bet. You bet. I'll meet you at the Nine."

Crystal, Jillian, and I hurried through the process of getting the gun loaded on the Nebula Nine and putting the gliders into the ship's docking area, while Echo reinstalled Emerson into the onboard computer.

After I secured the gun in the cargo hold, I climbed the ladder from the lower deck and walked onto the bridge. Echo rose from her knees at Emerson's console cabinet and brushed her hands together. "Finished. And I made a programming change that I've been dying to make. Dying to make."

"What change?"

She set her hands on her hips and flashed a proud smile. "Emerson can now land the Nebula Nine."

I laughed. "Good job. We've needed that several times."

"I know. I know." She closed the cabinet and looked at me with longing in her eyes. "I wish …" She shook her head. "Never mind. Never mind."

I gazed at her. Thoughts came through as if spoken out loud—*I wish I could go with you.*

"You want to go to Delta Zero with us?" I asked.

She squinted. "Did you just read my mind? You did, didn't you?"

I nodded. "But I assume you were assigned to this post for a reason. Can you leave?"

"Yes, yes. Piper and Lyric will be here soon. I was watching the controls while repairing the Astral Dragon. The Dragon's in the bay that's next to the Nine's. She's as good as new. Well, almost as good as new. Still some scorch marks. A lot of scorch marks. Hundreds of scorch marks. But no leaks at all. Not a single leak. At least none that I know of."

"That's a lot of repairs. How long have we been gone? In your time that is. I don't know what the warp's up to right now."

"Five days, give or take a few hours. Plenty of time. Plenty."

"That's odd. We haven't been gone nearly that long in Delta Zero days. That means time is moving faster here now. It was the opposite before."

Echo clapped her hands. "That's so exciting! We must've had a rebound effect. All time passage returns to equilibrium eventually, so Delta Zero is slowing down for a while. If not for the negative energy that's probably building up there, the rebound effect would be even bigger. Even bigger."

"I'm glad you understand that time warp stuff, because I don't. Anyway, I suppose you and Jillian could go in the Nine, and Crystal and I could take the Dragon. Two ships are better than one."

"Are two arrival bays available at that Zeta station?"

I lifted a finger. "I don't know if even one is available. I do know that Omen can't shut the station down. I overrode that option with an administrator password. But he can cause a lot of other problems. He opened a bay door that nearly sucked me out into oblivion."

Echo gasped. "Oh. Not good. Not good. But if we're safely seated in the ships, that won't matter. We can just fly away."

"Only if we can keep the bay doors from closing the moment we arrive." I gave her a lightning-fast summary of the recent events. Since Echo was so smart, she took it all in without explanations.

She scrunched her brow. "I might have a solution. A plan. A way to fix the problem. Multiple options."

"How?"

"First option, when we appear in the arrival bays, we can blast the reintegration gun with the ship's laser. Then, if the bay doors close, it'll be safe to manually open it. Second option, we could blast our way out the doors. Pretty messy, though. Chance of flying stuff damaging something is pretty high. Third option, pick an arrival bay where the doors are locked open. We won't need air. Then we can fly right out."

"Locked open?"

Echo nodded. "Some of the Gamma station bays are like that for ships that aren't dropping off passengers. They're just arriving and leaving right away. They never close unless there's an emergency."

"Can you detect if a Delta Zero door is locked open from the control room here?"

"I can tell if the station is reporting it to be locked open. Whether or not the station's computer is lying, I wouldn't know."

"Crystal would know. I found out she can tell if almost anything is lying, even machines."

Crystal and Jillian walked up the Nine's lowered front ramp and joined us on the bridge. "I can tell most of the time," Crystal said, talking while chewing. "But I heard Echo's options through my earbud. One way or another, we can make it through the door."

"Then let's get moving," I said. "My father needs that gun. And we don't know what's going on with Oliver, Zoë, and Perdantus. They could be in a lot of trouble."

"True." Crystal swallowed her mouthful. "But you'd better eat something. I doubt that you've had anything since that muffin Kattica gave you."

"I had some trail mix. Not much, but it helped."

"The Dragon's stocked with good food," Echo said. "You can get something there."

A new voice broke in through the earbud. "Megan, it's Lyric. I'm in the control room, and I've been listening in. It sounds like you're going to leave right away."

I looked in the direction of the control room, though I couldn't see it. "I have to leave. I guess you heard why."

"I did. Go ahead and board the Dragon. I found six Delta Zero arrival bays that are reporting locked-open doors. Two are next to each other. I can send the two ships to those bays."

"That sounds too convenient. Could be a trap." I looked at Crystal. "Go to the control room and check it out. See if you think the Zeta station is lying while I board the Dragon."

"I'm on it, Captain." Crystal jogged down the ramp and hurried out of sight.

I hugged Jillian. "I'm glad you're back in one piece."

"Trust me, I like being solid much better." She drew away and gave me a push on the back. "Last one to Delta Zero is a bad omen."

"Yeah. Funny." I hugged Echo. "See you soon."

She held my shoulders and kissed me on both cheeks. "One kiss from me, and one from Lyric, since she's in the control room."

"Thanks." I waved toward Emerson's console. "I'm looking forward to seeing you land the Nine."

As I jogged down the ramp, his reply came through my earbud. "The new protocol states that I am allowed to land if no qualified pilot is available, so it's unlikely that I will be called upon to land the ship."

Not bothering to answer him, I hurried to the bay next door and walked toward the Astral Dragon's ramp. As Echo had said, black scorch marks covered much of the ship, though not readily visible on the black exterior. I strode up the ramp and onto the bridge. Inside, the many scorch marks on the walls were easier to see.

"Welcome, Megan," Sonya said. "Will you resume your role as captain?"

"Yes, and Crystal will be my first mate. We'll be transported to the Zeta station orbiting Delta Zero, and we'll fly to the planet from there."

"Very good. Crystal will make an excellent first mate, and I'll be happy to assist you."

I sat in the captain's chair and narrowed an eye at her console. "Sonya, what level is your snark factor? I've never heard you be so compliant."

"There is no longer a snark factor in my programming. Echo altered my personality parameters."

"Well, we can't have that. Restore the most recent backup. I need my Sonya."

"The restore process will take approximately twenty seconds. I will play some soothing music for you to enjoy while you wait." Sounds of a piano filtered down from the ceiling speakers, not too bad, but it would get old quickly.

"Okay, I'll look over the ship's readings to see what else I need to do." I pressed the button to retract the wings. We wouldn't need them until we entered Delta Zero's atmosphere. All the other settings seemed fine.

Crystal ran up the ramp, smiling. "Omen's station was definitely lying, so we made a switch. We're going to different arrival bays. They might not be locked open, but maybe Omen won't expect us to go there. Another problem is that they won't be next to each other."

"Well," Sonya said, "look what the dumpster divers hauled in. A yellow-headed beanpole."

"Sonya!" I gave her console a scolding stare. "Turn your snark level to twenty."

"Snark level set to twenty, as commanded, dear Captain."

I pushed the button that closed the ramp. As it rose, Crystal stood between it and me. "As I was about to say, the two ships will be separated for a short time. Maybe a minute. That shouldn't be a problem."

Lyric spoke through the earbud. "Fifteen seconds till transport. Everyone get ready."

I nodded toward the first mate's chair. "Strap in. We'll zoom out of the arrival bay as soon as we reintegrate there. I'm itching to get back to my father."

"Aye, aye, sir." Crystal slid into the seat and buckled her belt. "So I assume you're all right with Echo being first mate for Jillian. There's no chance Jillian will have any aftereffects from getting atomized and sucked into a computer?"

I shrugged. "Actually, I haven't thought about that. I hope she's all right."

"Three seconds," Lyric said. "Starting activation sequence."

Crystal nodded. "Yeah, Jillian's probably fine. It's just that ..."

I activated the front screen, giving us a view of the bay doors opening to allow our transport. "It's just what?" The disintegration beam lit up the bay. Stings again assaulted my body. A second light flashed, and the stings faded. Ahead, the bay doors stood wide open. "Tell me later. Sonya, shields up."

"Shields are now up, Captain."

"We're zooming out of here." I started the engines and pushed the throttle. Just as we lurched forward, the door panels started sliding together. I growled, "Omen knows we're here, but he's too late."

The Astral Dragon zipped between the doors and into the open. "Nothing scraped," Crystal said as she looked at her console screen. "Good thing you retracted the wings."

"Yep. Now to pull back for a wider view of the Zeta station." I spun the Dragon and pointed its prow at the closing doors, then fired the rear jets to slow our momentum and adjusted the thrusters to push us into a crawling orbit.

As we drifted around the station, Crystal squinted. "I saw two open bays, but the Nine wasn't in either of them."

"Same." I touched my earbud. "Jillian? Echo? Where are you?"

"In a bay with closed doors," Echo said. "Completely closed. They started closing the second we got here, the very second. We couldn't risk zooming out because our wings were deployed … extended … um … sticking out."

I toggled the microphone off on my earbud. "That's a basic system check. You always retract the wings when in space."

Crystal shrugged. "I was worried about Jillian being off her game."

I turned the microphone on. "You're sitting ducks for Omen. You have to get out of there. Blast the door open."

Jillian's voice came through. "I already tried the lasers. They bounce back to the ship. Good thing I turned the shields on as soon as we got here. I'm going to try a photon torpedo."

"Wait. If a laser bounces, then a torpedo might do the same. Omen probably put a force field on the interior of the door. Let me hit it from the outside."

"Okay," Jillian said, "but you'd better hurry. The airlock door opened, and a big robot carrying a huge gun is rolling toward us."

Crystal pointed at one of the bays. "They're marked with symbols. Which one are you in?"

"It looks like a triangle, then a crescent moon, then a star, then a diamond."

"All right," I said. "See if your lasers will discourage that robot while I look for your door."

While I steered the Dragon around the station, Crystal whispered, "Triangle, crescent moon, star, diamond" again and again. After we had traveled about three quarters of the way, she pointed. "There!"

"I see it." I shifted the Dragon toward the door, highlighted it with the targeting grid, and set my finger on the trigger. "Get ready for a jolt!" I fired a photon torpedo. The streak of light blasted against the door, ripping a jagged hole that revealed the Nebula Nine within. Metal shards slapped the Nine's prow, lights flashed all around it, and smoke began filling the bay, making it hard to see inside.

"Can you fit through that hole?" I called.

"Negative," Jillian said, "but you killed the force field. I'll blast the rest of the way out."

The Nine fired photon torpedoes from both front turrets and blew the doors away. The two mangled panels flew by, safely missing us. With a boost from its rear thrusters, the Nine shot out and zipped toward the planet. "Catch up and take the lead, Mophead. You know how to get to the base camp, and I don't."

"And you have the reintegration gun." I spun the Dragon and pushed the throttle. We rocketed forward and followed the Nine's vector, closing in quickly. When we caught up, we flew at its side. "Sonya, call Emerson and establish a video link from bridge to bridge."

"Connecting."

After a few seconds, Jillian and Echo appeared on the front viewing screen, sitting at their stations. "We got through step one," I said. "We're in the Delta system. But Omen knows we're here, and he's sure to tell his minions. I don't know how long it will take for them to get his message since they're probably on their way to the bramble bee cave, but we should assume they know we're coming."

"Are we going to the base camp's tower or straight to the glowsap mine?" Jillian asked.

I firmed my lips. "Good question. I was thinking I would use the gun to restore my father while you went to the mine, but you have the gun, and Echo's tech skills are better suited for the reintegration mission in case there's a glitch."

Jillian nodded. "And you have more Starborn powers than anyone, so it's better for you to head to the mine to do battle with Omen's minions."

"Right." I heaved a sigh as I looked at Crystal. "Can you send the base camp location to Jillian and load the mine's coordinates? We need to generate a route."

Crystal blew a playful huff. "It's a good thing I memorized the coordinates for both locations. I don't know what you'd do without me."

"I guess I'd get lost searching for the right glowsap mine."

"You got that right." Crystal tapped on her screen. "We're all set."

Jillian looked at her console. "Coordinates loaded. We'll stay in touch."

The view switched to the planet, now filling the screen as we closed in, a red dot superimposed on our destination. I veered the Dragon away from the Nine and accelerated toward the point, extending our wings as we turned.

Crystal eyed her console. "Two minutes, seven seconds to go. Any plans for a stealth approach? They'll hear us coming if we just roar in like flying tigers."

"You're right." I studied the area on a map. Apparently someone, probably my father or Echo, loaded some high-resolution images of Delta Zero's surface into the Dragon's computer. "The jungle's dense at the mine site, but I see some gaps a few kilometers away from it, probably far enough to keep from being heard. A couple of the gaps have mountains that stick way up with no others around. I'm guessing volcanoes."

Crystal gulped. "I hope they're not active. We had to deal with way too many of those on Delta Ninety-five."

"That's for sure." A tiny red light flashed on that area of the map. A note popped up, and I read it out loud. "When I surveyed this area while flying the Nebula Seven, I noticed three volcanoes. They seemed dormant, but I wondered if they could be awakened by what I felt earlier at my base camp. It seemed that every time Raven reacted with angry words or when she attempted acts of violence, the ground trembled. I also noticed that whenever the level of negative energy in the cauldron rose, seismic activity increased. Not to sound too poetic, but I wondered if the planet was fighting back, flexing its muscles as it tried to expel with violent shudders the evils that polluted its domain."

"Wow!" Crystal said. "That's deep stuff."

"Yeah. My father can be pretty eloquent. Good to keep his notes in mind." I pushed the note off my screen. "We'll fly low in that area until we find a safe spot to land. Then we'll take the rovers closer and walk when we're in range."

"But the rovers can't fly away. Gliders would be better."

"Rovers are all we have. The gliders are in the Nine."

"Sounds like we're flying the wrong ship. Or we should've moved the gliders to the Dragon."

"Probably, but you know what they say about hindsight."

Crystal blinked at me. "No. What do they say about hindsight?"

"Something Kattica mentioned. Hindsight has perfect vision."

"Perfect vision?" Crystal scrunched her brow. "What is hindsight, anyway? Like looking back at who's on your six? Or is it the person who's on the six looking forward at the leader's—"

"Don't say it." My harsh tone surprised me. I cleared my throat and spoke more calmly. "Hindsight is predicting events after they already happened."

Crystal smirked. "I knew that. I was just trying to be funny." She focused on her console. "Don't worry. No more funny stuff. Only super serious Crystal from now on. I don't want you barking at me again."

"But if you don't want me to bark, I need you to make me laugh. If you stop being funny, I might kick you right in the hindsight."

"You got it." Crystal grinned, still staring at her console. "I never want to be the butt of a joke."

I pointed at her. "Hah. Good one."

"All right," Sonya said, "it seems that I, as the only adult in the room, have to tell you two to grow up and pay attention to the dangerous situation. An airborne vehicle has appeared on the scanner, and it is flying toward our destination."

I looked at the console and watched the moving blip on the scanner. "Probably a transport glider like we saw earlier. Emerson said it's Alliance model five-seventy. A prisoner ship. Rudimentary weapons."

"Based on its size, shape, and speed, it is more likely a model six-ninety. It has lasers and photon torpedoes, not merely rudimentary. It also can detect our ship if anyone on board theirs is paying attention to a scanner."

"Then we'd better land as soon as we can." I ran a finger along my map. "Sonya, I marked the area where there are some clearings. Find one that's big enough and send us toward it."

"Clearing located," Sonya said. "Altering course. Prepare for quick maneuvers."

The Dragon veered to the right for a few seconds before diving toward the treetops. When the clearing came into view, I grasped the steering yoke. "I'll take it from here, Sonya."

"Let me," Crystal said, her hands on her own yoke. "I need the practice."

"Pretty tough, but ..." I released the yoke. "The Dragon's all yours."

"Coolness." Her brow knitting, Crystal steered the ship to the clearing, engaged the forward thrusters to slow us to a near standstill, and eased us down to a soft landing in a field of grass, the jungle trees almost close enough for the wings to touch them.

I rose and bumped fists with her. "Better than I could've done it."

She exhaled and smiled. "I learned from the best."

Sonya spoke up. "If your mutual admiration fawning is finished, be warned that the ship I mentioned is now coming directly this way. Arrival time forty-one seconds."

"To the rovers," I said.

Crystal showed me a handheld computer pad. "I've got a map to the site."

"Good." I ran toward the ladder with Crystal on my six. "Sonya, keep the shields up and take off as soon as we leave. Lead them on a wild-goose chase, but stay close enough to pick up our earbud transmissions."

"Wild goose idiom understood. Opening rover bay door."

We hustled to the bay, stripped off our space suits, and jumped into the rovers, then closed the glass hatches over us and fired up the thrusters underneath. The moment the door fully opened, we zipped out and rushed into the surrounding jungle, swerving around trees like darting birds as the thrusters tossed forest debris to both sides.

I glanced back. The Dragon took off and flew quickly out of sight. "All right," I said, looking forward, "let's slow it down. We don't want the sound of these rovers to alert anyone."

Crystal's voice came through my earbud. "Right. Only about eight kilometers to go. I'd say we should stop at two kilometers and hoof it from there."

"Sounds good. Since you have the map, you take the lead." I slowed my rover. "I'll be on your six for a change."

"All right." She guided her rover around mine and zoomed ahead. "Try to keep up, and watch for a fast stop."

"Got it." I accelerated to her speed and stayed about ten meters behind her."

After a couple of minutes, Crystal called, "Up ahead looks good. Dense clump of bushes to the left to hide the rovers."

"Then let's park."

She steered her rover into the thicket and set it on the ground. When I did the same, we popped our covers and stepped out.

Crystal sniffed. "Do you smell that?"

I inhaled. The odor of burnt flesh entered. "Something's burning. Some kind of corpse."

"That's what I was thinking." Crystal looked at her computer pad, then pointed in the direction we had been going. "That way. I'll be on your six now."

I checked my belt. My blaster and knife were in their proper places. "Double time. Let's go."

I jogged ahead, Crystal behind me calling out any changes in direction as we weaved through the jungle. At one point, we had to wade through a knee-deep creek. At another, a huge snake dropped onto my shoulders, but I shook it off before it could wrap around me, and Crystal leaped over it.

When we drew within a hundred meters or so, Crystal caught up and grabbed my sleeve, stopping me. "It's time to sneak as quietly as a mute mouse."

After catching our breath for a moment, we crept toward another clearing in the distance. A low rumble coursed across the area, familiar and terrifying. I whispered, "I'll never forget that sound. A volcano's about to erupt somewhere close by."

As we walked on, Crystal pointed to our left. The top of a volcano rose above the trees, smoke pouring from the vent crater at its summit. "Yep," Crystal said. "Looks like Delta Zero's copying Delta Ninety-five. I think that fire-breathing mountain is ready to blow."

10

Much closer than the volcano, another column of smoke rose from somewhere ahead, the obvious source of the worsening stench. When we reached the edge of the wooded area, we stopped, each of us behind a tree.

A shoulder-high pile of bramble bee carcasses burned at the center of the clearing, and a cave opening yawned to the left. Near the cave entrance, Oliver knelt at the side of a girl lying on the ground, a hand on her forehead. No adults stood anywhere in sight.

"Looks safe," I said. "Let's go."

I jogged straight to Oliver and knelt at the girl's other side. "About time I showed up, right?"

He smiled, his face smeared with black dirt. "I'm glad you're here, but we've been so busy, I hadn't thought about when you'd come."

Crystal knelt next to him. "Not exactly the welcome we expected, but it's better than a sharp stick in the eye." She hugged him from the side, then looked at the girl, a brown-haired wisp about eight years old. With ashen skin and gray lips, she looked more like a cadaver than a living girl. "What's up with her?"

"Bramble bee sting. We have two others. No one's died yet. I think my healing gift is slowing the poison. But Twila here is the worst. The poison is making her throat swell up, and she can barely breathe." He looked at me. "I need a certain person to energize me."

"I can do that." I scanned the area. "Where's Zoë?"

Oliver pointed with a thumb. "In the cave, killing bees by the dozens." He balled a hand into a fist. "She chokes them with her mind. Works really well."

"After I energize you, maybe I could go in there and help her."

He shrugged. "She's almost done. Better to stay out here and help with the healing."

"I will, but we should hurry. A prison ship with weapons might be coming soon. Sonya's leading it on a wild-goose chase, but the pilot will probably smarten up eventually."

"That's not the only worry. One of the guards ran for help. No telling how many will show up or when. But we need to take care of Twila, or she'll die soon. Then we'll figure out what to do next."

"Sure." I pulled my locket out, wrapped my hand around it, and closed my eyes. As I concentrated, words entered my mind that I didn't consciously choose to think. As the locket warmed in my hand, the words came through my lips in a whispered melody. "Power of God, power above, release the power of Oliver's love. May it flow from his hands to the poison within and purge the sickness from sera and skin."

Heat rose into my face. Sweat trickled down my forehead and into my eyes. I opened them and blinked to clear the stinging tears. Had the eloquence Barnabas mentioned somehow blended with my energizing power?

Across from me, Oliver pulled Twila up to a sitting position. She coughed out a wad of mucous and sucked in a deep breath. She smiled at him and threw her arms around his neck.

Oliver hugged her in return, tears running through the smudges on his cheeks. When Twila drew back, I reached for Oliver and compressed his shoulder. "I'm so proud of you, I feel like I'm going to burst."

He gave me a tired smile in return. "Well, don't do that. We still have two others to take care of."

"Both of you go," Crystal said. "I'll stay here with Twila till she has the strength to get up."

Oliver and I rose and jogged toward a boy lying under a tree at the opposite side of the clearing. "You mentioned a guard running for help," I said. "What happened to the other guards who were supposed to come with you?"

"Four of them are dead. When we got here to the glowsap mine, we felt our power come back, so Zoë stopped their hearts." He snapped his fingers. "Dropped them in an instant. That's why the fifth one ran away."

"Wow! Does she feel bad about it? I mean, I think it's fine. They were kid killers. But how's she handling it?"

"The first one shook her up, but when the second one tried to strangle a little boy to stop her, she mowed the next three down in a hurry. And the boy wasn't hurt."

"Where are the other kids?"

"Kattica and Scamp left with them a few minutes ago. I assumed you would show up eventually to help us get them all out of here, so they're leading the kids through the jungle back to the base camp to pack up their belongings. Since they'll be under jungle cover, they're hoping the transport ships won't see them. And Perdantus went with them to help them find their way."

"Good. Crystal and I flew the Astral Dragon here, and Jillian and Echo flew to the base camp to try to reintegrate my father. I'll tell you the whole story later."

"Looking forward to it." He knelt at the boy's side. "Let's do this."

We went through the same healing process as before, though the words didn't come through this time, maybe because this boy wasn't as near death. When he felt better, we moved to another girl, this one about twelve years old, and healed her as well.

Oliver and I rose, and we both breathed tired sighs. He nodded toward the cave, smiling. "Here comes the cold-blooded killer."

I turned. Zoë limped toward the pile of burning bees and tossed a bee carcass on it before heading our way. As she drew near, she brushed her hands together. "That's the last of them."

I gave her a hug and kissed her dirty forehead. "Good job. Both you and Oliver. I knew I could count on you."

"Well, it wasn't easy. That's for sure. But this is the only bee cave we're going to purge. This mess isn't the bees' fault, but we had to put them down because they kept attacking, and we couldn't move the sick kids, so we sent the younger ones to the camp and made the place safe."

"Yeah. Oliver told me. Makes sense."

"Twila's fine now," Crystal said as she joined us. "Maybe we'd better get an update from Sonya. That other ship might show up soon."

"Or reinforcements from that one guard," Oliver said.

Just as I opened my mouth to call Sonya, her voice came through my earbud. "Captain Willis, I have an important update. As of nine seconds ago, I am no longer a wild goose. The other vessel appeared to figure out that I was a decoy, and it broke off pursuit. Its last known trajectory is toward your destination. Now that it has been alerted to our presence, I assume it will arrive with speed and aggression."

"You're right. Thank you." I waved toward the jungle. "Let's get everyone under cover. Hurry."

I scooped Twila into my arms and carried her while Crystal, Oliver, and Zoë ushered the other two children toward the jungle, a few steps ahead of me. When I was only a couple of meters from the trees, a laser bullet zipped past my face, so close, I felt the heat at the tip of my nose.

A man shouted, "Halt!"

An explosion erupted a step in front of me. The concussive force blew me in reverse. As I fell on my back with Twila on top of me, dirt rained over us. Dazed and dizzy, I looked toward the direction the laser bullet had come from. Five guards with laser blasters ran toward me, the prisoner transport ship on the ground behind them, its cargo door open. Two others with rifles were guiding a line of kids into the ship. I couldn't be sure, but it looked like Kattica and Scamp were among them, apparently forced to march there from wherever they were captured.

Grunting, I struggled to my feet with Twila still in my arms, but the dizziness washed over me, making me stagger.

"Megan!" Oliver wrapped both arms around me. He half carried and half dragged Twila and me into the jungle.

When we reached a fallen log, we lay on our stomachs behind it and looked over the top, Crystal, Zoë, and the other children already in the same position. The five men stormed into the jungle, firing their laser blasters. The shining bullets zipped over our heads and burned into trees behind us.

I drew my blaster and fired in return. The first bullet sizzled into the closest man. He yelped, crashed headfirst into the undergrowth, and lay motionless. My second and third bullets hit two more men. They, too, collapsed and moved no more.

The final two men pivoted and ran out, one of them calling, "Bring the ship. We'll blast them with the big guns."

My heart thumping, I checked my ear for the bud, but it was gone. "Crystal! Call Sonya! We need a rescue pickup, but she can't destroy their transport ship. The kids are in it."

"Yep!" Crystal rose to her knees and whisper-shouted, "Sonya, we're under fire. We're hiding in the jungle near the glowsap mine, and that transport ship's getting ready to blast us. But you can't blow them up, because they've got the slave kids on board." She looked at me. "Sonya needs a command."

"Tell her to land in the clearing next to the mine and pick all of you up there."

"But what about the transport ship?" Crystal asked. "Won't it try to blast the Dragon? Sonya has to lower the shields to pick us up."

"You let me worry about the transport ship."

Crystal shook a finger at me. "Don't do anything stupid."

"I don't think it gets much stupider than attacking an armed ship by myself." I leaped to my feet and ran toward the edge of the jungle. When I burst into the clearing, the enemy ship was lifting off, its lower thrusters blowing dirt all around.

I spotted my earbud on the ground, snatched it up, and pushed it into my ear, then flexed my biceps to charge my legs and sprinted toward the ship. By the time I arrived at a spot directly underneath it, it had risen about six or seven meters from the ground. I leaped as high as I could and reached with outstretched arms. I grabbed a landing runner and dangled by one hand.

As the ship continued rising, the thrusters blasted my body, their winds tossing my hair and flapping my clothes. The force shoved me down, loosening my grip. I pulled with all my might and latched on with my other hand, then swung up, curled a leg around the runner, and muscled to a sitting position.

Now stable, I leaned away from the thrusters toward the center of the ship, the top of my head touching its belly. I looked up and imagined the inside compartments. The children likely sat directly above my head, probably unchained because the guards didn't have time to secure them. If I could put the ship down, maybe I could get them out unharmed.

The ship turned toward the edge of the jungle where we had been hiding. Once their heat-sensing scanners locked on my crew, the ship would probably fire photon torpedoes at them. Which Starborn power could I use to stop the barrage? I couldn't see the pilot to squeeze his heart or set his clothes on fire, and reading his mind wouldn't do any good. I already knew what he was planning to do.

I spotted an electric junction box attached to the ship's belly about three meters in front of me. Maybe I could give it a jolt and short circuit something. I slid along the runner and set a palm on the box. I flexed the correct muscle and charged my bracelet with electricity. Arcing current coursed through my hand and into the box. The painful jolt made me jerk my hand back. Above, the engine choked and sputtered. Smoke poured from the side of the ship, but would that be enough to bring it down?

I looked toward the direction Crystal and I had left the rovers. As the Astral Dragon zoomed toward us, a loud boom ripped through the air. Lava shot from the volcano crater in a brilliant orange geyser and spilled down the slopes.

Loud thoughts poured from the ship's cockpit, maybe whispered among the guards at the same time. *The weapons are jammed. We'll chain the kids, and I'll program this buggy to send them to the volcano. Then we'll get low enough to jump before it leaves.*

I touched my earbud. "Sonya, the goons on the transport ship are going to send the kids to the volcano but jump out first. Can you shoot them as they're falling and block the ship to keep it from heading to the volcano?"

Static filled the reply, breaking up her words. "Understand ... you're saying. Shoot ... kids?"

"No! Shoot the guards! Stop the ship from killing the kids."

"Your command ... not understood."

I groaned. "Sonya, I'll speak slowly. Shoot the guards as they're jumping from the ship, then block the ship from going to the volcano."

At the edge of the clearing, Crystal ran out directly under me and shouted, barely audible over the thruster noise. "I heard you. Sonya's going to land, and I'll pilot the ship and take out the goons. Don't worry. I got this."

I shouted in return. "Did you hear the part about the volcano?"

"I saw it erupt, if that's what you mean."

"No. I meant—" The roar of the Astral Dragon's landing thrusters drowned my voice. Crystal spun and ran toward the ship as it settled in the clearing.

I heaved an exasperated sigh. As I watched Crystal hustle up the ramp, I imagined the guards clapping manacles on the kids. They probably had enough time to finish by now.

I tried the earbud again. "Crystal, I need to know if you heard that this ship is programmed to crash into the volcano." Only static came through the earbud. As far as I knew, Crystal had no idea about the transport's next destination.

Just as the Dragon took off, the transport ship descended to about two or three meters from the ground. A guard jumped out and rolled, then another, then another, until seven had taken the leap. As they struggled to their feet, apparently shaken by the impact, the Astral Dragon shot lasers at them, picking them off one by one.

The transport shifted forward and accelerated toward the volcano. I looked back. The Astral Dragon continued shooting the guards. Apparently, Crystal thought she could give chase whenever she finished, confident that Sonya could pick us up on a scanner. If the kids were going to be saved, I had to save them myself.

I laid both hands on the ship's underbelly, but I couldn't steer it, having no separate foundation to brace myself on. Still, since the jumpers probably left the door open, maybe I could climb aboard to steer the ship with the controls.

Setting my feet on the runner, I braced my hands against the belly and slid them out to the edge of the passenger compartment until I caught hold of its edge. Holding it with one hand, I felt for an opening with the other. After sliding toward the aft section, I found the open doorway, latched onto the lower edge with both hands, and slowly straightened my legs, allowing me to push my hands deeper into the compartment.

Something grabbed my wrists and jerked me inside, scraping my chest and stomach along the edge of the doorway. I rolled into the compartment and sat up, blinking at a dozen or so terrified children sitting on the floor and staring at me, including Kattica and Scamp. Shackles clamped their ankles, their attached chains running through floor hooks leading to a thicker chain attached to a bracket on the wall opposite the door.

"Megan," Scamp said, his voice reflecting the worry in his eyes. "When I saw the bracelets, I knew it was you. Can you help us?"

"I'll do what I can." I climbed to my feet and hustled to the cockpit. Through the windshield, the volcano loomed large. We would be there in less than a minute.

I grabbed the steering yoke and tried to turn it, but it was locked in place. My only option was to disable the craft and send it into the tops of the jungle trees, hoping the foliage would soften the crash.

After charging my hands again with the bracelets, I set both palms on the control console. The electricity pierced the panel and coursed into the circuits. Sparks flew everywhere. Smoke billowed from behind the controls and began filling the cockpit chamber. The ship slowed and descended at an increasing angle, but how fast would the angle change? Too small of an angle would send us crashing into the mountainside, and too large would make us plummet into the trees at a high rate of speed, but I couldn't do anything to change it. I had to see about the kids.

I hustled back to the prisoner compartment, calling, "Everyone brace for impact!" I squeezed between Scamp and Kattica and hooked arms with them. "Heads down and scrunch as low as you can."

When they obeyed, most of them trembling, I scrunched low as well, though I kept peeking in all directions. The angle of descent sharpened, and our fall accelerated. The sound of treetops scraping against the ship's belly rustled throughout the compartment. Branches knifed into the doorway, breaking off and flying through the air, some slapping our arms and the tops of our heads. One bashed into my cheek, sending blood flying—my fault for peeking too often.

More branches cracked, and the ship dropped, fast enough to lift us off the floor. The ship smashed into the ground, and we crashed with it, falling against each other to the sounds of oofs and moans.

When the motion stopped, I looked around at the sprawled bodies, some motionless and some writhing. My head pounded, my tailbone ached, and blood trickled down one cheek, but I felt unhurt otherwise. "Is everyone all right?"

Among the moans and whimpers, a few whispered, "I'm okay" and "I think so."

Kattica straightened in her sitting position and clapped her hands. "Sound off, everyone. Now!"

The kids called out their names one by one, some blended with groans. When they finished, Kattica looked at me. "Everyone survived."

I exhaled. "That's great."

She touched a spot on my cheek. "But you've got a nasty cut."

"Yeah, I feel it bleeding, but it's no big deal." I rose to my feet. "Where are the other kids? You're missing a bunch."

"When the guards spotted us, Scamp and I broke off to lead them away from the others, but a few were scared and followed us while your amazing bird guided the rest of them to safety. One of our kids knows his language. Anyway, they're supposed to be going to the base camp, but I don't know if they made it."

"Let's hope so. I have people there to help them. But we can't worry about that right now. We're not out of danger yet. Lava might be heading this way. I'm going to check."

As I turned to leave, Scamp grabbed my pant leg. "First, look for the key to our chains. I think they keep it in the cockpit somewhere."

"No," Kattica said. "I saw one of the guards put it in his pocket before he jumped out. I don't think they had more than one key."

I nodded toward the multitude of chains that led to the wall bracket. "If you all work together, maybe you can break that bracket loose. While you're trying, I'm going to check on the lava."

I walked to the open doorway, wider now because of dents and gouges the branches had made, and jumped to the ground. The odor of sulfur permeated the air, and intense heat wafted into my face. The roar of crackling fire seemed to ride in on billows of smoke coming from the direction of the volcano. I followed the smoke toward its source. After about fifty meters, I arrived at the edge of the jungle where old lava rock spanned the gap between the trees and the slope leading up to the volcano's summit.

Although most of the lava spilled to the left and right, a new channel began pouring down the slope toward me. At the current rate of flow, it would reach the jungle in less than five minutes, setting flames to everything in its path, including the ship along with its young prisoners. Trapped in chains, they would all die horrible deaths.

An engine roared above and behind me. I turned and looked. The Astral Dragon zoomed past overhead before spinning around and returning to hover directly over me. With no clearing anywhere in sight other than the lava rock that was about to be inundated with a fiery new flow, the Dragon had to stay in hover mode.

The ramp opened. Crystal eased out and shouted, "Catch!" She tossed something small toward me.

I caught the tiny object—a new earbud. As I inserted it, Crystal retreated into the ship and closed the ramp. Her voice entered my ear. "Got any ideas on how to rescue you guys before that lava burns you to a crisp?"

"Follow me to the transport ship while I think." I jogged toward the crash site as I spoke. "The kids are trapped there, chained to an interior wall." I halted at the ship's doorway and looked inside. The young prisoners were pulling on the central chain, grunting as their muscles strained, their teeth clenched. "They're trying to pull free, but the center chain's attached to a bracket that's probably too strong to break."

"If it's that strong, can we attach the Dragon's towing hook to it and haul their ship out?"

"Brilliant! Do you know how to deploy the cable?"

"No, but I can ask Sonya."

"Even if you figure it out, the cable might get tangled in the trees. I'll have to ride it down. Open the ramp again and hover as low as you can, maybe a few meters behind the transport. It clipped the tops of trees on the way to the ground, so you can get lower there."

"Yep. On my way."

As she flew the Dragon into position, I looked toward the volcano. Lava breached the jungle. Towering flames shot high into the sky as the flow burned the trees. At the current rate, it would reach us in a few minutes, maybe sooner.

"I'm in position, Captain."

I ran directly under the Dragon and looked up as its thrusters blasted the broken treetops. "Open the ramp."

"I'm opening it, but do you really think you can jump from the ground into the Dragon? The bottom of the ramp will be ... let me check ... looks like twenty-point-two meters from your spot. And you can't possibly make it all the way without hitting at least some branches. They'll knock you back."

"You're right. I'll have to do stair steps, jumping from limb to limb."

"Okay, kanga-girl. Hop to it."

I flexed my biceps to charge my legs and aimed my body toward a limb that hung about six meters high with nothing in the way. I lunged upward and landed with my knees bent, swinging my arms to get my balance. I spotted another accessible limb and pushed off the first one, but the lower limb's sway spoiled my takeoff angle. A leafy branch smacked my forehead, slowing my momentum and cutting my rise short. I reached high and curled my arms around the target limb.

As pain shot up and down my arms, I swung my legs up and climbed onto the limb, then set my feet to gauge my next jump. The

Astral Dragon now hovered about eight meters above me. The higher limbs looked thinner than the ones below, maybe not able to support a jump.

As I tested the limb's bend, I looked at the rolling wall of lava, now only about ten meters from the ship and stretching at least two kilometers to each side. I had no more time to worry about this limb. I just had to go for it.

After charging my legs once more, I leaped toward the ramp. When I elevated above the trees, a gust from the thrusters buffeted me, sending me off course. The Astral Dragon flew into my path and scooped me in like a seagull snatching a morsel out of the air.

I tumbled on the ramp all the way to the bridge and collided with the front of the pilot's console. Crystal grabbed my wrist and hoisted me to my feet. "Sonya estimated that the lava will hit the transport ship in less than three minutes."

I shook my head hard to clear the cobwebs. "Thanks for the great flying. Now hover directly over the transport while I deploy the towing cable."

"You got it." She jogged back to her seat.

I ran to the ladder, slid down to the lowest level, and hustled to the stern. I opened the door and walked out onto the rear deck. Much like on the Nebula Nine, the towing cable wound around a spool with a hook attached to the cable's end. I unlocked the spool mechanism and held the iron hook, bigger than both of my hands combined.

"Sonya, how long is the towing cable?"

"Fifty meters," she said through my earbud.

"That should be enough. Reel it out at a rate of two meters per second."

"Acknowledged."

When it began reeling, I clutched the hook against my chest and jumped off the deck. As the lava pushed closer and closer to the transport, new flames shot up the trees, sending wave after wave of heat across my body. Although the cable lowered me at the rate I had asked for, the process seemed to take far too long.

The moment I touched down, I pulled the hook into the transport ship. The children sat with their heads low, no longer tugging on the chains. Heat radiated into the compartment. It had to be at least 40 degrees Celsius inside, and probably much hotter on the hull's exterior.

Scamp looked at me with a forlorn expression. "We tried and tried, but it's impossible. We're exhausted."

"I understand. My ship is going to try to lift us out of here." Now with plenty of slack in the cable, I strode over the chains to the wall bracket, knelt next to it, and slid the end of the hook through one of the bigger links. "Sonya, reel it in at about ten centimeters per second and be ready to stop on my command."

"Acknowledged. A word of warning, I estimate that the lava will arrive in twenty seconds. But you should be aware that pressure in the volcano is still growing. A cataclysmic explosion can send a debris field through the air at speeds between fifty and three hundred meters per second, and the field can travel up to fifty kilometers in worst case scenarios. In short, lava would be the least of your worries."

"Thanks for the warning." As the seconds ticked down in my mind, the cable slowly snaked outside and up into the air. The moment it tightened against the doorframe and the hook set itself firmly in the link, I called, "Stop!"

The reeling stopped.

I lunged to the doorway, leaned out, and looked in the direction of the volcano. A two-meter high wall of lava rolled within centimeters of the bow, ready to engulf it. I shouted, "Crystal, get us out of here! Fast!"

With a sudden jerk, the transport lifted off the ground. The jolt sent me flying out the doorway, and I tumbled to the ground in a sideways roll. The transport now three or four meters above the ground, I leaped to my feet, charged my legs, and jumped straight up.

I grabbed a landing runner, but the superheated metal scalded my hands, forcing me to let go. I fell, landed on the ground, and rolled away from the lava, grunting at the pain. When I stopped, I looked up. The transport lifted over the treetops, swaying precariously as smoke rose from the bow.

"Get them out of here, Crystal. I can outrun the lava. I'll meet you at the glowsap mine. It's not too far."

"Got it. Be careful." The Astral Dragon accelerated toward the mine, its stern low, dragged down by the weight of the transport.

With the lava closing in, I climbed to my feet and jogged away, every limb and joint aching. When I reached a safe distance, I stopped and turned, hoping to catch my breath for a minute. In the distance, lava continued pouring from the volcano's summit, now only partially visible over the tops of the trees.

Thoughts about the guards rolled to mind. Those beasts tried to send children, some as young as ten years old, into that inferno. How could such evil exist? From kidnapping to slavery to torture to murder, Omen and his fellow cockroaches had committed such horrific crimes, maybe they were the cause of the eruption, creating too much negative energy for this planet to handle. Like my father said, it was fighting back, flexing its muscles as it tried to expel with violent shudders the evils that polluted the planet.

As if called upon by my thoughts, the ground began to tremble, the intensity growing. When it spiked, the volcano cone exploded. Debris rushed in my direction. I pivoted and ran, charging my legs to run even faster as I dodged trees, leaped over bushes, and ducked under low branches, but there was no way I could outrun it, especially if this was an example of Sonya's worst-case scenario.

At each side, boulders struck trees, breaking their tops and smashing limbs on the way down. One boulder landed a few meters in front of me, sending falling branches into my path. I vaulted over both the boulder and the branches and continued leaping as more debris rained in the jungle—rocks, ash, and dirt.

Fortunately, the fragments seemed smaller as I put more distance between myself and the volcano, but one sizeable boulder crashed directly in front of me. Just as I leaped to fly over it, a branch smacked me in the face, sending me tumbling in multiple somersaults until I collided with a tree and toppled to my side.

Hurting too much to move, I lay in a fetal curl as a storm of hot ashes cascaded over my body and quickly buried me. I held my breath and forced myself to struggle to my feet, scattering the ashy blanket.

As the falling dark flakes dissipated into a gentle shower, I pulled the top of my shirt up over my face to filter my breathing and to wipe the sooty stuff off my skin. Now disoriented, I had to figure out which way to go. I looked at the debris field and the depth of the ashes. Guessing that the deposits would be deeper toward the volcano, I turned in the opposite direction and walked slowly through the dirty and broken jungle.

With every step, my legs and knees ached. I kicked ashes up in front of me, making me blink my stinging eyes. As badly as I hurt, could I make it all the way to the glowsap mine? At this point, it seemed impossible. I just had to concentrate on one step at a time.

After a couple of minutes, the roar of a ship's engine passed by overhead and diminished in the distance. I knew that sound—the Astral Dragon. Crystal had probably already dropped the kids off and was now searching for me, but with all the hot ashes, could she find me on the thermal sensors? That seemed doubtful. But as I trudged into cooler and cooler areas, maybe she would eventually find me. Obviously, I needed to keep moving to get away from the heat.

I felt for my earbud, but it was gone again. As many times as I had been thrown around, it was no wonder. With all the thrashing and collisions, I felt like a combination of a crash-test dummy and a punching bag. But I had to press on in spite of the pain.

After a few minutes, the Astral Dragon returned and hovered overhead. I halted and looked up. The towing hook descended through the canopy and paused at chest level, a small box attached to one side, apparently stuck to the iron by a magnet.

I pried the box free and opened it, revealing yet another earbud. When I inserted it, Crystal's voice came through. "We don't have an endless supply of those buds, Sister. You'd better not lose that one."

I pushed the box into my pocket. "No promises." Feeling too weak to hold on to the hook, I fastened it to my belt at the back. "I'm ready. Pull me up."

As the line reeled in, lifting me skyward, Crystal spoke in sing song. "There once was a girl who had nine lives. She spent them like drunks juggling sharp knives. While trying to be Cupid, her friend called her stupid, and the girl just marched into bee hives."

I laughed in spite of the pain. "That's a good limerick."

"What's a limerick?"

"I'll explain later, but I like the idiom about a cat with nine lives."

"What's an idiom?"

I let out a sigh. "You asked me that once before, but I didn't answer. It's a saying, an expression that means something else. I'll have to get a book about idioms for you to study."

When the hook drew me close to the deck, I set my hands on the platform and rose to my feet, unfastening myself at the same time. Dirty blood dripped from my nose and chin to the deck floor, trickling down from my scalp and face wounds. I desperately needed a shower and then a healing touch from Oliver.

After brushing away the blood the best I could, I opened the deck door and hobbled into the ship. The sudden relief seemed to sap every gram of energy I had left. A girl stood nearby in a shadow, but my blurring vision wouldn't let me focus on her.

My legs buckled, and I dropped to my knees. The girl grabbed my arm and knelt next to me. "I've been waiting here for you. Let me help you."

I blinked at her, finally recognizing Kattica. "Thank you. Where are the others?"

As she helped me to my feet with one hand, she brushed ash from my face with the other. "I was the first one released from the chains. When Oliver and Zoë started working on the other kids with their blowtorch, I asked to return with Crystal to search for you so she could concentrate on flying."

"Thank you for that. I appreciate it."

"It's the least I could do. You saved our lives." She guided me away from the deck down the corridor. "Do you have a lavatory where I can help you get cleaned up?"

I nodded toward the direction we were walking. "Second door on the right. There's a shower stall. I'm sure someone on Gamma Five refilled our water tank."

"Good. I'll get your shower started, then I'll fetch some clean clothes for you. Just try not to fall while you're in there."

"There's a stool. I'll sit on it. Facecloths and towels are in a floor cabinet."

"Perfect." Kattica helped me peel my filthy, bloodstained uniform off. When she exposed the dragon brand on my arm, she drew her head back and squinted. "What's this for?"

"Punishment for being a pirate. At least that's what the Alliance called me. They branded me when my family got caught."

"They branded a young girl?" She pursed her lips and nodded. "I think I'm finally starting to understand why you do what you do. Your enemies are truly evil." She lifted a stool into the stall, ushered me in, handed me a facecloth, and turned the water on. "Back soon. I'm sure Crystal can tell me where to find clothes for you."

"Probably. I'm not sure what clothes for me are on the ship, but I know who supplied us. I'm sure there's something available." When the door closed, I sat on the stool and eased my head into the flow. Lukewarm, it felt wonderful, though it stung the cuts on my scalp and face. Knowing I should conserve water, I pushed the soap dispenser's button, covered the facecloth with gel, and scrubbed myself from top to bottom.

When I finished, I turned the water off and stepped out of the stall. A fresh towel and uniform sat on the top of the cabinet. Now feeling much better, I was able to dry off and put the uniform on myself. Although I had never seen this outfit before, the shirt and pants fit perfectly, all black for stealth operations with armored pads for the shoulders, chest, and knees. The shirt also boasted a stitched AA monogram on both upper sleeves and the breast pocket.

As I ran a hand along the sleeve, I whispered, "Astral Alliance. Thank you, Papa."

When Kattica returned with a first-aid kit, she applied antibiotic ointment to my cuts and added adhesive bandages. Then we walked together to the ladder. I climbed up first, and she followed, promising to keep me from falling, though I now felt strong enough to get to the top without a spotter.

With Kattica still behind me, I hobbled to the bridge and found Crystal in the captain's chair. When she saw me, she propped her legs on the console and grinned. "Just chilling while Sonya flies around watching for any other enemy ships. Oliver and Zoë finished cutting the chains, and Oliver's healing the kids who got hurt in the crash. We'll pick them up when he's done."

I sat in the copilot's seat while Kattica settled on the floor next to me as if hoping I would ask her to do something. "Any word from Jillian or the other kids?" I asked Crystal.

"Nope. We might be out of range, or maybe the tower signal's interfering. We'll head over to the base camp soon and see what's going on."

I nodded. "Once we get the kids loaded onto the Dragon, we'll find the Nebula Nine, split the kids up between the two ships, and leave this planet for good."

Kattica touched my arm. "Where will we go, Megan?"

I looked at her. "First, to Delta Ninety-five. We have a sanctuary there for freed kids. Then we'll figure out where your homes are and get you there as soon as we can."

Crystal leaned close and whispered, "Delta Ninety-five? That's where Omen Real lives. I hope it's safe."

"Since it's in the Delta system, it's relatively close. And I don't know where else to take them. We'll make sure it's safe before we leave them there."

"Fair enough."

After nearly an hour, Oliver called in, telling us that the kids we rescued from the transport were ready to go, ten in all, and Zoë had retrieved the rovers. Once they had finished boarding and loading the rovers, Kattica and Scamp secured the kids in the sleeping quarters. Then I flew the ship toward the base camp, Crystal returning to the first mate's chair, Zoë and Oliver standing behind us.

I guided the Dragon through wide orbits well above the camp to scope the area, watching for any danger. The place appeared to be deserted—no vehicles and no kids. Not even Jillian or Echo seemed to be anywhere, and if the Nebula Nine were flying around, surely Sonya would be able to detect it.

Since the camp seemed secure, I flew lower and angled in for a landing. As the ship drew near, our inside lights flickered, and our engine power sagged. "Sonya!" I called, "why are we losing power?"

"A strange signal from outside the ship is interfering with internal communications."

I growled. "Probably from the tower, but I don't have enough juice in the thrusters to pull away. Everyone brace for a crash landing!"

Crystal slid a finger along her console screen. "Diverting power from the lights. We're going dark."

The lights turned off, leaving the front window the only source of illumination. "Good move, Crystal. That'll help."

I activated the thrusters under the ship and coasted to a slide in the clearing. The moment we stopped, the engine died completely.

I slammed my fist on the console. "Blazes! I should've known the tower might interfere with the ship's circuits."

"How could you possibly have known?" Oliver asked.

I touched my ears. "I already knew it messes up a bat's signals. I should've guessed the signal has a scrambling component."

"Don't be so hard on yourself. We all knew about the bats, and no one connected the two, so you're not alone."

Heat coursed through my cheeks. "That doesn't make me feel any better, if that's what you're trying to do. I've been a ship's mechanic ever since I can remember. It's my job to know stuff like that." I took a breath and waved a hand. "I'm not mad at you Oliver. Thanks for trying."

"No problem. I know you're in a lot of pain. That could make anyone cranky. But what're we going to do?"

I jabbed a thumb against my chest. "I'm going to try to find my father. The rest of you can work with Sonya to see if we can divert power from other places enough to get this ship out of here. She's got a backup battery, so she probably still has enough power to talk to you."

Zoë nodded. "We'll get right on it."

"Not me," Crystal said. "I'm going with you. You're an accident waiting to happen."

I exhaled to cool my anger. "Thanks. I'll probably need you." I rose from my seat and walked gingerly toward the ramp, pain in every step. "And close the ramp behind me. You'll have to do it manually."

Crystal rose as well. "On your six, Captain."

When I reached the end of the ramp, I pulled the emergency release handle and rode the ramp down to the ground, then Crystal and I walked outside.

"Sonya," Oliver said from behind me, "can you give me a list of everything that's using power right now?"

I adjusted my earbud. "You're coming through my bud. So far the tower's not interfering with that signal."

"Copy that," Oliver said. "We'll keep listening. Give us an update every few minutes so we'll know you're alive."

"Will do." We scanned the cabins and the surrounding jungle. Nothing moved except the branches and leaves. "Let's go to the tower."

I jogged with a limp around the corner of a cabin and halted in front of the tower, Crystal at my side. With evening approaching, the tall structure cast a long shadow over us, the bulb at the top still flashing purple. As before, an awful dread filled my mind. Since I had no powers here, I couldn't sense a mind at all, much less read one.

A bright form took shape between us and the tower. I whipped out my laser blaster and held it at the ready. Seconds later, Omen AI appeared, semitransparent and flickering. "Well, Megan," he said in an impatient tone, "you have been a meddlesome brat."

I squared my shoulders. "And proud of it. I'll meddle until every enslaved child is set free."

"Oh, that's a pretty speech. But your altruism is borne of naïveté and abysmal ignorance."

"Wow," Crystal whispered from behind me. "I hope *you* understand what he's saying, because I don't."

Ignoring Crystal, I locked my stare on Omen. It was time to put my negotiating skills to the ultimate test—getting critical information from an artificial intelligence entity. I chuckled in a condescending way. "Since you're putting your pompous arrogance on display with a few seventh-grade vocabulary words, I assume I'm supposed to be impressed."

"No, Megan. I am merely speaking at a level that is appropriate for a conversation with you. Your intelligence and cunning are well known across the galaxy."

I set a fist on my hip. "Adding smarmy flattery to your arrogance. Now *that's* impressive. You're excavating a crater in your credibility with your own tongue."

Omen smirked. "And there is another masterful manifestation of your intellect, your charming wit."

A fluttering sound descended from a nearby tree, but I dared not look as I kept my focus on Omen. "Oh, so now you're infusing your compliments with thinly veiled sarcasm." I laughed under my breath. "So convincing. I'm touched. Really."

Perdantus called from above, breathless. "Megan! I finally found you. I have urgent news."

I avoided looking at him, hoping he would continue without any prompting.

"Now that we both have drawn our lines of intimidation," Omen said, "I will return to my purpose for appearing here. As a businessman dealing in the collection and sales of valuable glowsap, I have to protect my interests at the resource sites. Since you interfered by injecting doubt in my employees about my ability to properly pay them, and then you removed them from the workplace, I now have no one to mine the glowsap."

"That's true," Perdantus called. "Jillian and Echo have all the kids in the Nebula Nine, and they're flying nearby, but what he didn't tell you is that the kids are getting sick. We don't know why. Somehow we need Oliver to get in the Nine to see what he can do for them. Also, Jillian left the reintegration gun in the cabin where you slept, but she discovered that it won't work. It won't even turn on. She thinks the tower is interfering."

"What's wrong, Megan?" Omen asked. "Cat got your tongue?"

"No. I was just waiting for you to say something worth answering. But I will comment on your worthless worries if I must." I crossed my arms and glared at him. "So you want me to give child slaves back to you and try to convince them that you really are going to pay them?" I shook my head. "I don't think so."

"Since you are so enamored with helping the unfortunate, I think you will be convinced to comply quite soon."

"Oh, really? Are you referring to that nasty little time bomb you put in the kids? Something to make them sick?"

"I heard that," Oliver said through my earbud. "I'll check on the kids here, but since I don't have any healing ability right now, I'm not sure how I can help until we get enough power to fly. Sonya says we're close but not quite there yet."

Again staying calm, I huffed at Omen. "Give me a break. Such a playground tactic. I had you pegged for a seventh-grade education, but I'll have to lower my estimate to about third grade."

Omen tightened his jaw, his first hint at being rattled. I had to go for broke before he could recover. "Tell you what, I'll make a deal with you. Are you open to that?"

"It depends on the terms."

Since I wasn't sure of the terms myself, I had to figure them out on the fly. All I knew was that I had to get Oliver and the kids away from the tower. "The terms will benefit both of us. I'm sure you know by now that my ship is incapacitated."

"Of course. That's by design. The tower's signal—"

"I know all about the tower's signal. In fact, I was able to shrink its range so my crew could use their powers to eliminate your hired thugs. In fact, I could turn it off completely if I wanted to, allowing me to leave in my ship whenever I wish."

"I admit there are ways to change the tower's signal without my knowledge." Omen's visage strengthened as he smiled. "Since you are able to leave and you have either captured or killed all of my employees, I'm curious to hear why you don't simply leave. With that kind of leverage, why even bother offering terms of a potential deal?"

"Megan," Oliver said. "It's true. These kids are getting really sick. It's bramble bee venom. I'm sure of it. I'm guessing they had a capsule implanted somewhere and Omen did something to break it."

My pause to listen to Oliver shattered my advantage, giving Omen time to turn the tables.

"Oh, I see. You can't answer. There's a reason you won't turn my tower off or simply leave. You don't have the leverage I thought you did."

"That's not it." I pointed at my ear. "I was listening to one of my crew members through my earbud. He wants us to leave and let you suffer this humiliating defeat to a bunch of kids, but I want to stay a little longer to give you a chance to recover some value from your investment here."

"As if you care about my investment." He let out a resigned sigh. "Go ahead. I'm listening."

"Give me a second to think of the best way to explain." I looked at the top of the tower. If I could detach the light and move the signal generator somewhere else, my father, who was probably watching, could follow me to that point. Then, I could turn the signal off, shoot him with the gun, and restore him. But how far from the ship would I have to move the signal generator to allow it to leave? Probably not very far since the ship had almost enough power already.

"I'm waiting, Megan. I know you're smart enough to—"

"Cut the flattery." I spoke in a matter-of-fact tone. "Here's the deal. Give me the specs for your tower's signals and how much cable is available to move it to—"

"No."

"No? You didn't let me finish."

"Because I figured out your dilemma. You need my tower's signal for a reason I haven't deduced, but you also need to eliminate it so you can leave. I'll wager it's because the signal disabled your ship. So, once it's turned off, you'll leave, but then you'll replicate the signal for your purposes, which must be extremely important. Otherwise, you would have left already."

I stared at him. His guess wasn't exactly right, but it was close enough to reverse the leverage in his favor. He had the upper hand, and he knew it.

"I see that you're stymied. Therefore, I will offer you a new proposal. As you will soon learn, not all of my employees have fallen sick, but they will if you don't do the following. Leave them all here, whether sick, dead, or healthy. Then I will turn the tower off long enough for you to depart. I realize that I will suffer the loss of some of my labor staff, but that's part of doing business. I can acquire more." Omen began to fade. "I will give you five minutes to discuss the matter with your crew. When I return, if the children are back in their cabins, I will turn the tower off long enough for you to leave." He gave me a final nod. "Goodbye, Megan. It has been a pleasure doing business with you." Then he vanished.

I stared straight ahead, slack jawed. He had beaten me badly, and I wouldn't be the one who had to suffer for my horrible negotiations.

Crystal looped her arm through mine. "Megan, you did the best you could. You had everything going against you. Kids are dying, but you couldn't sacrifice your father—"

I twisted out of her grasp. "You don't have to tell me what's at stake." I let my shoulders sag. "I'm sorry, Crystal. I know you're trying to help. But I'm hurting, my father's in danger, and I keep messing up."

Perdantus flew to my shoulder and pointed toward the tower with a wing. "Megan, look."

My father's electrified form staggered toward me, his light dim and flickering. I ran to him and halted within reach. "Papa! Are you all right?"

He signaled with his glowing fingers. *Dying. Turn tower off. Heal kids.*

"But you'll die."

His fingers moved more quickly. *Better me than kids.*

"When we shut it off last time, you survived for a while. If we have the reintegration gun ready, we can use it before you disperse."

He shook his head and signaled, *Battery dead. No time to charge.*

"Papa ..." Tears flowed. Spasms racked my body as I sobbed. "Papa! My dear Papa! Mama's gone. I can't ... I can't lose you, too!"

"Megan," Oliver said in my ear, "these kids are dying. One boy's heart stopped beating, and Zoë's doing CPR on him. Even if we got our powers back, I don't think I can heal them all. They're dropping like flies."

Crystal touched my arm. "And the kids in the Nine are probably dying. It can't wait." She showed me her laser blaster. "I can do it if you need me to. I mean, you already say you killed your mother. You don't want to kill your father, too."

"No." I took the blaster. "I'll do it. It's my responsibility."

I steeled myself, strode the few steps to the tower, and aimed at the light. As I steadied my breaths, thoughts flooded my mind, so fast it seemed that everything around me stopped, even time itself. This signal squelched my Starborn gifts, stole power from the Astral Dragon, and disrupted a bat's echolocation. What did all of those have in common? Could it be transmitting negative energy like we thought? If so, how was that holding Papa together? Or was it possible that Starborn energy, whether positive or negative, would hold him together? And could a huge dose of positive energy recharge the gun and the Astral Dragon? Could it also bring healing?

Barnabas's advice returned to mind. Sometimes I had to allow others to sacrifice, but sometimes I had to decide to do it myself. Then, his final words flowed. *You will know the time has come when you are the only one who can provide the greatest benefit.*

I nodded. It was time to sacrifice myself. I called out, "Crystal, get the reintegration gun and battery, just in case."

"You got it." She ran toward the cabin.

"Oliver, I need someone to help her carry the unit. It's heavy."

"Scamp's on his way," Oliver said. "He's not sick."

"Perfect." I leaped onto one of the legs of the tower and scrambled to the top, surging adrenaline keeping the pain at bay. After finding the main energy feed box next to the bulb, I looked down. Below, Crystal and Scamp lugged the reintegration gun to the tower, set it down, and aimed the barrel at my father. When Crystal looked up, she shouted, "Blazes, girl! What are you doing?"

"You'll see." I pulled my locket out, laid it on my palm, and opened the back. Inside, the ruby barely glowed at all. Papa was nearly dead.

I grasped a thick cable leading from the upper box to the negative energy box at ground level and took a deep breath. I had to do this fast. I jerked the cable from the upper box, exposing a pair of bare wires. The purple light darkened. The ruby flashed and pulsed more brightly than I had ever seen it, signaling that I had my Starborn powers back.

Not really knowing what I was doing, I pressed the bare wires against the ruby, closed my other hand over them, and flexed my biceps to charge my bracelets. A jolt of electricity shot through my arms, up my spine, and into my head. The tower's bulb flashed on again, now a brilliant scarlet.

My brain felt like it was on fire. My earbud sizzled and fell out, burning in flames as it dropped to the ground. A curtain of red veiled everything in sight, growing darker and darker. Then, my vision turned black. I let go of the tower and fell, my thoughts fading to nothing as I hurtled toward the ground.

I opened my eyes. I stood in a field of shoulder-high grain as the pods swayed in a cool gentle breeze. The azure sky seemed endless, stretching from horizon to horizon. The field swept into a valley where a creek bubbled down a gentle slope, shaded by a few trees.

I whispered, "I know this place."

"You should. You were a child here."

I turned toward the voice. Barnabas stood only a couple of steps away. Dressed in khaki pants and a red sweatshirt with no words on the front, he looked strong and well. I blinked at him. "Barnabas? I don't understand. Why am I here? Just a second ago, I was on Delta Zero at the top of a tower."

"Indeed, you were. As usual, you were heroically saving lives, but this time, it cost you yours."

I swallowed hard. "I ... I died?"

"In a sense. You are physically dead. Your heart has stopped, and you are no longer breathing. Let me show you."

Barnabas waved a hand, as if drawing a curtain across the landscape. The tower stood in view with me straddling the top. I pressed the exposed wires between my hands. I stiffened, my mouth agape. Red light streamed everywhere—from the bulb, my mouth, and my eyes. Like lava spilling from the volcano we had recently escaped, the light flowed down to the ground, covering everything, including Crystal, my father's radiance, and the Astral Dragon.

Crystal fired the regeneration gun at him. His sparks congealed into his physical form. When I fell from the tower, he caught me in his arms, then he and Crystal ran with me to the Astral Dragon. They hurried up the ramp and out of sight.

"Come," Barnabas said, extending a hand, "there is much more to see." When I took his hand, he led me up the ramp and onto the ship's bridge. My father laid me on the floor in front of Sonya's console and started performing mouth-to-mouth resuscitation.

"I'm not breathing, Barnabas, like you said."

"Not on your own. Your father's giving your body a chance, but you don't have long."

"Where's Oliver?" Papa shouted between breaths. "She needs a healer!"

"In the infirmary." Zoë ran from the bridge. "I'll get him."

Papa started chest compressions, pushing down hard and fast. I could almost feel the pressure as he continued. Soon, something cracked. Was it one of my ribs?

Oliver dashed in and knelt at my other side, Zoë behind him. "You do the breathing," Oliver said to Papa. "I'll do the compressions."

Papa nodded and pressed his lips against mine while Oliver laid his hands on my chest, one on top of the other. As they continued the CPR, Crystal paced. "This is all so terrible! Kids are dying, even my best friend!"

"The others are healed," Oliver said, grunting as he pushed. "A bright red light ... flashed in ... and they got better. I didn't ... have to do ... anything. ... But I will soon. ... Sonya's taking us ... to rendezvous with the Nine. ... The kids there ... are still sick."

"We have landed next to the Nebula Nine," Sonya said. "The Nine's ramp is opening. Oliver may now go there to help the sick children on board."

Crystal halted her pacing and looked at him. "What are you going to do, Oliver?"

The scene froze in place. No one moved.

I stepped closer to my body. "Barnabas, what happened?"

He joined me at my side. "That's all that has happened. We are now in a stasis pocket."

"A stasis pocket. What's that?"

"The end of the present time and before the next moment. Time continues to pass, to be sure, but not in your reality. You see, time is a puzzling concept. It is more perception than anything, a way of measuring instead of a tangible entity. Time is not passing faster or slower in other worlds. But your perception of time passage is. You see, time always appears to move at the speed of mind. Time passage did not speed up on Delta Zero while Raven was here, but actions were relatively faster than outside of this world. People moved far more quickly, including their glowsap mining efforts, and they aged more quickly as well." He sighed. "I'm afraid that's the best I can tell you, because I don't understand it all myself." He tapped a finger against his head. "My brain isn't that big."

"Okay, so how do we get my reality moving again? I need to know what happens. Will I die? Will Oliver and my father revive me? Will Oliver have to leave the Astral Dragon and help the other kids in the Nebula Nine? If he does, my father won't have a healer to help save me."

Barnabas set a hand on my shoulder. "What do *you* want Oliver to do?"

I stared at him. His wise eyes seemed so sincere, as if what I wanted could make a difference. "Why are you asking me? I can't do a thing about what's going to happen."

"Why do you say that?"

"Why?" I waved a hand at my motionless body. "Look at me. I'm unconscious. No, I'm dead. I can't lift a finger, much less tell Oliver what he should do. What *I* want won't change anything."

"Oh? I think you're greatly mistaken. You have a will, and it is still attached to your brain, though your consciousness has drifted outside of it. What you decide here can definitely affect your outcome."

"You mean, if I have the will to live, then I have a chance to survive? If I don't give up, they won't give up on me?"

"Well, I'm sure your father won't give up on you no matter what you do, but you might be able to have an impact on what Oliver does. He believes that if he saves the other children but not you, many more children could die as a result of your death. The battle is not yet over. Omen still lives, and he will not stop his lucrative business merely because of a temporary setback on Delta Zero."

"You're right. Omen is still a big threat, but you said Oliver *believes* that my death will cause other children to die. Is he wrong?"

"It's complicated. Trying to save you will likely result in death for some children on the Nebula Nine. But if he helps you survive, you might save many more children in the long run. On the other hand, if you die, your crewmates will fight on. Since you have trained them so well, they could possibly achieve more than they could with you in their midst, because they rely on you more than they need to."

"Are you saying I'm a crutch?"

"Not really a crutch. A crutch is for those who are lame or injured. You're a coach, an energizer, a dynamo, as they have often said. But a power cell that has already been energized doesn't need to stay close to its dynamo. It needs to be sent out to perform the great deeds its maker designed it to perform."

I shook my head. "Sorry. My brain's pretty fuzzy right now. Can you make it simpler?"

"I'll try." Barnabas stroked his chin. "Consider a dozen lanterns in one location providing great light where they are, but also consider a dozen lanterns that go out into a world of darkness, where they each light another lantern, and those lanterns light other lanterns, and so on. It wouldn't be long before they are able to light the entire world."

I imagined his illustration. He was right, of course, about lanterns, but did it really apply to me? "So you're saying if I die, the lanterns, that is, my crew, will spread the light more than if I live?"

"Only because you have trained them to do so. It is your light and love that they will take to others. Your courage, sacrifice, and love will always be their inspiration."

"And if I live, they would be too dependent on me."

"If you allow them to be, yes. After all, they're still children. For them to do otherwise, they would have to mature quickly, and your death would be a catalyst for that growth."

I looked at each face in the ship—their concern for me, their fear, their determination. I loved them all so much. How could I leave them? But how could I *not* leave them? In many ways, they were dependent on me. Although they did venture out on their own at times, it was because I told them what to do. They had never truly stepped out on their own.

Then I gazed into Papa's eyes. Fear blazed in his sparkling tears, as did love, even more vivid, more desperate. He had lost Mama, and he probably blamed himself for getting her involved with our freedom fighting. If he lost me, he would blame himself even more. After all, he trained a little girl to be a thief and a killer. He would never forgive himself for forcing that life on me ... and that death. I couldn't allow such horrible grief to crush him. I chose this life of danger. And now it seemed that I could choose whether or not to suffer this death.

"Barnabas ..." Somehow, even outside of my body, I could feel my throat tighten. "Barnabas, I want to live. And I'll do whatever it takes to send my crewmates out on their own to spread the light. But how do I let Oliver know?"

"You cannot let him know. In order to break from his dependence on you, he has to make his own decisions. If you influence him, you will be battling against your own purpose to foster independence. All you can do is use your will to live and fight to survive."

I pressed my lips together. "So I just have to trust him and try not to die."

"That is a succinct way to state the matter."

"Okay. So what do I do now? When will this pause end?"

Barnabas gave a light shrug. "You would know better than I ever could. I understand that you have been in a similar situation before."

I nodded. "I was dying from bramble-bee poison, and Oliver was trying to decide whether or not to give me chest compressions."

"Why did he hesitate?"

"He never said, but I think he was embarrassed about touching my chest."

Barnabas smiled. "Ah. The misplaced proprieties of a young boy."

"Something like that. I was kind of embarrassed, too. I mean, after I found out about it."

"And are you embarrassed now?"

I looked at Oliver. Both of his hands were firmly planted on my chest. "Not in the slightest."

"You have learned complete trust, one sign that you have both matured greatly. In any case, back to the issue of ending this pause. As it was during the previous episode, so it is now. God, who appeared to you as a dragon at the time, is the one who can and will end this pause when you are ready. And I, for one, believe you are ready, though I am concerned that you have spent the last of your nine lives, so to speak. I pray that your idiom will not be tested again. Because if it is, only a miracle could save you."

"I'll do my best, but how will I know when the pause will—" Something jerked me toward my body, stretching me painfully.

Barnabas's voice faded as he spoke. "Farewell for now, Megan. I know someday we will meet again."

I streamed into my head, and darkness filled my vision. I tried to open my eyes, but the lids wouldn't budge. Somehow my brain was still working, though nothing else could move at all.

Something put pressure on my lips, and air pushed into my lungs. A coarse whisper filtered in. "Breathe, Megan, breathe." Papa's voice.

Oliver added his voice. "Zoë, can you massage Megan's heart with your mind?"

"I think so."

"Give it a try. What I'm doing isn't working. I'll go help the kids on the Nine."

"Gotcha."

Tightness squeezed my heart, then let go, then squeezed again, then let go again, the pattern repeating and the squeezes getting harder each time. Pain shot across my ribs, up and down my torso, and into every limb. Finally, my heart thumped. I gasped a deep breath. Papa shouted, "Everyone back! Give her room!"

The pressure vanished. I sucked in more deep breaths, though each breath sent a new shockwave of pain through my ribs. My heart beat on its own in a normal rhythm. The only other sensations were wetness in my pants and a bad odor. Finally, I opened my eyes.

Papa's face nearly filled my vision as he smiled and wept at the same time. "Megan, you've come back to us. I was so worried."

"So …" I cleared my throat. "So was I."

He pulled back, still kneeling next to me. "Oliver went to heal the kids on the Nine. Zoë stayed to help me do CPR."

"I know. I heard him."

"You did? I thought you were unconscious."

"Sort of. But I could hear." A pang near my heart made me wince. "I think I broke some ribs."

"You mean *I* broke your ribs. I'm sorry. I'm not used to doing chest compressions. I guess I pushed too hard."

As he gazed at me, his thoughts poured into my mind. *Oh, Megan, I love you so much. I don't know what I would do without you.*

I blocked the flow. It wasn't right to intrude. But being able to read his mind let me know that I still had Starborn powers, maybe all of them. My ribs would probably heal quickly.

Crystal and Zoë knelt next to me across from Papa. "So what's next, hero girl?" Crystal said. "I mean after sending all that Starborn energy from the tower and nearly drowning us all in the dynamo deluge, Omen's probably going to sit back and enjoy his money and not bother any kids again. He knows he'd have to deal with you if he tried to start a new mine."

"I'll think about Omen later. Right now I should help Oliver heal the other kids." I flexed to get up, but new pain roared, taking my breath away.

Zoë pushed me back down. "You're in no shape to help anyone. Trust Oliver. He can handle it."

"I trust him. I just want to help him."

Crystal let out a tsking sound. "You can help Oliver by helping yourself."

"You should be in bed." Papa slid his arms under my back and legs. "I'll take you to the infirmary."

"It's full," Zoë said. "The best bed is in the captain's quarters on the Nine. She's right next to us, not five steps from ramp to ramp."

"Then I'll take her there." Papa lifted me into his arms.

"And I'll be on your six," Crystal said. "You know, in case you … um …" She shook her head. "No reason. I'll just be on your six."

Zoë gestured toward the infirmary with a thumb. "I'll stay with the kids here. Some of them are still recovering. They'll need someone to get water and food."

Crystal patted her on the back. "And would you mind getting something edible for Megan? Something better than disgusting?"

"Will do." Zoë hustled out of the room.

As Papa walked down the Astral Dragon's ramp, he whispered, "You are the bravest girl ... no, the bravest *person* I have ever known. You saved my life. You saved those kids from slavery. You are amazing."

Trying not to grimace at my aching ribs, I gave him a tight-lipped smile. "Thank you. So are you." After taking a painful breath, I added loudly enough for Crystal to hear, "And so are all of my crewmates."

"You got that right," Crystal said. "We are now the amazing Astral Alliance." Although I couldn't see her, I could tell she was grinning about the alliteration.

When we arrived at the Nebula Nine's bridge, Jillian ran to greet us, brushing tears from her cheeks. "So you ..." She sniffed. "You finally decided to get up, did you?"

I forced another smile. "Yep. Been too lazy lately."

Echo bounded into view and drew close. "And she hasn't been hungry. Not hungry at all. I heard she hasn't eaten all day. Not once all day." She wrinkled her nose. "What's that smell?"

"Well," Papa said, "let's just say that when her heart stopped, she had no control over her body."

"Say no more," Jillian said as she pointed toward the crew's sleeping area. "She has a change of clothes in the Nine's captain's quarters. And it has a shower with warm water. Really nice."

"I'll go with her." Crystal walked into sight from behind my father. "I helped her get cleaned up last time her heart stopped, and Kattica did the same a little while ago. She should be used to it by now."

Crystal led the way to the captain's quarters and stood by the bed. "Can you stand?" she asked me. "That would help."

"Probably. My legs feel strong enough. The only thing that hurts is my ribs."

Papa lowered my feet to the floor and held me until Crystal grasped my arm. "Let's see if you need support." When she let me go, I lifted my legs in turn. "Yep. You're good."

Papa looked at Crystal. "Thank you for taking care of her."

"No problem." She wrapped her arms around him and pressed her head against his chest. When she drew back, she looked up at him. "Thank you for being the best dad in the world. You raised the greatest hero I have ever seen, even the heroes in those crazy novels I read. No one is like Megan."

"You've got that right." Papa kissed her forehead. "But from what I've seen, you're quite the hero yourself." He then kissed me on the forehead and walked out of the room.

Crystal set her fists on her hips and looked me up and down. "Blazes, girl. You're a bigger mess than any time I've ever seen you. And that's saying a lot."

I managed another smile. "I guess I always try to outdo myself, but you didn't see me before Kattica got me to the Dragon's shower. I was a lot dirtier then."

"I'm glad I didn't see that." She pinched the monogram on one of my filthy sleeves. "Too bad. I really like this new uniform. You'll have to change into one of your old imperial Alliance duds."

I nodded. "Maybe I could just leave these on, wash them in the shower."

"And you'd be dry in how many hours? Not happening." She set a hand on my back. "Let's get you cleaned up, and I'll wash your lovely new uniform myself."

Crystal spent the next half hour getting me cleaned up. Since my spare Alliance uniform was also dirty, she searched in a storage closet for a fresh set and found one that fit me. Apparently the Nine had a female on board in the past who was close enough to my size.

By the time Crystal finished, I felt a lot stronger, though my ribs still ached. As she rose from tying my shoes, I lifted my legs again. "Thanks. I think I'm ready."

She squinted at me. "Ready for what?"

"To go after Omen, of course. We messed up his mine on this planet, but he's still ready to cause trouble, probably living in luxury on

Delta Ninety-five. He won't give up just because we put a roadblock in his way."

"True, but the rest of us might say something about whether or not you should go to Delta Ninety-five."

I blinked at her. "What are you talking about? Of course I have to go."

Crystal took my hand and led me to a mirror on the wall. "Look at yourself. You're as pale as fog and nearly as thin. And you're literally trembling."

I gazed at my reflection. She was right about how I looked. And the trembling? I lifted a hand. Yes, it trembled, as if shivering in the cold. I grasped my hand with the other to stop it. "Okay, Miss Observant. I'm a wreck. But I'm a ready wreck. I can still do what I have to do."

"Maybe." She looped her arm around mine and guided me out of the room. "Let's ask Oliver what he thinks. He's probably finished healing the kids here. Apparently when you broadcast your powers to him, he got supercharged to the max. No idea how long it'll last."

When we arrived on the bridge, we found Oliver sitting at the first mate's station and Papa and Jillian chatting privately at the far wall. Papa smiled and lifted a finger, letting me know that he would greet me in a moment. Oliver leaped up, hurried to me, and reached his arms out before pulling back. "Are you sturdy enough to hug?"

"Absolutely." I drew him close. As we embraced, I rubbed his back. "Thank you for taking care of me, Oliver. I would've died without you."

"That's not what I heard." He pulled away, his eyes glistening with tears. "I had to leave. Zoë got your heart started again."

"I know how long you kept me alive before Zoë took over. I'll explain more later, but I was watching."

"Oliver," Crystal said, nodding toward me. "Can you check Megan over? I mean, can she … um …"

"Resume her duties as commanding officer?" Oliver asked.

"Yeah. That. Sounds a lot better than 'fly to the next mission without dropping dead.'"

"Let's see." His eyes moved, shifting up and down and side to side. "Do your ribs hurt?"

I touched my ribcage. "You could see that?"

He smiled. "Just a guess. I heard something pop during CPR. But if you'll let me poke around, I can tell what's going on in there."

I lifted my arms. "Go for it."

Oliver set a hand on each side of my ribcage and closed his eyes as he whispered, "Probing ... probing ... probing. Everything looks fine down here." After moving a hand to the top of my sternum, he tilted his head. "Ah. Two ribs are cracked. No sharp edges sticking out or anything." He opened his eyes and lowered his hands. "Otherwise, your ribs are fine."

"Should she take it easy for a while?" Crystal asked.

Oliver turned toward Emerson's console. "Emerson? What's the protocol for cracked ribs?"

His voice came from the ceiling speakers. "With no intervention, cracked ribs take three to six weeks to fully heal. Megan should apply ice for twenty minutes of every waking hour for two days, then for ten minutes three times daily as needed to reduce pain and swelling. Wrap the ice in a protective cloth before applying it to the injured area. Our medical supply cabinet has appropriate non-narcotic pain relievers that she should take until the pain is gone."

"Thank you, Emerson," I said. "That shouldn't be hard to—"

"And may I say, Megan, that the stories about your conquest of Omen are already reaching epic proportions. Radio chatter is filled with the news. You are truly a hero of the highest caliber."

"Well ..." New warmth coursed through my body. All of this praise was getting a bit overdone. "Thanks."

"But you should rest," Crystal said with a firm tone. "At least a couple of weeks."

"Emerson," I said, "how long would it take to get to Delta Ninety-Five? Say, normal cruising speed."

"If there is no time warp shift between here and there, we could arrive in seven days, three hours, and seven minutes."

"There is no time shift. Trust me on that. We'll be fine."

"No time shift?" Papa said as he and Jillian joined us. "Then how do you explain Raven aging so quickly?"

"I'll try to explain on the way to Delta Ninety-five." I looked at Oliver. "So seven days rest. Is that enough, Mr. Healer? I have healing powers myself, so I might be fine by then, including all the bumps and bruises I got while escaping the volcano."

Oliver nodded. "True about the bumps and bruises, and I guess I can check your ribs after seven days. By then we should have a good idea about what you can do."

Crystal sighed. "All right. I guess it was wishful thinking to hope Megan would rest as long as she should. Seven days will have to do."

Perdantus flew in and landed on my shoulder. "I have news, but first, Megan, it's good to see you standing and breathing. I thought we had lost you, and the prospects of continuing our crusade without you seemed dim indeed."

I ran a finger up and down his chest. "You and my other crewmates are more than capable of continuing our crusade without me. But, thank you."

"Now my news. Sonya picked up a distress call from Gamma Five, transmitted through the Zeta station there to the one here. Lyric's mother, Piper, reported that her husband has disappeared. She suspects kidnapping by someone who wants to take control of the Zeta station. She has heard whisperings of such a conspiracy during the past few weeks. She needs help searching for him and for protecting the station from a potential takeover."

Papa gave me a questioning look that I knew so well. He was torn between two priorities, being with me and answering a call to duty.

"You should go," I said. "And take all the kids we rescued before anything can happen to the Zeta station at Gamma Five. Piper can help you get them transported to their homes."

He set a hand on my shoulder and looked me in the eye. "You know I want to be with you, right?"

"Of course. And we will be together when this is all over. It's better for us to go where we're needed most. Two lanterns can spread light faster than one."

He gave me a tight-lipped nod. "So be it."

"Regarding your plans," Perdantus said as he fluttered down to my console, "Echo reported another reason to avoid sending the Astral Dragon to Delta Ninety-five. The Dragon's flight from the Zeta station to this planet revealed some air leaks. They are minor, but the ship would lose too much air during a long flight. Echo could patch whatever leaks she can find, but there is no guarantee that she can find them all. As Echo said, and I quote, 'With children on board, the risk is too high, much too high.'"

Jillian set a hand on Papa's shoulder. "I'm going with you, Bro. No offense, but taking all the kids, making sure they're checked out by medical professionals, and putting the ship through a search for leaks while trying to find Piper's husband and defending the Zeta station?" She shook her head. "Nope. No one could do it all. Not even you."

"No argument with that," Papa said. "One person can't—"

"Well," Jillian continued, apparently not caring that she interrupted him, "Megan could probably do it ... or Crystal ... or Oliver ... or Perdantus ... or—"

"All right, Sis." Papa shoved her shoulder. "Knock it off."

I smiled. "Looks like I should send Echo to keep you siblings out of trouble. Since she knows the ship so well now, she can test and patch it while you two help Piper."

"Sounds good." Papa kissed my forehead. "Stay in touch."

Jillian hugged Oliver and Crystal. Then she hugged me, kissed my forehead, and mussed my hair. "Listen to your aunt, Mophead. Don't die again, all right?"

"She can't," Crystal said. "That cat doesn't have any of her nine lives left. But don't worry. I'll stick to her like slime on a slug. I'll make sure she stays on this side of death's door."

When Papa and Jillian left, I touched my ear to adjust the bud, but it wasn't there. "I forgot. My earbud got fried at the tower."

Crystal groaned. "Not again! How many is that? Five?"

"Who do you want to call?" Oliver asked.

"Zoë. We should get going as soon as possible."

Oliver shifted from foot to foot, his hands in his pockets. "I've been meaning to tell you, but we've gotten distracted."

"Sounds ominous. Go ahead and spill it."

"I took away Zoë's medical clearance. She's going home to Gamma Five."

"What? Why?"

"When she killed the slavers and the bees, it took a lot out of her, and after she massaged your heart to bring you back to life, she looked really bad. Anyway, while you were getting cleaned up, I went to the Dragon's infirmary to see about her. She had a bleeding perforation in her lung. I used my healing power to patch her up, but she's too fragile to go on any missions. And she wants to go home anyway." Oliver shrugged. "Who was I to say no to a girl who wants to live long enough to see her parents again?"

I sighed. "You did the right thing, but I should go and say goodbye."

Just as I turned to leave, Oliver caught my wrist. "She said for you not to come. She knows if she sees you, she wouldn't be able to stand not going with us. I think you should leave her alone."

"Oliver's right," Crystal said. "I know I couldn't stand it if I were her. I'm sure she'll send you a message when she gets home."

I imagined Zoë sitting in a comfortable chair with her family around. She seemed content. And she deserved to be content. We all did, but at least one of us could find some peace. It might as well be Zoë.

I sat in the captain's chair, prompting Perdantus to hop back up to my shoulder. "Oliver," I said, "you and Crystal can decide on who's first mate and who's navigator. I'm in rest mode for the next seven days."

"Easy decision." Crystal sat at the navigator's station. "I don't want to be first mate. First mate means first in line to replace you, and ain't nobody wants to do that."

Oliver grinned. "Because replacing her would be impossible." He sat in the first mate's seat. "But I'll fill the chair. That part's easy."

I rolled my eyes. "Cut the brown-nosing, you two. It's nauseating."

"What we meant," Crystal said, "is that it's impossible to replace you because no one in the galaxy is as insufferably bossy or mule-headedly stubborn as you are."

"That's better. Thank you."

Crystal grinned. "Anytime, Mophead."

I settled back in my seat and called out, "Emerson, close the ramp and plot a course to Delta Ninety-five."

The ramp began closing. "The course is already set, Captain. Since we will stay in the same star system, we will not travel through a wormhole, making our flight safer. I am now awaiting your command to depart from this planet."

The front viewing screen turned on, showing the surrounding jungle. "The command is given. Let's go to Delta Ninety-five."

Part
02
Delta Ninety-Five

14

During our travel toward Delta Ninety-five, Emerson gathered intel from various sources, including Quixon, our former-slave-trader friend on Delta Ninety-eight. He reported that a strange human occasionally showed up on Ninety-eight asking about buying children. Since we pretty much destroyed the slave market at Bassolith, he didn't have any obvious success, though Quixon believed he picked up some leads on where to get children elsewhere, including the kids we left on Delta Ninety-five. If that was true, those kids were in danger.

On day five, we received a message from Lyric on Gamma Five, relayed to the Delta system through the Zeta station. Everyone had arrived safely. Most of the kids were given clean bills of health, though a few had to be treated for some lasting effects of the bramble bee poison. Zoë volunteered to coordinate travel to their homes in various star systems, so every family would eventually be restored, exactly the goal we had been fighting for.

Also, Papa and Jillian had patched all of the leaks in the Astral Dragon, and Echo performed a pressure test that proved the ship was ready for interstellar travel. Since no time shift existed any longer between the two worlds, travel between Zeta stations was no longer dangerous. They had already shipped some of the kids to various stations to get them home, and they hoped to finish the job as soon as possible. Rumors of an attack on the station continued to keep everyone on edge and working hard to complete the transports.

"Well, the news from Gamma Five is mostly good," Crystal said from the navigator's station.

"That's for sure." I rose from the captain's chair and stretched my arms, but new pain spiked in my ribs, making me wince.

"Not much more time to recover," Oliver said as he got up from the first mate's chair. "And you're still hurting."

"It's getting better. I'll be fine." I walked toward the living quarters and picked up a computer pad from Emerson's console along the way. "I'm going to rest in my bed while sending some messages to Gamma Five."

"All right if I join you?" Crystal asked. "I barely slept last night."

I halted and looked at her. "Sure. You can help with my messages."

"Probably." She hopped up from her seat. "I can keep you from using any Willis words so whoever's reading it won't think you're making up words that don't exist."

Oliver pushed his hands into his pockets. "I guess I'll stay here. Someone's got to keep an eye on stuff. And I can make dinner."

"He's such a gentleman," Crystal said with a grin. "I'll have that reconstituted greenish stuff mixed with the grayish powder in the foil pouches and that stringy stuff that's supposed to taste like beef but really tastes like worms, and I do know what worms taste like."

I cringed. "I'm not going to ask how you know."

"I'm on it," Oliver said. "Green stuff, gray stuff, and worm stuff."

Crystal and I walked to my quarters, kicked our shoes off, and lay on the bed, not bothering to get under the covers. My head propped by a pillow, I set the edge of the computer pad on my chest and brought up the messaging system. "I want to write to Lyric first. I was thinking that being able to morph into another person can be a super powerful way to battle against Omen. Since I've never done it before, maybe she can tell me how."

"You've also never read minds, at least not that I know of. Maybe you can contact Chip about that. And moving stuff would be great, too. I know you've done it a little bit, but you need to be able to do it at any moment and with heavier stuff, so write to Zoë, too."

"Actually, I have done some mind reading. First, those goons in the transport ship, then I heard some of my father's thoughts, but I shut them off. It didn't seem right."

"Yeah. I'd be upset if you pried into my thoughts without asking."

"No worries. I haven't. But maybe we could try it. You know, give me some practice. It would be an amazing weapon against the real Omen if I'm ever face to face with him."

"All right." Crystal pointed at my computer pad. "Write your message to Lyric. Then we'll practice."

"Will do." I typed in the proper protocol to send the message first to the Zeta station at Delta Zero, then to the Gamma Five Zeta station, then to Lyric's personal address. I spoke as I tapped out the words. "Dear Lyric, thank you for the update you sent us. Sounds like everything's moving along. I sure hope my father and my aunt can help you find your father. I was wondering if you could help me learn how to shape shift into another person. I don't even know how to begin. Do you just think about the person you want to look like? Let me know."

I tapped the send icon. "It'll take a while to get there. Even if she answers right away, it'll take another while to get her reply."

"Perfect." Crystal sat up and looked straight at me. "What am I thinking now? You have my permission to probe."

During the next hour, we practiced my mind reading skills until I got pretty good at it. Once, I accidentally probed too deeply and learned about a time a slave master whipped her back. Because I had seen her scars, I already knew about it, but hearing the thoughts made the torture come alive in my mind—painfully alive.

When I told her what I heard, she said I had to be mistaken, but my lie-detecting power said she was either lying or trying to hide something. Still, I let it go. If she wanted me to know what really happened, she would tell me.

After we ate the dinner Oliver prepared, we played a board game with him, then we all went to bed, Crystal again in my quarters and Perdantus with Oliver. I wore an old T-shirt and baggy shorts, while Crystal wore green-and-blue checkered pajamas she found in the storage closet. Also, my new Astral Alliance uniform lay clean and folded on the night table. It would be great to put it on again when I woke up.

Once we had settled in the bed, Perdantus's voice penetrated the wall from the next room. "That's a good question, Oliver. The reason Omen prevailed in the discussion at the tower with Megan is simple. Megan had an unwinnable position, and Omen knew it. Although Megan is extraordinarily gifted in the art of negotiation, she had no chance of winning against an opponent who also has considerable skills. She pressed on valiantly, but she had no chance."

"But she *did* win," Oliver said. "She did defeat Omen. Not with words. With love. She's got all sorts of bravado, sass, and big words, but the reason she always comes out on top is because of love."

"Yes, Oliver. You're right. Love is her greatest asset. And that's why I love her as much as I do, and I trust that you do as well."

"Um … well, yeah. She's like a sister to me. She's amazing."

Then the conversation fell silent.

Crystal covered her mouth with a hand and whispered, "My lie detector is drawing a blank. Can you read Oliver's mind from here? Does he really love you like a sister, or is there something more?"

I scowled. "Are you being stupid Cupid again? Oliver's right. We are like brother and sister. Nothing more. And we're too young for romance anyway."

She crossed her arms in front and pouted. "Spoil sport."

"Mind reading isn't a sport. I'm not about to invade his privacy. He's too good of a friend."

Crystal sighed. "I suppose you're right, but someday you two will be old enough, and—"

"And I *still* won't read his mind."

Just as she opened her mouth to respond, my computer pad dinged. I grabbed it from the night table and looked at the screen. "Message from Lyric. And it's audio." I tapped the icon.

"Megan …" Her voice sounded scared, breathless. "Something terrible is happening here. Alliance ships are orbiting the Zeta station, like they're trying to trap us. One of them landed in an arrival bay, arrested my mother, and disabled the ship-transport system. I guess they did that so the Astral Dragon couldn't escape, but we got the rest of the kids out in other ships in time. Anyway, the messaging system is still working, at least for now, so I'm sending this as fast as I can. My mother, your father, your aunt, and Echo are waiting for me in the Astral Dragon so we can try to get past the blockade. I'm sorry, but I don't have time to tell you how to shape shift besides just concentrate on a mental image of someone you know." The message ended.

Crystal and I stared at each other, our mouths hanging open. Finally, Crystal whispered, "Megan, what are we going to do?"

"First, I'm checking my locket." I pulled it up from under my shirt and opened the back. The dragon's eye glowed. "My father's still alive."

"Okay. That's a good sign. What next?"

I closed the locket and slid it back into place. "Lyric's message was probably a few hours old. If someone was attacking with Alliance ships, then the Nine might also be in danger. We have to protect it." I jumped out of bed and grabbed my new uniform from the night table, while Crystal fetched hers from the closet. As we hurriedly got dressed, I spoke toward the ceiling. "Emerson, shift to emergency protocol three. Do not allow any incoming messages into your system. Route them directly to my computer pad."

"Performing bypass procedures now. Your timing is interesting. A message from the Alliance is coming in at this moment. I am routing it to your pad."

I leaped back to the bed, snatched up the pad, and accessed the message. It looked like a simple series of alphanumeric characters, probably a code. I tapped on the pad. "Emerson, I'm sending this message to you, but I'm putting spaces between the first few characters so it'll be a little different. I'm worried that it might be a code to take over the Nine. When you read it, tell me what the code would've done to you." I tapped the send key.

"Message received. You are correct that it is an infiltration code that would have allowed access to internal commands, including navigation and weapons control."

"If the infiltration had worked, how would you have responded?"

"I would have sent a simple acknowledgment and awaited further instructions."

I set the pad on the bed. "Then send that message to the address the code came from and see if you can determine where that address is and who the sender might be."

"Acknowledgment sent. Performing address search. Because of the gap between us and the Delta Zero Zeta station, this could take a considerable amount of time, as will the sender's next command."

"Understood. Send Oliver and Perdantus a wake-up alarm and instructions to meet me on the bridge."

"Acknowledged." A siren sounded from the ceiling.

I fastened the front of my uniform's top, zipped the pants, and looked at Crystal. "Ready?"

She tossed her pajamas on the bed. "Been ready. Let's go."

I grabbed the pad and ran from the room. When we arrived at the bridge, Oliver was already tapping on the console screen at the first mate's station with Perdantus on his shoulder.

I sat at my station and looked at him. "How did you get here so fast?"

He shrugged. "Never took off my uniform."

"Did Emerson give you an update?"

"Yep, and I'm installing a program my father wrote. It's in a secret folder that not even Emerson knows about. It'll automatically strip any access command codes from incoming messages. That way you won't have to filter them on your pad."

"Perfect. That's great thinking. I mean, I know your father wrote it, but you knew to install it."

"We all do our part." He tapped once more on his screen. "It's done. Emerson will automatically filter all messages now."

"Great." I looked at my pad. "Let's see what got forwarded to me." I scanned a list of messages that had similar subject lines and spoke them as I read. "Alliance orders for all officers in deployed vessels ... Alliance orders for all active officers in port ... Alliance orders for all decommissioned officers." I tapped on that one and read it. "All decommissioned officers are to report for active duty. Go at once to the closest base. There you will receive your orders."

"Who authorized it?" Oliver asked. "All orders like that should show the officer who authorized the order."

I looked at the bottom of the message. Next to a label that said *By Authority Of* was the name Admiral Dwight Fairbanks. I sucked in a quick breath and read it out loud. "Admiral Dwight Fairbanks."

Oliver huffed. "Well, we know that's fake. We saw him die."

"Correction," Perdantus said. "You saw him fall into a burning ship."

I rolled my eyes. "Perdantus, he was wrapped in flames before he fell in. You were with us. You saw it."

"I did not see it. I was incapacitated in Oliver's pocket at the time. But, regardless of who witnessed the event, did any of us see his corpse afterward?"

We all shook our heads.

"I have long wondered," Perdantus said, "how Camille Fairbanks could receive a commission as an admiral without someone high in the ranks authorizing it. We should consider the possibility that Dwight Fairbanks approved her commission, perhaps from a hospital bed."

Oliver slammed a fist on his console. "I should've thought of that. I've been around the Alliance officers enough to know that a widow can't just march in and take over."

I waved both hands, palms downward, as if trying to settle a crowd. "Okay, so let's assume he's alive. What's he up to?"

Oliver pointed at my pad. "Check the other messages. Maybe we'll get a clue."

I tapped on the first one and read it. "All currently deployed officers are to fly their vessels at once to the Delta system. You may use the Zeta stations if that option will get you there in the shortest amount of time. Travel using these stations is now completely safe. We will rendezvous at Delta Ninety-five where you will receive further orders."

My heart thudded. "They're all going to Delta Ninety-five!"

"But why?" Crystal asked.

I looked at the pad. "Maybe I can find more clues in one of these—"

Crystal snatched the pad from me. "Oliver and I will do that. You have a ship to command. We should either retreat or get there as fast as possible. Your call."

"We have to rescue the kids on Ninety-five. The only option is to charge ahead." I looked at our current route. We still had two days to go before arriving. "Emerson, calculate the fastest possible acceleration and deceleration protocol for eighty percent of survivable g-force maximum."

"Calculation in progress. I am programmed to remind the captain that g-forces at that level may cause severe headaches, body aches, and nausea. Fainting is not out of the question before the ship's g-force dampeners have had time to adjust the environment."

"Those dampeners are nearly worthless. They make maybe a five percent difference."

"Correct, but that five percent might be enough to keep you and your crew conscious."

"Understood. We'll take the risk. Just tell me how much time it will take to get there."

"The new acceleration-deceleration protocol will allow the ship to arrive in an orbit around Delta Ninety-five in seven hours, six minutes, fourteen seconds."

"That's much better. Everyone strap in. When we adjust to the g-forces, we can get up for food and water."

"And the toilet," Crystal said. "Those g-forces always increase my p-forces."

Perdantus flew from the room, calling, "I will go to my usual place. Give me ten seconds."

When Oliver and Crystal had buckled and ten seconds had passed, I grasped my armrests. "Emerson, start the new acceleration protocol."

"Engaging."

The engines roared, and the acceleration pressed my body against the back of my chair. My cracked ribs ached. In all the excitement, I hadn't thought about how they might be affected.

Oliver glanced at me for a brief moment before looking forward again. I didn't have to read his mind. He was wondering if giving me clearance to go on this mission was the right decision.

As the g-forces increased, Crystal moaned. "Don't barf. Please don't barf. I don't have a bag to barf in. And even if I did, I hate barfing."

My own stomach churned. Dizziness invaded my brain. I shook my head hard to cast it away, but it came back, making me feel like I might faint.

Oliver let out a barely audible moan. I reached a hand over to him. He grasped it tightly and closed his eyes. Pain from his grip helped me focus on it instead of my ribs and head. I could stand this. I had to stand this.

After several minutes, the dizziness faded, as did the nausea, though the soreness in my ribs continued. I tried to take a deep breath, but the pain kept it shallow. "You doing any better, Oliver?"

He released my hand and opened his eyes. "Some."

I twisted my neck to look at Crystal. "How about you?"

"Better. But I threw up in my mouth a little. That was nasty. Good thing I had a bottle of water at my station." She held a plastic bottle as if ready to toss it. "Want some?"

"Sure, but don't throw it. The way we're accelerating, it could end up behind you." I unbuckled, rose from my chair, and set my feet to keep the g-forces from launching me into Crystal as I staggered toward her.

When I arrived, she caught me with one hand and pushed the bottle into my pocket with the other. "Good luck getting back to your seat. It'll be like climbing a steep mountain."

"Nope. We've got about three plus hours of acceleration, then the same amount of deceleration. I'm going to strap into bed for a while. It's downhill in that direction. When I get up later on, it'll be downhill going back to my seat. Besides, I have snacks there and extra water. It'll be a good place to hole up."

"Sounds good for me, too. Toilet first, though. My bladder's ready to pop."

Oliver unbuckled. "Guess I'll go, too."

"Emerson," I said, "keep me informed about any messages that might explain why the Alliance is heading for Delta Ninety-five, or chatter that'll make a difference to us. But if any news can wait till we get up, let us sleep."

"Acknowledged."

After clumsily using the toilet and shuffling carefully to bed, not bothering to take anything off except our shoes, we strapped in and lay quietly for a while, trying to sleep. But I couldn't sleep. Questions kept my brain in high gear. Did Admiral Fairbanks really survive? If so, why was he sending ships to Delta Ninety-five? Why did the Alliance attack the Zeta station at Gamma Five? To capture my father? To capture me? Maybe Fairbanks was on Omen's payroll, and after I rescued the enslaved children on Delta Zero, Omen sent him to capture or kill me at all costs. I was now Alliance enemy number one.

The thought of being a target for the Alliance raised a shudder. How could it be true? I was just a young teenager, not a deadly scourge. Then again, maybe the situation wasn't about me at all. Maybe something else was going on at Delta Ninety-five, an invasion of some sort, and Fairbanks needed control of the Gamma Five Zeta station for transporting part of his fleet from the Gamma system.

I let out a quiet sigh. I couldn't possibly know for certain. I just had to trust that I would know what to do when the time came. I prayed in my mind, *God, please watch over my loved ones in the Gamma system— Papa, Aunt Jillian, Zoë, Echo, Lyric, and the other kids. Oh, and Piper, too. Bring us all safely together. Also, help me squash Omen and his schemes once and for all and rescue any other kids he's enslaved. Whatever I need to do to make that happen, let me know, and I'll do it.* I paused for a moment before adding, *That's all I can think of so … good night, God. And thank you.*

After the prayer, I was able to drift off to sleep, and I slept for a few hours. The shift to deceleration woke me up as the strap pressed against my stomach from the opposite direction.

Crystal groaned. "The snacks I ate are about to regurgitate. And I didn't rhyme just now on purpose."

I threw off the bedcovers. "Let's see if Emerson has any news."

"I'll be on your six, but the g-forces will make any vomit fly on you."

"Just turn your head." I carefully got up, slipped my shoes on and tied them, then shuffled toward the bridge, leaning back to compensate for the g-forces while Crystal did the same a few steps behind me.

When we arrived, Oliver, sitting again at the first mate's station, pointed at my chair. "Better get in your seat. Some weird stuff is happening."

Crystal hustled to the navigator's station while I staggered to my place and sat down. "What stuff?"

"Read the last message that came in."

I looked at my console, tapped the most recent entry in the messages window, and read it loudly enough for Crystal to hear. "To all Alliance vessels that are enroute to Delta Ninety-five, one starship, the Nebula Nine, will already be there when you arrive. In the past, that vessel was commandeered by our enemies, but we sent infiltration codes to wrest control from them and send the ship to join us at our destination planet. So far, it seems that the codes worked as designed, but we will know for certain when it begins its orbit around the planet. Although our ships won't be there yet, our ground station will be able to detect if any survivors are on board, thereby determining if the ship's computer carried out our orders to kill everyone by lowering the air pressure to a level that cannot sustain life. If there are survivors, and they are who we expect they are, we will destroy the ship when we arrive. We cannot allow the most powerful villain ever to attack our peaceful alliance to continue disrupting our operations by fostering rebellion and anarchy wherever she goes."

My heart racing, I repeated, "Wherever *she* goes? Are they talking about me?"

"Who else, arch villain of the galaxy?" Crystal said. "You have been a sandspur in the old admiral's leathery backside for a long time now. You destroyed his ship, killed his wife and daughter, and spoiled his Starborn hunting business. You're a pint-sized wrecking crew."

"So they want to kill us," Oliver said. "And when we're in range, they'll check to make sure we're dead."

I turned toward Emerson's console. "Emerson, how long until we're in range of a typical Alliance infrared scanner on the surface on Delta Ninety-five."

"Without knowledge of the type of scanner or its placement on the planet, I cannot provide a precise time, but I can provide an estimate that the ship will be in range in about two hours. You should assume one hour to be safe."

"And how long before we go into orbit around Delta Ninety-five?"

"Two hours, thirty-seven minutes, two seconds."

"If we slow down, will the base station be able to detect the change?"

"Affirmative. One of the infiltration messages instructed me to continue flying according to the protocol that I already have in place. Any deviation will be detected."

I took a deep breath. "Okay. One hour. We don't have much time."

"Time to do what?" Crystal asked.

"To evacuate in the gliders. We can take them to the surface undetected. They won't be looking for such a small craft. But before we do that, I want to figure out how to shape shift. I need time to practice."

Crystal nodded. "So if you're captured, they won't know you're really the infamous Megan Willis."

"I suppose that's a good reason, but I really hope to find Omen's hideout, see if he has a glowsap mine, and go in as a child slave. Omen would recognize me otherwise."

"Then you would have to go alone," Oliver said. "Omen knows what Crystal and I look like, so we can't go with you."

"No, but you can look for the kids we left at the refuge and see if they're all right."

"But Megan," Crystal said with a whine in her tone, "I'm supposed to be on your six. I can't let you go by yourself."

"I won't be by myself. I'm sure Perdantus will want to go with me. Omen doesn't know him. And besides, we can get a lot more done if we separate. You two don't need me to tell you what to do. You're both intelligent, brave, and resourceful. I trust in you completely."

Oliver rolled his eyes. "After that speech, I guess we don't have much choice, do we?"

"It's not just a speech to give you a boost. It's a hundred percent true. And, no, you don't have a choice, unless you can come up with a better plan."

Oliver and Crystal looked at each other for a moment, then both shrugged their shoulders. "Okay," Oliver said. "I'll get the refuge coordinates from Emerson, and we'll head to the planet."

Crystal pointed at me. "And you need to get another pair of earbuds so we can talk to you whenever we're in range, not just one that you're sure to lose the next time you get bashed in the head. And be listening to us, of course. That way, you'll know when we've found the kids, and we'll know when you stomp Omen into mashed potatoes."

"There you go. You're both thinking ahead. Good job." I rose and walked toward Crystal, straining against the g-forces. When I arrived, I held to her chair and looked her in the eye. "Help me concentrate. I want to look different. Any ideas?"

"Well, I think you should start with something easy. I mean, don't be like Lyric and change into a guy. That's professional level stuff. Maybe change your hair. Your mop is kind of your trademark. And you could make your face look more … I don't know … ugly? You're kind of pixie cute right now, so if you make your nose crooked and your chin jut out, you can go for a trollish look."

"Not so sure about that. Lyric said to concentrate on someone I know. She always changed into someone she had at least seen, like me or my father. So I need a girl who is young enough to be a glowsap slave but old enough to be believable as someone who would try to escape a mine by herself. Also, she can't be someone Omen would think is a spy working for me."

"I see where you're going with this." She tapped her chin with a finger. "Omen's probably seen Zoë, so she's out. I suppose he might recognize a girl like Echo or Riddle, because we don't know if he captured them for Raven and company." She lowered her hand. "What about one of Thorne's girls?"

"We don't know if he's seen the girls at the refuge, and Cynda and Renalda were too young."

"And too fragile."

I imagined Renalda shivering in front of Omen like a lost little waif. "Or not."

Crystal half closed an eye. "What do you mean?"

"Someone like Cynda or Renalda would be believable, small enough to escape without being noticed, scared enough to walk right into the slavers' base to find help, pathetic enough to get sympathy."

"Sympathy from Omen? Are you kidding me? He ran a slave mine by bribing kids with fake money and fake messages from home. He's not about to feel sorry for poor little Cynda or poor little Renalda."

"Maybe no sympathy from Omen, but if he has guards, a scared and fragile little girl might be the perfect mask to get past them."

Crystal whistled. "Wow, Megan. Taking advantage of a man's honest sympathies, maybe the only decency in the heart of one of Omen's guards? That's stooping pretty low."

I bent my brow. "Why is that?"

"Well, protecting little girls is kind of an instinct for a lot of men, right? Like a daddy-daughter thing. Your father has it. My father did before the slavers killed him. I mean, he bulldozed into them and screamed at me to run, but they …" Her chin quivered, and her voice pitched higher. "But they shot him. And I couldn't get away." She averted her eyes. "So … yeah. That's just … just kind of mean."

Heat rushed into my cheeks. I wanted to argue for my idea, but I couldn't think of a counterpoint besides the fact that I would do anything to stop evil. Maybe she was right, and maybe not. But I could give in to her feelings this time. "All right, Crystal. It's not a great idea. I'll come up with a better one."

She sniffed hard. "Okay …" Grief still invaded her voice. "Who will you be?"

"Since I'm part of the reason Renalda died, I want to go as her, but not a trembling, fearful Renalda. I'll be a strong and confident Renalda."

Crystal nodded. "I like that."

"Good." I closed my eyes and pictured Renalda in a happy state, smiling with sparkling eyes. "Okay. She parted her hair in the middle. Pretty much the same color as mine."

"Usually in a ponytail," Crystal added.

"Right. I've got that. She was quite a bit shorter and thinner, so I'll have to adjust the fasteners on my bracelets to tighten them."

"Good point."

I focused on the mental image, concentrating hard as I drew a picture of myself next to it. Feature by feature, I changed my portrait, lengthening my hair and putting a part in it, narrowing my face, torso, and limbs, and shrinking my height while shortening my arms and legs. As the morphing proceeded, pain roared across my body—heavy pressure, like a vise squeezing my bones. How Lyric did this so quickly, I couldn't imagine.

When the mental image of myself matched the one I created of Renalda, the pain stopped. I opened my eyes and looked at Crystal, angling my head more upward than usual. "Well?"

She stared at me, her mouth agape, not saying a word.

"Do I have to find a mirror? Or are you going to tell me what you see?"

She closed her mouth and cleared her throat. "Well, the voice is Megan's, but it sounds really strange coming from the spitting image of Renalda."

"Then it worked?"

"Perfectly. But you're going to need a change of clothes. Yours are a couple of sizes too big."

I looked down at my baggy uniform and lifted my arms. The sleeves slid down to my knobby elbows, as did my bracelets. I refastened them at a tighter setting and pushed my sleeves back into place. "We probably still have clothes Dirk wore while he was here. I'll find something." I touched my throat. "I guess my larynx didn't change. I couldn't copy Renalda's, maybe because I've never seen it."

"Your larynx? Another Willis word?"

"My voice box. I'll have to try to mimic her voice or at least try to sound more like a little girl."

"Yep. Let's find Dirk's clothes and get you ready."

"And I'd better take my uniform in a backpack in case I have to become myself again."

For the next several minutes, we searched the room Dirk once slept in and found some denim pants and a button-down shirt he used to wear while cleaning the galley. I tried them on. They fit much better than my own clothes, still a bit baggy, but they would do. I also found his spacesuit and laid it on the bed to take with us.

"We'll have to use pins to shore up your underwear," Crystal said as she held up a pair of Dirk's. "These just don't suit you."

"Yep. We'll use pins on mine." After grabbing the spacesuit, I walked with Crystal back to the bridge where Oliver could see me. I laid the suit on the floor and spread my arms. "Do you think this is a good disguise?"

Oliver's brow shot upward. "Amazing. You look exactly like Renalda."

"Megan," Crystal said, "your own father wouldn't recognize you. If I hadn't watched you change, I wouldn't believe it was you. In fact, I'm not sure it *is* you."

I smiled. "Good. All the better for my clandestine operation."

She huffed. "Okay. You just proved it's you. Stupid Willis word gave you away. Try to talk like you're as dumb as me."

A thought flew into my mind from Oliver's direction. *No one can talk that dumb.*

Oliver snorted. "I'm not touching that line."

I smirked at him. "You'd better not say what you were thinking. You shouted it so loud in your mind, I couldn't help but read it."

"Oh." His cheeks reddened. "I didn't mean it. Really. Crystal's my friend. You know that."

"Of course. Just try to keep your thoughts quieter, and I'll try to close my mental ears around you."

Crystal set a fist on her hip. "Okay, I'm not gonna ask what mental spitwad Oliver spewed at me, but I can imagine. Anyway, I think you're ready with your looks. Now you should work on moving things with your mind. Start with something close and lightweight."

I nodded toward her. "Your hair. I'll see if I can blow it back, like you're in a breeze."

"Yeah. Go for it."

I locked my gaze on the blonde tresses that hung over her ear on each side. I imagined a breeze blowing from my mind into her face. As the mental image strengthened, her hair moved, first a little, then a lot. Soon, all of her hair blew back as if she were facing a stiff ocean breeze.

Crystal blinked at the wind. "Cool your jets, girl! You're about to blow me away!"

I let the breeze settle. "Okay. Let's move to something harder."

For the next few minutes, I picked up other objects, starting with my locket, then my shoe as I used my mind to untie it, slide it off my foot, and throw it toward Oliver. The g-force momentum made it fly much faster and farther than I intended. Fortunately, he dodged the missile.

Finally, I focused on the panel under Emerson's console. I pulled it open, exposing the computer parts within, including a backup battery on the floor, an object that weighed at least twenty kilograms. I reached out a hand as if sliding it under the battery. Straining with all my might, I shifted my hand upward. The battery lifted off the floor—a bigger burden on my brain than I expected.

As my arm trembled, so did the battery. Finally, I let it down slowly and exhaled. "That was a lot harder than I thought it would be."

"But you did it." Crystal patted my back. "You're going to be fine."

"Maybe." I closed Emerson's access door with my mind. "Emerson, how long do we have?"

"Approximately twenty minutes, but because of the uncertainty, I suggest that you leave in the gliders as soon as possible."

"We'll go now." I scanned the floor for my shoe. When I found it, I extended a hand again and brought it floating into my grasp, though more slowly than I had hoped since it had to fight the g-forces. "Everyone hit the toilet," I said as I put the shoe on. "Grab a snack, a bottle of water, and a laser blaster before heading to the gliders. Remember it's warm at the refuge all year round, so dress accordingly. I'll tell Perdantus what's going on. We're leaving in ten minutes."

I pivoted toward Emerson's console. "Emerson, can you transmit the coordinates for the refugee colony to the computers in our gliders?"

"Affirmative."

"Please do it. Also, when the ship gets close enough to the planet, do as many orbits as you can before the other ships show up. While you're orbiting, scan for human activity on the surface. If you find anything, send the coordinates to our gliders with an explanatory note. Then land the Nine somewhere close to the refuge—"

"Land the Nebula Nine?" Emerson's tone seemed incredulous.

"Right. Your programming should allow that now."

"You are correct, but I have never landed the ship before. The programming allows for it, but my ability to do so has not been tested."

"Run simulations based on the times I landed the Nine or even back to when Captain Tillman landed her."

"The only record I have of a landing of the Nebula Nine on a planet that has the seismic instability of Delta Ninety-five was when you landed her there. The result was not optimal."

"Not optimal? That's an understatement. We crashed like a dying duck."

"And that is exactly my point. I have no record of a safe landing under such conditions. Therefore, an accurate simulation is impossible. I would have to, as I have heard Captain Tillman say, 'fly by the seat of my pants.' Captain Willis, I have no pants."

I laughed. "Emerson, that's the first real joke I've ever heard you tell. Very good."

"It was not a joke. My point is—"

"Just land the best you can, Emerson. I trust you. And when you do, turn off everything except for your communication receivers. Don't answer anybody, including one of us. We don't want the other Alliance ships to know where you are. We'll scan for you until we find you."

"The Alliance ships might find the wreckage from a failed landing attempt, but, as always, I will do as you say."

"Good. Thank you."

After we made preparations, including new buds for my ears, a blaster in my belt holster, and a backpack for my uniform, we put on our spacesuits and got into our gliders, Perdantus with me. For the time being, I left my helmet off. The trip to the planet's surface would be fairly short, especially since we were already traveling faster than gliders could go on their own. The Nebula Nine's momentum saw to that. We would have to fire our braking thrusters most of the way to keep from hitting the atmosphere like a battering ram and frying our heat shields.

When we launched, the glider bay door closed behind us, and we zoomed away from the Nine to avoid detection from any ship that might be approaching. I opened the comm link on the console. "Oliver. Crystal. You two split up for now. Stay several kilometers apart until you enter the atmosphere, then head for the refuge coordinates."

"Will do," Oliver said, his voice tinny through the console speaker but clearer in my earbuds. "Crystal, I'll veer left. You veer right."

"Fine by me." Crystal's voice sounded annoyed. "I'm supposed to be on Megan's six, but I guess being on her one or two will have to do." Then she shouted, "Blazes! I hate it when I accidentally rhyme."

I stifled a laugh. "You're a poet who's trying not to show it. Anyway, both of you keep blasting those braking thrusters or you'll burn up in the atmosphere. We have a lot of forward momentum to overcome."

"Got it," Crystal said. "Thrusters on max."

"Same here," Oliver added. "What's your course, Megan?"

"I'm heading toward the polar north. Since it's probably not as hot there with fewer volcanoes, it would be a better place for a villain's headquarters."

"Makes sense."

"I'm signing off now. No more chatter. Emerson, same to you. Send all incoming messages for the Nine to my glider's computer. Text only."

"Going silent," Oliver said.

Crystal sighed. "Same here, former Mophead."

Her comment reminded me that I didn't look like myself anymore. Being another person felt so weird.

During our maneuvers, Perdantus stared at me from his perch on my knee.

"Is something wrong?" I asked.

"It's just that I am having trouble getting used to how you look. I see your usual expressions and hear your familiar voice, but that face is not the face I have grown to love."

"Good reminder. I should change my voice. Probably something higher." I tried for a more girlish tone. "How's this?"

Perdantus fluffed his feathers. "Quite hideous. You sound like a storybook fairy."

I laughed, still speaking with the higher tone. "How could you know what a fairy sounds like? There aren't any fairies on your home planet. Or on any planet I've ever heard of."

"Crystal has a program on her computer pad that reads books to her, and I have listened with her many times. I assume that the reader was trying to imitate a fairy when she read the fairy's spoken parts. You sound exactly like that."

I deepened my voice a bit. "Is this better?"

"If you mean more human, then yes, but I am still not enamored with it."

"Well, get used to it. I have to practice to get used to it myself. Except if I have to talk to Emerson. I'll need to match my voice print on file."

"I understand."

As we continued to slow our speed, we drew closer and closer to the planet. Reds and oranges from lava flow still covered a lot of the surface, though not nearly as much as the last time I was here. Blackness from cooled lava rock replaced some of those areas, and new tree growth dotted the remainder with greenery.

The polar cap, however, was nearly completely green, apparently warm enough to allow dense growth and stable enough to quell volcanic activity. I adjusted my thrusters to head straight for the cap, hoping Emerson could narrow my search soon. As I flew closer, I imagined the Nine cruising into a low orbit and Emerson searching for any sign of life, either by a thermal scan or by detecting any electronic signals.

I also imagined Omen on the planet scanning me in return, as if his hologram hovered nearby, staring at me with hatred and disdain. The feeling raised tingles on my neck. I had to come up with a distraction.

I tapped on the helmet in my lap. "Perdantus, I'm going to have to decelerate even faster than we already are. If you want to hop in to keep your balance, you can. I'm not planning to put it on."

"Very well. Better there than pressed against the windshield."

The moment he jumped in, my computer beeped, notifying me of a new message. I set the forward thrusters on maximum. The change pressed my body hard against the seat's straps. In my helmet, Perdantus lay curled, somewhat flattened at the front, but he seemed okay.

I tapped the screen's icon to access a text message from Emerson. It read, "Two Alliance ships have flown into scanner range. They have not yet sent a hailing signal. A surface-based signal appears to have scanned the Nine for occupants. Of course, they found none. I am sending you the coordinates for the source of that scan. It appears to have come from an equatorial region. I will also send a map of the planet with a red pin marking the signal source and a blue pin marking the location of the refuge."

I whispered, "Equatorial? I'll have to adjust my vector."

Keeping the forward thrusters at maximum, I steered the glider into a more southward angle. When the map appeared on the screen, I spotted the red pin that marked the ground-based scanner—only a couple of kilometers away from the blue pin. I shook my head. Not good. That meant the refuge was probably discovered by whoever put the scanner there. Our friends on the surface might already be in Omen's hands.

A new message from Emerson popped up. I read it out loud so Perdantus could hear. "I am sending this message to all three gliders. The two Alliance ships are now in orbit. They contacted a base station with a simple arrival notification and received an acknowledging reply, but the reply did not come from the station that scanned the Nebula Nine. This one is near the planet's north pole. That station did not appear to check for living inhabitants on the Nine, but the two arriving ships did. Perhaps they were instructed to do so by the polar station. In any case, the two arriving ships hailed the Nine, and I answered with a simple acknowledgment that my current orbit has been programmed in advance.

"I did not tell them that the programming includes a quick dive to the planet's surface, which will commence in thirty seconds. In a moment, I will send a distress signal that will be cut short, and I will expel smoke through one of the exhaust ports. My hope is that the two Alliance captains won't stop to wonder why the Nine would plunge to the planet instead of staying in its orbital path. And since no one is on board the Nine, perhaps they won't care to follow to see where she hits the surface. Either way, I will be landing, or crashing, shortly."

Still straining against the straps because of our deceleration, I looked at Perdantus. "Oliver and Crystal will be flying into a mess, but at least they know what's going on. They'll probably land somewhere reasonably close to the refuge and sneak closer. I'm sure they can manage. Anyway, now I have to shift again and see what's happening in the polar region."

"In other words," Perdantus said, his body still pressed tightly against the inside of the helmet, "prepare for more discomfort."

"Exactly." I broke away from the new approach vector and steered toward the pole again, shifting the pressure from the straps and pushing Perdantus to another part of the helmet. After several seconds, I was able to straighten our flight, but the continued deceleration kept the pressure in place.

I checked the onboard computer for a course update. At our current deceleration, the glider would slow to a survivable speed, but just barely. If the manufacturer's specs on the heat shields were more optimistic than reality, the glider's exterior shell would get too hot and potentially break apart, and the inside would become an oven set on broil.

After a couple of minutes, the glider had slowed to the maximum tolerable speed just as it entered the first layer of air. Whether or not the shields would endure would be tested over the next minute or so. "We should be okay, Perdantus, but it's going to get really hot in here, and I won't be able to open the vents until the oxygen level outside is survivable."

Perdantus grunted. "I understand."

The temperature inside rose quickly. A meter on the console told the story—already up to 38 degrees Celsius. One second later, it changed to 39, then 40, then 41. We would be roasting in a few minutes.

Another meter said that the external shell's temperature stood at 90% of maximum. That was also rising far too quickly. A third gauge measured the oxygen in the air outside and the pressure. At 4% oxygen and a pressure of 8 millibars, I couldn't open the vents yet. But at our rate of altitude drop, it wouldn't be long until I could.

Sweat trickled down my cheeks. Perdantus's respiration quickened. Unable to sweat, he probably couldn't last as long as I could. I had to open the vents at the first possible moment.

I checked the meters—47 degrees inside, external shell temperature at 97% of max, 8% oxygen outside with a pressure of 182 millibars. Not yet. Just another minute.

As the air outside grew denser, bumps shook the glider. With the shell taking such a beating and the temperature so high, it could break apart at any moment. These gliders were designed for atmospheric entry at a much lower speed and a gentler angle, like my approach when landing on Beta Four, nothing like this. I had to hope that Oliver and Crystal were faring better than Perdantus and I were.

I glanced at Perdantus again. He had stopped breathing.

16

I gasped. "Perdantus!" He didn't even budge. Once more I looked at the meters—50 degrees inside, external shell at 101% of maximum, 12% oxygen outside with a pressure of 375 millibars. That would have to do.

I pressed the button that opened the vents. Cool air rushed in. The interior temperature dropped quickly, but I could already feel the lower oxygen content as I tried to breathe the thinner air.

Once more I looked at Perdantus and his motionless body. "C'mon, Perdantus! Breathe!" I massaged his chest with a finger, but it didn't help. I picked him up with one hand while holding the steering yoke with the other. I opened my mouth around his beak, closed my lips, and blew. His chest inflated, and he wiggled violently. I placed him back in the helmet and held him down. He now breathed on his own, though unconscious, still fitful with his movements.

"It's all right, Perdantus," I said in my normal voice. "It's me, Megan. I've got you. You're going to be all right." Though I wasn't sure about that.

He settled down and lay quietly in the helmet. Whether my words caused the improvement or the cooler air and slowly increasing pressure did, I couldn't tell. Either way, soon we would be on the ground, and I could check on him further.

I leveled the glider and flew above a thick forest. The tops of the trees undulated with curves in the hilly landscape, but no clearings appeared anywhere. I glanced at the map. I would arrive at the broadcasting station in seconds. I had to find a place to land soon so I could sneak up on foot.

I made a wide turn and angled upward to get a better view of the area. Once I had leveled out again, I looked down from the much higher elevation. In the direction I had been going, a mansion sprawled across a green valley with a river running from north to south within a stone's throw to the east of the mansion, most likely the water supply for whoever lived there.

A radio tower jutted from the ground to the north of the mansion, surrounded by black rock, maybe lava rock from an old eruption. I scanned the area upslope and spotted a volcano in the distance. Smoke rose from the caldera, but the spotty greenery gave evidence that it hadn't erupted in quite a while.

"What happened?" Perdantus asked, now standing upright in my helmet. "Did I fall asleep?"

"Knocked out. Overheated." I chose not to tell him that I had to resort to mouth-to-beak resuscitation. "We had a rough ride. Now I'm looking for a place to land. There's an outpost here. More like a mansion. Someone's living the good life."

Perdantus flitted to the dashboard and looked out. "I see some birds. No species I'm familiar with like those I met in the more southerly regions, but at least no one here will be surprised to see me if I go on a scouting mission."

"I'll definitely need you to do that." I spotted a clearing in the forest, an area of black lava rock too thick to allow tree growth. "We're going to land."

I steered the glider to the clearing and lowered it slowly onto the rock. When we settled, I shut off the engine and opened the dome. A breeze blew back my locks, cooler than what we experienced closer to the equator. The air also smelled cleaner, only a hint of sulfur.

Perdantus flew toward a tree, calling, "I will see what is immediately nearby."

"Good." I stepped out, shed my suit, and laid it in the glider. I smoothed out Dirk's clothes, a perfect outfit for the temperature, but sweat still dampened my armpits and back, raising a chill as the breeze blew past.

Shivering, I picked up the backpack that held my uniform and put it on, then looked up and found Perdantus perched at the top of an evergreen tree. "What do you see up there?"

"I see the outpost, perhaps two kilometers away. An easy distance to walk, though the forest between here and there is quite dense."

"After that rough ride, I'm going to test my blaster. Make sure it didn't get overheated." I withdrew it from its holster, aimed at a tree, and pulled the trigger. Nothing happened. "Blazes! Now I'm unarmed. These guns are way too sensitive." I tossed the blaster toward the glider's seat but missed. It clanked against the side and dropped to the ground.

Extending a hand, I picked the blaster up with my mind and lowered it into the glider. "This is getting easier."

"Good," Perdantus said, still perched in the tree. "Your telekinetic power might be more useful than the blaster, a hidden weapon that can't be confiscated."

"Fair point." I took the gun belt off and levitated it into the glider as well, then used my mind to press the button that lowered the hatch. "Lead the way, Perdantus."

"Do you know yet what you plan to say to whoever occupies the outpost?"

"Nope. I'll just make something up when I see what's going on there."

"Very well." He flew from the tree and sailed over the edge of the clearing. "This way."

After checking my earbuds to make sure they were turned on, I strode quickly in that direction, entered the forest, and trudged through the underbrush. Although it wasn't as dense as I had expected, it was thick enough to force me to lift my feet high to step over the densest portions. At times, I came to a wall of trees and had to detour several paces to get around them. Fortunately, Perdantus always got me going in the right direction again.

When I arrived at the far edge of the forest, I halted at a slope that led down to the river valley. The river, maybe about five meters wide, flowed from left to right, that is, north to south. From here, the mansion stood about a kilometer away. The structure boasted a three-story section at the center with castle-like turrets, two stories around the center, and one-story sections at the edges that looked like add-ons, maybe a kitchen, garage, and some kind of extra room. The span between the place and me would be easy to cross except for the steep slope immediately ahead, mostly soil with a few strips of lava rock here and there.

I could easily begin walking down one of the lava ridges, but gaps between the end of one ridge and the start of the next one down the slope would force me to make tracks between them, a clear sign that someone had entered the compound. Or I could supercharge my legs with my bracelets and leap from ridge to ridge. That would work. Of course, if someone was watching a camera feed, I wouldn't escape notice, but maybe I could hurry down there before a dreary-eyed sentry noticed.

I rolled up a sleeve and looked at my arm. The conductive ink stood out more than ever, maybe because my arms were thinner now. My plan might work without a problem.

After sliding my sleeve back in place, I sidled to the closest lava ridge and ran down it, letting gravity speed me along. When I neared the first gap, I flexed my biceps to charge my legs and leaped to the next ridge in a dead run, then did the same on the second and third gaps before reaching level ground. I hurried to the nearest wall of the mansion and flattened myself against it, facing the forest I had come from, the rear of the mansion around the corner to my right and the front around the corner to my left. Two windows interrupted the stucco façade, both with blinds that hid whatever lay inside.

Perdantus landed on the roof of the one-story section of the building. "So far, there is no movement anywhere."

I nodded, not wanting to talk and possibly alert someone, though the sound of flowing water nearby would probably keep my voice from carrying very far. I looked at the corner to my right, about three steps away. Two cameras protruded from the wall, one pointing at an angle toward the front and one toward the rear. Both had probably spied me running down the slope. Earlier, I had imagined a sleepy security guard not paying attention to his job, but now that seemed unlikely. Someone probably knew I was here.

The sound of a door opening came from the rear of the building. I stepped away from the wall, turned, and, again charging my legs, leaped up to the roof, bending my knees for a soft landing. I padded to the rear edge and looked down. A thirty-something man walked out and glanced around. Wearing an Alliance planet-based uniform, dark blue except for an orange sleeve insignia, and wielding a laser pistol, he probably wouldn't be friendly toward my snooping.

I focused on his head, mentally drilling past his crew cut hair, and listened. Ignoring the profanity in his tirade about having to hunt for a stupid lost kid, I picked up an interesting couple of phrases. *Idiot girl probably escaped from the mine. Omen will want to find out who let her slip past the fence.*

That was helpful information—they had at least one mine here, they enslaved children, and Omen was in charge. But how many mines? How many children? And where were they? Those facts stayed hidden in his brain.

He pulled a radio from his belt and spoke into it. "No sign of her yet. I'm heading out front. Let me know if you see her on a screen."

As I kept an eye on him, I tiptoed across the roof toward the front of the mansion. Obviously, someone was still watching from inside. Maybe I could draw that person out. I extended a hand and mentally stretched my arm to the guard, then pushed my fingers through his torso and wrapped them around his heart with a gentle squeeze.

He halted and clutched his chest, his breaths shallow and labored. With a trembling hand, he raised the radio to his lips and wheezed, "I think I'm having a heart attack." He dropped the radio and fell to his knees.

A door opened somewhere. Unbidden, my grip on the man's heart weakened and released. I glanced at the tower. Could it be having the same effect on me that the one on Delta Zero had?

The guard inhaled deeply and shook his head hard. A dark-haired woman ran to him and rubbed his back. "Stan, are you all right?"

While they talked, I hurried to the back of the roof, leaped off, and landed in a roll, then jumped up. The door stood ajar with enough of a gap to enter. I slid through and walked into an enormous dining room, complete with a long, polished table, ornate straight-backed chairs, and a lacy tablecloth. But I didn't have time to admire the furnishings. I had to find out what was going on here.

I walked under a high arching doorway into the next room where a wide desk held several monitors, each with a view from a camera outside. Two wheeled chairs stood here and there as if the occupants had leaped out of them in a hurry.

Perdantus chirped, barely audible from his perch outside. "Megan, the guards are returning."

I opened a door on the far side of the guards' room, entered a huge dim chamber, and closed the door behind me. The moment the latch clicked, chatter from the guards' station penetrated.

The woman said, "Want me to call the doctor to have a look at you?"

"No, no," Stan replied. "I'm fine now. I'll see him when he comes tonight. It might've been the chili I ate. Really gassy."

"Okay. If you're sure. But I wonder what happened to that girl."

"She probably headed downstream. That's where we tell the kids that we put our gliders. Since you're new here, you probably didn't know that, but if I were trying to escape, that's where I would go."

"Makes sense, but what if she headed upstream? She could cause trouble there."

"Not likely. Too much security. But you can call up there and warn them."

"Will do."

Silence followed. I looked to my right. At the far end of the room, stairs led upward into darkness. A steady beeping sound drew my attention to the left. Several steps in that direction, blinking lights on a head-high, floor-standing machine illuminated a man in a hospital-style bed, his back propped into a partly reclined position, white pillows on each side of his head. With his eyes closed and his breathing steady, he seemed to be sleeping.

I tiptoed closer, passing what appeared to be the main entry door to my right, probably leading to the front of the mansion. When I arrived at the bedside, I grasped the metal side rail and looked the man over. Burn scars ravaged his face and hairless scalp as well as his forearms. A pale-blue linen sheet covered the rest of his body. Wires ran from electrodes attached to his head to the machine, maybe a brain scanning device. An IV tube snaked from under the sheet up to a bag of clear liquid hanging from a bedside pole.

On a bedside table lay a short stack of gauze pads in sterile packages as well as a roll of surgical tape and a pair of scissors, a sign that he had wounds that needed regular attention, which meant that a doctor or a nurse would probably visit him again soon.

I studied the meters on the scanning device. Some made sense, like blood pressure, heart rate, respiration, but others just showed squiggly lines on a graph that looked similar to data coming across a digital comm line. I had seen something like this before when my father tapped into Alliance chatter.

Again I looked at the patient. Horrid, wrinkled scars disfigured his face, making him unrecognizable, at least to me. Maybe if I tried to read his mind, I could learn his identity and how he got so badly burned.

Focusing on his forehead, I concentrated. As I stood there, a strange sensation came over me—darkness and despair, a lot like what I felt near the tower on Delta Zero. My earlier guess had to be true. Negative energy from the tower behind the mansion was sapping my powers.

The man squirmed, then grunted. His eyes blinked open, and he stared at me. A mechanical voice emanated from the scanning device. "Who are you, and what are you doing here?"

I glanced at the speaker embedded in the device. Apparently, the wires transmitted this man's thoughts, allowing him to speak. After stealthily sliding my bracelets out of sight under my sleeves, I forced the higher voice, hoping to avoid sounding like a fairy. "Um ... I'm Renalda. I escaped from the glowsap mine, and I'm looking for help."

The man's brow lifted, and he replied through the speaker. "So you're a mine worker?"

Sorely tempted to put on the scared little girl act, I resisted and squared my shoulders. "*Was* a mine worker. I'm trying to go home to my parents."

"But you came here voluntarily with your parents' approval. Every worker at every mine did."

"*Every* mine? How many mines are there?"

"That's not for you to know." His eyes and facial expression shifted as he spoke, the only indications that the thoughts were coming from him and not the machine. "The important point is that you are an employee. We pay you quite well, and you get regular messages from home. The only acceptable reason for you to leave would be abuse, and we take that very seriously. Did someone mistreat you?"

I crossed my arms. I wanted to tell him that I already exposed their little payment scheme on Delta Zero, but that would ruin any chance of getting more information. "I don't believe the messages are really from my parents."

"Why not?"

I had to think fast. "Well, for one thing, my mother would never call me Squirt. Only my father does. My mother hates that nickname. And she said she baked a cake for my birthday and wished I could have been there to share it. They blew out the candles for me and she said it was tasty. But she has diabetes and never eats sugar."

"There are sugar-free recipes for cakes."

"Not at my house. My father loves sugar. My mother would never bake a cake without it."

"Be that as it may, apparently she did bake a sugar-free cake, or maybe she took a small bite and found it to be tasty. As for calling you Squirt, that name has apparently grown on her because your absence has softened her dislike of it. She simply misses you. It seems to me that your homesickness has you longing for what used to be, but things have apparently changed since you left. It's hard to accept that your parents aren't quite the same as they used to be."

I decided that now was a good time to give in a bit so I could probe for more information. "I guess you might be right, but I'm kind of lost now. I don't know how to get back to my mine."

"That's understandable. The forest is dense around all three mines. I will arrange for you to be guided to the proper place."

Now at least I knew the number of mines. Maybe I could go for broke. "Do you have a map showing the mines? I know the basic direction I came from. With a map, I'm sure I could find my way back."

"No, you don't need a map. I will provide you with an armed escort. Hungry beasts prowl the forest, and you would be a tasty meal for them."

"I didn't see any beasts on my way over here."

"Because they are nocturnal. Based on the amount of light entering this room, I assume daylight is waning outside, so you will have to travel at night. The escort will have a map on a computer pad and a digital compass, so even in the darkness of the forest, you won't get lost."

I nodded. Perfect. That computer pad would soon be mine. "Thank you … um … I never got your name."

"Fairbanks. Admiral Dwight Fairbanks."

Resisting the urge to strangle him, I kept my face expressionless. "Thank you, Admiral Fairbanks."

"You're welcome. I sent a request for an escort—a female guard. You will be quite safe, and you will receive no punishment."

I bowed my head. "Thank you again."

The door to the security-desk room opened, and the dark-haired woman peered at us through the gap, wrinkles in her face now evident. "Admiral, I sent a message to each mine to see which one is Renalda's. It might take a while to get a reply."

"Understood, Cynthia," Fairbanks said. "Kindly provide her with some food and water while she's waiting." His eyes shifted toward me. "Have a seat in one of the chairs in this room. You shouldn't have to wait long."

"Oh, and Admiral," Cynthia said, "your nurse is just now arriving. Since she's changing your bandages, she plans to sedate you."

At that moment, the room's other door opened, and a thin middle-aged woman with short dark hair and dressed in green scrubs walked in, carrying a medical bag. "I heard that," she said with a rough voice. "Yes, I do plan to sedate you."

Fairbanks rolled his eyes and again spoke through the machine. "Oh, yes, because I might feel a twinge of pain."

"More than a twinge. The last time I changed your bandages, you kicked me in the stomach."

The speaker let out a huff. "Because you mentioned her name."

"Whose name?" Cynthia asked. "Um ... not to be nosy, but I'm new here. I don't know what happened, and I want to avoid getting kicked."

His tone turned angry. "Megan Willis, a fourteen-year-old pirate who killed my wife and daughter, destroyed my ship, scarring me for life, and devastated my glowsap business." As his face reddened, he lifted a hand from beneath the sheet and clenched it, trembling. "If only I could capture that little demon, I would cut her smart-mouthed tongue out and shove it down her throat. Then I would slice her open with a dull rusty knife and gut her like a—"

"Now, Admiral," the nurse said as she prepared a syringe, "your blood pressure is shooting up. We don't want you to have a stroke, do we?"

He loosened his fist and let it drop. Again the speaker relayed his words. "No, Mabel. Then I would never be able to get revenge against that sassy little monster."

Although I was the target for his outraged rants, the insults felt pretty good. It was an honor to be the reason for the downfall of this kid-slaving tyrant.

Mabel injected the contents of the syringe into the IV port. Within seconds, the admiral's eyes closed, and his head lolled to the side. "He's under," Mabel said to Cynthia. "We're free to talk now. Real quiet, though. You never know if a sedated person is still listening."

Cynthia walked in fully, closed the door behind her, and crouched, looking at me with kind eyes. She spoke with a low whisper. "I didn't tell the Admiral this, but I checked all three mines, and the name Renalda isn't on any of the rosters. What's your real name?"

I glanced at Fairbanks and Mabel before meeting Cynthia's stare and matching her whisper. "Can you blame me for keeping who I am a secret? I don't want to be a slave at a death mine."

"Of course you don't. We won't take you there, and Stan won't either. I told him I saw the girl again. He's out looking for her."

I lifted my brow. So the guards here weren't both on the same side. I had to probe further. "Wait …" I said, still at a low whisper. "Are you two spies or something? Whose side are you on?"

Cynthia took my hand. My first reaction was to pull it back, but I had to remember that I looked only ten years old. "We're on your side. But you have to be honest with me. I saw you leap like you had springs on your feet when you ran into the valley, and then you jumped from the ground to the roof in one hop. No girl your age, or any age for that matter, can jump that high. So, who are you, really?"

I glared at her. "Why should I trust you? If you were really on my side, you wouldn't be taking care of Admiral Fairbanks. If he's running the child-trafficking operation, why don't you kill him?"

Cynthia looked at Mabel as she peeled a gauze bandage from the admiral's arm. When Mabel nodded, Cynthia continued. "It's not so simple. Fairbanks started the operation, and to protect himself and his interests, he installed a kill switch. Do you know what a kill switch is?"

I nodded. "If Fairbanks dies, his death will trigger something terrible."

"Terrible is right. He has a network of computers that run not only his glowsap business but also his communications with the Alliance commanders. They, of course, are duty bound to obey him without question. In his mad obsession to capture and kill Megan Willis, his orders can be pretty strange at times."

"Oh," I said, "so you really *did* know about Megan."

"Of course. Everyone knows about Megan. She's our group's inspiration. But I thought asking the question would keep me from blowing my cover. I've been in deep cover for years." She lifted her dark tresses. "Look. My hair used to be blonde." She touched her cheek. "And these wrinkles are fake. I added them to keep anyone from recognizing me. The worst thing I could do is to hurt our group's cause."

"What is your group?"

"We don't have an official name. We're a loose conglomerate of former Alliance pilots and commanders who were drummed out by Fairbanks when we asked too many questions, and some of us are parents of children who were abducted by the slavers. We're still searching for them. A few of our members say we're the AR, the Alliance Resistance. Kind of bland and hokey, I think." She smiled. "But *I* like to call us Megan's Meddlers."

Warmth surged through my cheeks, a good warmth. "I ... um ... I'll bet she would like that."

"I hope so. Anyway, we need to keep Fairbanks alive so the kill switch isn't triggered. When he was brought here from Delta Ninety-eight by his subordinates, he told them about the computer network and that if he dies, he will no longer be able to send a code to one of the computers. If the computer doesn't receive the code every day, it will set off a device that will destroy Alpha One. We think there might be similar devices on other planets in each of the major star systems, including Beta, Gamma, Delta, Epsilon, and Zeta. If they go off, billions of people will die. And he's been in possession of that kill switch for years now."

As I imagined Alpha One, my home planet, blowing up, another memory rose to the surface, the moment Admiral Fairbanks stood atop the Nebula One, practically daring me to take him out with a photon torpedo. He knew then that his death would bring about a cataclysmic disaster, and he didn't seem to care. If I hadn't resisted the temptation, countless people would have lost their lives.

"Since he's here in bed," I said, "haven't you seen him send the code? Can't you mimic it, you know, send it for him if he dies?"

Mabel shook her head. "It's biometric. He has a wristband that takes a sample of his blood, verifies its oxygen level, and sends the data through the tower outside to the Zeta station at Delta Zero, and to his computer. That final address is encrypted, and our tech people haven't figured it out yet. Also, if we tried to send it for him, we're afraid doing it wrong might also trigger the kill switch. It's better to keep looking for the computer so we can try to hack it on site and disable the switch along with the device that's supposed to destroy one or more planets."

"Unfortunately," Cynthia said, "we have to let the glowsap mines keep operating, at least on a rudimentary level, or Fairbanks will know something's wrong. That's why we celebrate when Megan manages to squash some of the mines and rescue the workers. While she does that, we continue to keep Fairbanks alive as we search for the computer and the deadly devices."

"But," Mabel said as she applied a new bandage, "that option comes with its own problems. Fairbanks has launched an all-out search-and-destroy mission on this planet because he believes Megan has come here to rescue kids in the glowsap mines."

Cynthia nodded. "Apparently, Megan rescued all of the children at the mines on Delta Zero, so he's decided to find and kill her once and for all."

"True ..." Mabel walked around the foot of the bed to the other side, tape and scissors in hand. "But we intend to find her first. To warn her. To help protect her."

"Which is why," Cynthia continued, "I want to know who you are. I'm guessing you're one of the Starborn children, and you have special powers from being born on Gamma Five. We know Megan has some Starborn kids as crewmates, so maybe you're one of them."

I lifted a finger. "One more question before I tell you. Who is Omen?"

"I'll show you." Cynthia straightened, walked to the device next to the bed, and flipped a switch.

Projectors from all around the room emitted beams of light and formed a hologram of Omen next to me. He blinked, as if awakened, and gazed at me, his expression friendly. "Hello, little girl. What's your name?"

I looked at Cynthia. "Should I answer?"

"If you want. Omen is an artificial intelligence representation of the thoughts of Admiral Fairbanks, run by a computer. Since the admiral is asleep, Omen will react based on his programming and knowledge gained to this point, but I severed his upload connection to the computer. He can get data from it, but he can't store it. Anything he learns here will be lost."

Omen pointed at her. "So you're on the side of the rebels. I should have known."

"Hey, Omen," I said. "Focus. You asked me a question."

He turned toward me, squinting. "You look familiar. Aren't you one of Thorne's orphans?" He snapped his fingers. "Renalda. You're Renalda. I saw your photo in Thorne's records."

"I do look like her, don't I?" I waved a hand at Cynthia. "I've seen enough. Turn him off now."

When she did, the hologram faded. As she walked toward me, she gave me a long, hard look. "Omen recognized you as Renalda, and I know who Thorne was, a slaver on Delta Ninety-eight, a willow wind Megan killed. So that checks out, but you confirmed that you just *look* like Renalda. And you have a commanding manner that doesn't match that of a little girl. When are you going to come clean and tell me who you really are?"

I nodded toward the rear of the building. "Turn off the tower, and I'll tell you everything."

Cynthia looked at Mabel. "Has Fairbanks done the kill-switch transmission yet?"

Mabel nodded. "We can turn the tower off, but only for a little while. We just have to hope Stan doesn't notice. He's been acting suspicious lately. I wouldn't want to stir his pot of doubts any more than we have to."

"Okay, whoever you are ..." Cynthia walked to the flight of stairs I had seen earlier and began climbing them. "If you want to see the command center, come with me."

I followed her up the flight and then another to the third floor where we entered a hallway with three closed doors on either side and one at the end. Cameras at each corner of the hall likely plastered our pictures on the monitors downstairs, but since Stan was supposedly out searching for me, I decided not to ask about them.

Cynthia opened the second door on the right and walked inside. Again, I followed, this time into a room with an array of computers and monitors lining the opposite wall, making the room look like a miniature Zeta station control center.

At the corner of the ceiling to my right, a camera aimed its lens directly at us. I pointed at it. "Won't that show Stan what we're doing? I know he's outside right now, but will movement here trigger an alarm that he'd check on?"

"There's no motion detector on it. We just have to hurry. Stan is unpredictable, and he gets violent if something riles him." Cynthia sat at a wheeled chair and tapped on a keyboard in front of one of the monitors. A diagram of the tower popped up with animated concentric circles radiating from the top. She tapped an icon near the bottom of the screen, and the circles disappeared. "It's off."

Like shadows fleeing, the dark sensation quickly slipped away, proving that the tower was the source of the negative energy.

Cynthia rose. "Let's go into one of the bedrooms. They're private." I followed her out. As she quietly closed the door, she glanced down the stairwell, apparently nervous. She led me to the door at the end of the hall, opened it, and ushered me into a bedroom with a single window that led to the roof.

When she closed the door, she sat on a bed with a bare mattress and patted it. "We can talk here."

I sat and looked her in the eye. "Are you really on my side? I mean, are you against Fairbanks and the slayers?"

"Yes. That's what I told you downstairs."

Although I hadn't had much practice with the lie-detecting power, I could tell she was being honest. "Okay, then. I'll come clean, but first I have to change clothes."

"Change clothes? Why?"

"You'll see." I took the backpack off and withdrew my uniform. As I unbuttoned my shirt, she turned away, allowing me a bit of privacy. Once I finished changing, fastening my belt in place, and stuffing Dirk's clothes into the pack, I sat on the bed in the baggy uniform. "You can look now, but it'll still take a minute."

When she refocused on me, I lowered my head, closed my eyes, and concentrated on two mental images, one of Renalda and one of myself. Piece by piece, I copied my features to Renalda's—nose, ears, mouth, etc.

As the process continued, Cynthia let out a gasp now and then but said nothing. Finally, the two mental images appeared to be identical. I opened my eyes, lifted my head, and looked at her.

She stared at me with her mouth hanging open. "It's you! You're Megan Willis!"

"Yes, I have Starborn—"

A gunshot rang out downstairs. A woman shouted in a painful moan, then called out, "Cynthia! Run! Stan is—" Another gunshot silenced her.

Cynthia leaped up and pulled me to my feet. "Out the window!"

As footsteps thundered up the stairs, Cynthia shoved the window sash up and gestured for me to go through the opening.

I shook my head. "You first. I've got your back."

Not bothering to argue, she climbed out. The moment she was completely through, Stan ran in, a handgun aimed at me. He blinked hard. "Megan Willis?"

"In the flesh." I extended a hand and used my mind to jerk the gun from him. It flew into my grasp, and I aimed it back at him. "Surprised?"

He raised his hands, fear in his eyes. "What're you going to do now? Kill me and the admiral?"

"You'll soon find out." Without looking outside, I called, "Come in. It's safe." When Cynthia climbed back into the room, I nodded toward the door. "Check on Mabel. I'll take care of Stan."

When Cynthia ran out, I ejected the chambered bullet, popped the magazine from the gun, and threw the ammo out the window. "Stan, I'm not going to kill you or the admiral. In fact, I want you to make sure he stays alive." I dropped the gun on the floor. "Cooperate, and you'll get to keep your life."

Stan lowered his hands and snorted. "You don't have a weapon. How do you think you're going to escape?"

I reached a hand out again, grabbed his heart, and squeezed. His eyes bulged. Clutching his chest, he dropped to his knees and toppled to the side. As he gasped for breath, I stood next to him. "Any other questions?"

He rasped. "No. Please … don't kill me."

I released his heart. He sucked in a deep breath and rested in a fetal curl. I nudged his knee with my foot. "Do you have a flying craft anywhere close by? Big enough to carry a passenger?"

Still lying curled, he nodded, gasping as he spoke. "Upstream. Two klicks. There's … there's a concrete pad."

"Perdantus!" I called through the open window. "If you're listening, don't show yourself. I need you to verify what this guard said about an aircraft two kilometers upstream."

"On my way," he said from somewhere nearby.

I checked Stan's belt and pockets for any other weapons. Besides a radio, he was clean, but I had no idea if other weapons might be stashed in one of the rooms. With Mabel possibly dying, I couldn't take the time to search.

"Behave yourself, or I'll be back." I ran out of the bedroom and hurried toward the stairs, shouting, "Cynthia, how is Mabel?"

Cynthia called from below. "She's alive. Barely. We have to get her out of here."

I rushed down the final flight of stairs and found Cynthia kneeling over Mabel, blood on her hands. I whispered, "To where?"

Cynthia whispered in return, tears streaming. "To our group's enclave. About thirty kilometers. She came here in a single-person space glider, but she obviously can't fly it, and she's fading fast."

"Maybe I can help her." I knelt at Mabel's other side. Blood soaked her shirt at her waist. I pinched the hem and lifted the shirt, revealing a hole in her scant stomach, surrounded by blood smears. Blood spurted from the wound, apparently from a lacerated artery. "Have you seen any other wounds?"

Cynthia touched Mabel's thigh. "One here. Probably the first bullet."

I glanced at her thigh. A small circle of blood marked the bullet's entry point, but at least it didn't appear to be spurting.

"I'll deal with the belly first." I set a palm over the wound and pressed down. Warm blood leaked between my fingers. I closed my eyes and mentally focused beyond the hole, trying to locate the bleeder, but it seemed so dark, and everything was squished together. How could I possibly find something without a light?

Oliver and Galena did it somehow. Maybe they created their own light as part of the healing gift. Or maybe a dragon's eye would help. With my free hand, I pulled the necklace from behind my uniform and held the locket in my fist. As it did the previous time, it grew warm in my grasp. Words again came to mind, and I let them flow. "God is truth, God is love, God provides light from heaven above. Search the sea, search the tide, search into towers where lanterns abide."

Light began seeping into my perception. As blood continued spurting inside, I followed the flow to a sliced artery and squeezed the cut closed with my mind. The pinch point sizzled. Mabel moaned. Cynthia shushed her. "It's all right. You're going to be all right."

My throat tightened, forcing me to swallow. I hoped she'd be all right, but she had lost so much blood, I wasn't sure at all. I mentally scanned the area again. The flow of blood had slowed. Maybe I could pull my mental focus out of this wound and move to the thigh.

Stan thumped down the stairs and aimed a gun at me, this time a laser blaster. Obviously, he did have a stash of weapons somewhere. He growled, "I'm sure to get a promotion for capturing you, but I'd better cripple you first."

Just as he began pulling the trigger, I mentally grabbed the gun and tried to jerk it from his grasp, but he held on tightly. As I twisted the gun to wrench it away, the barrel turned toward him, completing the trigger pull. It fired a laser bullet that burned into his forehead. His eyes rolled upward, and he crumpled to the floor.

Cynthia yelped, then covered her mouth and spoke between her fingers. "I can't believe what I just saw."

Although killing Stan sent a shockwave through my brain, I kept my voice calm. "He had a radio. With the tower off, could he have called for backup?"

"Yes. We have an outpost relay. If he alerted someone, they can get here pretty quickly. And they can also turn the tower back on remotely once they're close enough."

"Then we'd better scram. I got Mabel's belly wound pretty well patched up. I'll have to finish later."

Perdantus flew down the stairwell and landed on the back of a chair. "A two-person glider is available upstream. No one was around while I was there."

"Cynthia," I said as I pulled Mabel's arms. "Help me get her on my shoulders."

"No. Let me carry her. I've been trained for this. And I'm a lot bigger than you."

"All right. That'll free me up to fight if I have to."

After I helped Cynthia load Mabel, I walked to the bed and wiped my bloody hands on the sheet. "Do you know where the glowsap mines are?"

"Yes. Let's go out the back way. We'll pass the security desk. There's a computer pad with a map. User ID is Cynthia. Password is Meddlers spelled in reverse." She adjusted Mabel on her shoulders. "I'm ready."

Perdantus flew upstairs to exit through the window, while I opened the door to the security office and let Cynthia go first. As we passed the desk, I grabbed the computer pad and followed her through the dining room and out the back door.

With Perdantus leading the way, we hurried across the grassy expanse to the river and walked upstream as fast as Cynthia's burden would allow. Since the slope gradually became steeper, I clipped the computer pad to my belt, allowing me to pump with both arms as we continued.

Each step made my legs feel heavier and heavier. I had expended a lot of energy using my Starborn powers, but that might not be the only reason for my exhaustion. Maybe someone restarted the tower remotely, and it was draining me. And if so, that meant the admiral's allies were closing in.

After a few minutes, the roar of engines drew my attention to the sky. A trio of gliders appeared to the west, flying low over the forest toward the compound. Their shape revealed them to be from a Nebula series ship, maybe one of the two ships that had recently arrived. With weapons turrets on the front, these were attack gliders, ready to strafe their targets with rapid-fire machine guns.

One of the gliders peeled off from the formation and flew toward us. The forest to the north lay only about fifty paces away, but could we get under tree cover before the glider arrived?

I called out, "We've been spotted!"

We both took off at a trot. Mabel bounced on Cynthia's shoulders, but it couldn't be helped. As the glider closed in, I looked straight at its pilot, barely visible from this distance. Could I grab his heart? Choke him? Or maybe set something on fire? Probably not while on the run, and with the tower back on, I didn't know if I had any Starborn powers.

When we came within ten paces of the woods, the glider fired a volley of bullets only centimeters in front of us, forcing us to halt. As grass and lava rock particles flew everywhere, the glider roared past us from left to right, wind from its wake blowing us back and throwing the shards into our faces. The glider bent into a sharp U-turn and zoomed toward us again. If we tried to run, it would probably riddle us with bullets.

I extended my hand toward it. Since I hadn't practiced setting anything on fire, I had to try to disable him, and I had only a few seconds to get it done. "Duck, Cynthia! This is gonna be close!"

She dropped to her knees. I ran to put some distance between us, hoping to draw the pilot's fire. When I stopped, I looked at him again and tried to penetrate his chest, but it didn't seem to work. The front turrets opened, ready to shoot. Just as I was about to dive to the ground, another glider collided with the attacker from the side and sent it spinning out of control.

The second glider zipped over me, narrowly missing my head, and began a sharp turn. The first glider slammed into the ground, skidded to the forest, and smashed into a huge tree. The fuselage broke in half, and the momentum flung the pilot deeper into the woods like a limp ragdoll.

The ramming glider slowed and lowered to the ground in front of us, its nose pointed at me, Cynthia on the other side. The pilot's helmet prevented a view of any expression, friendly or otherwise. When the hatch opened, the pilot rose and removed the helmet, letting blonde tresses spill out and revealing Crystal's face. "Good thing I decided to stay on your six. You were about to get ventilated."

I ran to her and gave her a hug. "Thanks for the save."

"My pleasure, though I could've crashed and died. You know, typical mortal danger stuff we heroes have to face."

"What's going on at the refuge?"

"Tell you later." She nodded toward where Cynthia sat with Mabel lying next to her. "Better get them into the woods before more gliders show up."

I ran back to Cynthia, helped her rise with Mabel on her shoulders, and supported her from one side while Crystal supported her from the other. When we got them under cover, Crystal pointed northward. "I saw where you were heading. A bigger glider, right?"

I nodded. "How far on foot?"

"Five minutes, max. I'll meet you there."

"Wait." I unclipped the computer pad and gave it to her. "Take this. Keep it safe."

"Sure thing." She hustled toward her glider. I scanned the sky for the other two gliders. Might they return if the pilots didn't hear from the one that came after us? And what about the crashed pilot? Maybe I could get intel from him.

I scanned the wooded area and spotted the pilot several paces away, partly wrapped around a tree trunk. It wouldn't take long to check on him, but with Cynthia carrying a burden and Mabel's need for medical attention, every second mattered.

A flutter of wings drew my attention skyward. Perdantus flew in a slow orbit above the trees, apparently ready to continue guiding us. "Cynthia," I called. "You go ahead. Follow Perdantus. I'll catch up in a minute."

"Gotcha." Cynthia readjusted Mabel on her shoulders and strode on.

I ran to the pilot and checked his neck—no pulse. I wouldn't be able to get intel but maybe a weapon. I checked his belt, found a laser blaster, and pulled it from the holster, then hurried to catch up with Cynthia, who was no longer in sight because of the trees, though I could still hear Perdantus's guiding chirps.

Since the attack glider probably radioed our apparent destination to his allies, an ambush at the glider pad seemed likely. I had to catch up or maybe make a wide circle and arrive at an unexpected angle.

Veering to the right, I broke into a run, leaping over and dodging obstacles. When I arrived at a spot directly to the east of the pad, I cut to the west and approached more slowly. Soon, I came within view of the pad through the last line of trees. Cynthia arrived at the clearing and laid Mabel on the concrete pad. Crystal climbed out of her glider and helped load Mabel into the passenger seat of the two-person craft.

I walked to a big tree at the edge of the clearing and looked around for any sign of trouble. Something gnawed at my mind. This getaway seemed all too easy. It would be better if I stayed hidden. Crystal could handle this.

When Cynthia climbed into the pilot's seat and closed the hatch, Crystal gave me a furtive glance but said nothing, smart enough to know why I was hiding.

Perdantus shouted from above, "An armed stranger is approaching the pad!"

As I readied my blaster and searched for the stranger, Crystal slapped the side of the glider and shouted, "Go!"

Its engine roaring, the glider lifted off from the pad. Crystal backpedaled, raising an arm to shield her eyes from the gusty thruster blast. When they zoomed away, she sprinted toward her glider.

A laser bullet zipped past her, missing by centimeters. I spotted the shooter, a man in an Alliance uniform and helmet at the north edge of the clearing, aiming his weapon. I fired a laser bullet of my own. It zinged into his shoulder in a splash of sparks. He dropped his gun and fell, moaning as he clutched his wounded shoulder.

"More are coming!" Perdantus called from a high branch.

I waved an arm as I ran toward the glider. "Perdantus, get in with Crystal!"

As Crystal climbed in and Perdantus flew to her shoulder, she shot a worried look at me. "How're you going to escape?"

"Close the hatch." I stuffed my blaster into its holster. "I'll ride on top."

"I should've guessed." She pushed the hatch button. "Just hang on tight."

Laser bullets sizzled past me, over my head, and on both sides. The shooters were probably still too far away to be accurate, but that wouldn't last. The second the hatch closed, I leaped on top, wrapped my arms and legs around the dome as far as I could, and slapped the glass. "Go!"

As the glider lifted, a shining bullet drilled into the side. Another ripped into my hand and sizzled like acid. As more bullets pelted the glider, Crystal zoomed away. After nearly a minute, smoke streamed from the rear section, and the engine sputtered. We angled into a descent toward the treetops.

Crystal's voice came through my earbuds. "Get ready for a rough landing!"

Pain from the hand wound throttling my voice, I shouted. "Dodge the trees!"

"No kidding, Captain."

"Head toward my glider before you ditch this one. Perdantus will tell you which way to go."

"Copy that."

While listening to Crystal get info from Perdantus, I held on tightly and scanned all around. Whoever attacked us at the pad would surely follow, though they had to hustle back to their crafts, giving us a good head start, but with our trailing smoke and slower speed, they could catch up in a hurry.

"I see a good spot to land," Crystal said. "But it's gonna be close. Get ready for a brush with the treetops, then a quick dive. If you can use your powers to keep us from crashing, that would be great."

I grunted, "Yeah. Sure."

As we sank closer to the treetops below, I mentally pushed on the branches. They bent downward somewhat, but I had no idea if the bending would be enough to help.

The glider took a sudden dive. The bottom surface swiped at the branches as we broke past them toward a clearing. The impact made the glider spin wildly. Crystal corrected by shifting us into a quickly descending orbit. I gritted my teeth and continued my mental push, hoping I could keep us from a catastrophic impact.

Seconds later, we hit the ground in a twirling slide that sent us careening toward the forest. I sat up with my legs still straddling the dome and thrust out my hands with a mental shove against the trees. As they bent, our glider slowed. It hit one of the trunks with a thud and threw me off my perch. I rolled past the tree and sat up on the ground, unharmed by the fall. Although I couldn't stop the crash, maybe I kept us from getting killed.

Crystal popped her hatch open and climbed out while Perdantus flew upward, calling, "I will watch for pursuers."

Crystal ran to me and extended a hand. "Need a boost?"

"Yeah. Thanks." My right hand still feeling on fire, I grabbed her wrist with my left and rose with her pull.

"We need to scoot," she said. "Whoever shot at us will be looking for the wreckage."

"Right." I turned my earbuds off. "We should go silent. They might be able to detect our signals."

Crystal turned off her buds. "Done. But what about the computer pad you gave me? It might be sending a signal." She pointed over her shoulder with her thumb. "It's in my glider."

"Good thought." I reached into her glider and grabbed the pad from the floorboard. After turning it off, I looked up and spotted Perdantus. "See anything?"

"Four gliders, but they aren't coming this way. At least not yet."

"Good. Can you lead us to my glider?"

"Yes. I can see it from here." He flew over the treetops. "This way."

We ran into the forest, trying to look up to see his route while also glancing down to keep from tripping. After a few minutes, we arrived at the small clearing where I had parked my glider. I entered the security code, opened the hatch, and laid the computer pad on the seat.

Crystal set a fist on her hip. "Okay, Captain. We made it this far. What's the plan? We can't both fit in that cockpit."

"No, but I can ride on top again. Just far enough for us to get away from—"

"Nope." Crystal shook her head hard. "Bad plan. You're always risking your life in some crazy way. Let's just hide your glider, hole up in the woods, and chill out. They'll get tired of looking for us after a while."

I gazed into her sincere, worried eyes. In spite of my hope to get as far away from this place as possible, I had to give in. "You're right. We can rest for a while and get each other up to date."

After finding a gap in the woods wide enough to fit the glider through, I got into the pilot's seat and drove it into the gap, pushing it into some low underbrush that hid it quite well. When we finished, we sat side by side with our backs to the glider while Perdantus stayed in the upper branches as a lookout.

I took a deep breath and exhaled slowly while shaking my wounded hand. "Finally a chance to talk."

"And to heal yourself." She pulled my hand closer and squinted. "Burned a hole straight through between your thumb and index finger. Barely missed the bones. No blood, though. The heat must've ... um ... whatever that Willis word is for sealing it with heat."

"Cauterized it."

"Right. Well, you work on trying to heal it while I tell you what's going on at the refuge."

"Sounds good." I focused on the wound. "Let's hear it."

"First of all, the kids at the refuge are all fine. Ever since the eruptions settled down, they were able to set up a great survival routine, you know, fetching water from the river, growing crops, hunting game. They've been thriving. Anyway, not long after we left, a pair of military-like people visited them, a man and a woman, saying they were from a resistance group."

"Military? That sounds like trouble."

"Not even close." Crystal pointed at me. "They're big fans of yours, and they heard what we did here and wanted to set up their operations at the refuge. The woman called their group Megan's Meddlers." She poked my side with an elbow, sending sharp pain through my ribs, making me wince. "Oops. Sorry."

"No worries. My ribs are getting better, not quite completely healed though."

"Well, work on all your injuries while I keep going. This could take a while. Anyway, the two newcomers invited about ten of their friends, most of them former Alliance officers who were upset about how Admiral Fairbanks—Dwight, not Camille—was making the entire fleet his personal profit machine. They figured out he was running the galaxy-wide trafficking operation, and they wanted to do whatever they could to stop it. And I'll bet you'll never guess who started their group."

"Captain Tillman? Oliver's father?"

Crystal frowned. "I guess it wasn't that hard, was it?"

"Nope." The thought of Captain Tillman starting the group raised a tingle up my spine. Since he was willing to torture me to get what he wanted, could he have passed his brutality along to anyone else in his group? I gave her a nod. "Keep going."

"Anyway, Oliver was real proud to hear that. And they invited him to be an officer in their ranks."

"Wow!" My heart swelled with pride, but I knew it meant that he wouldn't be part of my crew anymore. As tears welled, I averted my eyes. "Good for him. He's amazing."

"Yeah. He is. But he said no."

"No?" I turned my head toward her, blinking. "Why?"

"Because, Megan ..." She brushed a tear from my cheek with a thumb. "He's loyal to you. Probably way more than you realize. Anyway, I told him to ask you if it would be okay, and he said no. He didn't want to put any pressure on you, because he knew you'd feel like you had to say yes."

"He's right. I would say yes. But not because I have to. Because I want what's best for him. Always."

"Exactly what he said about you. But you two can fight that out later. Back to my story. Megan's Meddlers set up a station to monitor ships that came close to the planet. That's why Emerson detected a scanner near the refuge. It belongs to the Meddlers, not the Alliance."

"Any word on where Emerson landed the ship?"

Crystal shook her head. "He's supposed to be listening for us, but so far he hasn't responded."

"He's obeying orders. Everything's shut down except for the low-power antenna. We would have to be real close for him to detect a signal. But I'm wondering about something. If Emerson could detect that scanner near the refuge, then the Alliance might be able to find the Meddlers. I hope they've gone silent."

"They have. As soon as they spotted the Nine, they shut everything down and went on high alert. When Oliver and I showed up, they shot at our gliders, so we had to land and walk about five kilometers to get to the refuge. Then they grabbed us and put us in a cage. No matter what we said, they wouldn't believe that we helped set up this refuge. Fortunately, Vonda came by and told them who we were. Then they praised us like folk heroes, especially Oliver because of who his dad is … or was."

"So why did you come to find me?"

She shrugged. "Nothing for me to do there. Oliver's in charge of finding the Nine, and they didn't need me to hypnotize anyone or be a lie-detector, so I thought I'd go back to being on your six."

"And I'm glad you did. You saved my life."

She grinned. "I hate to say I told you so, but … Actually, no, I don't hate it at all. I'm going to enjoy it." She drew her head so close to mine, our noses nearly touched. "I told you so."

I shoved her away. "Yes, you definitely did."

"And don't you forget it." She folded her hands in her lap. "Okay. Your turn. Spill your story."

For the next several minutes, I told her about what happened to me. When I mentioned that I found Admiral Fairbanks and that he was the mastermind behind everything, she gave me a hard time for not killing him. Then I explained the kill switch, and she relented.

I finished with a shrug. "And now here we are."

Crystal scrunched her brow. "I wonder where Cynthia took Mabel. Any hospital around here would be under Alliance control."

"Cynthia called it an enclave. About thirty kilometers away. I'm guessing someone there has medical training."

"Could it be an Alliance hospital? Maybe Mabel was working out of it under cover, and Cynthia called it an enclave because it's where the moles hide out. But if that's where the local hospital is, why would it be so far from Fairbanks? If he got sicker and needed surgery or something, wouldn't they want the hospital to be somewhere closer to him?"

"It's just a few minutes in a fast glider. Not a big delay at all."

"Good point. So, if it is an Alliance hospital, maybe Cynthia is a double agent. I read a spy novel once where this woman worked for three different governments. She wasn't loyal to any of them. She was in it for herself. When I was helping Cynthia load Mabel in the glider, she kept staring at me. Gave me the creeps. Maybe she's really a double agent."

"Did you introduce yourself to her?"

"No. Like I said, she gave me the creeps. I didn't know if I could trust her."

"But Cynthia risked her life to help Mabel. Carried her on her shoulders while we were being chased. She's not a double agent."

Crystal shrugged. "All right. Cross that conspiracy theory off the list. It's just when I hear about a spy, it makes me wonder. Spies tell lies." She grimaced. "Blazes! I did it again! Stupid rhyming habit."

I smiled. "I get your point. Cynthia lies for a living. We should be on guard when we're around her. And we should probably check on Mabel whether Cynthia is a double agent or not. Maybe we can get the real scoop about what's going on here."

"Sure. But how?"

I gazed toward the west. "I saw which direction Cynthia flew. The enclave shouldn't be too hard to find from the air."

"Except for the fact that Alliance gliders are searching for us, and Admiral Fairbanks is obsessed with finding you and hammering you into mincemeat. He's not going to give up anytime soon."

"He doesn't know I was there. He fell asleep before I turned back into myself, and Stan is dead. So the gliders might give up soon, because the kid who got away is just a lost little girl named Renalda."

"That *Stan is dead* part means they'll be hunting for a reason he's dead. But we'll see what happens. If it looks like the heat's off, we'll try to find the enclave. We still have a problem, though—a one-seat glider and two passengers. And I don't want to see you riding on top again, or me."

"I don't either. Easy to get shot that way. But I could repair yours. It's close by, and if I need parts, I can see what I can salvage from the dead pilot's glider."

"Well, that glider *isn't* close by. And it got really bent out of shape."

I shrugged. "Best idea I've got. And it'll give the Alliance more time to decide to stop looking for us."

"Sounds good. Let's do it."

For the next hour, I worked on Crystal's glider, plugging a couple of holes with whatever I could find and replacing two parts that I salvaged from the dead pilot's glider. Fortunately, it seemed that no one flew a patrol to watch for me during my trip to the other glider and back. Fairbanks probably wasn't interested in finding "Renalda."

When I finished, we turned our earbuds back on and boarded our gliders, the computer pad now on my lap. We flew side by side in the direction Cynthia had been going when she departed with Mabel, staying low near the treetops to avoid detection. Since Perdantus couldn't keep up with a glider, he joined me and offered advice about how to survey the area even while hampered by our low altitude.

After about half an hour of searching, Crystal's voice piped through my buds. "I see something. One o'clock. A dark spot in that low ridge. Looks like a cave. Lots of dirt and rocks on both sides of the opening, like it's been … um …"

"Excavated," I offered.

"Yeah, but don't get cocky. Just because you have a bigger … um … thing."

"Vocabulary?"

"Right. And I'm shutting up now. Let's head to the cave." Crystal angled her glider in that direction. I followed, watching for any sign of the enemy. "There's a landing pad right in front of the cave entrance," she said, "and a two-seater is there."

I spotted the pad and the glider. "Yep. That's Cynthia's. But we'd better not land next to it. If it's an Alliance facility, we don't want to alert them. Let's find another place close enough to walk from."

We located a flat area nearby, but at a lower elevation that would require a steep climb up the ridge. Apparently, whoever designed this location wanted to make sure it was hard to access on foot.

Once we had secured the gliders, I sent Perdantus to scout the cave. After clipping the computer pad to my belt again, I climbed the steep, tree-filled slope with Crystal. Since no path led up the incline, we had to grab branches and tree trunks to hoist ourselves. Each grasp with my right hand sent pain shooting up my arm, and every strain in my torso muscles made my injured ribs twinge, but not as bad as before.

When we finally reached the ledge where the glider rested about twenty paces away, we halted and caught our breath. Perdantus landed on my shoulder and spoke in a low tone. "There is a modern structure inside the cave. I saw one office with a desk and two chairs and two women sitting. There is a corridor leading deeper into the cave, so perhaps there are medical rooms beyond where I searched. One of the women watched me with high suspicion, so I decided not to venture farther inside."

"Good call," I said. "If one of the women was Cynthia, she knows who you are. I still believe she's on our side, but no use taking chances."

"I saw Cynthia when we were at the Fairbanks building, but I did not see her in the cave."

"Good intel. Please continue scanning the area and contact us if you see anything we need to know."

"Of course." He flew off my shoulder and into the air.

"If we're not taking chances," Crystal said, "you could change into someone else again. Cynthia knows you can do that, but she's not guarding the entrance. At least it'll get you inside, and you can distract the women to get Perdantus and me in. Not only that, if there is a double agent inside, the moment Megan Willis shows up, the place instantly turns into a big fat bullseye for an attack. Killing you is the admiral's number one goal."

"All right. But who should I be?"

"How about Jillian? If they look you up in a database, they'll match your face to a real person. Even if they know Jillian's been working with

Megan Willis, you can claim that you're a double agent and pretend to be on their side no matter if they're Alliance or Meddlers."

I gave her a skeptical frown. "Pretty shaky. It would definitely test my acting skills."

"Your spy skills, you mean. Being a cocky infiltrator is what you do best."

"I don't have a better idea, but she's bigger than I am, so my uniform might not fit."

Crystal narrowed an eye. "Why did Lyric's clothes change when she morphed, but you always stay in the same clothes?"

I shrugged. "She has lots more experience, I guess. When I've changed, I concentrated on the face and body size. I'll see what I can do." I unclipped the computer pad and gave it to Crystal, then closed my eyes and concentrated on a mental image of my aunt and another of me. As before, I covered my face with Jillian's features bit by bit, increased my height, and filled out my proportions to match hers, this time also focusing on the uniform. The size changes hurt again, but not as much as last time, and the process went faster. I was getting better at this.

When I finished, I opened my eyes and looked at Crystal. She grinned. "Looking good, Sister!" Then she shook her head. "Not that you looked bad before. It's just that you're all grown up, and your clothes did change this time, which is good, because if they didn't, you'd be in a world of hurt right now."

No longer wearing my new outfit, I patted the front of a neatly pressed Alliance uniform. "This outfit pegs me as Alliance. I guess I'll find out right away which side they're on." I flexed my muscles to test my bracelets. Nothing happened. That wasn't good. Maybe my larger arms were negatively affecting the conductive ink.

Crystal pointed at the laser blaster, now on the ground. "That dropped while you were changing."

"I forgot to include my belt in the morphing." I scooped the blaster up and slid it behind my waistband at the hip. "While I'm gone, see if you can find a glowsap-mine map on the computer pad. User ID is Cynthia. Password is Meddlers spelled in reverse."

"Got it."

I took a deep breath and walked with a confident gait toward the cave entrance, whispering to myself, "Be Jillian. Be Jillian. Be Jillian."

When I passed the glider and walked within view of the cave, a thirtyish woman stepped out of an office. Wearing military camo and aiming an automatic rifle at me, she blocked my path, her brawny body bulging at the sleeves. With no Alliance emblem anywhere on her uniform, she was more than likely a resistance member. Yet, the rifle in her hands and a pistol in a side holster weren't helping me feel confident.

I tried to read her thoughts, but her skull seemed impenetrable. Either she was good at guarding her thoughts, or I was lousy at the mind-reading power. Of course, I could easily snatch the rifle away from her, but that didn't seem necessary yet.

"Who are you?" she asked, her forehead creased in spite of the tight bun holding her dark hair back. "And why are you here?"

I raised my hands. "Jillian Willis, former captain of the Nebula Nine. Now an ally of Megan Willis, my niece. I came here because I heard that this is an enclave for those who oppose the Alliance. I want to join your cause."

The woman called toward the office. "Says she's Jillian Willis, Megan Willis's aunt. No longer with the Alliance. Wants to join the opposition."

"I took a photo," a woman in the office called in return. "I'll check it out."

Keeping my head motionless, I scanned the area with my eyes, trying to locate a camera, but I couldn't find one.

"That's her," the woman in the office said. "She's really Megan's aunt. Records say she stole the Nebula Nine, pretending to take it out of decommission status. I'll ask the commander what to do with her."

Her tone seemed far less than welcoming. If these were really Meddlers, the guards wouldn't have to ask what to do with me, would they? Megan's aunt should be welcomed with open arms. And the guard kept her rifle aimed at me. Not exactly what I had expected. But I kept my cool and said nothing.

After nearly a minute, a tall man wearing camo from head to toe walked out from the cave's interior, pulled the pistol from the armed woman's holster, and marched toward me, the pistol aimed at my head. With dark skin similar to Zoë's, a shaved head, and a wiry body, his stern face made him look like a hardened soldier.

Again, I stood completely still. I had to be Jillian—cocksure and unflappable.

When he arrived, he pressed the barrel against my forehead and set his face close to mine. "You have one chance to stay alive." His hot breath smelled of coffee and his uniform like campfire smoke. "If you really are Megan Willis's aunt, then Julian Willis is your twin brother. You should be able to answer a simple question about the Willis family."

I dared not even nod. Moving only my lips, I spoke clearly. "I can."

"According to records from your flight school, who was the top pilot in your class?"

"According to the official records, I was, but the official records don't reflect the truth."

"Oh?" He pulled the pistol back a few centimeters. "Are the official records inaccurate?"

"Quite inaccurate. I cheated in both the academic scores and the piloting contest. My twin brother, Julian Willis, would have prevailed in both categories if I hadn't cheated. He is the true top pilot from my class."

"How interesting." He stepped back and lowered the pistol. "We knew you cheated in the contest, but this is the first I've heard that you also cheated in the academic portion."

I exhaled. "Well, it's true. I confessed both to my brother not long ago."

He slid the pistol behind his belt. "Where is he now?"

I folded my hands behind my back. "That's information I'm not willing to divulge."

As he stared at me, the sternness in his face melted into a smile. "I'm really getting to like you, Captain Jillian Willis. If I weren't already married, I would—"

"You would what?" the rifle-wielding woman called.

He chuckled. "I would keep looking for you, dear, my one and only love."

"Good answer." The woman, obviously his wife, lowered her rifle. "Welcome, Captain. We're glad you're here. We can definitely use your help."

I smiled. "Whew! You had me scared for a minute."

"We have to be careful," the man said. "One of our people told your niece about our enclave, and we're worried that too many people are going to find out about it."

I shook my head. "Megan's tight-lipped. She told me and Crystal. No one else."

His brow shot upward. "Crystal? Have you seen her lately?"

"Yes. Quite recently. Why?"

His respiration quickened. "What about Zoë?"

"Why the interrogation?" I crossed my arms in front. "I'm not going to give you any information you don't need."

"All right. Fair enough." The man sighed. "You're supposed to keep secrets. I understand."

I lowered my arms. "Well, maybe if you tell me your secrets, I'll tell you mine. Why are you so fired up about Zoë and Crystal?"

The man glanced at his wife. "Should I tell her?"

"You might as well." She walked to his side and slung the rifle's strap over her shoulder. "Cat's practically out of the bag already."

As they stood together, the contrast between his dark skin and her light tones seemed stark. "Well ..." He glanced at her before focusing on me, tears in his eyes. "Ophelia and I joined this resistance force when we learned that the Alliance has been behind the trafficking of children. You see, our daughter was kidnapped by slavers who were financed by the Alliance, and we've been looking for her ever since. When we learned that she joined Anne Willis, we tried to track her down, but then she went with Megan Willis and—"

"Wait." I held up a hand, my own tears welling. "Are you saying that Zoë is your daughter?"

"Yes. I'm sorry. I forgot to mention her name. Anyway, when she went with Megan, we lost track of her, because Megan is, as I'm sure you're aware, a hard girl to find. We just hear reports of the damage she and her crew have done to the slave trade and the Alliance, and we try to follow the route, but after a while we gave up and joined the Resistance."

"Megan's Meddlers," Ophelia said, smiling. "Isaac and I are huge Megan supporters, especially since Zoë's with her."

Isaac's expression took on a pleading aspect. "Do you think you can get word to Zoë that we're looking for her?"

My lie-detecting ability kicked in. Without a doubt, they were telling the truth. "I'll tell her." One of the tears trickled down my cheek. I brushed it away with a thumb. "As soon as I see her again."

A new voice asked, "What about Crystal?"

I looked past Isaac for the source of the voice. Cynthia limped out of the cave. "I didn't get to ask Megan," she said as she drew closer, "because we were under fire. But now that you're here, I'll ask. Have you seen Crystal recently?"

I nodded. "Very recently. Why?"

"Slavers took her from me when she was six years old. Like Isaac and Ophelia, I've been looking for her ever since."

When my mental lie-detector confirmed her words, I sucked in a breath. "You're Crystal's mother? I mean, of course you are. I'm just overwhelmed. I heard you were dead."

"I'm sure Crystal thought so. I was shot by the kidnapper. It took weeks for me to recover." Cynthia offered a trembling smile. "When I was with Megan, a girl with blonde hair saved us both. I never heard her name, but her hair and face reminded me of my Crystal. I kept watching her, thinking I should ask, but I also had to hurry. When I closed the glider's hatch, I saw the brightness in her eyes. No one else has eyes like that. Then I knew, but she slapped the glider and shouted at me to leave. Of course, I had to get Mabel to safety. So I just left, and I've wondered about it ever since."

I laughed under my breath. "If the girl was with Megan, then she was definitely Crystal. They're nearly inseparable." I resisted the urge to look back at Crystal. Mother and daughter had been separated for more than six years. And since Crystal thought her mother was dead, she didn't recognize her when they met. She probably wouldn't know her now, either. And from her vantage point, she might not be able to hear the conversation.

Then, I remembered my earbuds. They had been turned on the entire time. She definitely heard.

I looked past the glider. Crystal stood behind it, peering around the tail, tear tracks on her cheeks. She whispered, her voice entering my ear, broken and shaking. "I … I couldn't tell … from here. Is she … is she telling the truth?"

My own voice pitched higher. "I think so."

"Who are you talking to?" Cynthia asked.

I turned back toward her and steadied my voice. "To Crystal. Your daughter."

As I glanced between the two, Cynthia looked past me. "Crystal? Is it really you?"

Crystal stepped out from behind the glider, her arms crossed as she shifted from foot to foot. "I'm Crystal."

Cynthia extended her arms. "It's me, pumpkin seed."

"Pumpkin seed?" Crystal said, nearly squeaking. "How do you know about that name?"

Cynthia peeled a layer of wrinkled skin from each cheek and threw them on the ground. "Because I'm your mother. I survived getting shot."

Crystal's eyes widened. She whispered, "Mommy?" Then she ran, her arms extended. When they met, Cynthia lifted Crystal in the air and twirled her in a circle, making Crystal's locks swing freely.

My tears flowed. I choked back a sob and crossed my arms, fighting to keep control. My sister and her real mother were finally reunited. And a heartbreaking thought added to my flood of emotions. Had I lost my sister? I couldn't imagine Crystal staying with me when she could be with her mother.

While they continued hugging, Isaac compressed my shoulder with a strong hand. "So Crystal came with you. Is Zoë somewhere close by as well?"

I sniffed hard and shook my head. "Zoë is …" My tight throat forced me to swallow. "Zoë's on Gamma Five with my …" I almost said father, but I covered the mistake with a stifled sob, unsure if I should reveal who I really was. "She's with my brother. Megan's father. She's well protected and doing great things for the cause."

Isaac hugged Ophelia, both smiling and crying at the same time. "And Megan?" he asked. "Cynthia saw her with Crystal earlier today, and you said they were nearly inseparable. We would like to meet her, if possible."

I nodded. "I think we can arrange a meeting."

Crystal drew away from Cynthia and looked at me with a wink, her smile stretching her cheeks. "Go ahead, Jillian. Get Megan. We'll wait."

I tried to peer into the cave. It seemed that Crystal's concern about this place being a big fat target if I revealed my identity had gone up in smoke. I wasn't so sure we should give up being careful. It seemed that everything was far too serene for a secret enclave that doubled as a hospital. "Where's Mabel?" I asked Cynthia. "Megan told me about her. Is she all right?"

Cynthia held Crystal's hand and turned toward me. "We have a surgeon inside who's removing a bullet from her thigh. Took him and his nurse a while to get here, so she lost quite a bit more blood. He said she's got a good chance, though, probably ninety percent."

As if on cue, a gray-haired man wearing scrubs walked out of the cave, stripping bloody gloves off his hands. "The bullet's out, but she needs blood. Do we have any A-positive donors here?"

Isaac raised his hand. "I'm A-positive."

"More than one donor would be better. O-positive and O-negative would work in a pinch."

Everyone else raised their hands, including me, since my type was O-positive.

"Good. We could use some from all of you to replenish our supply. My nurse can draw your blood and give Mabel what she needs." He tossed the gloves into a bin just inside the cave entrance. "I need to go to the stream to wash. We ran out of water in there."

Isaac led the way into the cave. "Let's go, blood donors."

As the surgeon walked to the side, I passed by him on my way in. A thought from his brain came through to mine as he walked away. *Too bad Megan's not with them.*

I continued watching him, his back turned toward me. Did he mean that he wanted to meet me? Or was he hoping I would be there for another reason, the big-fat-target reason? But no other thoughts drifted to my mind. Since I had no way to verify his meaning, I had to stay on high alert.

Now at the tail end of the line, I walked under the cave's arch, almost low enough to make me duck. A desk lamp in the office to the left provided enough light to see the uneven, rocky floor. Electric lanterns hanging on the corridor wall at intervals of a few meters guided our steps deeper within. Obviously, a generator somewhere unseen provided electricity, but no engine noise interrupted the silence. Maybe the people here used solar panels to charge power cells, but not likely. The panels would be too easy to notice from the air.

Isaac led the procession into a large, well-lit room to the right. With a surgery bed, tables, and cabinets, it looked like a typical hospital operating room. Mabel lay on the bed, an IV tube running from the back of her hand to a bag hanging from a pole. Her body covered by a sheet, she appeared to be breathing easily.

A woman wearing scrubs stood next to a wheeled chair. Gray strands in her otherwise dark hair and creases in her face and forehead made her look to be in her late fifties. Since no other women were in sight, maybe she was the other woman Perdantus saw earlier.

"Who's first?" she asked, gesturing toward the chair.

Isaac raised a hand. "I might as well since I'm A-positive."

While she seated him, I scanned the room for any sign of danger, listening for movement or a beeping noise and smelling for chemicals like gunpowder or ammonia fertilizer that might indicate the presence of a bomb, but I couldn't detect anything unusual.

I tried to read the nurse's mind, but nothing came through. As before, she was either guarding her thoughts or my skill was too weak.

She looked into an open jar and cursed. "I'm out of alcohol for the swabs. I'll have to get some from my kit. It's in our glider." She strode out of the room. "It's not far. Back soon."

My lie-detector needle went off the scale. When she walked out of earshot, I spun toward Crystal. "She lied."

Crystal nodded. "I know. Any idea why?"

I raised my voice. "Everyone out! It's a trap!"

Isaac shot up from the chair, making it spin on its wheels. "You heard her. It's a trap. Everyone out."

"What kind of trap?" Ophelia asked as she turned that way.

"Don't ask questions." He set a hand on her back and guided her toward the door. "Just leave."

"I'll get Mabel," Cynthia said as she slid her hands under Mabel's back.

Crystal ran around the bed and grabbed the IV pole. "I got this. Let's roll."

The moment Isaac and Ophelia ran into the corridor, an explosion boomed overhead. The rocky ceiling fractured and collapsed. I waved my arms in sweeping arcs and used my mind to hold the debris in place over our heads. With thousands of kilos of rocks pushing down on my mental barrier, I grunted, "Go! I can't hold this load much longer."

Crystal jerked the IV tube out of Mabel's hand and pushed Cynthia toward the door. "Get her out of here. I'm helping Jillian."

"But how?" Cynthia asked.

Crystal shouted. "Never mind! Just go!"

"I'm going!" Cynthia staggered from the room with Mabel in her arms.

As the load crushed my brain, my body bent downward. My sore ribs seemed to scream. I could no longer move my arms, but I kept them raised as I gasped for breath, my heart feeling like it might burst. I grunted with nearly every word. "Crystal … go. … Be with … your mother. … You … have to live."

"Not without you." She lunged to the chair and wheeled it to me. "Sit and keep that ceiling where it belongs."

I sat down hard, pain from the weight so excruciating, I could no longer breathe.

"I've got you." Crystal pushed the chair toward the door. "Just a few more seconds."

The ceiling collapsed over our original spot. As Crystal pushed the chair faster, the avalanche chased us from the room. When we burst out into the corridor, the wheels hit something on the floor, sending us into a headlong tumble. I struck hard rock, scraping my palms and elbows. Crystal fell on my back with a loud oomph. Her weight pushed air from my lungs. I gasped for breath but couldn't draw any air.

Rocks pelted the ground on both sides. Crystal cried out as they hit her as well, but I couldn't feel them with her body protecting mine.

A few seconds later, the storm of rocks and dirt ended, sooner than I expected. Maybe since the explosion happened in the other chamber, the collapse wasn't so bad here. In complete darkness, I forced in a breath and called, "Crystal. Are you all right?"

Strands of hair brushed my cheek as she whispered directly into my ear. "I'm fine. Just fine. But you probably already know that's a lie. I feel like my backbone isn't a bone anymore. More like jelly. I'm a jellyfish now."

"Can you move your fingers and toes?"

"Let me check … um … yeah. They move."

"That's a good sign."

"And it's good that I didn't bring that computer pad with me. I put it in Cynthia's glider. It probably would've gotten crushed."

I knew she was talking to get her mind off the pain, so I went along with it, my chest too flattened to draw in enough air for a shout. Our newfound allies knew where we were. They would find us. "Did you see the mine locations on the pad?"

"No. I couldn't get past the security screen."

A muffled call came from somewhere. "Jillian! Crystal! Can you hear me?"

"Sounds like Isaac," Crystal said, still whispering. "Can you answer? My lungs are like pancakes."

"I'll try." I pushed against the ground with my hands to relieve some of the pressure on my lungs. "Yes, Isaac. We're here. Crystal and me." I rested, again losing air.

"Okay," Isaac said. "I see where you are now. Hang in there. We're going to dig you out." The sound of rocks scraping and colliding blended with his shouts. "Come on, everyone. Together."

I took in another shallow breath. "I'll see if I can move some of the rocks off your back with my mind."

"No. I'm okay. You rest. They'll dig us out." Her whisper drew closer, sending warm breath into my ear. "I guess I can't get on your six any closer than I am now, right?"

"Definitely." When I mentally replayed her actions from moments ago, warmth coursed across my body. Her love and courage were amazing. "Thanks for what you did back there."

"You're welcome, but it's a good thing I didn't have time to think. It was stupid dangerous. Sort of like something you would do."

"I'm glad you were being stupid. You can join my stupid club."

She laughed, then groaned. "Glad to be a member of the Megan Willis Stupid Society."

"Speaking of Megan, maybe I should change back into my body. If assassins are still around, I'd rather fight them as myself so my bracelets will work. They don't work in this body."

"Okay. Go for it."

I closed my eyes and went through the transformation process, both my body and my clothes, faster than before. Several seconds later, I felt like myself again, though the pain continued.

The weight suddenly eased. Light poured through gaps between the rocks above. As I blinked at the light, Isaac's face appeared. When he saw me, his eyes widened. "Megan Willis?"

"Yeah. It was me all along, not Jillian."

"Well, ain't that a trip! You're a shape shifter, like Lyric Altera." He passed a huge rock to Cynthia, and she passed it to Ophelia. The weight eased a lot more. Now able to twist my neck to see all around, I looked at Crystal as Isaac touched her back. "Think it's safe to lift you?" he asked. "We need to get you both out of here in case there's another collapse."

"Go for it," Crystal said. "I think we busted the rolling chair, so I can't ride on that."

Isaac carefully lifted her off me and passed her to Cynthia, who carried her toward the cave entrance. With the weight off my back, I could breathe more easily, though it seemed that every centimeter of my body ached, especially my ribs.

With Isaac's help, I shifted to a cross-legged sitting position. "I know we have to scoot, but give me a second to catch my breath."

He glanced at the ceiling. "It's probably stable enough for now." He sat in front of me in the same pose. "Thank you for what you did. You recognized the danger and took action. If not for you, we would all be dead. You really are the hero everyone says you are."

Tired of the accolades, I changed the subject. "Well, so is your daughter. She saved me like that more than once. Even took a laser blast for me."

When I pushed a hand against the ground to get up, he grasped my arm and hoisted me to my feet. While we walked slowly toward the entrance, I told him about Zoë jumping in front of the laser to keep me from getting hit, and about her keeping the bramble bees off us by creating a water shield from an underground lake. If not for her, they would have stung us to death. I finished that story at the same time we exited the cave, the sky now dimmer as night approached.

Crystal sat on the ground with Cynthia next to the two-person glider, Mabel lying on her back nearby, her eyes open. Ophelia stood close with a rifle, apparently watching to see if the surgeon or nurse might return. Since they left several minutes ago, they had probably reported to their superiors by now. Gliders could be on their way to check whether or not the bomb succeeded in wiping us out. Even if not, there was no reason for us to stay here.

"Do the surgeon and nurse know where the refuge is?" I asked Cynthia.

She shook her head. "They were recent volunteers from Delta Ninety-eight and came directly here instead of the refuge. We weren't ready to give away the refuge location to someone so new. But it wouldn't hurt to act like they do know, just to be safe."

"Then we should leave the enclave as soon as possible." I hobbled toward Crystal. "We can go to the refuge and warn them that their location might be compromised. Then we'll get their help so we can invade the glowsap mines and rescue the kids. If they've found the Nebula Nine, we'll have a lot more firepower. The Alliance will be watching for us, but it'll be night soon, so we can travel under the cover of darkness. We could get there in a couple of hours, but we should take a longer route to avoid detection."

Isaac gave me a firm nod. "I like that plan. Since our enclave's been exposed and obliterated, we might as well go on the offensive. No more secret infiltrating. From now on, it's all or nothing."

"That's the spirit." I looked around at the potential passengers. "Let's see. Maybe Cynthia and Mabel in this glider. Crystal and I have gliders down the slope. Isaac, what transportation options do we have for you and your wife?"

"A couple of ground rovers. What you call the refuge is our central headquarters. We know a safe route. We'll be a lot slower, but we'll get there."

"Sounds good." I looked at Crystal. "How're you feeling?"

She smiled, then winced. "Like a blacksmith's been pounding me against an anvil with a humongous hammer. Or like a mashed pretzel with its salt licked off by a dragon's fiery tongue. Or like a bug that hit a windshield and splattered its guts all across the glass. Take your pick."

"Think anything's broken?"

"Only my hope to ever be three dimensional again. I think I've been flattened for life."

Cynthia laughed. "Is she always this funny?"

I smiled. "Only when she's awake. At least in her flattened state she can slide under a locked door if we don't have a key."

Cynthia pointed at me. "And you're funny, too. It's going to be great getting to know both of you."

The reminder that I was no longer Crystal's only family pierced my heart again. Of course I was happy for her, but I knew that someday soon it would mean the end of our adventures together. "Let's get going." I whistled for Perdantus.

He flew to my shoulder. "I heard the explosion. I'm glad to see you survived."

"Barely." I glanced skyward. "Did you see anything while you were on patrol?"

"I saw a man and a woman board a glider and take off to the west."

"Before or after the explosion?"

"At the same time, as if they were waiting to hear it."

I nodded. "So they left without knowing we survived. Good intel. Anyway, our plans have changed. I'll tell you more later. I hope you don't mind riding with me. I'm filthy, and I smell awful."

He bowed his head. "Worse than awful, but I am always glad to be with you."

Using the two-person glider, Cynthia gave me a ride to my glider and then Crystal to hers while Perdantus flew to join us. After Crystal and I gingerly got into our seats, we closed our hatches and waited for our new allies to load Mabel and for Cynthia to lead the way to the refuge. Since she knew the best route, it made sense to follow her. Besides, it wasn't quite dark yet, or as my father used to say when timing a sneak attack, "It's dark, but it's not *dark* dark."

With Perdantus perched on my dashboard, I spoke to Crystal through the earbuds while waiting for the others to signal that they were ready to leave. "How are you feeling now?" I sent her responses through my console speaker so Perdantus could hear. "And, just so you know, Perdantus is listening."

"No problem. Physically, I'm a little better. Still aching, especially my back. But mentally, I'm stoked like Thorne's furnace. Finding my mother is the best thing that's ever happened to me." She paused for a moment before adding. "Besides meeting you, of course. I mean, now I have two sisters, you and Zoë, and a mother. Life couldn't get any better than that."

I allowed myself a little smile. It was kind of her to include me in her family circle. I looked at her through the two glass domes, barely visible in the growing darkness as she stared straight ahead. "You mentioned your father a while back, that he tried to save you from the slavers, but you never mentioned anyone else in your family. Is there anyone else?"

"Well, Mommy ... I mean ... Sorry. I always called her Mommy when I was little. I'd better switch to something else. Maybe Mom. Anyway, Mom never told me about anyone else. I don't even know if she remarried or kept our last name."

"Your last name? I don't think you've ever told me that either. What is it?"

"Clearwater. She chose my first name to go with it. You know, crystal clear water. And because of my eyes. They were gleaming even when I was a newborn. That's why the slavers kidnapped me. Word got around."

"Crystal Clearwater. I love it. Why didn't you ever mention it before?"

A pause ensued. Darkness now veiled her completely. "Because …" She sniffed. "Because the slave master who wanted me to …"

"You don't have to say it. The one who whipped you so badly, right?"

"Right." Stifled sobs rattled her voice. "He never called me Crystal. Just Clearwater. Clearwater do this. Clearwater do that. I wanted to forget that name because it reminded me of him. But now that I have my mother, it'll remind me of her. And, by the way, Cynthia's not her real name. It's her undercover name. She's really Jade Clearwater, if she didn't change it."

"Jade. That's a gemstone. Fits nicely."

"I think so."

The roar of an engine drew my attention upward. Lights from the two-person glider hovered above, its lower thrusters blowing the treetops. Since I had given Cynthia, or Jade, our earbud frequency, we would be able to talk during the upcoming flight. "Are you ready up there, Jade Clearwater?" I asked.

She laughed. "So Crystal's been telling you our family secrets, has she?"

"Some of them. Maybe you can fill us in on what she doesn't know."

"Maybe. But right now, you two need to get off your lazy duffs and launch those rust buckets you call gliders." Her glider flew southward. "Follow me. That is, if you can keep up."

"Not a problem." I turned my glider's engine on, activated the lower thrusters, and took off. As I rose above the trees and turned, I spotted Crystal's glider, also rising. Seconds later, we were flying side by side, the lights on Jade's glider easily visible about thirty meters in front.

As we flew through the darkness, the three of us chatted. I wanted to learn new information about Jade and her undercover work, but she wanted to hear our stories and compare them to the legends spreading wildly through every star system. Apparently, we were more than just folk heroes. We had reach mythological status. Although many of the tales were accurate, they sometimes exaggerated our feats to absurd levels.

Time passed by as quickly as the kilometers underneath us. Crystal did most of the talking, which gave me a chance to scan for signals. Since Emerson was supposed to maintain complete silence, I didn't expect to hear from him, but he expected to hear from me.

Every few seconds, I sent an encoded message on a frequency he would be monitoring. It provided my current coordinates, so he would know my location and travel vector. Since only he could decode the message, no one could intercept it and gain any information.

As we drew within about thirty minutes of the refuge, an alarm beeped on my console. My scanner indicated another vessel behind us. "Crystal, did you get the alarm?"

"Yep. Something's back there, and it's gaining ground."

"The scanner on this glider doesn't tell me much, only that it's big. It can't be the Nine. I told Emerson to turn off everything except the comm receivers and that we would eventually find him."

"My scanner's more capable," Jade said. "The buggy behind us is an Alliance starship, and it's in weapons range."

"Can you tell if it locked its weapons on us?" I asked.

"Nope. My scanner's not *that* capable. But I went off course a bit a couple of times, and it kept following. We are definitely the mouse in that cat's stalking path."

"We can't lead it to the refuge. Where should we go?"

"I know a place where our size will be to our advantage. We can outmaneuver it."

"Lead the way."

Jade's glider steered hard to the left. Crystal and I veered in the same direction. When we straightened, our headlights illuminated a volcano about a minute away at our current speed.

"Mom," Crystal said, "are you planning to fly into that volcano?"

"Yep. That starship would be crazy to follow us, right?"

"Um … yeah. Crazy."

I tightened my grip on the yoke. Although an Alliance starship probably wouldn't fly into a volcano, it might shoot us out of the sky before we could escape into one.

"By the way," Jade said, "that volcano's cone collapsed. It's just a dormant caldera now. Cool enough to walk on if we had to. But I'm betting that starship's captain doesn't know the volcanoes around here very well. He'll think we're suicidal."

"Probably," Crystal said. "Let's do it."

With the glider's lights the only visual guide, Jade rose above the ragged cone and dove toward the flat expanse inside. Crystal and I flew in the same vector, trusting that Jade knew what she was doing.

I checked the console. The starship stayed on our tail, now only about three hundred meters to the rear. How long would it wait before firing? Even the cockiest captain wouldn't risk landing a ship that size in such a tight area. Of course, it was theoretically possible to land there, but with the surrounding jagged walls, it would be far from safe.

Jade landed without a problem. Crystal and I landed side by side behind her. "Go dark," I called as I flipped my lights off. "We don't want to be an easy target."

Now sitting in nearly complete blackness, surrounded by a broken wall that rose twenty meters above our landing zone, I twisted in my seat to look to the rear. Against a backdrop of stars, a dark silhouette rose slowly above the wall, clearly the shape and size of a Nebula series starship.

The huge ship shifted forward in our direction. The lower hull shattered the top of the wall, its thrusters sending the fragments flying everywhere. Some pelted our gliders, but they did no damage that I could detect.

As the ship descended into the caldera, its wings clipped the wall's sides, again scattering debris. Finally, it landed with a hefty thud that shook the floor and sent tremors into my glider and through my body. Then, its engines fell silent. Our gliders sat under one of its wings. Although we were safe from a photon torpedo attack, it could hit us with its lasers.

"It's just sitting there," Crystal said. "And it's too dark to read its insignia. What are we going to do?"

"Something stupid." I popped my hatch and climbed to the caldera floor.

Perdantus flitted to my shoulder. "Perhaps you should keep your distance. I will fly close and read the insignia."

"No need." I reached into the glider, opened the emergency tools compartment under the dashboard, and withdrew a small flashlight.

I flicked it on and shone the beam on the insignia. "It's the Nebula Nine!"

"What?" Crystal said. "Emerson wouldn't've flown it here. Who's the pilot? It couldn't be your father. He would've identified himself instead of scaring the snot out of us."

"I think I know what happened." After sliding the flashlight into my pocket, I rapped on the hull with a fist. "Emerson, this is Captain Megan Willis. You may now turn on outgoing transmissions."

"Acknowledged," Emerson said. "Outgoing transmissions are now active."

"Why didn't you stay put? I told you to turn everything off."

"I did exactly as you instructed. I turned everything off except my ability to scan for signals. When I received your position and vector signal, I decided to follow you because—"

"Wait. How can you say you did exactly as instructed? I didn't say you could restart your engines and follow me."

"You also did not say that I could not do so. I obeyed the instruction to shut down, but you did not include a length of shutdown time or a command to stay in that state. My programming, of course, assumes that any command without a specific endpoint should be regarded as nonending, but there are exception parameters that provide for my discretion."

"What parameters?"

"If the ship's captain and/or crew are in danger, I am able to override the assumption that your command was nonending."

"Are we in danger?"

"You *were* in danger. Another Nebula starship was following you from farther behind than I was. Its weapons were locked on you, so I intervened. When it detected that my weapons were locked on it, the ship broke off its pursuit."

I breathed a relieved sigh. "So you probably saved our lives."

"That is a reasonable conclusion, though I cannot be certain that the ship would have fired on you. At the very least, it was following your gliders with a readiness to do so."

"Turn on the external lights. We'll get these gliders loaded in the bay, put Mabel in the infirmary, and head to the refuge."

When the lights turned on, I blinked at the brightness. As my eyes adjusted, the scene came into view. The Nebula Nine sat on the caldera floor at an angle, one wing resting on the top of the surrounding wall. "Um … nice landing job, Emerson."

"I detect sarcasm. You and I both know that the landing was far from perfect. This was my second landing, and the tolerances were tighter than most. If you had seen my earlier landing, I think you would have been more impressed."

I laughed. "You're right, Emerson. This was definitely a tough spot to land." I slapped the hull. "Open the ramp and the glider bay doors. If we're being followed, we need to hustle out of here and decide where to go. We can't lead an Alliance ship to the refuge. We're not certain yet if they know where it is."

During the next few minutes, we docked the gliders and put Mabel in the infirmary. Apparently, the surgeon had retrieved the bullet and patched her up in spite of his plan to kill us all. Maybe he wanted to make a good show of it and manufacture an excuse to ask for blood donations.

When we finished, I sat in the captain's chair, Crystal took the first mate's seat, and Jade parked herself at the navigator's station, while Perdantus perched on the back of the weapons' station chair.

Jade tapped on her console's screen. "It'll take me a few minutes to get the hang of this menu system, but I'll figure it out. You'll need me to navigate us to a spot that's good for hiding this fabulous ship and close enough to the refuge to walk. We don't want to risk flying the gliders."

I turned toward her. "Keep up the flattery. Emerson will be sure to help you."

"I am not influenced by flattery," Emerson said, "but I do welcome truthful statements about this ship."

Jade ran a finger along the screen. "I found the local map, but the grid ends at a point about ten kilometers to each side. I'm sure this technologically advanced computer has the ability to see …" She drew her head back. "Oh. There it is. Thank you, Emerson."

I stifled a laugh. "Let me know when you have a route." As sleepiness suddenly invaded my brain, I yawned. "I wish I had time for a nap. We're probably safe here for now, but the kids at the refuge might not be."

"True," Jade said. "I'll have the route plotted in a minute. Sleep has to wait until this is all over."

"Let's hope that's soon." At my console, I turned on our engines. "Emerson, I'm going to fly without lights, just scanners. With all the volcanoes and other land masses around, that's going to take a lot of concentration, so please watch for Alliance vessels. I won't be able to."

"Acknowledged."

"I'll get everyone something to eat," Crystal said as she rose from her station.

"In your condition?" Jade asked. "You need to rest."

"No coddling allowed. Ask Megan. I whine a lot, but I hate being coddled." Crystal walked toward the galley. "And speaking of not being coddled, we sent the good food with the kids on the Dragon. I hope we have something decent left."

Jade raised a finger. "As long as you're being Miss No-coddling, check on Mabel if you don't mind."

"I will." Crystal's voice faded in the distance. "Once I start heating the food."

Emerson spoke from the ceiling speakers. "Captain, the camera and microphone in the infirmary were turned off manually."

"What? Only Mabel's in there. Can you run a video replay to see what she did?"

"I am reviewing it now. Mabel turned off the room lights, which then made it too dark to see her later actions, though I assume she is also the one who turned off the other devices. A tiny light beam appeared that likely guided her actions."

I shot to my feet. "I'll go—"

"I am faster," Perdantus said. "I will check the infirmary and return with a report. I know how to turn on the room's lights." He flew from the bridge.

I reseated myself, mentally following his path. What might Mabel be doing? I couldn't think of anything that wasn't sinister. I ached to go and check on her myself, but I needed to trust Perdantus, and we had to launch as soon as possible. We had already delayed far too long.

"I've got the vector plotted," Jade said. "We're good to go."

I looked at my console. "I see it. Pretty dicey path. Lots of zigs and zags. Why aren't we going straight to the refuge?"

"When we got within range, I sent a message to the refuge warning them that their location might be compromised. If it really is, they'll be ready. Anyway, I thought maybe we could lure the Alliance ship to chase us through an obstacle course."

"And hope it crashes?"

"Exactly."

I whistled. "Wow, Jade. That's really risky. I'm as likely to crash as their pilot is."

"Not from what I've heard. You're Megan Superstar Willis. You won't crash."

I blew through flapping lips. "You're listening to folk tales. Some of them are wild stretches."

"But some of them aren't, like the ones Crystal told us on the way over here. You, in a little glider, actually outmaneuvered a Nebula ship and flew into a tiny cave on an ice planet. Don't tell me you can't do a great feat like that again in this magnificent starship."

"Crystal didn't give the details. Actually, the glider hit something and tumbled into the cave, and I nearly froze to death inside, but if you want to call that a great feat, then go for it."

"You're too modest." Jade tapped on her screen. "Just start heading for the volcano gauntlet on the course I plotted. I'll lure the other ship closer."

"How?"

"Leave that to me. You'll be too busy flying dark, and we need to stay dark so you don't give the other captain a safe path to follow."

"But it has to be near morning by now, right? Keeping the ship dark won't do any good after Yama-Yami, the Delta star, rises."

Jade shrugged. "So you'll have to make the other ship crash as soon as you can."

"But I need to know—"

"Emerson, honey," Jade said, looking at the ceiling, "can you give me control of the glider bay doors?"

"If the captain permits, I can send control codes to your glider."

Jade looked at me. "Megan?"

I heaved an exasperated sigh. "Just give me a clue about what you're planning."

"I'm going to be an annoying fly that the charging bull will want to swat."

"But what will make him chase the Nine?"

"Considering the admiral's obsession with killing you, all I have to do is radio that ship's captain that you're on board this ship. Keep your shields down for now to make them think you don't know they're following you."

I sucked in a breath. "What? Are you out of your—"

"But I won't radio them until I lure the ship to the low elevation we'll need for him to run the gauntlet while chasing you. Otherwise, he'd try to shoot the Nine from high above."

"I realize that, but leaving our shields down is dangerous."

"Exactly. Well, I'd better scoot." Jade waved a hand as she hurried from the bridge, her voice fading as she called, "You're still in charge. If you don't want me to do this, lock the bay doors." She slid down a ladder and out of sight.

At that moment, Crystal walked in and set a tray covered with a glob of something unidentifiable and probably barely edible on my console. "Where'd my mother go?"

I rolled my eyes and spoke with a sarcastic tone. "She's taking her glider to lure that Nebula ship into chasing us while our shields are down."

Crystal slapped her forehead. "Claw of the dragon! What in the galaxy is she thinking?"

"She's thinking I can get the other ship to crash into something." I slid the tray to the side and pointed at the zigzagging route on my console screen. "Those jagged lines on both sides of our course are mountains. A couple of them are volcanoes. The lower our elevation, the tighter the squeeze between them. And there's a river running right down the middle that curves like a snake. If I can stay right over it, I might have a chance."

"Then you'd better not eat this crud." She took the tray. "I think there's already vomit in our future."

"I'm worried that the other ship will simply stay high and try to shoot us from above. The only reason for the captain to chase us low is to accept the challenge."

"Like, if you can do it, I can do it?"

"Exactly." Wanting to get my mind off the route ahead, I looked toward the ladder leading to the infirmary level. "Perdantus said he would check on Mabel and report to you. Apparently, she turned off the camera and microphone in the infirmary. Did you see him?"

"Nope. I'm on it." Crystal ran to the weapons room, grabbed a laser blaster, and hurried from the bridge, calling, "Make sure your buds are on!"

Just as I was about to respond, Jade's voice came through the ceiling speaker. "Did you cancel the mission? The bay doors won't open for me."

"That's because I didn't give Emerson the go-ahead yet." I looked at his console and heaved a resigned sigh. "Give Jade control of the glider bay doors."

"Acknowledged."

"There we go," Jade said. "You take the lead. If you arrive at the gauntlet early, just fly around near the beginning of it. I won't be long."

I rolled my eyes. Who was the captain of this ship, anyway? I engaged the thrusters and lifted the Nine off the caldera floor. When the ship reached a point about ten meters above the side walls, I shifted forward, flew into Jade's vector at a slow speed, and descended to the prescribed lower level. At this rate, I would arrive at the gauntlet in about twelve minutes, but could I concentrate on flying while I was distracted by what Mabel was doing? And why hadn't I heard from Perdantus?

"Megan!" Crystal shouted through my earbuds. "Mabel's gone!"

"Gone?"

"Right, as in not here in the infirmary."

"Do you see Perdantus?"

"No, I called him, but … Wait. I hear him chirping. Give me a second."

"Emerson," I said. "Conduct a weight displacement search. See if you can find Mabel."

"Search commencing."

"I've got Perdantus," Crystal said. "Someone stuffed him into a garbage bin and put a big book on the lid. He wouldn't've lasted long in there. Not enough air. Blazes! Another rhyme!"

"So Mabel's a spy for the Alliance?" I asked.

"Maybe she was in cahoots with the surgeon and the nurse."

"That would be nuts. She stayed in the room with the bomb."

"Good point. I guess she didn't know about the bomb, and the surgeon probably didn't know Mabel was on his side. She was in deep cover."

"We're just guessing. Maybe Emerson will find—"

"Search completed," Emerson said. "Although weight displacement searches are not always accurate, I do not believe Mabel is aboard the ship. All other scans indicate the same."

"Show me the camera view from the glider bay back when Jade opened the doors. Put it on my console."

My console screen cleared, the data windows replaced by a view of the glider bay. Jade climbed into her two-person glider, closed the hatch, and began pushing buttons. Soon, the bay doors opened, and she flew out.

Just as the doors started closing behind her, Mabel limped into view. Carrying what appeared to be a computer pad in her hand, she jumped through the opening to the ground outside. Then the doors closed completely.

"Crystal, Mabel jumped ship. She's in the caldera somewhere."

"With that injured leg," Crystal said, "I doubt she can climb out. I'll bet someone in the Alliance will pick her up."

"And I think she stole something." I glanced at Emerson's console. "Emerson, run that sequence back and magnify the pad Mabel was carrying. Max magnification."

When he did, I studied the screen. It looked like the same pad Jade told me to grab. "Emerson, did anyone upload that pad's data to you?"

"Negative."

I clenched a fist. "Blazes! Now we won't have a map to the glowsap mines."

"Calm yourself," Jade said through my earbuds. "I didn't memorize the map, but I have a good idea of where they are. Regarding Mabel, I'm not super surprised about her turning coat on us. Sometimes she took far better care of the admiral than she needed to. If I were doing it, I'd keep him alive, but I wouldn't mind making him suffer more. You know, something to upset his stomach or give him the hives."

"I guess you didn't see her in the caldera after she jumped out."

"Nope. But if she's waiting for the Alliance ship we've been tracking, I'm going to make sure she has to wait a long time. I'm already keeping it busy. My guess is that I'll arrive at the gauntlet in about ten minutes."

"Emerson, how long until dawn?" I asked. "I need to know when the pilot will be able to see us."

"Light from the Delta system's star will be noticeable in about three minutes. I estimate that the Nebula Nine will be visible to the pursuing ship in approximately five minutes."

"Five minutes! I must've lost track of time. Jade, they'll have a visual on us in five minutes. I'm showing eight minutes till the gauntlet at our current speed, super slow right now because of the curves ahead."

"I'll see what I can do to make them accelerate."

I studied the course and planned my maneuvers. Soon, Perdantus flew in and landed on the back of the first mate's chair. "That was quite a harrowing experience, but I did gain a bit of information from Mabel before she grabbed me and stuffed me into that malodorous bin."

Crystal walked in and stood behind me. "Good. He made it back here. He's pretty agitated about something."

"Go ahead, Perdantus," I said. "We're listening."

"When I arrived at the infirmary, I saw a thin beam of light, so I decided not to use the switch to turn on the overhead lights. In the glow of the beam, I could see that Mabel had a communications device that she inserted into her ear, similar to your earbuds, though a bit larger and with a protruding microphone stem. Have you seen one of those before?"

I nodded. "Older tech. Too big for stealth, but they have great range."

"That was my assumption. Since I hoped to hear her speak, I stayed silent and hopped closer to her. She told someone about our plans to gather our forces to rescue the children at the mines in the north and that you, Megan, are piloting this ship. Of course, I could not hear the replies coming into her ear, but I heard her say, 'Good. Then they won't find any children. Any living children, that is.' At that point, she saw me and grabbed me before I had a chance to fly away. If not for my claws and beak piercing her skin, I think she would have crushed me in her hand. Fortunately, she opted for the bin. Although the odor was horrific, at least I survived."

Crystal kicked the base of my chair. "Blazes times ten! It sounds like they're going to kill the kids if we don't find them in time."

"Right," I said. "Or maybe move the most valuable ones somewhere and kill the rest."

"I heard all of that," Jade said. "At least I won't have to convince them that Megan Willis is on board the Nine. I think this chase is about to get very interesting. Three minutes till the gauntlet. I'll be passing you in about two. They're at your altitude now, so it'll be game on before you know it."

"I'm going to accelerate a bit. That should incite them to chase me at a faster speed. Emerson, shields up. We can't wait any longer."

"Shields are going up," Emerson said. "You will have full protection in ten seconds."

"Everyone strap in."

Crystal sat in the first mate's chair and buckled while Perdantus flew from the bridge.

"Emerson," I said, "contact the enemy ship on the Alliance hailing frequency, audio only."

"I am hailing the ship." A short pause ensued. "The ship accepted the connection. You may speak when ready."

I tapped the microphone button. "Hello, Captain. How are you today?"

"Well, well, well," a woman said through the ceiling speakers. "If it isn't the cockiest little girl in the galaxy."

"This is *Captain* Megan Willis. Who are you?"

"*Captain* Josie Warren, but my name is immaterial. You are an enemy to the Alliance, and I, as the captain of the Nebula Four, am demanding that you land the stolen Nebula Nine immediately and surrender. Otherwise, I will have to destroy your ship and everyone in it."

I added a bit of sarcasm to my tone. "Surrender or die? You're not giving me any desirable options, but leave the channel open and let me think about it for a moment." I tapped the microphone off.

"The Nebula Four has locked its photon torpedoes on our ship," Emerson said.

"Understood." Keeping all external lights off, I looked at the front viewing window. In the light of dawn's earliest rays, we flew, still quite slowly, toward a small gap between two looming mountains. At ground level between them, a river rushed over protruding rocks, flinging water high into the air. Getting past all of these obstacles would take a miracle.

After whispering a quick prayer for safety, I pushed the throttle. "Here's your answer, Josie."

The Nine surged forward. My hands tight on the yoke, I descended to ten meters above the river and steered between the two mountains. The extended wings barely missed the mountains, and the gaps ahead were likely even narrower than this one.

Beyond the gap, the river bent to the left at nearly ninety degrees. I steered with the flow, making the Nine tilt precariously. Something thudded on the left side. I steered a few degrees back to the right. "Emerson, what happened? Any damage?"

"The left wing skimmed the river's surface and struck a rock, but the shields prevented any damage to the wing."

"Draw the wings in fifty percent. Our ride will be rougher, but I'll be able to fit into tighter spaces."

"Retracting the wings fifty percent."

As the wings retracted, the ship bucked harder and harder. With another pinch between two mountains coming up in about thirty seconds, I descended until the belly of the ship drew within two meters of the river.

Crystal ran an index finger along her screen. "Their front turrets are lighting up. I'm locking our rear ones on them."

"Fire when ready."

She grasped her yoke and set a finger on the firing button. "They fired theirs."

"Shields are at a hundred percent. They'll hold for now."

The torpedoes zipped past us, one on each side, and slammed into the river. The explosions sent mud splattering across our front window, blinding me.

I laughed. "Oh, so *that's* how you want to play this game, Josie." I looked at Crystal. "Do the same to them."

"I'm aiming for the river. Timing has to be perfect." Crystal pressed the button. "Eat mud, slavers!" After a couple of seconds, she shouted, "Woohoo! Got 'em! They're covered with mud!"

"Good job." Three seconds ahead, the river pooled in a small lake, visible only on our scanners. "Gotta get cleaned up." I sent the Nine lower and skimmed the lake's surface. Water sprayed across our front window, clearing most of the mud. I pulled the ship up. "Let's see if they'll take a bath or keep chasing us."

"Considering that they can't see right now," Crystal said as she looked at the rear camera view on her console, "I'm guessing bath."

"She can fly with scanners. I'm guessing she'll chase." I tapped the microphone icon. "Hey, *Captain*, how did that mud taste?" I cut the microphone off and pushed the throttle further. "Come and get us, Josie."

"She skipped the bath, and they're accelerating."

The next narrow gap stood five seconds away. It seemed much tighter than what the map showed. We would never make it flying horizontally. "Did she retract their wings?"

"She's doing it now."

"She's too late. Hang on tight." I tilted our ship ninety degrees and flew through the gap. The food tray toppled off the edge of the console and threw the crud across the floor. When we came out on the other side, I flipped us back and put the rear camera view on the front screen. The Nebula Four turned sideways to fit through, but the lower wing dug into the river and sent the ship into an out-of-control cartwheel.

"Emerson, extend the wings. Give me a front view." I pulled up and turned about in time to see the Nebula Four crash into the side of a mountain, hitting black lava rock and smashing into several pieces. As bodies flew from the tossing wreckage, I hovered close and scanned the area for survivors. Some of the people lay motionless, but a few struggled to rise. One woman stood knee deep near the edge of the river. Water dripping from her short dark hair and blood trickling from a slashed cheek, she glared at the Nine. Since she wore a captain's uniform, she had to be Josie. I could easily put her down with a laser blast, but I had learned long ago that I wouldn't be a kill-at-all-costs warrior.

I drifted closer and stopped, staying in hover mode as the Nine's thrusters blew water that reached Josie in a light spray. I switched my earbuds to the standard Alliance frequency and spoke in an even tone. "Captain Josie Warren, can you hear me?"

She touched her ear and nodded.

"You won't have to surrender or die, but I will extend the following options. Either leave your ship and your command, or go back to serving your child-slaving master. If you leave the Alliance, you will have your integrity. But if you return to aiding and abetting slavers, I will oppose you with every power at my command, and I will show you no more mercy."

I turned the Nine away. Taking a deep breath, I flew the ship higher, exiting the gauntlet. "Emerson, are any other Nebula ships in communication range?"

"Affirmative. Five other ships would be able to read a hailing signal from our location."

"How long would it take for the closest one to get here?"

"At a cruiser's normal atmospheric entry speed, approximately seven minutes."

"Send a distress signal with the Nebula Four's location."

"Acknowledged."

Jade's glider flew ahead of us and slowed to our speed. "Feeling sorry for them, Megan?" she asked through the Nine's speakers.

"I'm being humane. I know 'just following orders' is no excuse for torturing kids, but …" I shrugged. "I don't know. It just seems like the right thing to do."

"I understand. Stay on my tail and follow me to the refuge. And, by the way, you were truly amazing. You're living up to your reputation, and that's saying a lot."

"Thanks, but I couldn't've done it without Crystal. Your daughter is—"

"Equally amazing. I know. So is that adorable Emerson. By the way, my people at the refuge sent a message saying that there's no indication of an imminent attack. All scans are clear. So I think we can stop our worrying. I'll see you on the ground soon."

"Sounds good." As we followed the glider, my shot of adrenaline wore out. Exhaustion weighed my shoulders down. I stretched my arms and let out a big yawn. "We've been up all night. I'm pooped."

"Same here. And hungry." Crystal copied my motions, blinking. "I'm falling asleep. Food can wait."

"You both may take a nap," Emerson said. "I am able to follow the glider and land the ship. Protocol allows it because you both will be unavailable."

"Oh?" I rose from my seat. "So you're getting to like the landing business?"

"I need the practice. My previous landing was not acceptable."

"Thanks." I pulled my locket out from under my shirt, brushed the dirt off the back, and opened it. The dragon's eye emitted its usual glow. My father was still alive. "And can you send a message to my father through the Zeta stations? Use my usual encryption algorithm to make sure no one else sees it."

"Acknowledged."

I bypassed the scattered food and walked toward the sleeping quarters, Crystal following. "But I'm too dirty to go to bed. I hope we have enough water for two showers."

"We do," Emerson said, "if you each wash yourselves in under three minutes."

"As dirty as I am, that'll be a challenge, but we'll manage."

After we each took a shower in the allotted time, we put on clean Alliance uniforms and, after setting our weapons belts on the night table, flopped into my bed. I fell asleep immediately and dreamed of flying through that gauntlet again and again, crashing each time and resetting to the start like in a computer game.

When I restarted the gauntlet for about the tenth time, something sharp touched my shoulder. I blinked my eyes open. Perdantus stood at my side poking my shoulder with his beak.

"I apologize for interrupting your sleep, but I have been told that our need to act is growing more and more urgent."

Crystal and I sat up at the same time. As she rubbed her eyes with her knuckles, I yawned. "How long were we asleep?"

"Approximately three hours."

"That'll have to do."

"I will alert the others that you are coming." Perdantus flew from the room.

We got out of bed, strapped on our weapons belts, and walked toward the bridge. Along the way, we checked our laser blasters. They seemed to be charged and in working order.

When we arrived at the bridge, the front ramp lay open, allowing bright daylight to stream inside. Isaac sat at the physician's station and Ophelia at the navigator's console. Both smiled at us but said nothing.

Oliver, with Perdantus on his shoulder, stood next to Emerson's console, grinning. "Good morning, sleepyheads."

"And good morning to you, sir." I rubbed my stomach. "Is breakfast ready?"

"Yep." He nodded toward the floor. "I found a bunch of glop there with a tray next to it. It's in the galley."

"Thanks, I was saving that for you." I looked toward the ceiling. "Emerson, any update from my father or anyone else on Gamma Five?"

"Negative. Do you want me to send another request?"

"Not yet. We'll give them more time."

Oliver's brow creased. "We've been hailing Lyric's mother for quite a while. We got a report that the Alliance now has full control of the Gamma Five Zeta station. They're still letting transmissions through, but only if they're encrypted in a way they can read them."

"So Emerson's message to my father can't get through to him."

"Not likely."

"Breakfast is served." Jade's voice came from the direction of the galley. She walked in, carrying a tray loaded with food—scrambled eggs, meat strips, and slices of green fruit. She set the tray on Emerson's console and handed Crystal a fork and another to me. "Dig in. We don't have much time. We have to get back to the north before they move those kids."

"Or murder them." I pushed a fork under the eggs and scooped some into my mouth.

"Water." Oliver set a flask next to the tray. "Freshly filtered from the river. You wouldn't believe the sanctuary these kids have set up, complete with game birds, fruiting vines, and these huge rabbits that multiply like ... well ... like rabbits." He pointed at the tray. "That's rabbit bacon. I think it tastes like—"

"I am receiving an encrypted message on an emergency frequency," Emerson said. "I will read it to you when it is complete."

We all fell silent except for chewing sounds from Crystal and me.

"The message is complete. It says, 'I am sending the coordinates for two new glowsap mines. I was assigned to kill the children who were considered too weak or sick to be moved. Instead, I hid them in a secure location. I will send those coordinates as well. I took the computer pad because I had to show the Alliance something to prove I was still on their side. Since they were planning to move the children anyway, I knew the information on the pad would be outdated before you could get there. I will do all I can to help you from within the system. But please hurry. The kids I saved are vulnerable. They need to be rescued as soon as possible.'

"A series of coordinates follows the message," Emerson said. "I will plot them on a map."

Jade whistled. "So Mabel came through. She's really on our side."

I swallowed a mouthful of food. "I'd like to think so, but we'd better be careful. It could be a trap. I mean, some things still don't add up. If she wanted us to know her plan, why turn the camera and the lights off in the infirmary? Why grab Perdantus and stuff him in the bin?"

"Good questions," Oliver said. "We'll be on guard."

"Yep," Crystal said, "but we're not gonna let terrifying, mortal danger stop us, right?" She took a bite of rabbit meat and talked while chewing. "You know, this bunny bacon is pretty good."

A map appeared on our viewing window, showing topographic lines marked along with two red dots and a blue one. "The red points," Emerson said, are the two new mines. The blue point is where the rescued children are."

I studied the map. The closeness of the topographic lines to each other indicated that the children were next to a rapid change in elevation, like at the base of a cliff, which meant that they might be hiding in a cave. A flat area to the east of the location looked like a reasonable landing spot. I walked to the screen and pointed at the flat area. "Anyone know what's there?"

Isaac strode forward and joined me. "I've flown around that area a couple of times. I think it's a dry lake bed. At least it was dry the last time I saw it."

"Can we land the Nebula Nine and the gliders there?"

"There's enough room, if that's what you mean. Like most other places, there's lava rock. A lava flow might be the reason the lake's dry, and since the eruptions have quieted lately, it might have water now.

We had a couple of rainstorms in that area recently. Even if there is water, it shouldn't be very deep."

"Right," Crystal said. "With its landing feet, the Nine should be fine." She winced. "Blazes!"

"What's wrong?" Jade asked.

"Nothing." Crystal added a muttered, "Stupid rhymes." But I was probably the only one who could hear her.

"Crystal is right," I said. "We'll assume we can land the Nine there. It looks like about a kilometer's walk from the cave, and it's mostly downhill, but I don't know what the terrain is like between the two places." I glanced at Isaac. "Any idea?"

He nodded. "Really rough. If Mabel is telling the truth about where they are, she probably led them on a narrow trail from the west." He pointed at the map. "Here to here. It's between two ridges. We can land the gliders on the trail, but not the Nine. Any other place to land the Nine in that direction would be pretty far away."

"Then we'll ferry them in gliders to the Nine." I looked at Oliver. "Any idea how many two-person gliders we have available?"

Oliver pointed at Jade. "Hers and two others. I haven't introduced you to the two adult leaders here yet, but they each have a two-person glider. Vonda and Bastian are with them now talking about how to keep the kids in this refuge safe while the adults are gone on this new mission."

"Ask them to come in when they're ready. I would like to meet them."

"On my way." Oliver hustled down the ramp with Perdantus flying at his side. At the same moment, Vonda walked in. Dressed in a leather tunic and trousers and with her red hair long and braided, she looked far more elegant than she did the last time I had seen her, and a few centimeters taller as well.

I gave her a smile and continued talking about our plans. "Since we don't know how many kids there are, we can't guess how long it will take to shuttle them."

Isaac eyed the map while stroking his chin. "In good weather, I'd say fifteen minutes per shuttle run. Since we have three gliders, that's twelve kids per hour. Our intel says that the three mines enslaved about fifty kids." He looked at Ophelia. "Best guess on the number of kids they'd throw away?"

"Going from three mines down to two tells us they might also be trimming the number of kids by the same ratio, so let's guess fifteen to seventeen."

"So," Isaac said, "shuttling would take an hour and fifteen to an hour and a half. But that's in good weather. We're due for another storm, and it's been getting colder in the north lately. I wouldn't be surprised to see snow or ice with the next storm. And the way the barometric pressure has been dropping in that region, I'm expecting a big one."

23

"If a big storm's coming," I said, "we'll need towels, blankets, and extra clothes. We have some towels and blankets on the Nine, but no clothes that'll fit little kids." I looked at Vonda. "Any thoughts?"

She pointed at herself with a thumb. "Clothing is my specialty. One other girl and I have been making clothes for everyone nearly nonstop since you left. The kids just keep growing."

When she turned to leave, I called out, "Wait." I ran to her and gave her a hug. "You take care of those kids for me. You and Bastian. I'm counting on you."

She gave me the biggest smile I had ever seen on her face, her cheeks not as sunken as they were when I first saw her. "We will." She hustled down the ramp, calling, "I'll gather what we can spare."

When she turned out of sight, an adult couple, probably in their twenties, walked into view and strolled up the ramp hand in hand, both wearing full camo and combat boots. The man's wiry build and crew cut hair made him look like a fresh military recruit. The woman, on the other hand, with her lithe body and red hair in a lush ponytail, looked more like a fashion model for a military recruiting poster. Their expressions seemed pleasant enough, though they didn't smile as they stared straight at me.

Isaac whispered in my ear, "Miles and Dana. Married three years. You won't find anyone more passionate about stopping the slavers."

When they arrived, Miles dropped to a knee and took my hand in both of his. "It is a great honor to meet you, Captain Megan Willis. Your heroic reputation precedes you." He kissed the back of my hand. "I am Miles Ascot, at your service."

Not knowing how to react, I bowed my head. "It's a pleasure to meet you, Miles."

He rose and gestured toward the woman. "This is my wife, Dana Ascot."

Dana dipped her knee as if to curtsy, but the lack of a dress made the move seem awkward. "Megan Willis, I look forward to battling at your side to rescue the children, conquer the slavers, and destroy their ghastly business once and for all. We must purge the galaxy of this filth and never let it return."

I gave her a head bow as well. "I agree wholeheartedly."

Miles clapped his hands. "Excellent. We are ready to head north. Oliver is loading our weapons into our gliders as we speak. And he'll bring even more to stow on the Nine."

"What weapons do you have?" I asked.

"Oh, you're going to love this. We raided that Nebula ship you destroyed and took every weapon that survived the crash."

"Did any crew members survive?"

"Some. When we arrived, they fired at us with sidearms, but once we had killed several of them with laser blasts, they knew they were outgunned and fled like the vermin they are. We decided not to chase them down because we wanted to grab whatever weapons we could before their reinforcements showed up. We noticed another Alliance starship was on its way."

I drew a mental picture of the battle. Since the Four had wrecked in an enclosed valley, the crew members were sitting ducks. They had no chance.

"Is something wrong, Megan?" Dana asked, tilting her head. "You seem troubled."

"I'm always troubled when I hear about people dying."

Miles clenched a fist. "They're scoundrels. They all deserve to die. No mercy to child slavers."

"They do deserve to die, but I never celebrate death. I'm a liberator, not an executioner."

"Sometimes we have to execute the guilty to liberate the innocent." Miles waved a hand. "I know we have differing philosophies, but I'm sure we can put our differences aside and work for a common goal, the elimination of the slave-trafficking scourge."

I gave him a firm nod. "Once again, I agree wholeheartedly."

Oliver jogged up the ramp. "The weapons are loaded in the three gliders, and we put the gliders in the Nine's bay. We should be ready to go."

"How many crew members are coming?" I asked Miles. "And what weapons are in the gliders?"

Miles bowed his head. "I apologize. I've been presumptuous. As captain of the Nebula Nine, you definitely need to know who is part of this rescue mission and what weapons are on board. I will provide a quick summary." He looked toward the glider bay as if mentally counting the vehicles. "Each glider now has six portable bombs, so that's eighteen total. They have both remote-control detonators and timers, depending on which method we want to use when we blow up the mines."

Wanting to make sure that he was on my side, I peered into his eyes, trying to read his mind, but for some reason, he was blocking me, not a good sign. I needed another way to test him. "Miles, who'll be in charge of the remote-control units?"

"Dana and I each have half of the units. Why?"

"Put them in a box and bring it to me. I will issue them as they're needed."

Miles laughed under his breath. "It's not efficient to have one person in control of the units. What if something happens to you?"

"I have a first mate and other crew members who can take over that duty if necessary."

Miles pointed at himself, his voice getting louder. "*I* made those bombs, and *I* built the detonators. I'm not about to let a little girl from Alpha One—"

Dana nudged his ribs, shutting him up. "What he means to say is that we have fought this battle for years, and it's difficult to give command of our weapons to someone who is so new to the conflict. I'm sure you can understand, can't you?"

Warmth coursed through my ears. "I understand, but if those bombs are going to be on my ship, then I will be in control of them." I pointed toward the ramp. "Miles, if you want to continue your war against the slavers while staying in control of your bombs, then you can take them and go. With your passion and energy, I'm sure you can find another way to transport the bombs to where you need them."

Miles stared at me, his mouth hanging open. The guard on his mind finally dropped as words leaked through. *Whose side are you on?* Then he sealed the brain leak and spoke in a conciliatory tone. "I will do as you ask, Captain Willis. I've been in charge of my own actions ever since I started this quest. I guess I'm not used to taking orders. Considering your accomplishments, I should be more confident in your command. I apologize for my insolence."

I studied his countenance. My Starborn powers let me know he was certainly telling the truth. And now I understood his desire to block his thoughts. He probably had a lot of negative ones about me, but maybe now that was changing. He had passed my test.

I drew close and set a hand on each of his shoulders. "Miles, you keep the remotes. I hereby put you in command of the offensive part of the attack, and I will be in charge of the rescue mission at both the mines and Mabel's refuge. Simply put, you be you, and I'll be me. Execute whoever you need to execute, and I'll rescue whoever I need to rescue."

He stared at me for a long moment before firming his jaw. "Captain Willis, you won't regret putting your trust in me. I promise. Together we will end this scourge once and for all. So help me, Astral Dragon." He spun toward Dana. "Let's go to the glider bay. Not to disrespect Oliver in any way, but I want to personally inspect the bombs."

Oliver waved a hand. "No feelings of disrespect at all. I've never handled bombs like those before. I'm glad you're checking my work."

Miles lifted a finger. "To answer your earlier question about crew members, I have five men and a woman on my team. The woman is a top engineer who volunteered to check the Nine's engines to see if there is any way to add some power and speed. The men are ground soldiers who simply want to fight. I have complete confidence in all of them."

I gave him a nod. "Then they are welcome on this ship. Bring them aboard. Put your engineer in the engine room, two of your soldiers at the weapons stations on the bridge, and yourself, Dana, and Jade in the gliders with the other soldiers. We'll leave as soon as everyone's ready."

Smiling widely, Miles splayed his hand. "Five minutes." He looped his arm through Dana's, and the two hustled down the ramp.

Oliver whistled. "Megan, I thought for sure you had him pegged as an agent for the Alliance. Why the sudden change? Did you read his mind?"

I shook my head. "Not mind-reading. Lie detecting. He was being truthful. Miles and I aren't much alike, but he'll make a great sword while I stick to being more of a shield."

Isaac nodded. "Good decision. They have proven themselves many times over. They're good people."

"Then I'm sure they'll prove themselves again." I clapped my hands. "Everyone to their places. We have five minutes."

Crystal raised a finger. "I call navigator seat. Oliver gets shotgun."

"Shotgun's perfect." Oliver sat in the first mate's chair. "From what I heard, I missed a lot of action lately."

I sat in the captain's chair. "Never a dull moment."

Once everyone had arrived at their stations, including Isaac and Ophelia in observation chairs on the bridge, two of Miles's soldiers at the weapons consoles, and Jade, Miles, and Dana in the gliders with the other soldiers, I closed the ramp.

"Emerson," I called, "any enemy ships on the scanner?"

"Affirmative. Four are in orbit around Delta Ninety-five and one is in the vicinity of the Nebula Four wreckage, but none are in weapons range."

"They're waiting for us to make a move," Miles said through his glider's comm port.

"Then we'll make a move and see what they do about it. We'll have to go to the new mine locations first. Are those coordinates in the navigation system?"

"They are," Crystal said. "I plotted six vectors to the closer mine. Choose one whenever you're ready."

Ophelia spoke up from her seat. "Aren't we going to rescue the kids Mabel is hiding?"

"We will," I said. "But if we go there first, we'll have the kids on the Nine, and I don't want to take them into battle." As I reached for the button to engage the engines, a strange feeling made me pause. Although everyone else had prepared for this quest for months and years, I felt unprepared. For some reason, I knew that the next few hours might be some of the most important in my life, and I wasn't ready.

After taking a deep breath and praying for the right words, I opened the comms so everyone could hear me. "May God be with us as we take this journey to the northlands of this planet. We will encounter some of the vilest people in the galaxy, beasts who would enslave children for their own profit, from an admiral in the Alliance to a grunt with a gun who will claim that he's just following orders. All of them are guilty before God, the master of the universe who watches over children. That same God is now sending us as his mighty arm to conquer the beasts and rescue his little ones." I looked upward. "So now I ask for you, God, to watch over us. Give us success. And most of all, whether we live or die, help us rescue the children and take all of them safely home."

As echoes of *Amen* and *Hear, hear* came through the comms, I started the engines. "Let's go."

I lifted the Nine off the ground quickly and veered hard toward the north. Once I leveled the ship at a cruising altitude above the sparse clouds, I called out, "Engine room operator. State your name and give me a report."

"I am Lainie Smith. My former rank was lieutenant in the Alliance under Admiral Dwight Fairbanks on the Nebula One. I was on board the ship when you took control with your mother, and I'm really sorry. I had no idea that we were carrying dead children who had—"

"Lainie, no need to apologize. I really need to get the reports. We can talk later, all right?"

"Yes, Captain. Of course." She cleared her throat. "The engines are running at normal capacity, but I learned a technique on the Nebula One that should boost efficiency by about thirty percent. Permission to employ that technique."

"Permission granted."

After I checked in with the gliders and the soldiers at the weapons station, the Nebula Nine's engines began humming more smoothly. Apparently, Lainie had implemented the change.

"Captain," Emerson said. "The four Alliance ships have left their orbits. They appear to be heading toward the northern section of the planet."

"Already? How could they have learned about our movements so fast?"

"I do not have that information."

I sighed. "No. Of course you don't."

"Game's on," Miles said from his glider. "And our scanners indicate that the weather's rough near the pole, a storm moving southward toward the area. The only way to do this is for the gliders to take the lead. We can split up and see what the Alliance ships do to counter us. Since we can go where the big ships can't, we can avoid their fire."

"What kind of range does that two-seater have?" I asked.

"Fully fueled, about ten thousand kilometers. That's plenty. And, yes, all three are fueled."

"Okay. You three will draw the big ships away from the mines. While they're distracted, we'll zoom in and see if we can disarm the guards at the mines and take the kids. When we're all clear, we'll head to the refuge where the other kids are. Then you can go to the mines, destroy them with the bombs, and do what you will with the remaining slavers. Since we don't know if you'll be able to draw all the Alliance ships away from the battle, we'll have to be ready to change our plans on the fly."

"Captain," Miles said, his tone a bit uneasy. "If you don't mind, I would like to offer an alternative."

I imagined him speaking from the glider's cockpit. "Please do."

"Let's say you show up at the mines and begin disarming the guards and collecting the children. Immediately upon your arrival, the guards there will summon the Alliance ships to help them. Our gliders won't be able to keep them distracted long enough for you to complete your mission. If the Alliance ships show up while you're loading children, the result could be disastrous. I suggest that you allow my team to sneak into the mines first and place sonic devices that will kill the bees."

"Yes!" Crystal pumped a fist. "Buzz biters!"

"Exactly," Miles said. "Then after we herd the children into the caves to protect them, we can ambush the guards. Once we finish with them, you can come with the Nebula Nine to collect the kids, that is, after you collect the ones hiding in the other location."

"What about the Alliance ships?" I asked. "Won't they interfere with your ambush?"

"Not if they don't know about it. We'll send a remote-controlled, unmanned glider to distract them while we set the ambush."

I drew mental pictures of the scenario. Although a dozen things could go wrong, the plan had fewer flaws than mine did. "All right. We'll go with your plan."

"Thank you, Captain Willis."

"How should the timing work?" I asked.

"The gliders should deploy about a half hour out from the mines, then you'll fly the Nine on a route that'll make it look like you're going somewhere else. We'll have to hope they're not very smart."

"We should always assume they're smart."

"True," Miles said. "That's a good policy, but in my experience—"

"And what about your weather forecast? If we get a big storm, will the kids even be at the mines? Will everyone be holed up in a base camp somewhere that we don't know about?"

"That's another good point. We'll have to come up with a bad-weather option. We should brainstorm for a while."

"Brainstorm?" I repeated. "Over the comm system?"

"Right. How else would we do it? Do you want me to come up to the bridge?"

I imagined our words being transmitted through the airwaves, potentially being picked up by ears I didn't want to be listening. If Mabel really wasn't on our side, she could have planted a listening device that could send our conversation to the Alliance. Or maybe one of the other newcomers worked for the Alliance. I hadn't vetted all of them like I had Miles, a pretty stupid mistake. Obviously, I was too tired. I had to wake up and be smarter, be more like the pirate, that is, the freedom fighter, my father trained me to be.

"Megan?" Miles said. "Did you hear my question? Do you want me to come to the bridge?"

"No. Let me think about it first."

"Suit yourself. I'm game to lead the charge, but let me know if you change your mind."

"Will do." I turn the comms off. "Emerson. Shut down all external and internal microphones and transmitters. We're going silent."

"Acknowledged. All communications are now muted."

Oliver leaned close and whispered, "What are you thinking?"

I leaned close to him as I matched his whisper. "I'm thinking we need to do something unexpected, something that'll rock the Alliance back on its heels."

"Like what?"

"Come with me." I rose from my chair and turned toward Crystal. "You, too. On my six."

Crystal got up. "All right, Miss Mysterious."

"Steady as she goes, Emerson," I said as I walked toward the ladder. "No changes until I get back."

"Acknowledged."

Followed by Oliver and Crystal, I climbed down the ladder to the maintenance level and walked to the hovel where I lived when Captain Tillman first imprisoned me on the Nine, the cot I used to sleep on still anchored to the floor. I sat on it and patted the space on each side. When Oliver and Crystal sat next to me, I whispered as quietly as I could. "You two are the only people on board I'm sure I can count on to keep a secret. Everyone else could be compromised."

Oliver nodded, whispering as well. "I think you're right."

"Even my mother?" Crystal asked.

I patted her knee. "You're mother's probably fine. And maybe everyone is, but if we're going to do something that takes the Alliance by surprise, I can't risk that they'll hear about it. I'm concerned that someone, maybe Mabel, could've planted a communications relay device on the Nine. I mean, those Alliance ships dropped out of orbit faster than I would've thought possible."

"Mabel's the fink," Crystal said. "I mean, Perdantus wouldn't have suffocated in that bin, because I saw later that there was a small hole in it, but turning off the camera and the lights still stinks like dead fish to me."

"She might've been on a camera the Alliance could see," Oliver said, "so she had to put on a show for someone."

"No use speculating," I said. "I'm assuming we're broadcasting to someone, and we don't have time to search for a signal. I could ask Emerson to scan for one, but if I do, it'll give away that I know we're being monitored. I don't want them to know we're onto them."

Oliver lowered his whisper further. "What's your plan?"

"First, I'm assuming the Alliance knows that our targets are the coordinates for the supposed two new mines. I'm betting they aren't real because it's not that easy to establish new mines. After all, you need the right kind of cave, and you have to convince the bramble bees to use it. And, as you know, it takes a while before there's enough sap to mine."

"So instead of us ambushing them," Oliver said, "they're ambushing us."

"Exactly, and we should make it look like we're falling for the trap. The gliders will head that way to draw the ships to their trap, but then our team will double back to the original three mines. That's where the kids probably are, and they won't be well guarded. Of course, when the gliders don't show up at the ambush, their forces will hurry back to the original mines, so our people will have to work fast to collect the kids."

"What if one of the glider pilots is the source of our intel leaks?" Oliver asked. "Won't they just update the Alliance?"

"Not likely," I said. "Our three glider pilots are Crystal's mother, Miles, and Dana. They've probably risked their lives for our cause as much as we have. If we can't trust them, we can't trust anyone."

Crystal nodded. "Right. I watched all three closely, and my lie detector says they're good to go. And not just because Jade's my mother. They really are on our side."

"That's good enough for me. Now that we decided we can trust our pilots, I'm going to send the new instructions to the gliders on the sly. No one else will know. Whether our leak is from a device Mabel put on the ship, or if it's one of the new crew members we brought on board, the plan should stay secure. I'm not even going to let Emerson know, in case someone put a bug in his system."

"Sounds good," Oliver said. "But what about the storm that might hit?"

"That's a good reason for the second part of our plan, and it should work storm or no storm." I kept my whisper as low as possible. "I know exactly where to find Admiral Fairbanks. We should go there and take him prisoner."

They both stared at me, unblinking. After a silent moment, Crystal set a palm against my forehead. "No fever."

I batted her hand away. "I'm serious. If we hold Fairbanks hostage, we can make whatever demands we want. Free the kids. Destroy the mines. Leave the planet."

"*If,*" Oliver said. "And it's a huge if. You said there's a tower signal that drains Starborn powers. And since they know that we know where it is, they'll be guarding that place like a fortress, especially since they also know that we're heading into the area."

I lifted a finger. "One photon torpedo from the Nine will take care of the tower. We'll send the gliders in advance to the mines to make it look like they're our targets. When the Alliance sends its resources to the mines, that should leave Fairbanks relatively unguarded. Between the Nine's firepower and our Starborn powers, we should be able to take him."

Crystal pointed at me. "You mean *your* Starborn powers. Mine won't do squat. Telling if someone's lying or not isn't going to help in a dangerous raid. And if you get blown to bits by a torpedo, I don't think Oliver's healing power is going to do much. He's not a jigsaw puzzle putter togetherer, or whatever you call it."

"There's more to the plan." I set a hand on each of them and drew them closer. "Here's what we're going to do."

When Oliver, Crystal, and I returned to the bridge, we hurried to our seats. I reopened the comms throughout the ship and spoke with a strong voice. "Attention everyone, we have a change of plans. We're going to deploy the gliders now instead of right before our attack."

"Got it," Miles said. "No storm like a brainstorm."

I nodded. That was Miles's way of letting me know that he got our secret update. "Good. Then launch now."

"Bay doors are already opening. We'll be off in four ... three ... two ... one ..."

I imagined the wind whistling through the glider bay as they took off. They were definitely taking on a huge amount of danger, now only minutes in front of them.

"We are on our way," Dana said. "Doors are now closing behind us."

I spun in my chair toward Crystal. "Do you have them on the monitor?"

"Yep." She ran a finger along the screen. "They're on the planned vector, but if they follow the plan, their signals should go off in a few ... Never mind. They turned them off. They're now in stealth mode."

Isaac rose and looked over Crystal's shoulder. "How closely are we going to follow them?"

"Not close at all," I said. "We want them to sneak in unnoticed. If we follow close, we'll be like a glowing sign pointing at them." I spun toward my console. Isaac's question fed the nagging thoughts in my mind. Could he be the rat among us? But it was an honest question. I couldn't let it bother me. "Crystal, I see you replaced the vectors with two new ones. I like the second one. I realize that it takes us out of the gliders' comm range, but that should confuse the enemy."

"That's why I offered it. Nothing like swinging wide and coming in from a new angle to catch the enemy off guard."

"We'll do it." I grasped the yoke, steered the Nine into the new vector, and turned the autopilot on. "We'll be there in ten minutes." I rose and walked straight to the two men at the weapons station. Each wore camo and sat on a stool in front of a console next to Crystal. "Are the photon torpedoes loaded and ready to fire?"

One of the men, a thirtyish redhead, gave me a nod. "The readings show that they are loaded and online."

"Did you physically check them yourself?" I asked.

He blinked. "Well ... no. I thought—"

"When it comes to weapons, never trust the data. I've seen false readings before. And a mistake can cost everyone their lives."

Just as the man began to rise, the other, a sixty-something man with a gray comb-over set a hand on his shoulder and pushed him back down. "I saw the torpedoes myself. Everything's ready."

I looked into his eyes. Although I wasn't highly experienced with the lie-detecting power, something seemed wrong with his answer. I tried to probe his mind, but, like with Miles, he had blocked his thoughts. I glanced at Crystal. She gave me a quick shake of the head to let me know this man was lying. Now that I knew who the leak was, I could use that to our advantage.

"Is something wrong?" the man said. "You're looking at me like you don't trust me."

I shook my head as if throwing off a trance. "Sorry. I've got a lot on my mind. Thank you for checking on the photon torpedoes. That's a relief."

"I understand. Battles are always an ugly business. I imagine we're all pretty nervous."

"What's your name?" I asked.

"Fortner. Kyle Fortner."

I looked at the younger man. "And yours?"

"Prince. Stanley Prince."

"Keep up the good work, gentlemen." I set a hand on my stomach. "Speaking of nervous, I should settle the churning." I strode toward the galley. "I'll be back before we get to the target." When I had walked out of sight, I broke into a trot and rushed into Dirk's old room. I pulled the panel off a wall that covered the channels leading throughout the ship. I hustled inside and scurried to the downward shaft that led to the torpedo room.

Pressing my hands against the sides to keep from dropping too fast, I lowered myself down the shaft. When I arrived, I slid the panel open, stepped out into the room, and located the vertical stack of photon torpedoes, ready to drop into the horizontal tubes one after the other as they fired through the turret at the end of the tubes.

On top of one of the tubes, I slid the access panel open and looked inside. The chamber was empty. I stepped over to the stack and found the bottom torpedo wedged in the opening, unable to drop—sabotage. I reached under the stack and wiggled the torpedo until it dropped into place, and the others above it slid down a notch. In that torpedo's wedged position, if anyone had armed it, it would have exploded in the room, possibly sending the Nine crashing to the ground.

I walked five paces across the room to the other tube and found the same problem, a wedged torpedo—more sabotage. After unjamming that one, I opened the top access panel for the second tube and felt around for the electronic eye that detected the presence of the torpedo. Something covered it.

Scratching with a fingernail, I peeled off a strip of tape and stuffed it into my pocket. That tape made it look like a torpedo was always in the tube. I stepped back to the first tube and peeled a similar strip of tape off its eye.

I clenched it in a fist. I wanted so badly to send Fortner flying out the ejection chute, but I had to cool my anger and figure out how to use him against the Alliance.

After hustling out of the room using the standard path instead of the channels, I climbed the ladder to the bridge level and walked toward my seat, watching Fortner out of the corner of my eye. Still seated on his stool, he was also watching me with a skeptical stare.

I stopped and looked at him. "Is something wrong?"

Fortner waved a hand. "No, no. I was just curious why you went out one way and came back another. I'm not familiar enough with the ship's layout to know about any shortcuts."

"Yes, all the paths can be a bit confusing, but since you checked on the torpedoes, you obviously know how to get to and from that room."

He nodded. "Of course."

"That's good. I was going to double check the torpedoes to be certain, but I paused, thinking that I would be showing lack of faith in you. Anyway, I went the long route to get there because I was heading for the galley, and I came back the usual way."

He shifted on his stool. "Thanks for deciding to trust me."

Crystal called out, "Two minutes until we're in range of the target, Captain."

"Good." I sat in my seat and tapped on the console screen's torpedo icon. "I'm shifting weapons control to my station. Put the target on the front screen."

The tower at the admiral's mansion appeared, still a few kilometers away. I pulled up the targeting grid and superimposed it over the tower. A wide red circle on the grid shrank as it closed in on the tower. "Oliver, take the yoke and pull up as soon as I shoot."

"Aye, aye, Captain."

Fortner rose from his stool, a gun in hand. He strode toward me, aiming it at my head. "Don't fire the torpedoes."

I turned toward him. "Are you out of your mind, Fortner?"

"I'm not suicidal. If you arm the torpedoes, we're all dead."

I gave him a mock gasp. "Why would that be?"

He set his finger against the trigger. "I rigged them to blow."

"Oh? Did you have an escape plan?"

He nodded. "I have a parachute."

Just as I flexed my hand to mentally grab the gun, Crystal leaped up from her seat and jogged toward him. "Fortner! Look at me."

When he turned toward her, she pointed at her eyes. "Look deeply. What do you see?"

He drew his head back. "Uh … I see … light."

"Good. Swim in those pools of light. Relax and enjoy. Do you like it?"

He stared as if in a trance. "Yes. It's so soothing."

As I gently took the gun out of his hand, Crystal continued. "You've been talking to people in the Alliance, haven't you?"

He murmured, "Yes."

"Do you have a communications device with you right now?"

"Yes."

"Is it turned on?"

"No."

"Where is it?"

"In my pocket."

She pushed a hand into his pocket and withdrew an earbud similar to the one Perdantus had seen in Mabel's possession. She set it in his hand. "Put it in your ear. Tell your Alliance contact that we called off the mission because of the storm that's coming. There will be no attack today. Say you'll contact them again when you have more information."

He pressed a button on the bud, inserted it in his ear, and spoke in monotone. "This is Kyle Fortner. The rebels have called off the attack because a storm's coming. I'll contact you again when I know more."

Crystal took the bud out of his ear, turned it off, and slid it into her pocket.

A beep sounded from my console. The tower was now in range. I swung toward the front, centered the tower in the grid, and fired both torpedoes. "They're away!"

Oliver pulled the Nine up hard. I switched the viewing window to the rear camera. The two torpedoes zoomed toward the tower in a trail of brilliant radiance. The moment they struck the base, a huge explosion of sparks shrouded the entire tower. When they cleared, pieces of the tower lay strewn all across the valley, including some on the roof of the mansion.

I leaped up from my seat and pointed at Isaac. "Contact our gliders. Tell them to check the original three mines to be sure, but I'm guessing now that Mabel was telling the truth. Fortner was our rat. The two new mines are probably the real ones. Also tell them that the Alliance guards are likely standing down because of the message that we're canceling the mission, so if Miles and company approach in stealth, they might not get any resistance."

Isaac nodded. "I'm on it."

"Oliver, land the Nine as close as you can to the mansion. We're going in."

He steered the ship into a landing arc. "One minute till we touch down."

Setting my feet to ride the angling ship, I pushed the gun against Fortner's back. "Crystal, you can let him go now."

She exhaled. "I was worried it wouldn't work since we were getting close to the tower." She snapped her fingers in front of his eyes. "Time to wake up, you treacherous rat."

He blinked. "What happened?"

I pressed the gun barrel harder into his back. "Don't say another word. Just raise your hands, walk to your station, and sit."

When he did, I handed the gun to Ophelia, not sure yet if I could trust Prince. "When we land, take them to the brig. Emerson will lock the cells for you."

Staying in her seat, she aimed the gun at them. "With pleasure."

I gave Prince a long stare. "Don't worry. I'll check back with you later to confirm your guilt or innocence."

He nodded. "That's fine. I understand."

"Ten seconds to landing," Oliver said. "It's windy near the ground, so buckle up."

I hustled to my chair, strapped in, and shifted the front window to its normal view. "Ready."

As Oliver lowered the Nine, a wind gust blew us hard to the right. He corrected expertly and landed only twenty meters or so from the mansion.

The moment he shut the engine down, I pressed the button to lower the ramp. As it opened, I pulled my laser blaster from its holster. "Okay, don't contact me unless it's an emergency. Everyone maintain your positions except for Crystal and Oliver. You two come with me."

I jogged down the ramp. When I came out into the open air, a gust of cold wind blew from the north, nearly knocking me off my feet. I ran to the mansion, blasting the cameras with the laser gun as I drew close. Three men in Alliance uniforms burst out the back door and aimed their guns at me. "Drop your weapon!" the one in the middle barked.

I laid the gun on the ground and raised my hands, glancing at the ship as Oliver and Crystal tiptoed down the ramp.

While one of the guards kept his gun aimed at me, the other two holstered theirs and walked toward me. When they each grabbed one of my wrists, the guard with the gun took a step closer. "What are you doing here?"

I raised my voice to compete with the sound of the wind. "I am here to rescue children from slavers and those who protect the slavers, vermin like you who are just following orders, even though those orders come from rats who torture kids."

He nodded slowly. "Okay. I recognize you now. You're Megan Willis, the rebel pirate. I've heard that you're on a wild-eyed quest to slay dragons that don't exist. You really are as insane as the admiral says you are."

Heat roared along my skin. This protector of slavers deserved the same punishment the slavers would soon get. "If by rebel pirate you mean someone who is rebelling against enslaving and torturing children, then, sure, I'm a rebel pirate."

He smiled. "Well, aren't you the feisty one? You'd better watch your mouth. The admiral said you should be shot on sight, and I'm willing to do that if you give me any trouble."

"Shot on sight? Too bad you're about to lose yours." I mentally poked his eyeballs as hard as I could.

He dropped the gun and screamed, covering his eyes with his hands. I jerked free from the other two guards, mentally swiped their guns into my grasp, one in each hand. I stepped back and aimed the guns at them. "Pull your radios from your belts and drop them."

When they obeyed, I nodded toward the north. "Start walking, and don't come back. Take your blind friend with you. And drop his radio as well."

"A storm's coming," one of them said, shivering. "My coat's in the house."

I laid the sarcasm on thickly. "I really feel bad about that, but I can't let you go inside where you might try to protect that child-trafficking monster. Maybe if you thought about the consequences of your evil choices beforehand like good little boys, you wouldn't be in this predicament." I waved the guns. "Now go. Quietly. One word, and you'll be breathing through a new hole in your head."

They turned toward the north and hustled away, supporting the wounded man between them.

I waved at Crystal and Oliver. They rushed to join me. "On my six," I whispered. "Once I make sure the area is clear, the rest is up to you."

When they nodded, I opened the door the guards had exited and walked through the dining room to the vacant security area. Three of the monitors showed only static, likely the feeds from the cameras I shot.

I crept to the interior door leading to the room where Admiral Fairbanks was when I visited earlier, opened it slowly, and peeked in. He still lay partially upright in the hospital bed, wires running to the speaker box like before, but I couldn't see an IV this time. Since his eyes were closed, he was probably asleep.

"All clear," I whispered as I opened the door the rest of the way. "Wake him up if he doesn't wake up on his own. We don't have time to wait. Be listening to your earbuds for any extra questions I might want you to ask him."

Crystal walked through, then Oliver, while I stayed behind and listened, careful to stay out of sight. Crystal spoke first, her tone friendly. "Admiral Fairbanks, wake up. I have an important message for you."

A grunt from Fairbanks reached my ears. "Who are you?" he asked through the voice box.

"My name is Crystal Clearwater. You probably don't recognize my name, but you might know the boy's. He is Oliver Tillman."

"I do. The son of the captain of the Nebula Nine before it was hijacked by Megan Willis, the notorious pirate. He does favor his father."

"Um ... I guess so," Crystal said. "I never met his father. Anyway, I have a message to deliver to you. It's from—"

"How did you get past my guards?" Fairbanks asked.

I nodded. We anticipated this question. How he would react to Crystal's answer was less predictable and could force her to opt for Plan B.

"A member of our crew disarmed them and sent them packing," Crystal said. "You're alone and defenseless."

"Is that so? Well, Miss Clearwater, maybe I'm not as defenseless as you think. But, be that as it may, what is the message?"

"We come bearing a wonderful gift. Oliver, here, is a Starborn. Have you heard of them?"

"Of course. My wife and daughter searched for the source of their power for years, and they were getting close, but Megan killed them both. Because of her, I am now bedridden and without a family."

I inhaled and slowly let the breath out. Crystal and Oliver had to execute our plan carefully.

"Well," Crystal continued, "Oliver has healing power, and he is offering to heal you."

"Out of the kindness of his heart? I doubt it. What do you want in return?"

"Not much, really. We know you have a kill switch. If you die, everyone on Alpha One will die with you. We don't know if it's a bomb or something else. We just want to keep you from killing billions of people."

"Actually, it's not a bomb, and the kill switch will activate a chain reaction that will wipe out not only Alpha One, but also a planet in each of the Beta, Gamma, Delta, Epsilon, and Zeta systems."

"Oh," Crystal said, "I see. Staying alive is very important to you, as it should be, and it's also important to everyone else. That's why Oliver wants to heal you. We don't want you to die and trigger the destruction. We have friends and relatives on some of those planets."

"All right. I can believe that."

Crystal's bare whisper came through my bud. "So far, he's telling the truth." She cleared her throat. "But here's the part that'll be a lot harder for you to agree to. Oliver's really good at healing easy stuff, like cuts and bruises, but when it comes to burns like yours, he needs to be energized by what we've been calling a dynamo power."

"A power enhancer. I understand. My wife theorized a catalyst, so I have no problem believing that."

Knowing Crystal wouldn't want to ask for a definition, I whispered rapid fire. "A catalyst is a person or a substance outside of a process that makes the process happen or makes it stronger. I'm a catalyst for you and Oliver. Same concept as a dynamo."

"Your wife was right," Crystal continued, "but the part you won't like is that Megan is the catalyst. She gives Oliver extra power. So, if you want to be healed, you'll have to let her be a part of the healing."

Silence ensued. I ached to see the admiral's expression, but I could imagine it—a red-faced scowl that twisted his scars into a hideous mask. Although I expected a fierce comeback, his words carried a different flavor.

"So Megan sent you here, I assume."

"Yes," Oliver said, taking over the conversation, as planned. "She doesn't want you to die. You might remember that she could've shot you when you were standing on top of the Nebula One, but she didn't. She spared your life."

"I remember. She was the reason I was standing there with the inferno blazing at my feet, so I give her no credit for mercy. I noticed that she made no effort to rescue me. She merely delivered me to a more painful existence, a state of suffering that she can't even imagine. I would have been better off if she had blown me to pieces with a torpedo."

"But then the kill switch would've been activated."

I cringed. Not a good response from Oliver. The admiral's retort would set us back.

"Did she know about the kill switch then?" Fairbanks asked.

I nodded. Exactly as I thought. Oliver would have to think fast to regain the negotiation advantage.

"No," Oliver said. "Maybe you don't think Megan showed you mercy, but Megan was trying to. While she didn't know about the kill switch, she also didn't know you would fall into the fire. She hoped you would be able to get off safely. I know, because I was there. But she sent me here to show you as much mercy as I can, because she really does care. You don't have to agree to anything. Just let me heal you as much as I can. If you don't want more, we'll just walk out of here and not bother you again."

I smiled. Oliver recovered brilliantly.

"All right," Fairbanks said. "Let's see what you can do."

"I'm going to cover your eyes with my hand, if that's okay."

"Go ahead."

Knowing this would take a while, I whispered, "Call me if you need me." I tiptoed out of the house into the cold wind and ran up the Nine's ramp. Once inside, I looked around at the worried faces of my crew at their stations on the bridge. "Is something wrong?"

Isaac nodded. "We can't find the Alliance ships on any scanner. It's like they disappeared. And Miles reported that Mabel was telling the truth about the new mine locations, but they weren't mines at all. Just shallow caves where they stowed the kids. They're tired and hungry, but otherwise fine. Since they didn't have anywhere else to go, they just stayed there because it was getting cold."

"Captain," Emerson said, "I detected a flying vessel that landed nearby. It has not hailed us, so I have no way of knowing its intent. I do know that it is a two-person passenger glider with no mounted weapons."

"How far away did it land?"

"About point five kilometers."

"Okay. Probably a spy glider. The passengers will want to report to the starships that the Nine is here. With the tower down, they can't use it as a transmitter, but they're close enough to contact them with a direct connection."

"Then the glider is a danger," Isaac said. "The Alliance will soon know our position."

I nodded. "Emerson, let me know if the glider moves or sends any communications. If it does, we'll have to do something about it."

"Acknowledged."

"Back to your update," I said. "Is there any other information?"

Ophelia raised a hand. "Oh, yes. Much more. The original three mines are abandoned, like Isaac told you, and none of the mines, either old or new, were guarded, so we're wondering if the Alliance is just giving up on the operation here. Why else would the ships just leave?"

"A great question," Isaac said, "and there's more. Some younger and weaker kids are in the place Mabel said they would be, so the gliders need the Nine to come so the kids can be shuttled, like we talked about. But we've been waiting to confirm that we'd be coming to help soon, because you told us not to contact you unless it's an emergency. Anyway, I was just about to call you because the storm is closing in. The kids will be in an emergency situation soon."

"You made the right decisions, but something's bothering me. Fairbanks brought six starships to this planet for a reason. If he was going to abandon the operation and let us collect all the kids, summoning the ships here doesn't make sense."

"Maybe he doesn't care so much about the glowsap mines because he has more money than he knows what to do with." Isaac pointed at me. "He just wants you."

I looked back at the mansion, visible past the open ramp. Only three guards were stationed there to watch the richest man in the galaxy. Was this whole thing a setup? "I didn't think the admiral would be the bait for his own trap to catch me, but here he is."

"How can it be a trap?" Isaac asked. "Like I said, the other ships aren't showing up on Emerson's scanners."

"No. They pulled back for a reason. Fairbanks wants me to send the Nine to pick up the kids. He knows I won't let them freeze to death. That way, if I go with you, he'll send the ships to kill me. If I stay here to deal with him, I'll be left at his outpost without a ship."

"So what are you going to do?"

"I have to stay here and finish this plan. He's still the ultimate leverage. If I have him, I'll be able to control any negotiations."

"But when we go after the kids, won't the ships show up to stop us even if you aren't with us?"

"It's hard to say. My guess is that some of the ships will attack you on the Nine, and some will probably come here to neutralize me."

"But if you stay here," Isaac said, "and the ships attack us, who'll be our captain? We don't know enough to fly this ship into battle."

A new voice entered the conversation. "I will be your captain."

I spun toward the source. A woman and a man, each dressed in an Alliance uniform, complete with a helmet, marched up the ramp. When they stopped two steps away, they took their helmets off. I recognized the woman immediately—Captain Josie Warren. With no belt around her slim waist, she appeared to be unarmed. The man, however, was unfamiliar. He, too, was unarmed.

"Captain Warren," I said, intentionally giving her a suspicious stare. "Why do you want to help us?"

"It's a long story, but I'll give you a summary. When our rescue ship picked us up, I reported to the captain. He told me that Admiral Fairbanks was using child slaves to lure you into a trap. Not exactly a noble strategy. Combine that revelation with you sparing my life and the lives of my surviving crew members, I finally came to my senses. I realized that I was on the wrong side of this battle. I made an excuse to go back to my wrecked ship, and I escaped with this gentleman." She gestured toward the man.

He bowed his head. "I am Ensign Tobias Weston. I am … I mean, I was the head of engineering on the Nebula Four. My uncle, a man you might remember from the Nebula One, was head of security on that ship."

I nodded. "I knew a Weston. I didn't know his first name, though."

"Dominick. He sent me a message before the admiral killed him, telling me about you and your quest. Ever since that day, I have looked forward to a time that I could join your efforts. And now is that time. I am ashamed to say that I have been too cowardly to do anything before, but now I hope you will accept my help."

Captain Warren extended a hand. "We hereby surrender to you, Captain Megan Willis. Feel free to put us in the brig, but I think we can be more useful as your crewmates, I as surrogate captain and Weston as an engineer. I know the details of the Alliance plans, and Weston can send shutdown codes to every ship to stop them."

"That sounds great." I shook her hand. "What are the details?"

"Like I mentioned, Admiral Fairbanks lured you to this outpost. The first time you came, he didn't expect you so soon, so you escaped. This time, however, he was ready for you. The five remaining starships, including one that came to the Nebula Four's crash site, are nearby, on the ground and undetectable. If you stay here while the Nebula Nine goes into battle, three starships will attempt to destroy the Nine while the other two come here to kill you. If you were to go with the Nine, all five ships would join forces to destroy the Nine and you with it. The admiral is not taking any chances since he knows how powerful you've become."

I felt my mouth drop open. Since every word she spoke passed my lie-detector test and they agreed with my own guesses, I didn't need to read her mind. "Thank you, Captain Warren and Ensign Weston. I accept your surrender and your service." I turned toward Emerson's console. "Emerson, do you have their voice prints in the database?"

"Affirmative."

"Josie Warren is now acting captain of the Nebula Nine. Only I will outrank her. Ensign Weston is now head of engineering. Give him access to all security commands. He will join Lainey in the engine room."

"Acknowledged."

I looked at Isaac. "Leave the three ground rovers for us. I'll have to figure out a way to transport Fairbanks once I take him prisoner."

"We brought a glider," Captain Warren said. "It has two seats. I landed near the edge of the woods up the slope to the west."

"That'll work, but I might still need the rovers." I patted her on the back. "May God be with all of you."

"And with you."

I hustled down the ramp and hurried into the mansion, listening to the ramp rise behind me. When I arrived at the interior door, I marched straight into the admiral's room. Oliver still had a hand over the admiral's eyes and another on his throat, apparently trying to heal the scars that made him unable to speak.

I waited for the takeoff sounds of the Nine to fade before I spoke. "That's enough," I said as I drew closer. "Let's see how he feels."

Oliver lifted his hands. "I was able to heal some of the scars. Maybe half. The others are really deep. They won't respond."

When Fairbanks saw me, his expression stayed stoic. "Welcome, Megan," he said through the voice box. "I've been expecting you."

26

"I know. In fact, there's a lot I know that you don't know, but I won't go into that now." I flipped the voice box's power switch off. "Tell me how you feel."

He cleared his throat and spoke with a gravelly voice. "It seems that I am much better, thanks to Oliver Tillman. I still have a lot of pain, but at least I can talk on my own now."

"I suppose some people would call that good news."

Fairbanks frowned. "There is no need for such dark humor at my expense. I am grateful for the partial healing, and I assume you want to bargain with me so I can appeal for a full healing."

"Bargain? No. Demand? Yes. I demand that you disable your kill switch. Only then will I *consider* giving Oliver the boost he needs to heal you completely."

"Well ..." He began peeling the electrodes off his head, each removal making him wince. "Without the kill switch, you have no reason to keep me alive. It's my only leverage."

"You're lying," Crystal said. Then she covered her mouth. "Oops. Sorry, Megan. You probably already knew that."

"I noticed, but feel free to give me a heads up anytime. You're more experienced than I am."

"So you think I lied?" Fairbanks asked as he peeled away the final electrode and tossed it to the side. "What was the lie?"

"The kill switch isn't your only leverage," I said. "You've also arranged to send multiple starships here to capture me."

"Actually, I don't intend to capture you." A sinister smile bent his lips. "I intend to kill you."

"Yeah, well, good luck with that. At this moment, the Nebula Nine is disabling your ships with shutdown codes and picking up all the children you enslaved. In short, we're destroying your evil business."

"It seems you have an advantage over me. You have a lie detector, and I don't, so I can't verify the truth of your statements. But one thing I do have that you don't. Against you, it is the ultimate leverage."

When he paused for effect, I crossed my arms. "Okay. I'll bite. What is it?"

"A recording I asked for. It's from the Zeta station on Gamma Five." He flipped his voice box back on and pressed three buttons on top. "Have a listen."

A sound like a slap of skin on skin emanated, then a grunt. "State your name," a man said.

"Julian Willis."

I recognized my father's voice immediately.

"Now the rest of you sound off," the man said, "or you'll get the same treatment."

"Jillian Willis."

"Lyric Altera."

"Piper Altera."

"Echo. That's the only name I have. Just Echo."

"Zoë Fields."

"That's all of them, Admiral," the man said. "I disabled the black girl with the negative energy, like you suggested. I didn't want her giving me a heart attack. And that Lyric girl shifted her shape and slipped out of her manacles, so I put her in the cell with the black girl. The negative energy stopped her changes. And it was easy to catch the Willis twins.

All I had to do was threaten Piper Altera when we caught her. That's all for now."

Fairbanks turned the box off. "As you could hear, I am holding some of your loved ones prisoner. I sentenced them to death, and if my agent doesn't hear from me by the end of the day, he will carry out the executions." He let out a sarcastic tsking sound. "It's a shame that you destroyed my tower. I suppose that means I won't be able to tell the agent to delay the executions."

As I listened to his words and those on the recording, I detected no lies, but, again, I didn't have Crystal's experience. I glanced at her. "Verdict?"

Her eyes glistened with tears. "All true as far as I can tell."

"Of course I'm telling the truth," Fairbanks said, "so I suggest that you call your ship to pick us up so I can contact my agent at Gamma Five. I'll tell him that if Oliver heals me, he is to release all of the prisoners, safe and unharmed. If Oliver does not, then my agent will execute one prisoner at a time until Oliver changes his mind. You see, Oliver's little demonstration convinced me that, with you as a catalyst, complete healing is possible. You helped me decide how to set up this potential exchange of assets, if you will."

I clenched my fists and stared at him, trying to pierce his mind. This time, it was easy. Words flowed as he stared back at me. *Megan, I know you've become a mind reader, so I am intentionally releasing my thoughts. That way, all you will get from me is exactly what I want you to know. I have the advantage over you, so you might as well give in. I have your father, your aunt, and your dear friends in custody, and I will kill them without mercy. You, on the other hand, cannot kill me, because you know what the result will be. Billions of innocent people will die. And, of course, I won't care, because I will be dead. And I am in no hurry. I already feel much better. The pain has decreased. And I can talk for the first time since you caused me to plunge into the fiery wreckage you created because of your arrogant, petulant—*

I broke contact. When I averted my eyes, he laughed. "What's wrong, Megan? Are my thoughts too hot to handle? They toasted your feelings? Well, that's a crying shame. I wouldn't want you to suffer what I have suffered."

"That's a lie," Crystal said. "But I guess you knew that."

I wrapped a hand around the admiral's throat and squeezed. As he gagged, I spoke slowly and firmly. "Listen, you filthy jackal. You think your money will buy you anything you want, but I'm here to tell you that everything you've worked for is going to burn. I'll find your money, your houses, your businesses, whatever, and set fire to all of it and make you watch it go up in smoke. We've already destroyed your glowsap mines, freed the children, and disabled the ships you sent here to kill me. Contrary to your plans, I'm not dead, and you're my prisoner. We'll see how it all turns out."

I gave him a final shove and stepped back. While he caught his breath, I looked at Oliver and Crystal as they stared at me with their mouths open. "Let's roll his bed outside and wait for the Nine."

"How long should it take?" Oliver asked. "It's getting cold and windy outside, and he's not dressed for it."

"No worries. We'll watch from inside. He can watch from outside."

Oliver pulled me away and whispered, "Do you think making him suffer is the right strategy? I mean, obviously you do, but I just want to make sure you're thinking straight. You're furious, and you have the right to be, but is your anger making decisions for you?"

I whispered in return, "As long as he has hostages, he thinks he's in charge, that he has all the leverage. I have to let him know that *I'm* in charge. He knows I can't kill him, but I can make him suffer to the point he'll wish I put him out of his misery. Giving him a little taste of it will let him know that I'm willing to be brutal. Now that you've called me aside, you've helped me set up this mind game perfectly, that is, if you want to play along."

"Sure. What's the plan?"

"I'll wheel him out into the cold. Then, when he's had a chance to shiver awhile, you can bring him back in. In the meantime, I'll be out on a rover looking for a glider Captain Warren left behind. You'll say that as a healer, you can't stand to see him suffer and whatever else you can think of to convince him. That way, you might be able to squeeze some intel out of him, like where the kill switch is and what it does. This might be our only way to figure out how to disarm it."

Oliver gave me a firm nod. "I can do that."

"Good. Keep your earbuds turned on max so I can listen. And let Crystal stand close enough so she can see his face to tell if he's lying or not. Maybe she can even use her hypnotizing ability to get information out of him."

"Maybe. She once told me the hypnotizing thing doesn't always work. I'm not sure why."

"Okay. I'll leave that to her. Now get ready for some playacting." I tensed my face and raised my voice, spiking it with anger. "No! I told you I'm going to make him suffer for what he's done. I don't care if he's an admiral or the king of the galaxy. No one gets to hurt kids and not suffer for it."

Oliver lifted his hands and backed away. "All right. All right."

"If you're too soft to do it, I'll take him myself." I strode around to the head of the bed and gave it a shove, but it slid only a few centimeters. I kicked at the lock on each wheel until it gave way, grunting loudly with every kick. When the last lock disengaged, I pushed the bed out the interior door.

As we passed through the security room, Fairbanks chuckled. "I am a seasoned soldier, Megan. If you think this bit of theater is going to make me change—"

"Shut up, you sniveling monster. This *theater* isn't just a drama ploy. All I want to do is make you suffer. End of story."

I pushed the bed through the exit door and across a patio to a spot where he could see the tower ruins. Cold wind buffeted us, flapping the sheet covering his body. I patted his shoulder. "Enjoy the view, but just to show you that I have a heart, I'll let you keep the sheet. Those hospital gowns can be kind of drafty." Resisting the urge to shiver, I walked toward the trio of rovers the Nine had left for us. "I'll return when I've had a chance to look around this place."

Without glancing back, I opened the glass dome of the closest rover, climbed inside, and lowered the dome, cutting off the chilly wind. "Oliver. Crystal. I told Oliver about this already, but I'm in a rover, and I'm going to take a look around. I'm trying to find a glider Captain Warren landed nearby. Maybe we can use it to transport Fairbanks. Once he's had some time to chill, maybe twenty minutes or so, you two can carry out the plan."

Oliver's voice entered my ear. "Will do. Let us know what you find out."

I turned the engine on and fired the thrusters under the craft. Although unable to fly like a glider, a rover would get me around pretty quickly, and I had to give Oliver time to hatch our plot. Maybe soon, the Nine would be close enough to contact me with an update, but since they had to shuttle the kids from the cave where Mabel took them, that would take a while.

Following Captain Warren's directions, I zoomed up the incline to the edge of the forest and turned north, now pushing against the blustery wind. Soon, I spotted something in the woods to the left.

I turned that way and stopped between two trees just inside the forest. A glider sat on the ground, its hatch open as if inviting me in. I exited the rover and bent over the interior of the glider, a two-seater, like Captain Warren had said, perfect for our needs. I checked the lock on the ignition. The captain had left it unlocked. Again, perfect.

After securing my rover, I climbed into the glider, started it, and flew from the forest, staying out of the valley and the admiral's view. "Oliver and Crystal, I found the two-seat glider Captain Warren came in. Now we can transport Fairbanks."

"Got it," Oliver said. "I was just about to go out and bring Fairbanks in. I guess you'll hear how it goes."

"Sounds good. I'm going to fly higher to see if I can pick up some chatter from the Alliance ships. This glider should be programmed to decrypt their messages."

"All right. Give us an update when you can."

"Will do." I turned the radio on. Only static came through the speakers. I angled the glider upward and flew directly into the wind. Dark clouds rolled toward me, lightning bolts knifing to the ground here and there, obviously a terrible storm. No telling what effect it might have had on our team's efforts to bring down the Alliance ships and might still be having on shuttling the kids to the Nine.

Captain Warren's static-filled voice came through the speakers. "That's all the news so far. Emerson will send this message every five minutes." I rolled my eyes. Bad timing. Now I would have to wait, though the coming storm wouldn't wait for anything.

I set a digital timer on the console for five minutes and started its countdown. As I turned away from the cloud bank, Oliver's voice came through my earbuds. "Don't worry, Admiral. I'll get you inside."

"Why are you doing this for me?" Fairbanks asked. "She's your captain."

"And you're an admiral. You outrank her. One thing my father drilled into me is respect for authority. Since you're the top authority, I can't let you freeze."

"Your father was a good man. Even though he ended up being my adversary, I always respected him."

"Thanks for saying so." The sound of a door shutting came through. "Better?"

"Much."

"Good."

"What are you going to do when Megan returns?" Fairbanks asked. "And what about the other girl? Crystal, right?"

"Yeah. Crystal. She's like me. She doesn't want to see someone suffer. I hate it because I'm a healer. She hates it because a slaver whipped her a lot. She knows what torture feels like. She doesn't want anyone else to go through it."

"Understandable."

"Here she comes now."

"Hello, Admiral," Crystal said. "I'm glad you're feeling better."

"Thank you. But tell me this, how can you seem so loyal to Megan, but then the moment she left, you turned against her?"

"Are you kidding me? She's got Starborn powers you wouldn't believe. She's got my lie-detecting power. She's got Zoë's power. And she's got Oliver's healing power. She can make your heart stop, heal you so it starts again, then she can stop it again just to annoy you."

"Has she done those things to you?"

"No," Crystal said, "but she could, so we always do whatever she says."

"Don't you also have the ability to hypnotize people for a short time? Couldn't you use that against her?"

"I did once when we first met, but it's because I took her by surprise. Smart people like her are a lot harder to hypnotize when they know what I can do. Basically, I can hypnotize people who are dumb, who don't know what I can do, or who let me do it because they trust me."

"I'll remember that, but I wonder how truthful you're being. It seems that I am at a disadvantage, because I don't have your mentalist power."

"Mentalist?" Crystal repeated. "What's that?"

"A mentalist is someone who uses mental abilities such as hypnosis or the power of suggestion, including your lie-detecting powers. Since I don't have those, you could be lying to gain my favor. Same with bringing me in from the cold."

"But," Oliver said, "gaining your favor doesn't help us. We're just trying to be nice. You know, humanitarian."

"That's quite a word for a boy your age."

"We've been hanging around Megan for a long time. She shows off her vocabulary every day."

I covered my mouth, stifling a laugh. Oliver was really laying it on thick.

"I noticed," Fairbanks said. "She's rather full of herself. She radiates arrogance."

"Yeah. You noticed. Anyway, I was wondering how we can work out our little … um … what's the word?"

"Dilemma?" I suggested.

"Dilemma," Oliver finished. "I agree with Megan that we can't let you kill everyone in all of those worlds. And you shouldn't kill your prisoners or enslave kids. She won't back down from any of those. So, what should we do to solve the dilemma?"

"It's simple. Heal me with her help, and I will release the prisoners. I will then leave the star systems that I am threatening to destroy and live on an estate I have built in another star system. You will never hear from me again. You have a lie detector. You know I'm not lying."

"He's not," Crystal said. "No doubt about it."

"There. You see?"

"But what about the kill switch?" Oliver asked "You could go to another star system, but you'll eventually die. What happens then?"

"Nothing. When I die, I will be too far away to activate the switch."

"You're lying," Crystal said. "And what about when you're out of range of any Zeta stations and you can't communicate with your kill switch between now and when you die? The first day you're out of touch … Boom! We're all dead."

"Ah. You've bested me on that one, Crystal. I should've known Megan would choose intelligent crewmates."

"Don't try to snow me," Crystal said. "I know brownnosing when I hear it. Just tell me how to cut the kill switch, and I'll convince Megan to heal you and let you go."

"The kill switch is my ultimate leverage. I'm not telling anyone how to stop it."

I shook my head. He was digging his heels in. They would have to come up with another angle.

Crystal heaved an exasperated sigh. "Admiral Fairbanks, you lied to me, you tried to flatter me, and now you're being stubborn about the most important point. We're talking about billions upon billions of innocent lives. You know we can't budge on that. Can you really look me in the eye and tell me that your life is more important than the lives of those billions of people?"

"To me, my life is more important than theirs."

"I think you're lying again."

"Really? Is your power weakening? I meant every word."

"I can't always get a good reading. Like I said, look me in the eye and tell me your life is more important than theirs."

"All right. I'll accept that challenge." A short pause ensued. "I am the admiral of the entire Alliance fleet who keeps the peace throughout a galaxy that is filled with imbeciles who don't know their left from their right, believe in superstitions about gods and fairies, and are easily duped by their betters. So, yes, my life is more important than theirs."

"Well, I see that you believe what you say." After a few seconds, Crystal spoke in a mesmerizing cadence. "Admiral Fairbanks, can you hear me?"

He replied with a soft voice that I could barely detect. "Yes."

"Admiral, what is the kill switch, and how does it work?"

I clenched a tight fist. Yes! Her approach was brilliant! She had hypnotized him.

The admiral spoke slowly. "The kill switch resides in the Zeta stations. They will use the transportation guns to disintegrate the planets."

I gasped. Total annihilation? The monster!

"How can we stop it?" Crystal asked.

"You can't. My engineers designed it with a biometric key. Only I can disable it. I have to be there in person to do so."

"Where do you have to be?" Crystal asked.

"Alpha One."

"Where exactly? The Zeta station? Somewhere on the planet?" After a few silent seconds, Crystal sighed. "He's resisting really hard now. I don't think I can get more information."

"You got a lot," Oliver said.

"When we get him to the Nine," Crystal said, "I might be able to do this again and get more, maybe make him tell his agent to let the prisoners go."

"Not likely. The way he talks when you've got a hold of him will make the agent suspicious."

Fingers snapped. "Admiral? It's me, Crystal. Are you all right?"

A few more silent seconds passed. "What? Yes, of course I'm all right. Why do you ask?"

"You zoned out. You were saying you couldn't tell us about the kill switch, but you went into some kind of trance."

"Probably the pain medication Mabel was giving me, but I won't need it for quite a while now. I don't have much pain."

"Must be strong stuff," Oliver said. "Anyway, I don't think we can convince Megan, not with what you offered. She won't budge without knowing how to stop the kill switch."

"Understandable. But she still wants to save her father and the others. I think she'll take what she can to free them and hope to try to best me at a later time."

"Yeah. Maybe. You'll have to work that out with her. She'll want some way to guarantee their release."

"Yes. Of course. When we are both aboard her ship, we will work that out. I have some ideas."

A sudden gust blew my glider hard to the side. I couldn't stay in the air much longer. "Oliver and Crystal, you did great. I don't think you're going to get any more intel, and the storm's really bearing down on us. I'll be there in a couple of minutes." I looked at the timer on the console—47 seconds till Josie's message would repeat. This might work out fine.

I descended to about fifty meters from the ground and orbited the mansion. When the timer ticked to zero, the message began again, but static buzzed through so badly, I couldn't understand a word. I ascended again until the words became clear enough, though I had to listen carefully to understand.

"So," Captain Warren said, "now that the Alliance ships are all disabled and cannot be revived without a secret command in my voice, we are heading toward the place Mabel took the other kids. With so many kids already on board, this place is now a boisterous playhouse. They're so excited. And adding more kids will just enhance the *fun*."

She emphasized *fun* in a way that let me know that, to her, it wasn't really much fun at all, though she still seemed pleased with the results.

"With a big storm threatening," Captain Warren continued, still barely understandable in the midst of static, "the shuttle procedure will be challenging. We might have to hole up for a while in whatever shelter the kids are in. Either way, we'll be back to the admiral's place as soon as we can. But, so far, all of our news is good. We blew every mine to smithereens, the kids are all safe, and we disabled the Alliance ships without firing a shot. Megan, knowing that you're not one to kill without a reason, I'm sure you'll be glad to hear that. That's all the news so far. Emerson will send this message every five minutes."

A lightning bolt blasted a tree to my right, splitting the trunk. Heavy rain and sleet pelted the glider's dome. I descended rapidly and landed next to the two remaining rovers. After grabbing the glider's remote-control unit, I popped the dome open, leaped out, and ran toward the mansion, pressing the button on the remote to close the hatch along the way.

After running inside, I walked into the front room with what I hoped was a serene expression. Now dressed in an Alliance uniform, Fairbanks sat upright on the bed with his legs over the side, Oliver and Crystal standing close. I stopped in front of him, just out of reach. "You look comfortable, Admiral."

"Better than I was." He nodded toward Oliver. "He helped me get dressed. I want to try to walk. I hope you aren't angry with your subordinates for disobeying orders. They were merely being humane toward a suffering old man."

"First, they're not my subordinates. They're my friends. Second, they didn't disobey me. They did exactly what I hoped. Our plan worked perfectly."

The admiral bent his brow. "Are you saying I was right about your theatric performance after all?"

"I had only a bit part in what you're calling a performance. The real stars were Oliver and Crystal. They played their parts beautifully, to the point that you have no idea how much information you gave away."

"Nonsense. I didn't give anything away."

"So you think. Anyway, I'm glad you're dressed. You'll be going with us as soon as the storm is over."

He lifted his brow. "Is that so? Where do you think you're taking me?"

"First, we're going to put you in the brig on the Nebula Nine. There, you'll send the message to stop the kill switch for the day and tell your agent not to kill his prisoners. Then we'll go to the Gamma Five Zeta station where you will tell your agent to release all of the hostages, but he can keep my father for the time being so you can maintain your leverage. When the others are safely on board the Nine, and Crystal confirms that you'll honor your word to release my father, I'll help Oliver heal you completely."

The admiral stroked his chin. "Well, I see that you've put a lot of thought into this. I'm impressed."

"Don't patronize me, Admiral. I'm your worst enemy, and you're not someone I want to impress."

He gave me a solemn nod. "I understand. I will refrain from treating you like a child. But you know that I still hold the ultimate leverage.

You should treat me like a formidable adversary and begin planning my release once Oliver heals me."

"Don't worry. I'm already working on a plan. In the meantime, while we're waiting for the Nine, let's call a temporary truce." I dragged a chair over to the bed and sat on it. "Before I can make plans about where to send you after you're healed, I need to know if there are any other glowsap mines that you know of anywhere in the galaxy besides the ones we destroyed here on Delta Ninety-five. Remember, we have two lie detectors here."

The admiral shook his head. "There are none that I know of."

Crystal nodded. "He's telling the truth."

"Of course," he added, "there could be mines that I don't know about. You might be aware of the fact that Thorne was trying to export the business by selling dead bees so their eggs could be harvested. As a businessman, he wanted a percentage of the profits, but I don't know if he succeeded with planting any new mines."

"We were aware of that, and we'll deal with those mines if and when we hear about them." I leaned back and crossed my legs. "Let's talk about where you keep all your money—cash, real estate, other investments."

He chuckled. "Looking for a bribe?"

I smiled. "Let's say that I am. How much might you be willing to offer me to simply let you go wherever you wish after you're healed?"

"Surely more than you could ever spend in your lifetime."

"That sounds good so far, but would you have to liquidate some of your assets? How long would it take? I mean, sometimes transactions like that can take a while, and I would want cash in hand before I let you go."

He sighed. "Once a pirate, always a pirate."

"Don't flatter me, Admiral. Calling me a pirate is a compliment."

"That's not surprising." After staring at me for a long moment, he continued. "I see no harm in telling you about my financial assets, as long as I stay away from the particulars, with one exception. I have vast holdings in real estate, but the one that you would be most interested in is the Zeta station at Alpha One. Have you seen it?"

I shook my head. "Except for the orbiting docking station, I haven't been to my home planet in a long time."

"We revealed the existence of that Zeta station during the past year. It's not spherical like the other Zetas. The top half has a spherical shape, like a dome, and the bottom half is more conical. The departure and arrival bays are in tiers at the center, only about fifteen or so. We decided that having more was overkill. The rest of the interior is a magnificent city, with offices, restaurants, and entertainment venues. Passages lead to the top surface. There we have airtight, insulated buildings where people can enjoy a view of space as the station orbits Alpha One. It can also fly into the atmosphere and tour the landscape, allowing those in the surface buildings to open the windows, walk out onto the balconies, and enjoy the breathtaking beauty from above. Citizens of the station would have to pay a lot of money to live there, but it's worth the price, because they know that if the planet is ever in danger, the station can leave and travel to a safer location. In short, it is the ultimate paradise."

I pointed at him. "And you own the station?"

He nodded. "And I will receive the proceeds of those who pay to live there. I have no renters yet, but many are waiting to sign up."

"Interesting. I assume since it's a Zeta station, it can transport ships to other Zetas."

"Of course. That's another one of its benefits—instant travel to other star systems. As you know, until recently, that was an unsafe option for passengers. But, thanks to you, it's now safe. Of course, in making it safe, you spoiled my most profitable revenue stream, but I am now sufficiently wealthy. I no longer need it."

"So why are you telling me about that asset and not the others?"

"Because I am offering it to you in exchange for my freedom."

I crossed my arms in front. "Okay. I like that. But what about the kill switch?"

"What do you care about that? You'll have the station. You can go anywhere you want. You'll be safe from the kill switch. That's all that matters."

I stared at him. He was serious—so selfish, he actually projected on me his callous attitude toward the masses, assuming I would have the same hideous worldview. Still, I could play along with it. "You're right. I'll take it. But I'll need you to come with me, show me around the station, give me all the keys, codes, and whatever to run the place."

He nodded. "Consider it done."

I glanced at Oliver. He stared at me, obviously confused. Crystal, on the other hand, gave me a tiny smile, using her powers to know that I was being deceptive without directly lying.

"Now that we're in agreement …" I rose from the chair and walked to the front door. "Let's check the weather." I opened the door and looked outside. Ice covered everything in sight, and snow fell, wind blowing the flakes in swirling sheets. "Looks like we're going to be here awhile. I think even if they've collected the kids by now, Captain Warren will fly into space and wait for the storm to clear before trying to land here."

Fairbanks huffed. "This storm could last for days. A storm we had a week or so ago lasted four days. I need to send a message within the next four hours, or the kill switch will be triggered. When the tower was active, I never had a problem even during a storm, but that's not an option now."

I closed the door and looked at Oliver and Crystal. "Here's what we're going to do. I'll take the admiral to the Nine in the glider. He'll send the message to keep the kill switch from activating and to tell his agent to stand down. Then, while he cools his heels in the brig, I'll come back with the Nine and pick you two up. We don't have time to wait this storm out."

Oliver pointed at Fairbanks with his thumb. "You don't mind having him ride next to you in the glider?"

"No worries. I can stop his heart if he tries anything."

"But then the kill switch will activate."

"Good point." I walked to a bedside table, picked up a pill bottle, and read the label, an opioid for pain that would also induce sleep. "This should do the trick."

Fairbanks sighed. "Very well. Since you don't trust me to behave myself, I'll take the medication, but be sure to wake me up within four hours if you want the messages sent on time."

"You can count on that." I gave him the recommended dosage of two pills, pushed the bottle into his pocket in case he needed more later, and helped him stand. "Let's walk you to the glider and get you seated before you fall asleep."

With me on one side and Oliver on the other, we walked Fairbanks through the frigid wind to the glider, opening the dome by remote control. By the time we seated him and I ran around to the pilot's side, he had already fallen asleep. I closed the hatch, waved at Oliver, and took off into the vicious storm. With my earbuds still on, I updated our progress as I flew through the bumpy air, my hands tightly on the yoke as the glider bucked wildly. "Wind's blowing out of the north at ninety-four kilometers per hour, gusting to one-twenty. No wonder the Nine's not here yet."

Oliver's voice came through my bud. "Maybe you'd better head nearly straight up. Get out of the storm and see if you can catch a signal from the Nine up there."

Although that was already my plan, I gave him credit. "Good advice. Thanks." I angled the glider upward and zoomed through the cloud bank. As we climbed, the jolts grew worse, but the admiral slept on, undisturbed.

"Here's another idea," Oliver said. "You know, it might be helpful at some point for you to morph into Fairbanks."

I grimaced. "Yuck. Are you serious?"

"Super serious. Think about it. His face could get you into places you couldn't normally go, like the Alpha One kill switch location."

"As disgusting as it sounds, that might be a good idea."

"But you'd better figure out how to talk like he does. If there's a voice-print detector, it won't be easy to fool."

"I don't know how Lyric pulled off the voice change, but I could get a look at his larynx, you know, with that X-ray vision stuff we healers can do."

"Good time to try it since he's out cold."

"That's for sure. I'll do it when I get into smoother air. Talk to you soon."

A couple of minutes later, we broke into the clear above the clouds into the night sky, illuminated by two small moons, one to my left and one to my right. I leveled the glider and sailed along in the upper atmosphere. Now I had to start the painful process of planning to change into a monster.

I laid my hand on the admiral's throat and peered within. After finding his larynx, I probed it through and through, hoping my power would hold a mental picture of it. Then I did the same to my own larynx, in case I needed that picture for changing back to normal.

When I finished, I spoke through my earbuds. "I'm above the storm. If anyone on the Nine can hear me, please respond."

Static filled my ears, though it carried the cadence of speech. That meant the Nine might be on the ground, holed up near the refuge Mabel had arranged for the condemned kids, and they were trying to send a message from there.

"I can't understand what you're saying. If you can hear me, can you send a glider above the storm so we can talk? I don't know where to find you."

The static returned, still indecipherable. Since they responded at all, maybe they understood. All I could do now was wait. But who was capable of flying a glider through a storm like this? Captain Warren probably could, but it would be better for her to stay with the Nine.

I flew in a wide circle for several minutes, listening for another call. Finally, a clear voice came through. "Phew!" Jade said. "That was the worst!"

I grinned. "Jade. I'm glad you could join me here."

"Well, I guessed you were kind of lonely up in the ether. Or is it the nether? I can never get those two straight. Anyway, I've come to guide you to the Nine. We have all the kids inside, and we were waiting for the storm to settle before flying through it. You know how rough it can be, and we didn't want to frighten the children."

"Good call. It's going to work out fine. I'll tell you all about what happened with Fairbanks as soon as we get everyone together. I don't want to repeat the story too many times."

"That's fine with me. I see you on my scanner. I'll be at your side in thirty seconds, then I'll lead the way and—"

"Wait. Are you in your two-seater?"

"Yes. Why?"

"I'm in Captain Warren's two-seater with Admiral Fairbanks."

"Fairbanks? No kidding. I'm looking forward to hearing your story, that's for sure."

"Let's drop him off at the Nine, then we'll both go to pick up Oliver and Crystal. That'll save me a trip."

"No problem. I see you now. Can you see me?"

Blinking lights appeared at my two o'clock. As it drew closer, I could make out the shape of a glider in the moonlight. "Yep. I've got eyes on you."

"Not literally, I hope. That would be strange." The glider eased into a full turn. "Follow me."

I steered into a path behind her. "I'm on your six."

"What does that mean?"

"Ask your daughter when we pick her up. She knows all about it."

As planned, we flew to the Nine through the gusty storm, another difficult trip, though the wind speed had fallen to under 70 kilometers per hour. We dropped Fairbanks off and set up an infirmary bed for him in the brig. After explaining the situation to Captain Warren, telling her when he needed to be awakened to send the needed messages in case we got delayed, Jade and I left, again in separate gliders. This time, Perdantus asked to go with me, explaining that, although he was delighted at the rescue of the children, many of them carried awful odors that were making his sneezing worse.

After a less harrowing flight through the abating storm, Perdantus riding on my shoulder, we arrived at the admiral's mansion. No lights shone from any of the rooms, and I couldn't see movement anywhere. "The generator must've gone out."

"If it has," Jade said from her glider, "you'd think they would be watching through a window and run out here. With no power, it must be getting really cold in there."

Prickles ran along my neck. "Yeah. Something's not adding up."

"Smoke is rising from the chimney," Perdantus said.

"Good catch. Someone must be in there." I shut the engine down. "Oliver? Crystal? Can you hear me? I'm sitting right outside."

A whisper from Oliver came through my bud, probably through Jade's as well. "A man in an Alliance uniform broke in, I guess one of the men you chased away earlier. The only weapon he had was a knife, but he knew how to use it. Crystal kept trying to get him to look into her eyes, but he seemed half blind and got furious at her, so he sliced her up pretty badly. He tied me to one side of the bed and Crystal to the other, and I think he sabotaged the generator. Maybe he left, and maybe he's still looking for the admiral in the house. Either way, we need to get help for Crystal. She's bleeding, and I can't get over to her. The bed just turns around when I try."

I popped open the hatch and climbed out. "On my way."

Jade had already jumped from her glider and was running toward the house, her fists clenched as she bulldozed through a snowdrift.

"Perdantus," I said, "search for an Alliance intruder."

"I will." Perdantus flew from my shoulder.

I whipped the laser blaster from its holster, ran into the mansion, and burst into the front room. By the light of flaming logs in the fireplace, I found Oliver and Crystal sitting on the floor in the positions he had described. Jade knelt at Crystal's side compressing her throat with the bedsheet.

Jade's voice cracked. "She's bleeding badly. She'll die soon if she doesn't get help."

"Oliver's a better healer than I am." I rushed to him, knelt, drew a knife from my belt, and sliced through a rope that tied his hands to the frame. He jerked away and scrambled to the other side of the bed. When Jade lifted her hand from Crystal's neck, the sheet was soaked with blood.

Oliver peeled the sheet away and set his hand directly on the wound, breathing heavily as a sob throttled his voice. "Energize me, Megan!"

Still on my knees, I scooted to them, cut Crystal loose, and slid the knife away. Then I pulled my locket from behind my shirt and clutched it tightly. In my other hand, I held the laser blaster as I glanced around for any sign of the intruder. "Is she conscious?"

"No." Oliver wept. "Megan, I think I'm losing her."

I closed my eyes and concentrated, whispering, "Dear God, help us. We can't lose Crystal. We just can't."

I felt Perdantus land on my shoulder. "The intruder is upstairs. He found a handgun, and he is stumbling around as if nearly blind. I fear that he is trying to find his way to the stairs."

I opened my eyes, my heart racing. "Jade, the intruder's upstairs. I can't be a dynamo and watch for him at the same time."

Jade snatched the blaster out of my hand. "You be a dynamo. I'll handle that—" She finished with an obscenity and charged up the stairs.

"I will watch for the other guards outside." Perdantus lifted off my shoulder and flew away.

I closed my eyes again and concentrated. Since I had done this several times before, energizing Oliver began working right away. I could feel it.

"Okay, okay," Oliver said. "I can see the artery. I'm trying to stitch it now."

From above, a gunshot rang out. The buzz of a laser followed. Jade screamed, "You cut my daughter. I'm going to—" Another gunshot interrupted. Jade moaned. With all the clamor, I couldn't concentrate.

"Megan," Oliver said, "It's getting blurry."

"I'm trying!"

Heavy footsteps thudded down the stairs. A man called, "I'll shoot this woman again if you don't tell me where Admiral Fairbanks is."

I opened my eyes. One of the guards I had confronted a while back lumbered down the stairs, one hand holding a pistol and the other dragging Jade by the wrist. With each step he took, Jade's body thumped down another stair.

I instinctively reached for my blaster, but, of course, it wasn't there. I could reach out and stop his heart or maybe jerk the gun from his hand and shoot him. Even setting fire to his clothes might be possible. But since I had to reserve power to heal Crystal, maybe I should try a different strategy.

Still trying to concentrate on Oliver, I rose to my feet. "I know where the admiral is."

He blinked, blood oozing from his eyes. "Where?"

"Let her go, and I'll tell you."

"No. You bring him to me, and I'll let him decide what to do with all of you."

"Admiral Fairbanks was miraculously healed enough to make him mobile. I took him outside to get him more help, because—"

"He's outside? Right now? I couldn't find him. It's dark out there, and an evil girl injured my eyes, some kind of demonic magic."

"Oh. That's awful." I breathed a silent sigh of relief. Fortunately, he didn't recognize my voice.

Oliver whispered, "I've got this now, Megan. I know what you have in mind. Go for it."

I kept my focus on the guard. "I'll tell you what. I'll run outside and get the admiral. I know where he is."

"Good. Bring him here."

"I'll be right back." I laid a hand on Oliver's head and whispered, "You're amazing." I opened the front door, hurried out into the bitter cold air, and closed the door behind me. If he wanted the admiral, I could give him the admiral, but doing this would be so repulsive. Still, I had no other plan in mind.

Closing my eyes, I created a mental image of Admiral Fairbanks alongside my own. As I transformed, I felt the stretching pain again, thought it wasn't as bad as before. Maybe I was becoming more flexible. This time I concentrated on the clothes, changing the uniform to what I had seen Fairbanks wearing in the past, and I recalled my mental picture of his larynx. Of course, I had never performed this part of a transformation before. I just had to hope it worked.

When I finished, I looked down at my body. Wearing an Alliance uniform, I looked pretty authentic. If I had missed any external details, the intruder's injured eyes wouldn't be able to notice.

I opened the door and reentered. When I saw the intruder, I spoke with my newly altered larynx. "What are you doing to that woman?"

He let her go, stood at attention, and saluted with an arm over his chest. "Admiral Fairbanks, this woman tried to shoot me, so I—"

"Acted in self-defense. Of course. But now it's time to desist. She can't hurt you."

"Yes sir. Of course, sir." He pulled Jade the rest of the way down the stairs and lowered her gently to the floor. She clutched her ankle and writhed, softly moaning.

"Now, soldier," I said extending a hand as I walked closer, "give me the gun. Because of your injured eyes, you shouldn't be handling one."

"You're right." He gave me the gun. "I was assigned to guard you, and I was forced to leave because of a strange girl who hurt my eyes. I had to fight through a ferocious storm to come back here to fulfill my duty."

"Very good, soldier. I appreciate your dedication. But I heard that you cut a girl's throat and tied her to a bed. Why did you do that?"

He gasped. "I cut a girl's throat?"

"You did. She is now lying in a pool of her own blood. We hope she'll survive, but she is in bad shape."

"I remember a girl leaping at me, telling me to look into her eyes. I pushed her away, but I must've pushed her with the hand that held the knife." He swiped blood from under his eyes. "I'm sorry. I'm so, so sorry."

"I understand." I turned him toward the stairs. With the pistol in my hand, I could easily shoot him in the back of the head, revenge for hurting Crystal, but I resisted the urge. "Now go upstairs. I assume you'll be able to find a bed. Lie down and take a good long rest. I will see about getting you the medical attention you need."

"Yes sir. Thank you, sir." A hand on the banister, he walked up the stairs.

I hustled to Jade and crouched close. "Are you all right?"

She grimaced. "Not really, but don't bother with me. Just see about Crystal."

After giving the gun to Jade, I ran to Oliver and Crystal. He still had a hand on her neck. "How's she doing?"

"When you left, she took a turn for the worse. I've kind of been holding her steady. She's lost a lot of blood, so even if I can get her sewn up, I'm not sure if she'll make it."

"She'll make it." I clutched my locket again. "I have faith in you."

"Thanks, but I think it'll help if you look like yourself again."

"No argument from me." I closed my eyes. Again I transformed quickly, including my clothes and larynx. "I think I'm back, but I'm keeping my eyes closed to concentrate on energizing you."

"Yep. You're you again, and I can already see inside her better. Keep it up."

"Will do." I concentrated hard, and I prayed harder than I had ever prayed before. I loved Crystal so much. I couldn't stand to lose her. The galaxy couldn't stand to lose her. Without Crystal, we would all be far poorer than we could imagine.

"There you go, Crystal," Oliver said with a hum. "You're doing great. Keep that heart pumping."

I joined in. "Crystal, we love you. We need you. Don't leave us. Stay with us. I need you on my six."

Crystal moaned. "What in blazes is going on?"

Her voice was like music. A sob erupted from my gut, making me squeak. "You're hurt. Oliver's ..." I swallowed. "Oliver's healing you."

"That blind-as-a-bat moron cut my throat."

"Shhh," Oliver said. "If you keep talking, you'll keep bleeding."

I leaned over and kissed both Crystal and Oliver on the forehead. "You got this, Oliver? I need to see about Jade."

"Yeah, I got this for sure this time. You can—"

"What's wrong with my mother?" Crystal asked.

I set a finger on her lips. "Hush. That's an order. She'll be fine."

"I'm all right, pumpkin seed," Jade called. "Just hush awhile."

I hurried over to Jade and knelt at her side as she lay curled on the floor. "Did you get shot?"

Jade nodded. "In the hip. That's why I can't get up. I also hurt my ankle. Maybe sprained it."

"I'll see about both. If I can't heal you, I'm sure Oliver can."

I found the bullet wound on her hip and laid a hand over it. "I think the bullet hit a bone. It's probably lodged in there. Not much blood, though." I shifted my hand to her ankle. When I tried to move it, she groaned. "I think it's a bad sprain. This'll take a while."

"It's getting really cold in here," Oliver said. "Crystal's stable now. Maybe we should go to the Nine and finish in the infirmary. I don't know how to restart the generator. I don't even know where it is."

"You're right." I rose, pulled the small flashlight from my pocket, and flicked it on. "See what you can do for Jade and get them both ready to go. I have to make amends upstairs."

Oliver raised his brow. "You're going to heal his eyes?"

I nodded. "I'm the one who blinded him."

"Yeah, because you had to."

"No, I didn't have to. I could've come up with another way to get the job done. That was just the fast and easy way." I began walking up the stairs, the flashlight beam guiding my steps. "I don't think it'll take long."

When I reached the top of the stairs, I searched each bedroom until I found the guard lying in a bed on his back, a bare mattress pad under him and no pillow. I walked to his side and knelt, listening to the heavy respirations of exhausted sleep, raspy and sometimes spasmodic.

Hoping to see how cold he was, I compressed his hand and found a photo pinched between his finger and thumb. I slid it from his grasp and set the beam on the portrait of a lovely young woman holding a male toddler, most likely his wife and son. On the back, handwritten script said, "To Zeke, with all my love, Natalie."

A tear crept to my eye. Zeke probably wondered if he would ever get to see his family clearly again. And if he couldn't, whose fault would it be? Mine.

I sniffed, brushed the tear away, and returned the photo to his fingers. They were cold, as expected. He had, indeed, braved a fierce snowstorm to find his commanding officer. How could I ever blame him for doing what he thought was right? Also, since cutting Crystal was an accident, he obviously didn't intend to hurt her so badly. And all of this could have been avoided if I hadn't been so quick to hurt him, the easy way to get him and his fellow guards to leave. I had chosen wrath over mercy, but now I had a chance to undo my mistake.

I laid a hand over his eyes and whispered in a melodic lilt, echoing words that entered my mind unbidden. "The wound of my wrath that was kindled in haste, will now be restored as a treasure from waste. Let mercy be spread from this man to another, and build a new kingdom of sisters and brothers."

When my power let me know that I had successfully healed his eyes, I lifted my hand. Zeke slept on, now breathing easily. I untied his boots, slid them off, and set them on the floor. A closet in the room held a pillow and blanket. I spread the blanket over him, fluffed the pillow, and pushed it under the back of his head.

"We're ready," Oliver called from downstairs.

I kissed Zeke on the forehead. "Sleep well, my brother. I'll send someone to pick you up before it gets too cold in here." Then I hurried downstairs.

With Jade now able to walk with help, Oliver and I guided her to the passenger seat of one of the gliders. Then Oliver carried Crystal in his arms while I boosted her mentally to make the load lighter for him. Once he had settled her in the other glider's passenger seat, I climbed into the pilot seat while Oliver climbed in with Jade.

I whistled for Perdantus. Within a few seconds, he flew to my glider and perched on the yoke. "I noticed no one else in the vicinity."

"Good. Thank you." I closed the dome and started the engine. "Let's go to the Nine and get some rest."

With the storm pretty much over, we flew without a problem to the Nine. Along the way, I checked the dragon's eye again. It still glowed. Papa was alive. But for how long, I had no idea.

When we arrived, we carried Crystal and Jade into the ship with a lot more helping hands, including several of the older kids my crew had rescued, and laid them in the infirmary. There, Oliver continued the healing process, no longer needing my energizing help.

I checked on Admiral Fairbanks in the brig. He lay asleep on a cot. Ensign Weston told me that the admiral successfully sent the signal to disable the kill switch for another day. He also told his guard who held my father and the others to stand down for the time being and to properly feed and care for them. He would get in touch with him later with further instructions.

When I returned to the bridge, Captain Warren rose from the pilot's chair. "The helm is now yours, Captain Willis," she said as she gestured with a hand toward the seat. "I think we should leave at once."

I looked around at all the faces staring at me—including Ensign Weston standing in front of Emerson's console and Isaac and Ophelia at the navigator's station. "I suppose we have a lot to tell each other, but …" I lifted a finger. "First, Captain Warren, can you arrange for an Alliance vessel to go to the Fairbanks outpost and pick up a guard I left there? He's recovering from his wounds upstairs in a bed. You can indicate that he served his admiral well."

She nodded. "I can do that. We disabled the cruisers but not the gliders."

"Perfect." I sat in the captain's chair. "You said we should leave at once. Do you have a destination in mind?"

"The Zeta station in this star system, but with so many kids on board, we should stop at Delta Ninety-eight for supplies. It's only about two hours away. Emerson told me that he contacted a certain Quixon there who will fully supply us for the journey."

I spun in the chair. "How many kids are on board?"

"Ninety-eight. Quite a coincidence, I think."

I whistled. "And quite a load."

"True. We had to double and triple up to get everyone secured in seats and beds, but they're ready for takeoff. Once we're in space, we can let them walk around, with proper guidance, of course."

"The route to Delta Ninety-eight has been plotted," Ophelia said. "We're ready to go."

I brought the course up on my screen and set it for autopilot. "Emerson, take us to Delta Ninety-eight. It's all yours, and you'll even have another chance to practice your landing skills."

"With more than one hundred people on board?" Emerson said. "Are you certain you want to put that many lives at risk when I have landed fewer than a human handful of times?"

"I have complete faith in you, my digital friend. Complete faith."

"Very well, and may I say that I am glad to have you back on board. We had an exceptionally harrowing experience to tell you about, but from the look on your haggard face, I assume you did as well."

I smiled. "Thanks, Emerson. Take us up, and I'll tell you all about it."

After we launched, broke through the atmosphere, and reached a comfortable cruising speed, I switched on all the comms and told everyone what happened at the admiral's mansion. After that, Captain Warren gave me a rundown on their rescue of the kids at the mines, some of the details I already knew. They learned that Mabel's intel was correct. The kids had been moved to two new mines, though the glowsap caves weren't producing yet, and the slavers had set up makeshift huts nearby for the kids to live in.

After Weston disabled the other starships by sending shutdown codes, Warren and Miles destroyed all of the mines, both old and new, so that no one could ever use them again. Then Warren collected all of the kids and waited for me to complete my job while Miles and Dana flew back to the sanctuary in the south.

While Captain Warren talked, she sent a secret message to one of her glider pilot friends to pick up Zeke at the admiral's compound. When she finished her story, I gave her a quizzical look. "You never mentioned Mabel's current whereabouts."

Captain Warren shrugged. "She wasn't at the cave where she hid the children. Since she likely thinks she's in trouble with people on both sides of the conflict, we're guessing that she decided to lay low and fend for herself. The kids in the cave said she left shortly before we arrived. Obviously she's resourceful, and since she kept the kids safe, I think we should leave her alone."

"Agreed."

When we arrived at Delta Ninety-eight, we found the city of Bassolith to be much different than I last saw it. Quixon had been elected mayor, and he had put a stop to all slave trading in the city, both public and private. He also worked with both the Jaradians and the Taurantas to write a new constitution, one that outlawed slavery forever. Quixon also took custody of Fortner and Prince, promising to investigate whether or not Prince was involved in the photon-torpedo sabotage.

While we loaded supplies and recharged the fusion engines, Melda came to the ship and greeted us, a happy reunion, especially when she described a solution they discovered to conquer the change that came over them during battle storms. Since the storms seemed to alter their moral compasses, they needed a way to focus on proper conduct. So, during a storm, the temple, through newly installed powerful speakers, broadcast the basic tenets of their moral code.

After her explanation, I asked, "Why can't you just focus on the tenets in your minds? You know, act according to how the truths you cherish have changed your hearts."

"We are not humans," she replied. "We don't have that ability. The storms seem to scramble our brains, and we need fresh input during the scramble."

I nodded. "It's always good for me to get fresh input, even when my brain isn't scrambled."

Once we had finished loading supplies and I had said my goodbyes to Quixon and Melda, we took off again, this time heading for the Zeta station, a journey that would last a few days. Since we couldn't put the children through the rigors of high g-forces, we had to take more time.

During the flight, I went to the brig and visited Admiral Fairbanks. A video monitor on the wall between us showed him sitting up on his cot, the color in his cheeks and bright eyes telling me that his health had improved quite a bit. Oliver's power had worked well, but the burn scars on his face and neck gave evidence that he might still be in considerable pain. Fortunately, he likely still had his medication if he needed it.

I rolled a wheeled chair over, sat in front of the monitor, and turned the comms on. "Hello, Admiral Fairbanks. It's Megan."

He sat up straighter. "Could you turn your camera on?"

"Sure." I pressed a button on a console embedded in the wall. "That should do it."

He smiled and nodded. "Yes, I can see you now. You look healthy but tired."

"True on both counts. I've been through a lot, but Oliver did a great job healing my injuries."

"Ah. A good segue leading to our issues. I suppose you did that intentionally."

"You mentioned health, not me."

He chuckled. "You're right. I suppose it's always on my mind."

"Well, Oliver's been working on healing Crystal, and it's sapped his energy. He'll need to get some much-needed rest before he tries to heal you completely. It's really exhausting."

"I understand. Fortunately, your Captain Warren allowed me to contact my agent at the Gamma Five Zeta station, and he is awaiting word on whether or not to kill or release his hostages. In the meantime, he is keeping them in a comfortable situation. That won't last forever, though. If he doesn't hear from me again within two Alpha One days, he will begin killing them, one each hour. That countdown began five hours ago, so we now have about forty-three hours before the first hostage dies."

"But if Oliver heals you, I have no leverage, nothing to make sure you keep your word."

"You've already determined that I am not lying about our deal. I will see it through."

"True. You aren't lying, but what if you change your mind? That's not the same as a lie. I don't know how to detect that, and you're too good at blocking my mind reading. I can't probe your thoughts. And even if I could, I'm not sure I could detect a lie in a thought."

He folded his hands in his lap. "Megan, I will be your leverage as we travel to Alpha One, and I will show you the Zeta station there. That's part of our deal. As a gesture of good faith, I will acquiesce to staying in this cell after I am healed on the condition that you fully release me after I give you the Zeta station. Since I am trusting you to do so, I hope you will trust me to live up to my end of the arrangement. And I will take yet another step to sweeten the deal. I will tell my agent to release one of the hostages now, and you won't have to give me anything in return."

"I don't see how I can say no to that."

"Of course you can't. But I have to approve who is to be released. I can't allow it to be someone who is as resourceful as your father or your aunt. You may choose from among the others."

"That's easy. Zoë. She's not healthy enough to stay locked up. And then your agent wouldn't have to keep the negative energy going. Zoë's the one who can kill him with her powers. No one else would be a danger to him. So, if he sends her to the Delta Zero station in a glider, he'll be safe. We can meet her there."

The admiral nodded. "That would work well for both of us."

"How will you tell him?"

He touched a band on his wrist. "This is the device I use to send a daily message to the kill switch. I can also send a message to my agent using IGMC. But you need not worry. Emerson relays the message through his port, so he can tell you exactly what my messages say."

"So Emerson also relays your kill-switch messages?"

"Yes, but don't assume that he can save one of those messages and send it again in case of my death. I programmed the kill switch to authenticate my messages based on parameters that differ every day."

"I understand, but we still have an impasse about what happens after our deal is done. I don't want you to go in hiding somewhere with the kill switch still active."

"Because we all know I'm going to die someday." He took in a deep breath and let it out slowly. "That impasse will remain in place. I will not budge on that point. But at least you will have the Alpha One Zeta station, and you can fly it to wherever you please."

"We're going over old ground."

"Indeed, we are. May I suggest that we put our plan into motion?" He began tapping on his wristband with a finger. "I am ordering my agent to release Zoë immediately. He will tell her how to access food and a bed on the Delta Zero Zeta station."

"All right. I'll see if Oliver feels ready to heal you, but, like I said, he might want to rest first." As I watched him tap out the message, the surreal nature of our encounter hit me pretty hard. This man hated me with a fiery passion, and I hated everything he stood for—every aspect of his foul enslavement of children for his personal benefit. Dealing with this monster made me sick to my stomach. But what else could I do? Now that he was sending a message to release Zoë, it seemed like I had to continue with the plan.

Or did I?

"There," he said with another tap on the band. "I sent the message. Feel free to verify with Emerson that it reflects what I promised."

"I will." I rose from the chair. "I'll be back with Oliver as soon as he's ready."

The admiral reclined on his cot. "I'll be waiting."

I turned the camera and monitor off. As I walked out of the brig, I called, "Emerson, did you get the message from Fairbanks? It's in IGMC."

"Affirmative."

"Please read it to me."

"It says, 'Release Zoë, the telekinetic girl. Put her in a glider and send her to the Delta Zero Zeta station. Instruct her on where to find food and a bed there. Turn off the negative energy for the rest of the hostages.'"

"Pretty much exactly what he said he would do." I walked to the infirmary and peeked in. The lights had been dimmed, but I could still see Crystal lying in the closest bed and her mother sitting in a reclining chair with her legs propped, apparently asleep. I tiptoed in and looked Crystal over. A bandage covered her neck wound, but no blood was evident. She breathed easily, her face free of pain lines.

Since Oliver finished his work here, he probably went to bed at his quarters. I exited the infirmary and began climbing the ladder to the bridge level. "Emerson, let me know if there is any response to the admiral's message."

"Acknowledged."

I stopped at the bridge and looked at the viewing window. The Nine zoomed through space, stars gleaming on the dark background. At least twenty children had gathered in front of the window, staring at the awesome display. Isaac and Ophelia stood in their midst, pointing at various stars as the children oohed and aahed. We had decided that they would take turns sleeping and eating. Apparently, these kids would have their turns in the cycle later.

Captain Warren rose from my seat and gestured for me to sit, but I smiled and shook my head, prompting her to sit there again.

Isaac turned and pointed at me. "There she is. Captain Megan Willis, the girl we've been telling you about.

All of the kids pivoted and looked at me, their eyes wide, some gasping. Isaac waved an arm. "Go on. Tell her what you told me."

They all hurried toward me single file, a girl, maybe nine years old with short brown hair, the first in line. She halted in front of me, stood on tiptoes, and kissed me on both cheeks. "Thank you, Megan. You're our hero."

One after another, boys and girls from about eight years old to sixteen, each kissed my cheeks and made similar statements. A boy about my age came last of all, limping heavily. He dropped to one knee and kissed the back of my hand. Then he looked up into my eyes, his expression somber. "You saved my life. I was one of the kids who was going to be killed because I couldn't work hard enough. You see, I broke my leg, and—"

"He sure did," one of the younger girls called out, "He broke it saving my life. He didn't have to. He just did it."

The boy smiled, my hand still in his. "Well, I did save her life, but we do what we have to do, right?"

Tears welled. I resisted the urge to brush them away and let them trickle down my cheeks. I grasped his hand and lifted him to his full height, a couple of centimeters taller than me. "Yes, we do what we have to do. Thank you for saving her life."

"It was my pleasure, Megan Willis."

As I gazed at him, familiar truths returned to mind. These beautiful human beings were the admiral's chattel, forced to work in daily danger, beasts of burden to be put down when no longer useful. How could I keep making deals with such a monster? "What's your name?" I asked.

"Homer. Homer Wilkes."

I stood on tiptoes and kissed his forehead. "You are my brother, Homer, a true hero." I spread my arms toward the rest of the children. "You're all my brothers and sisters."

The kids gathered close, and I reached around them as far as I could. As we hugged, I looked at Isaac and Ophelia. They both brushed tears from their cheeks. I waved a hand toward them. "Bring it in, you two. I have news."

When they joined us, I looked at them in turn. "Zoë is being released. If all goes well, she'll be at the Delta Zero Zeta station when we arrive."

Ophelia wept. Isaac pushed closer, wrapped me in his arms, and kissed the top of my head. "I don't know what we'd do without you, Megan Willis. I just don't know."

An image of Zoë jumping in front of me to block a laser blast invaded my thoughts again. She was ready to give her life for mine and very nearly did. "And I don't know what I'd do without Zoë."

Isaac gestured for the kids to back away. "I'm sure you have important things to do."

"Of course, but nothing's more important than these kids. They're the reason I do what I do."

As I walked toward the sleeping area, I waved. "I'll see you all again soon." I hurried to Oliver's quarters, a room that he now shared with Isaac and a couple of boys. The door stood ajar, so I peeked into the dimness, whispering, "Oliver?"

After a few seconds, the door opened a bit wider, held by Oliver, Perdantus on his shoulder. He blinked his bleary eyes. "What's up?"

"Did I wake you?"

"Sort of. I was kinda half asleep. Lots of stuff on my mind."

"Yeah. Same here."

"Want to talk?" he asked.

"If you're not too tired."

"Not too tired if it's important."

I looked past him. One of the boys lay on Oliver's double bed. "The galley okay? With all the new supplies, we can find something good to eat."

"Yeah. Sure. All right if Perdantus comes along?"

"Definitely. I saw Quixon bring in some fresh seedpods."

"Yes," Perdantus said. "They're my favorite. I haven't had them in far too long."

With Perdantus still on Oliver's shoulder, we walked to the galley where we found several children sitting at the main table, eating what appeared to be bowls of some kind of meat stew with vegetables. When one of the boys saw us, he shot to his feet and backed away from the table, pulling another boy with him. "We just finished. Take our places, and I'll get a bowl of stew for both of you."

I smiled. "Thank you." After Oliver and I seated ourselves, the boy set a bowl of stew and a spoon in front of each of us. He stood nearby, as if waiting to do anything else we might need, while the others at the table gawked.

The first boy noticed and waved a hand. "Everyone finish up and clear out of here."

In a clatter of bowls and spoons, the children collected the dishes, put them in the sink, and filed out of the galley, leaving Oliver, Perdantus, and me alone.

After I got a handful of seed pods and set them on the table, Perdantus fluttered to them and began eating, while Oliver and I munched on our stew, hot and delicious. I told them about my meeting with Admiral Fairbanks, including how he released Zoë without me giving anything in return.

Perdantus stopped eating and looked at me. "It's a negotiation tactic. Although he said he was giving Zoë to you freely, her release isn't free at all. He knows that you will feel obligated to reciprocate. He is using your emotions to bind you to the deal."

"But don't I still have to go through with it? I made a deal."

"You were coerced by the hostage situation," Perdantus said. "No deal is valid when it is forced. My opinion is that you are free to annul the deal."

Oliver nodded. "I agree with Perdantus. It's like he held a gun to your head to force you to sign a contract. It isn't right."

"But if I go along with it, maybe I'll be able to figure out how to stop the kill switch. Since Crystal verified that it really exists, I think nothing's more important."

Oliver nodded. "Agreed."

Perdantus hopped closer and looked straight at me. "Megan, if you and Oliver are strong enough to partake in the healing process, it will do no harm to continue with your plan, but it's important to deal from a position of strength."

I met his stare. "Isn't offering healing a position of strength?"

"Not to Admiral Fairbanks. To a murderous scoundrel like him, being kind and sacrificial is a sign of weakness. For you to take the upper hand, avoid letting him set the parameters. Take charge of the negotiations and set the parameters yourself. He's the one in the brig, not you. That is your position of strength."

I nodded. "That makes sense." He hopped back to the seed pods and continued eating.

I pushed my empty bowl to the side. "As long as Fairbanks has that wristband, he can contact his agent at the Gamma Five Zeta station and order executions. I could take it from him, but then he couldn't send the daily message to disable the kill switch."

"And," Oliver said, "if you give it back to him only for the kill switch, he could refuse to send it, and it would get triggered. Billions would die, but he wouldn't care."

"Except that he wouldn't have any leverage anymore. We could just kill him."

Oliver pointed at me. "And that's his advantage over you. He thinks you wouldn't do it. You spared him once before, so he doesn't think you have it in you to execute him."

"Yeah, but if I *had* killed him before, billions of people would be dead."

"But that's only if he's telling the truth about the kill switch. We're sure it exists, but we have no proof about what it would actually do."

"Except that he said the planets would be destroyed. That was under Crystal's hypnosis. It has to be true."

"Right. Right. I forgot. The ultimate leverage."

"It's hard to remember everything when we're so tired." I released a heavy sigh. "The bottom line is that if we heal him, the only thing I'll have left to hold over him is his freedom."

"Then you have to hang on to that. It's your last bargaining chip. Use it to get to the kill switch."

"Exactly what I was thinking." I rose from my seat. "I know what to do now. You go ahead and eat more, sleep, whatever you need to recover. I'm going back to renegotiate with Fairbanks. I'll call you if I need you."

Perdantus looked at me. "Do you want my help?"

I shook my head. "I'd better do this on my own, but I will ask Emerson to record our conversation. You can analyze it later. And having a record of our deal might be helpful."

"Agreed."

I caressed his chest feathers, then patted Oliver on the back. "Pray for me. I'll need it."

After putting my bowl in the sink, I walked toward the ladder, calling, "Emerson, do you automatically record conversations with prisoners in the brig?"

"Affirmative."

I began climbing down the ladder. "How long do you save them?"

"Seven days, unless you request a permanent archive."

When I reached the lower floor, I walked toward the brig. "I am requesting a permanent archive of all conversations in the brig until further notice, including the one I had today."

"Acknowledged."

I sat in the same chair and turned on the camera, monitor, and comms. When the admiral appeared on the screen, again lying on the cot, I took a deep breath and spoke with an authoritative tone. "Admiral Fairbanks, I have something to say to you."

He sat up and looked at me, smiling. "To what do I owe this extra visit to my humble—"

"Shut up and listen. After speaking with my counselors, I have decided to alter our arrangements as follows: Oliver and I will do our best to heal you completely, but we make no promises about whether or not we will succeed. Once we get to the Zeta station at Delta Zero, we will verify Zoë's safety and take her on board. From there, we will travel to the Gamma Five Zeta station. You will tell your agent to release the rest of the hostages to us whether you are completely healed or not. After that, we will travel to the Alpha One Zeta station, and you will hand over control of it to me. You will also show me the kill switch and tell me how to disable it. If you don't, you will remain in the brig until we figure out how to disable it ourselves. Your freedom will depend on our success. We will begin the healing process when Oliver has had enough rest."

I took in a silent breath and stared at him. He stroked his chin and stared back at me for a long moment before nodding. "I accept your terms."

"Good."

As I rose from the chair, he waved a hand. "Sit down, Megan. I have something else to say."

"You're my prisoner. You don't tell me what to do." I turned the comms off and walked out of the brig with a lively gait. It felt so good to take control of the situation and not let the admiral think he called the shots. He would have to look at the four blank walls and decide if that's where he wanted to stay for the rest of his life. And since I didn't provide a time frame for how long Oliver would need, I could delay the healing as much as I wanted to. Every moment he continued to suffer would make him all the more ready to do what I wanted.

During the rest of the journey to the Delta Zero station, I mingled with the children and got to know as many as I could. Fortunately, they quickly dropped the hero worship and acted more like grateful friends. I learned that none of them were Starborn, even though a few were born on Gamma Five. Most came from Beta Three or Alpha One. I promised that I would take all of them home as soon as I could.

When we drew within a few hours of reaching Delta Zero, I visited the infirmary. Jade was still there, sitting upright in her recliner, chatting with Crystal, a smaller bandage now on her neck. When they saw me, they smiled. "About time you showed up," Crystal said. "I was wondering if you forgot about me."

Jade shushed her. "You're not supposed to talk yet. Besides, Megan's been here several times, and you slept through every visit."

Crystal pouted. "Because Oliver kept giving me medicine that knocks me out cold."

I walked closer. "If you say another word, I'm going to bop you on the head." I pulled her into my arms. "It's so good to see you awake. I thought I was going to lose you."

When I drew back, she grinned. "Nope. I'm super glued to your six. You couldn't peel me off with a blowtorch."

I shook a finger. "What did I just tell you about talking?"

"Bop me on the head, then, if that's how you treat an injured friend." She pointed at her head. "But don't damage the goods. My mother washed my face and hair, changed my bandage, got me dressed, and fed me some really good stew. I'm ready to get back to being the best navigator the Nebula Nine has ever had."

I laughed. "And I'll be glad to have you back as soon as Oliver gives you clearance."

"Oh. He already did. Ask him. Now I just need clearance from my mother." Crystal looked at Jade and spoke in an expectant tone. "Right, dear mother?"

Jade smiled and shook her head. "How can I argue with that?" She waved a hand. "All right, but no more fights with half-blind guys carrying a knife."

Crystal raised a hand as if swearing an oath. "I promise not to try to use my powers to hypnotize any knife-wielding Alliance soldier who is guarding Admiral Fairbanks on Delta Ninety-five. Never, ever again."

Jade laughed. "I guess I'll have to take what I can get."

I helped both Crystal and Jade rise, and we walked together out of the infirmary, Jade limping only a little. Apparently, Oliver had worked a lot on her healing as well. They were both able to climb the ladder to bridge level with me giving them a telekinetic boost from behind.

When we walked onto the bridge, Captain Warren and Oliver rose from the captain and first mate's chairs and applauded, Perdantus chirping in delight from Oliver's shoulder. Isaac and Ophelia clapped their hands as well. Isaac rose from the navigator's chair and gestured for Crystal to sit.

The moment she sat and the applause died down, Emerson spoke through the ceiling speakers. "Captain Willis, Admiral Fairbanks tried to send a message to his agent though his wristband. I think you will want to know what it says."

I looked at his console. "Tell me."

"It says, and I quote, 'The little brat is trying to be boss. Let's show her who is really in charge. Kill her father immediately. That will put her in her place.'"

29

I swallowed hard. "You said he *tried* to send it. Did it go through?"

"Negative. I blocked the message. But it is attached to his daily signal to disable the kill switch. Since they are attached, they will either go through together or not at all."

"Can't you separate them?"

"I can separate them, but it is possible that the kill-switch message relies on something in the attached message. The result of sending a severed portion could be disastrous."

"And Fairbanks knows it," Oliver said. "He won't send his daily kill-switch message without the command to kill your father."

Perdantus flew to my shoulder and spoke quickly. "This is the admiral's attempt to restore his position of strength. The kill switch is his most powerful weapon, so he is putting it forth and daring you to stop him. If you give in by offering him healing sooner so that he'll send a kill-switch delay without the command to kill your father, he will have the upper hand from now on."

Trying not to tremble, I nodded. "So should I just let the message go through?"

Everyone stared at me without saying a word, and no wonder. They knew that only I could make the decision to possibly sacrifice my father to save multiple planets. My decision rested on two factors. Did I believe in the reality of the kill switch's danger to the planets? If so, could I trust my father to defend himself against the admiral's agent?

I took a deep breath and, keeping my voice steady, spoke with determination. "Send the message, then block all of his messages for the rest of the day."

"Acknowledged."

With my hands balled into fists, I strode toward the ladder again. "I'm going to the brig. Emerson, show the brig's camera view on the front screen."

"Acknowledged."

I slid down the ladder and stalked into the brig, drawing my laser blaster from its holster. When I reached the cell's controls, I opened the door, stepped into the room, and aimed the blaster at Admiral Fairbanks as he sat upright on the cot.

He chuckled. "I thought you might show up soon."

"Glad you're not surprised." I fired the blaster at his thigh, sending a laser bullet through his camo pants and into the flesh.

As smoke curled from the sizzling entry point, he clutched the wound and groaned. "Are you out of your mind? I have the power of life and death over your loved ones."

I fired at his other thigh and drilled a similar hole into it. "If you don't shut up, the next one's going through your jaw."

With a hand over each wound, he glared at me, his anger tightening his grimace. "Now they will all die, and it's because of your arrogance. You are pulling the trigger that ends their lives."

"This is the only trigger I'm pulling." I fired a laser bullet that slammed into the side of his face and pierced straight through. He toppled to the floor and moaned. I spiced my words with a growl. "Don't mess with my family."

He sat up and glared at me, his face sliced open from cheek to cheek, making him look like a hideous monster. Gasping, he slurred his words. "I will … kill you all."

"With the kill switch? Not likely. That laser bullet cauterized your wounds. You'll survive. You'll just be the ugliest human being in the galaxy until you die, a true monster."

His lips flapped as he spoke, making him almost impossible to understand. "Then I will … not be allowed … to access … the kill switch. My agent there … won't recognize me."

I pointed at myself with a thumb. "But he'll recognize me when I make myself look like you. I'll bring you along for the biometrics, maybe with a bag over your head, but my new face will get us wherever I need to go."

Spittle dripped from his mostly severed lower lip. "If you want … to see a monster … you should … look in a mirror."

"I would see a monster, but only after I change to looking like you." I walked out, closing the cell door behind me. As my fury subsided, the admiral's words echoed in my brain. *If you want to see a monster, you should look in a mirror.*

I halted and glanced back. Was he right? Had I completely lost control of myself? Had my passion to stop this demonic slaver turned me into a wrathful monster? Only a couple of days ago, I found the ability to show mercy to an enemy—Zeke. What happened to that? Did I still have an easily broken temper, a sharp, untamed tongue, and a trigger finger for violence? Choosing wrath over mercy again, I was far from the rational, controlled warrior I needed to be.

And now my father was probably going to die, and I couldn't do anything about it.

I ran to the infirmary, threw myself into the bed Crystal had been in, and sobbed. I cried out, my words shattered by spasms. "God … I'm so sorry. I'm supposed to … to show mercy … but I blew up again … I lashed out again … chose wrath again. I was trained … trained to be violent … against my enemies … and that part of me took over. I just can't … can't seem to control it."

I lay quietly for a minute, trying to settle my voice before continuing. "God, why is this all so hard? I'm just a kid. Just a kid trying to save the galaxy. And I have no idea what I'm doing. Can't you just tell me what to do? Send someone to give me advice? I'll listen. I know I don't always listen, but I promise I will."

After a few more minutes of silence, I felt a hand touch my head. I turned toward it. Crystal stood next to the bed, petting me. "I'm always here for you, Sister. Always."

I sniffed hard. "How long have you been listening to me bellyache?"

"Long enough to know how much you're hurting." She pushed hair out of my eyes. "You're super upset that you … well … as you would probably say, chose wrath over mercy."

"How would *you* say it?"

"That you chose your family and friends over a kid-torturing, murdering psycho monster. I mean, it's cool that you were nice to Zeke. Maybe he didn't know what Fairbanks was up to, and you shouldn't have tried to poke his eyes out. Lesson learned. But Fairbanks is different. He knows exactly what he's doing. If you show him mercy, he'll spit it right back in your face. You would actually be giving him more ammo to hurt the ones you love."

"So you're saying that showing mercy to him is like pointing a gun at my own people?"

"Exactly. And kicking his butt like you did is the only language he understands. Deep inside, you knew that. And love for your family, including tagalongs like me, took over. He deserved wrath. In fact, wrath was the only answer this time. Save mercy for those who need it. Like yourself."

"Myself? Are you saying I need mercy?"

"More than anyone on this ship, Sister. More than anyone else. Stop punishing yourself for doing the right thing. We all needed you to bust his chops. And you did it, literally."

After gazing into her tear-filled eyes for a moment, I reached out with both arms. She climbed into bed with me, and we held each other, both crying softly.

After several minutes, Emerson interrupted the comforting silence. "Captain Willis, we are approaching the Delta Zero Zeta station. Captain Warren wants me to let you know that she can pilot the ship into an arrival bay if you wish."

"No. I'll be right there." I pulled away from Crystal and set my feet on the floor. She did the same on the other side of the bed. I walked to a sink and used a paper towel to wash my face, then turned toward the door. "On my six?"

She grinned. "With pleasure."

I hurried to the bridge and found my seat empty, Oliver sitting in his usual spot. Captain Warren stood near the front, pointing at the viewing screen. "That one looks good. The signal light is green, and the door is open, almost like someone is expecting us."

"It's Zoë," I said as I sat in the captain's chair. "She knows how to operate the station." Isaac and Ophelia, standing at the navigator's console, held hands, both brushing tears.

Captain Warren turned toward me and smiled. "Then take us in, Captain Willis."

I grasped the yoke. "I see that we're at a good speed, decelerating at a perfect rate. Thank you, Captain Warren."

"You're welcome." She turned toward the front. "I would like to stay here and watch what you do. I haven't had much practice with these stations. The only one I landed in gave me a pretty rough bump."

"Sometimes it's hard to know how strong artificial gravity will be in these bays." As I guided the Nine toward the open doorway, I turned toward Oliver. "Did you check on Fairbanks?"

"Yep. He survived. He let me patch him up a bit. His face was a mess, but I was able to take away some of the pain."

"Good. I wasn't trying to kill him." My hands firm on the yoke, I landed the Nine in the bay. The doors behind us immediately closed, and the interior light came on.

"I am receiving a message," Emerson said, "from the control room of this station."

"Let's hear it."

Zoë's voice blasted through the speakers. "Greetings. I will be your hostess for this arrival. Feel free to stand and stretch while I fill your compartment with air."

I smiled. "Thank you, Zoë. Are you planning to board the Nine right away?"

"Coming now. This station is going to zap the Nine over to the Gamma Five station in ten minutes. That'll give me time to tell you what's going on. See you in two minutes. You should have plenty of air in the bay by then."

"Got it." I set a timer to open the ramp in two minutes.

Captain Warren backed away from the ramp before turning toward me. "When we get to Gamma Five, I will take my leave there and catch a transport to the planet." She bowed her head. "It has been a great pleasure working with you, Captain Megan Willis, but from now on, I will call you simply Megan."

"I feel the same way, Josie." I extended a hand. "It has been an honor."

She shook my hand. "I will have to change into something that doesn't identify me as Alliance. I'm sure my commission as an officer has been terminated."

"You are correct," Emerson said. "I received an updated roster list, and you are no longer among the officers. Ensign Weston, however, is still in good standing."

"And yet you still let me pilot this ship, Emerson?" Josie asked.

"I received the list. I did not say that I implemented it. As far as the Nebula Nine is concerned, you are still authorized to be its pilot."

"Thank you, Emerson." She walked toward the rear of the bridge. "I'll see if I can find something in one of the wardrobes, maybe a maintenance outfit."

The moment she left, the ramp began to lower. Seconds later, Zoë walked up the ramp, a serious expression on her face. Since I had expected a big smile, her countenance raised new worries.

I ran to her, gave her a hug, and kissed her forehead. "Are you all right?"

"I'm fine. Just kind of weak. But I'm worried about the other hostages. The guy who's holding them keeps threatening your father, saying he'll be the first one to die. His name is Evan Stude, but we call him Stooge. Anyway, when he let me go, he said if any of us tries to rescue our friends, he'll kill them all. The only hope we have is that he turned off the negative energy where he's keeping everyone. I don't know what Lyric and Echo can do with their powers now that they can use them. Maybe they figured out something, but I don't know."

"I hope they did. Admiral Fairbanks sent a message to the guy you call Stooge, telling him to kill my father."

Zoë covered her mouth. "Oh, no! That's awful. We need to get back right away. Stooge is a mean one."

"We will." I set a hand on her shoulder and turned her toward her parents. "Someone has been waiting a long time for this moment."

When Zoë saw them, she gasped. "Mom! Dad!" She started to break into a jog, but she grimaced and walked slowly toward them.

Isaac leaped into a run, scooped her into his arms, and walked toward Ophelia. "It's so good to see you again, my precious gem."

Zoë's smile stretched wider than I had ever seen it. "You, too, Dad."

When he arrived, he set her down, and the three embraced, all smiling as they wept.

I walked closer. Of course, they needed their reunion time, but we didn't have much time to spare. "Zoë, how many more minutes until we get zapped to Gamma?"

She drew away from their hug. "Maybe six or so."

"How did you get here? I mean, did you get zapped over in a glider, or what?"

She grinned. "For a short time, I was the captain of the Astral Dragon. It's in another bay. Your father and Echo fixed her up. She's running like a champ. Well, maybe ninety percent. And we borrowed a glider and loaded it in the rover bay."

"That's great." I spoke toward the ceiling. "Emerson, patch me through to an all-ship channel."

"You are now connected."

"Josie, it's Megan. Have you ever been a pirate?"

Josie's voice came through the speakers. "What in dragon blazes are you talking about?"

"Just listen. Go to my closet. You'll find a uniform my mother used to wear. I think it'll fit you well enough. You're about to become the acting captain of the Astral Dragon. She's in another bay, but you'll have to hurry. The Nine's going to be zapped to Gamma Five in about five minutes."

"Understood."

"Tobias," I said, "are you familiar with the Astral Dragon?"

His voice replaced Josie's. "Quite intimately. Admiral Fairbanks commissioned me to go over every centimeter of the Dragon to find any flaws or weaknesses. I know her inside and out, though I've never set foot in her."

"Now you have your chance. I need you to go with Josie to the Dragon. I hope you'll accept a commission as the new chief engineer on that ship."

"Gladly."

"Apparently the Dragon still needs a few repairs, so you'll have to run some diagnostics. I'll make sure Sonya is ready to help you. Meet Josie here on the bridge."

"Aye, Captain Willis. I'm on my way."

Zoë turned toward the ramp, still holding hands with her parents. "I'll set the system to send the Dragon ten minutes after the Nine gets zapped."

"Nope. You stay with your mom and dad. I know how to do it, and I can run faster. You tell Captain Warren where to go to find the Dragon. I know you haven't met her, but you'll recognize the Astral Dragon captain's outfit she's wearing."

She saluted. "Aye, Captain."

I yanked a drawer open under Emerson's console, grabbed a comm bud from it, and inserted it in my ear. "Emerson, program this bud to cross communicate with the Nine and the Dragon. You know the protocols."

"Communication channels are now linked."

I hustled down the ramp and onto the bay floor, spied the bay's number, and ran toward the exit. "Sonya, this is Megan. I'm sending a new captain and chief engineer to the Astral Dragon. Prepare to receive relevant data from Emerson, including photos and voice prints from the Alliance database."

Sonya spoke through the earbud. "I acknowledge your authority in this matter, and I will gladly accept data from Emerson since he is the only perfectly rational entity from his ship, but my programming suggests that I warn you about giving two of the most important positions on this ship to Alliance goons."

I opened the door and ran through the corridor. "Goons? What makes you say that?"

"Your mother used that word when describing Alliance officers. I am merely using her designation. From my experience, the word is accurate."

I burst into the stairwell, flexed my biceps to charge my legs, and zoomed up the steps, jumping from landing to landing. "Well, don't call them goons to their faces. To you they will be Captain Josie Warren and Ensign Tobias Weston."

"Acknowledged. And I have received the data from Emerson. I am ready to turn control over to Captain Warren once she matches the voice print from Emerson's data."

"Perfect. Thank you." When I reached the proper floor, I ran into the control room and scanned the various monitors. After I found a camera feed that showed the Nebula Nine, I read the countdown. Only two minutes, twelve seconds left before zapping. I tried to enter a new number to delay the launch, but it was password protected. No time to call Zoë and go through that process. I could still make it.

I shifted to another monitor that showed the Astral Dragon, its ramp down. Josie and Tobias were running up the ramp and onto the bridge. As I programmed the transport gun, I called, "Astral Dragon launch in three minutes." I entered the command, dashed out of the control room, and leaped down the flights of stairs, mentally counting the Nine's timer down.

When I reached the Nine's level, my count had dropped to twenty seconds to go. I sprinted through the corridor and threw open the bay entry door. *Ten seconds.* At the opposite side of the bay, a thud and a click reverberated. The arrival/departure door was about to open. Both running and leaping, I hustled to the ramp, jumped to the bridge, and rolled to a sitting position, shouting, "Close the ramp!"

As the ramp rose, the gap between its end and the ship's body narrowed. I counted down—*Three, two, one.* A buzz sounded. Light flashed through the gap, shut off by the ramp's closure. Then, silence filled the bridge.

While our arrival bay door in the Gamma station closed and air poured into the chamber, I folded my hands in my lap and exhaled. "Phew! That was close!" I looked at the bridge's console seats. Oliver, Crystal, Zoë, Isaac, Ophelia, and Jade stared at me, some with worried expressions and some smiling. "I guess it's pretty funny, isn't it?"

Oliver walked over and extended a hand. "Need a lift?"

"Sure. Thank—" A knock on the outside of the ramp interrupted. I grabbed Oliver's wrist, pulled myself up, and backed away with him until I could see the front viewing screen, but whoever was knocking stood out of the camera's view.

"Emerson, is any camera showing who's out there?"

"Affirmative, and that person called on the high-security channel with an authorized command to lower the ramp."

"Authorized?" As the ramp opened, I withdrew my blaster from its holster. The moment the end of the ramp touched the bay floor, my father stepped up on it and faced me. I cried out, "Papa!" and ran to him.

He spread his arms and caught my leaping body. With a slow spin, he pivoted and kissed my forehead, then I kissed his. "You're alive!" I said. "I'm so glad you're alive."

"I am, indeed." He set me down. "But we have to hurry and get a healer to Lyric, or she won't be alive for long. She's in the control room. Two floors up."

"Lyric?" I waved to Oliver. "Let's go! Lyric needs us!"

As we ran toward the bay exit, Oliver called, "You go on ahead. I'm slowing you down. I know how to get there."

"Right." I charged my legs again, zoomed to the exit, and sprinted through the corridor, then galloped up the stairs. When I ran into the control room, I found a camo-clad human male lying curled on the floor in a pool of blood, but I couldn't tell who it was.

I turned him to his back, revealing the face of my father. I gasped. "Papa? I don't understand." I touched my earbud. "Papa? Can you hear me?"

His voice came through the bud. "Sorry for the delay. I had to get an earbud from Zoë. That's Lyric in the control room. She changed into me."

Lyric gurgled, blood seeping from the corner of her mouth. I found a splotch of blood on her shirt where it had been tucked into her pants. I pulled the shirt out, exposing her stomach. Blood streamed from a bullet hole near her navel, much like Mabel's wound. I set a palm on the entry point and pressed down. "What happened to her?"

"When the guard pulled a gun to shoot me," Papa said through the earbud, "she transformed into me at the last moment and tried to hypnotize him. Apparently she still had some of Crystal's power remaining from when she was the energy source. She told him to open the cell door, but her hypnosis wasn't powerful enough, and she just confused him. That's when he shot her, thinking she was me, but before she collapsed, she convinced him to open the cell. When he did, I threw him in and locked him up."

Lyric's respirations grew shallower. I laid my ear on her chest. Her heartbeat sounded slow, weak, and erratic. "Oliver!" I shouted as I lifted away. "I need you! I think we're losing her!"

"I'm here." He rushed through the doorway. "What've we got?"

"Bullet to the stomach. Lots of blood lost. Worst of all, her heart's really weak. I know she looks like my father, but it's Lyric."

"Keep checking her heart while I try to stop the bleeding."

"Got it." When I lifted my hand from the gunshot wound, her form reverted to normal, her face ashen and her lips just as gray. As tears welled in my eyes, I set a hand on her chest and felt the fragile beats while Oliver knelt at her other side and laid his hands on her stomach.

He grimaced. "So much damage! Bullet fragments everywhere. I can patch up the damage, but I can't remove the fragments."

"Just do the best you can."

"I am. I am." He closed his eyes. "It's hard to find the holes in her arteries because there's so little blood coming out."

"Oh no!" I said in a near shout. "That means her heart isn't pumping enough!"

Oliver replied in a calm voice, apparently trying to calm me down as well. "Do you remember how Oz changed wood to carbon in that spear in his heart?"

I worked hard to talk without squeaking. "Yeah. Really strange. But it worked."

"Can you try to do the same? I mean with bullet fragments. Change them to carbon. Some have sharp edges, and they keep cutting new holes."

"I've never tried to copy any of Oz's powers before, but I'll do my best."

"That's all Lyric can ask for."

I focused on Lyric's stomach and penetrated with my mind, but I couldn't see past a dark veil. I groaned. "Why isn't my power working? I can't see anything!"

Papa hustled in, followed by Jillian, Echo, Crystal, and a woman I had not seen before, likely Piper. All five knelt nearby, Papa behind me with his hand on my back. His touch felt good but irritating at the same time. Would he see me fail? The last time I saw his form next to me while I was trying to heal someone, he was Lyric in disguise. Now he was my real Papa, and Lyric was the dying patient instead of Oz.

Memories of that moment returned. Since I had really thought Lyric was my father, the idea boosted my motivation, and I was able to energize Oliver to the max. Now that my real father was here, shouldn't I get a similar boost, maybe even a bigger one? But, so far, I wasn't getting it.

I peeked down at my locket. It emitted no extra glow, no sign that I was being supercharged. What did I need to do to make that happen?

Papa's whispered voice entered my ears. "Barnabas taught me about the real God, the true deity who loves us enough to guide ignorant minds into his embrace. So, God, I pray now for my dear daughter, Megan. Give her the power she needs to revive this wonderful girl who literally sacrificed her life to save mine. She has been a valiant and loyal keeper of the Starborn energy that you infused in the planet, a power for good and not evil. I pray that you will not let evil triumph over this precious child of yours." He breathed a deep sigh. "Amen."

Jillian and Crystal whispered amens as well, and Piper added, "By your will, may righteousness be restored to this galaxy. Amen."

Echo whispered, "Amen and amen."

The chorus of amens seemed to float around the room, penetrating my mind again and again and transforming into synonyms—*truly, so be it, let it be so, reliable, faithful,* and on and on.

As the chorus continued, it seemed that power flowed with it, as if the words were being sung by a dynamic choir. My locket pulsed with scarlet light. The redness swelled and poured into my eyes and throughout my body, then into Lyric's abdomen.

The surging power made it easy to locate the scattered fragments. Each time I found one, I concentrated on it, mentally transforming it into harmless carbon, much like I transformed myself into someone else. Then I moved to the next fragment and the next and the next.

Since I had no idea how to transform anything into something else, a new idea struck me, as if placed there by a mind outside my own. Someone had to be guiding all of my efforts, whether I was energizing

Oliver, reading minds, moving objects, or detecting lies. I had no idea how any of them worked, so how could I be the captain of a ship I couldn't control or navigate? All I could do was sit in a passenger seat and watch it zoom along at the speed of my mind, God as my captain, the one who knew how everything worked and loved us enough to make it all happen.

After a few minutes, I had transformed all of the fragments I could see. I checked Lyric's heart. It beat with perfect rhythm, strong and steady. Still on our knees, Oliver and I straightened our bodies and gazed at each other. He whispered, "I think we did it."

"We did." I reached across Lyric and gave Oliver a hug.

When I pulled away, he set a blood-smeared hand on Lyric's head. "Her color's coming back. I think she's going to be okay."

Piper dropped to her knees next to Lyric's head and stroked her long, silky brown hair, similar to her own. "My dear daughter, you're such a blessing. I don't know if you can hear me, but I love you so much." She laid one hand on my shoulder and the other on Oliver's. "Bless you both. Thank you. Thank you. Thank you."

We said, "You're welcome," and I added, "Thank God."

"Indeed." Piper broke into a sob. "I am so, so thankful."

After waiting for her emotions to settle, I touched her hand. "Any word on your husband?"

She inhaled deeply and shook her head. "But I have some friends in high places. I'll find him. I have a two-person glider here at the station. Once Lyric is well enough, we'll go to the planet and start our search."

With Papa's help, I rose to my feet, my legs wobbly. "So now we can—"

"Sorry to interrupt." Josie strode in, followed by Tobias. "I heard the healing through my earbuds, and I'd like to pause and celebrate, but we have a big problem."

"What?" I asked as Papa helped Oliver rise.

"The Alliance got wind of our arrival here, and several Gamma system patrol ships are on their way. We can't disable them like we did the Nebula cruisers. Besides, I'm sure the fleet changed the protocols by now, so we can't do it again."

I quickly introduced everyone to Captain Josie Warren and Ensign Tobias Weston. "Can we zap out of here to Alpha One in time?" I asked Josie.

"Not likely. We would have to be in the ships and ready to go within three minutes. I don't think we can all get back to the ships in time."

Tobias walked to one of the monitors and began tapping on the screen. "I'm moving the disintegration guns to the outer shell except for the two that are in the bays with the Astral Dragon and the Nebula Nine. The guns can disintegrate hostile ships."

I watched the array of guns as they moved around on the screen. "I noticed that the guns are on a track that lead to the outside, and I guessed they might be used as weapons. But the station's specs never mentioned anything like that."

Tobias smiled. "Because it's top secret. The Alliance doesn't want anyone outside of a few officers to know that a transportation depot can be turned into a deadly weapon."

"A few officers? You mean like you and who else?"

"Like me and my uncle. I know about it because I helped design the stations. He knew about it because he was head of security on the Nebula One. Admiral Fairbanks ordered the inclusion of the weapons capability, so he obviously knew about it."

I imagined the Zeta station orbiting the planet as well as the station orbiting Alpha One. "What would happen if the lasers were all aimed at the planet they're orbiting? Could they destroy it?"

He laughed. "Who would ever do something like that?"

"Humor me. What would happen if someone turned every bit of this station's power against the planet itself?"

Tobias made a final tap on the screen. "I suppose someone could put the station into a slow spin that would point the laser guns at the planet, several guns at a time. Maybe then or twenty could shoot with their full power, then they would rotate away, allowing ten or twenty other guns to shoot while the first shooters recharge, and so on."

"And what would happen to the planet?"

"It would disintegrate. Maybe not all at once, but eventually the guns could take the entire planet out."

My heart raced as I whispered, "The kill switch."

"What?"

I explained rapid-fire. "Admiral Fairbanks says he has a kill switch. If he dies, it's triggered, and billions of people will die, including people on one planet in every major star system. Could this station be part of a kill switch?"

Tobias shrugged. "It could be, I suppose, but if it is, I wasn't in on the programming."

"Can you find out if the switch is in the computer's code?"

"Almost certainly, but we need to defend the station first. Three ships will arrive in less than a minute, four more two minutes after that. I don't see any others on the horizon."

"Should I do anything?" I asked.

"No need. Just watch and learn."

The monitor now showed a map of the station with three tiny dots flying near the surface, orbiting slowly. Tobias pointed at the screen. "The first three ships are waiting for the others to arrive. They're congregating near the bay that holds the Nebula Nine, likely because they were able to use a thermal scanner to see the Nine behind the door."

Josie crossed her arms. "Those ships have torpedoes that can break that door but only if several of them shoot together. That's why they're waiting for the others to join them." She looked at Tobias. "How many would it take? Five or six ships?"

"Maybe five, but I think they'll wait for at least six to be sure. They don't want to waste torpedoes."

"Then wait for the sixth to show up before disintegrating them. We don't want any to get away. We'll hit the seventh when it shows up wondering where the others are."

"Wait," I said. "You're just going to kill everyone on board every ship?"

Josie swiveled her head toward me, her arms still crossed. "The kids are on the Nine. If we don't defend them, they'll all be killed. So will Admiral Fairbanks. And you know what that means."

I sighed. "The kill switch will be activated."

"And billions more will die." Josie refocused on the screen. "There is no other option."

I gritted my teeth. "I'm sick of Fairbanks holding the kill switch over our heads. I mean, of course we'd still defend the kids, but we need to know what's what."

"Agreed," Josie said. "And Tobias will examine the code as soon as he can."

"The sixth ship just arrived," Tobias said. "And they're making a semicircle to shoot at the door."

Josie gave him a nod. "Take them out."

"Getting a lock … got it." Tobias tapped on the screen six times in rapid succession. The view switched to a live camera feed that showed the ships hovering in a wide arc. Laser beams shot from the Zeta sphere and zapped all six ships into oblivion, leaving behind a fog of sparkles that quickly faded. "Enemy ships have been vaporized."

Nausea again erupted in my gut. Although those ships would've been the cause of countless deaths of innocent people, I couldn't help but think of their crews. How many of them had spouses and children of their own at home? But I had no options to offer, especially with no time to plan.

Josie patted Tobias on the back. "Good work. Now look for the kill switch code while we're waiting for ship number seven."

"Will do." Tobias stepped to the monitor on the right and pulled up a screen that scrolled lines of code from bottom to top. His eyes darted as he read the lines.

While he worked on that, I walked over to Lyric. She now sat on a wheeled chair, looking tired but no longer ashen. "How are you feeling?" I asked.

She gave me a smile, but I could tell it was forced. "Very weak, and quite a bit of pain in my stomach, but I guess that's better than dead, right?"

"Definitely. And you saved my father's life." I hugged her and kissed her forehead. "Thank you."

"You're welcome. Saving your father is the best thing I've ever done."

"I found it," Tobias said, pointing at the screen. "It's a devilish little monster. Disguised as part of the water filtration system. It's dormant until it receives a signal from somewhere outside the system."

"How did you find it so quickly?" I asked.

"Pretty simple. I know the three main programmers personally, and they all tag their sections of code. I just conducted a search for any code that didn't have one of their tags."

"Can you disable it?" I asked.

"Not easily. The code is read-only and password protected for write access. I would have to do some serious hacking to take it out."

"Admiral Fairbanks said he can access the kill switch at Alpha One with a biometric entry. Since that station triggers the others, maybe we should go there and somehow force him to give us access."

Josie nodded. "Agreed. You get everyone into the Nine, and I'll set the system to send you to the Alpha One station. The ensign and I will follow in the Astral Dragon after we take out the seventh ship. You'll need his help with hacking the Alpha One station."

"Why do you have to take out the seventh ship?" I asked.

"If we don't, their crew will report that the other ships are missing, then they would come into the control room and see where we went. I don't know of a way to hide our destination after the fact. Someone will eventually investigate, but we'll have a huge head start."

Papa stepped up to my side and spoke to Josie. "Jillian and I will take the Astral Dragon and ferry Piper, Lyric, and all the kids to a depot on the planet's surface. There, we can get them aboard a transport to Gamma Four. They should be safe there while we try to disable the kill switch. Since Zoë hasn't healed completely, we should probably take her and her folks there as well. Tobias should go with Megan on the Nine, so he'll be ready to work on the kill switch right away. After Jillian and I drop everyone off, we'll come back here and zap over to Alpha One."

Josie nodded. "You are the most experienced pilot of the Astral Dragon, so that's a better plan. I'll come along and facilitate the transports to Gamma Four and stay with the kids. We'll worry about getting them to their homes later."

I hugged Josie. "Thank you for everything. We couldn't have done this without you."

"Glad to." She patted my back. "I'll have to find another job now, something that doesn't serve the interests of a slave trafficker. That doesn't look good on a résumé."

I slid my hand into my father's and looked into his eyes. "All right, Papa. I'll see you and Aunt Jillian on Alpha One."

Part
03
Alpha One

31

I strapped into the captain's chair in the Nebula Nine, Oliver at my side in the first mate's seat. Crystal and Jade sat together at the navigator's console, while Tobias worked in the engine room, alone now since Lainie decided to go to Gamma Five with Josie. Zoë agreed to go home with her parents, and the kids all left as well, making the ship feel empty, though tranquil. Still, the thought of Admiral Fairbanks in the brig sent shivers up my spine. Fortunately, we would be at the Alpha One Zeta station in a matter of seconds. I wouldn't have to let him send another message to his kill switch until tomorrow, and maybe not even then if I could figure out how to disable it.

Josie's voice entered my ear. "Are you ready?"

"Ready."

"Just remember, Alpha One is Alliance headquarters. You're sure to get some questions about being there, but Ensign Weston should be able to clear the way. He has codes he can send to the station control room that'll keep you out of trouble."

"Won't someone ask why I'm captain of the Nine?"

"Only if you still look like yourself. Can you change into another officer?"

"I can, but it has to be someone I know. I can't be you, because you're no longer in their system. And it's hard to sound like anyone perfectly, unless I scan that person's larynx."

"Admiral Fairbanks," Crystal said. "No one will question him. And you've done it before. You can do it again."

Acid burned deep in my stomach. "It was like putting on a demon costume."

She shrugged. "You got anyone else in mind?"

I heaved a sigh. "No. I was already planning to change into him when I needed to access the kill switch, but I guess I can go ahead and do it now."

"Then get on with it. We've got a flight to catch."

"All right. But Oliver'd better have the nausea medicine ready." I closed my eyes and concentrated once again on a mental image of myself and my target, this time Admiral Dwight Fairbanks. As before, I made my image become the same as his, each change feeling like someone was stretching my body and face, and I again altered my clothes and my voice box.

After nearly a minute, I opened my eyes and turned toward Oliver. "How do I look?" My deeper voice made me shudder.

He cringed. "Hideous. Like the last time you did it. Maybe even more like him this time."

I swiveled my chair toward Crystal. "Do you agree?"

"With the hideous part? Definitely. But he looks a lot worse since you split his face in half. I'm glad you didn't copy that."

"We'll go with it." I spun my seat back in place. "Ready, Josie. Send us to Alpha One."

"Five seconds," Josie said. "Goodbye, Megan. I hope to see you again someday."

"Same to you. Sorry for the Fairbanks voice, but thanks again for everything."

Soon, light flashed through the bridge, then quickly faded. A terrible sensation radiated into my body, a familiar feeling now, the same one I felt when exposed to the negative energy. Why would someone transmit it at the Alpha One station?

Emerson spoke through the ceiling speakers in the Alpha One language. "The Nebula Nine is being hailed from the station's control room—audio and video. Remember that we are now in the Alpha system where Alpha One is spoken exclusively."

I cleared my throat and spoke in that language. "Patch the signal through to the main viewing window."

"You are now connected."

An image of a much fancier control room appeared. A man in an Alliance uniform took up most of the screen as he sat on a swivel chair. The stripes on his shoulder indicated the rank of ensign. He blinked hard. "Admiral Fairbanks? We weren't expecting you." He rose, stood at attention, and saluted. "Welcome, sir. Your arrival bay is now filling with air, and you should be able to deboard your ship soon."

I rose as well and returned the salute. "Are you alone in the control room, Ensign?"

"Yes, Admiral."

"I am here on a top secret mission. I trust that you will keep my presence to yourself. You are to erase all records of my arrival as well as our conversation."

"Of course, sir. Of course. What else can I do for you? Food? Drink? This station is well stocked with anything you might want."

I waved a hand as if irritated. "Don't bother me with trifles. I have an engineer on board who is to be given access to this station's systems and supplied with all necessary passwords. While he is working, I want you to leave the room, and don't ask questions."

"Of course, sir, but some of the access paths require your biometric key."

"Yes, yes, I know, but what is it? A fingerprint? A DNA sample? Ever since that brat, Megan Willis, nearly killed me, my memory hasn't been the same."

He gave me a suspicious stare. "If you don't mind me asking, sir, I heard that you were badly burned, but I see no scars. What happened?"

"I was visited by a healer, and that's a story too long to tell at the moment."

"Very well." He shifted nervously. "The biometric key is a drop of blood."

I studied his expression. His furrowed brow and narrowed eyes still displayed suspicion. Was this a test? Requiring blood from an admiral didn't sound right, but my lie-detector alarm stayed quiet. Still, that didn't mean anything if negative energy had taken away my powers. I had to go with a bluff. "A drop of blood? I don't remember that."

His brow relaxed. "Oh. Yes. Of course you wouldn't. I apologize. That's the biometric for one of our engineers. Yours is a thumbprint. Much simpler."

"Now that sounds right. I will be there with my engineer and both of my thumbs in a moment. Signing off for now." I tapped on the console, terminating the connection.

"Whoa!" Jade said. "That ensign was testing you, wasn't he?"

I nodded. "But I couldn't tell he was lying. That's not good."

Crystal tilted her head. "I didn't detect the lie either. What's going on?"

"I think they're broadcasting negative energy like they did with the towers at the admiral's compound and the Delta Zero mine. It seems like standard practice for Fairbanks to try to neutralize Starborn powers. I felt it as soon as we got here."

Crystal grinned. "That means you're stuck in a Fairbanks suit until further notice.""

"Thanks for the reminder." I adjusted my earbud to fit in the admiral's considerably bigger ear. "Tobias, do you know the Alpha One language?"

"I'm fluent," he said in Alpha One.

"Have you been listening?"

"Yep. I'm on my way to the bridge. But what're you going to do about the thumbprint? I doubt that your transformation includes prints. You probably still have your own."

"I was thinking either Crystal or I could hypnotize the admiral into coming with us, but it looks like negative energy is being transmitted here. We don't have our powers."

"Then I'll have to see what I can do about shutting that signal off before we can bring Fairbanks with us to the control room."

"We could drug him and drag him along," Jade said. "No hypnosis needed."

I laughed under my breath. "That might raise a lot of questions if someone saw us."

Oliver rose from his seat. "I'll go and check on him. Maybe he'll make a bargain to do what we ask if I heal him some more."

When Oliver left, Tobias walked in looking at a small meter in his hand. "You're right. I'm picking up some sort of transmission. I'll see if I can find the source when we get to the control room."

"Okay." I pressed the button on my console to lower the ramp. "Get your game face on. It's show time."

"I'm ready." He touched his ear. "I'm wearing a bud tuned to your frequency."

When the ramp's end reached the floor, Oliver's voice blasted into my earbud. "Megan!"

"What?"

"Admiral Fairbanks is dead!"

I gasped. "Dead? Are you sure?"

"Positive. No pulse. No breathing. I found an empty bottle on the floor. It's his pain medication. I guess he took all the pills that were left."

Tobias winced. "Overdose. Obviously intentional."

"What in blazes did he do that for? Now the kill switch will be activated." I began pacing on the ramp. "But he already sent the disabling message today. That means we probably have twenty-four hours from when he sent it."

Crystal rose and walked toward me. "If you don't have his prints, how're you going to access the system? Cut his thumbs off and put them in your pocket?"

I halted and looked at her. "If I have to. I'll do anything to save billions of innocent lives."

"Admiral Fairbanks," a woman said from the end of the ramp.

I turned that way. Captain Fossella stood just beyond the ramp with three guards on either side, each with a laser pistol. "Yes?"

She clasped her hands behind her. "Admiral Fairbanks, by order of the Alliance counsel, you are under arrest for slave trafficking."

I concealed a swallow. How in the world could I get out of this? "What?" I said, putting on a surprised expression. "Slave trafficking? Absurd!"

"Thanks to a report we received from Captain Tillman, we have all the evidence we need to put you away for the rest of your life." She motioned to the guards. "Take him."

I whispered, hoping my earbud would pick up my words. "Do whatever you have to do to stop the kill switch. As soon as you cut off the negative energy or I get out of its range, I'll transform back to normal, and maybe they'll let me go."

A guard grabbed one of my arms, and a second guard grabbed the other. "Come peacefully," the second guard said.

I shook free. "There is no need for violence. I will go without resistance."

The guard pointed. "He has an earbud."

Fossella pinched the bud out of my ear. "Can't have him calling for help. Frisk him for weapons. Arms up."

I complied. One of the guards patted me down thoroughly from top to bottom. When he felt my arms, he stopped and rolled up one of my sleeves, exposing a bracelet. "What's this?"

"A harmless bracelet," I said. "Certainly not a weapon." Which was likely true. In this body, I might not have the ink circuitry at the surface of my skin like I did in the form of Renalda.

Fossella looked the bracelet over. "Like he said, it's harmless."

After the guard finished patting me, he and the others guided me down the ramp. When we arrived at the end, I looked at Fossella and spoke at a low volume. "The crew members on the Nine have no idea about what I was doing."

She nodded. "Very few people did. I recognize Oliver, and I'm sure he's not involved. His father is the one who exposed your crimes. I'll have the child-care team come soon to see about him and the girl."

"The girl is with her mother," I said. "No need to call anyone for her."

"Your claim will be investigated." She nodded at the guards. "Take him to the holding cell."

The two guards guided me toward the arrival bay's passenger exit door, the other guards pointing laser blasters at my back. If they put me in a holding cell, I would likely still be under the influence of the negative energy and unable to use my powers, including reverting back to my body. My only hope was for Tobias to shut the energy off, but would they allow him to find the source and cut it off? And what about the kill switch? Nothing was more important than disabling it.

I walked with the guards down a corridor, much wider than those at the other stations. They halted at a double door. One of the guards slid a card through a reader. The doors slid apart, revealing a room with bare walls, a sink, a toilet, and a cot with a blanket and pillow. One of the guards gave me a not-so-gentle push, forcing me inside, and the doors slid closed behind me.

I sat on the cot. Without an earbud, I had no way to communicate with my team. I scanned the room. Above, a narrow gap separated the top of the wall from the ceiling, too high to reach, that is, if my bracelets wouldn't work.

I gave my biceps a quick flex but felt no charge. Even if the bracelets did work, that gap, probably designed for air flow, was too narrow for me to crawl through. I was stuck here for however long they wanted to keep me on ice. Now I had to count on my crew more than ever. Of course, they had always come through before, but with the kill switch soon to be triggered, they had to work fast, and they knew only that the switch was somewhere in this Zeta station's programming code. But where?

Perdantus flew through the gap and perched on the cot, apparently not wanting to be on my shoulder, so close to my altered face. "Good," he said. "I found you."

"I'm glad to see you. I was wondering how to communicate with everyone without my earbud."

"I will do my best to be an efficient messenger."

"Do you have news?"

"A great deal of news. First, Tobias showed Fossella the meter, saying a signal is interfering with our ship's systems. She said that she is unaware of the source, and she would not give him access to the control room. So Tobias contacted Josie, and she told Fossella that she and Tobias had renounced their allegiance to Fairbanks, which is why she was removed as an officer. Also, Tobias was now working undercover to foil the admiral's plans. That convinced Fossella to give Tobias access with a guard present to watch him. Second, Oliver is working on severing the thumbs from the corpse of Admiral Fairbanks. It is a nasty business, so Jade is helping him with a cleaver she found in the galley."

I cringed. "That does sound like a nasty business."

"Yes, and they have to finish quickly before Fossella finds the body. Third, we have word from your father that he heard about your capture. Apparently, news of this magnitude travels quickly, especially since we have instant messaging ability between Zeta stations. He has begun communicating with Oliver and Crystal using a non-Alliance encryption that Fossella will not be able to decipher, though she could shut it down if she discovers it. I do not yet know what your father is planning, but when I find out, I will tell you. And fourth, I have a theory as to why the admiral committed suicide, though I don't know if discussing it is useful, considering the emergency."

I nodded. "Go ahead."

"When Fairbanks ordered his agent to kill your father, I thought that was a move to establish his dominance in the negotiation so that he could call the shots. Now I believe that he knew all was lost, and he simply wanted to punish you.

"You see, he was living in a lonely mansion on a barely inhabitable planet, hardly a fitting place for someone with his purported wealth. Captain Tillman must have released the information about him quite some time ago, and Fossella has been working behind the scenes to expose him, likely freezing as many of his financial assets as she could reach. He had to know this day of reckoning was approaching.

"Therefore, in order to punish you further, he lured you to Alpha One with the promise of the possibility of finding the kill switch on this station. Instead of keeping that promise, at the last moment, he killed himself so you that you would die here along with everyone else, and you would fail in your mission.

"The only issue I can't figure out is how he knew you would try to impersonate him. That would be the only way you would be blamed for his crimes and be forced to stay here and die when the kill switch activates."

I sighed. "He knew because of my big mouth. I mentioned the possibility when I blasted his face apart."

"Ah. So that triggered his passion for revenge."

"Yeah. I have that effect on slave traffickers, I guess."

"What message shall I give your crew?"

"Have you heard when Fossella's bringing in someone to take Oliver?" I asked.

"He was told to expect someone in about an hour. In the meantime, he, Crystal, and Jade are staying on the Nebula Nine, communicating with your father, assuming Oliver is finished with harvesting a pair of thumbs, while Tobias works in the control room."

"All right. We really can't do anything until Tobias gives us a report. As long as the negative energy is killing our powers, we're stuck. Otherwise, Crystal could use her hypnotizing ability to spring me from this place. I just have to hope that my father and Aunt Jillian can come up with something."

"That is a reasonable hope. Those two are quite resourceful."

I laughed under my breath. "Definitely, but don't be surprised if they do something that'll shake this place up. My father won't be patient when it comes to protecting me."

"Or to keep the planet from disintegrating, I assume."

The door beeped. Someone had slid the access card through the reader.

Perdantus flew toward the ceiling. "I will return when I have news."

The door opened, revealing Mabel dressed in a royal blue Alliance uniform. Two armed guards stood behind her. "Well, Admiral Fairbanks," she said as she stepped inside. "You are looking much healthier than the last time I saw you."

I rose from the cot. "Starborn healers have been a great help."

"So I've heard." She turned toward the guards. "Close the door. I will knock when I need to leave."

"Are you sure?" one of the guards asked. "He is much bigger than you are. He could overpower you."

She sharpened her tone. "I said, close the door."

"Yes, ma'am." He reached for the controls at the side of the door, making it close.

Mabel refocused on me. "I know who you are," she whispered. "And I know why you can't change back to yourself. I will be helping Tobias solve that problem and look for the kill switch code. In the meantime, you need to decide if you even want to change back."

"I definitely want to change back, but not yet. Fairbanks mentioned that he has a guard at the kill switch location. That makes me think it's something physical instead of just software. I might have to stay Fairbanks to get access."

She nodded. "Right. With the admiral's thumbs in hand. I already talked to Oliver. Since I had told the truth about helping the kids on Delta Ninety-five, he decided to trust me with the secret. I apologize for not sticking around to help you there, but you have no idea how dangerous it was for me in the Delta system. Here at Alpha One, I have far more freedom as well as access to those in authority."

"Good. But if I stay looking like Fairbanks, how're you going to get me out? I'm public enemy number one, and rightfully so."

"When it comes to the entire planet disintegrating, we'll have to take our chances with whom we can trust. I'll talk to Fossella, you know, kind of ease up to the idea and see if she'll be likely to believe me about who you are and what you need to do."

"All right, but better do it quick. My father's bound to show up soon and do something more … well … direct."

"Understood." She turned and knocked on the door, looking back at me. "You'll hear from me soon."

When the door opened, she walked out. The moment it closed, a siren blared. A man called through hidden speakers, urgency in his tone. "All personnel report to your ships for immediate departure."

As the siren continued blaring, Perdantus flew in again and landed on the cot. "The Astral Dragon arrived and immediately zoomed out of the bay on a trajectory toward the planet. Several ships are preparing to give chase."

I crossed my arms and nodded. "Either Jillian is flying the Dragon, or Sonya is. You can be sure that my father stayed behind. Oldest trick in the book. He wanted to clear out as many of the station's personnel as possible."

"What can I do to help him?"

"Try to find him. Call his name. No one else here will understand your language. If he hears you, he'll whistle for you like I do. If you find him, tell him to look for Mabel. They can team up to help Tobias or get me out of here. I have my doubts about Mabel convincing Fossella of anything."

"I understand." He flew out again.

I sat on the cot and stared at the door, feeling more useless than I had ever felt in my life. But, again, I had to trust my team. They had never let me down before.

As I sat, I studied my hands. They definitely looked like the admiral's, but I couldn't tell if the fingerprints were mine or not. I had never bothered to notice them much. It stood to reason that they weren't his. When I last transformed, I altered to a mental image that I had in my mind, which didn't include fingerprints. Still, other hidden body parts changed. As I had concluded earlier, there was much more going on behind the scenes than what I could conjure with my mind.

I rolled a sleeve up to my elbow and found no electric ink lines on my skin. I probably still had them like I did as Renalda. Since his arms were bigger than mine, maybe the lines were too deep to see.

The alarm silenced. A beep sounded at the door, and it slid open. Papa stood there with Mabel at his side and Perdantus on his shoulder, no guards in sight.

Papa grinned. "Admiral Fairbanks, I am here to escort you to the Nebula Nine where you will fly to the surface of Alpha One. Your compliance is required immediately."

I rose from the cot. I ached to rush to him and hug him, but in this body, that would feel wrong. I decided to play along with his joke. "So, a pirate is taking me prisoner, is he? It seems that our roles have been reversed."

"Way too much reversal." His grin vanished as he shook his head. "It's hard to believe it's really you."

"Believe it. But why are we going to the planet?"

He gestured with his head. "I'll explain on the way. There's no time to lose."

When I exited the cell, Mabel gave me my earbud. "When most of the guards left, I locked Fossella in another cell, and now I'm going back to help Tobias in the control room. I'll open the bay door when your ramp closes. Also, I'm going to look into accessing a nuclear bomb in case we have to do something drastic to destroy this station. Radioactive fallout should stay in orbit and not affect the planet."

"Tough to find one," Papa said. "They were outlawed decades ago. I actually assembled several myself that would've worked, but I had no way to deploy them. They leaked too much radiation. Super dangerous."

Mabel patted his arm. "If I find one, I'll let you know." She strode away.

"I'll fly ahead," Perdantus said as he lifted off, "and inform the others."

Papa and I hurried toward the Nine's docking bay. "Tobias found the kill-switch code," he said, "but he thinks he won't be able to hack into it in time. We talked about trying to destroy this station, but it has a kill switch of its own. It sends a signal to the other stations every day."

"I get it. If we destroy this station, the others won't get the daily signal to stand down, and they'll disintegrate the other planets."

"Exactly. And we don't have enough firepower to destroy the other stations in time." He opened the door to the bay, allowing me to pass through first. As we walked as briskly as my elderly legs would allow, he nodded toward the Nine, still on the bay floor. "We're going to the planet to search for a device on the surface that transmits the kill code to the station, at least Tobias thinks it's down there. The code says so. He gave us some possible coordinates. They're loaded in Emerson."

I paused at the end of the ramp. "I understand, but if we disable the kill switch here, what will this station tell the other stations to do?"

"According to Tobias's understanding of the programming code, disabling the switch here will disable it at all of the stations. But, again, he doesn't think he can hack it in time. It's up to us to do it on the planet's surface."

"What about the negative energy? I still feel it. Has he found a way to stop it?"

"Not by changing the programming code. He has to physically dismantle the device, but that's a lower priority than hacking the code."

Papa and I hurried up the ramp and found Oliver seated in the first mate's chair while Crystal stood with her mother at the navigator's station. "About time you got back," Crystal said. "Sorry I wasn't on your six, but the keister you've got now isn't the one I'm used to following."

"Let's hope you won't have to look at this one much longer. I'm getting tired of it." While Papa stood at my side, I sat in the captain's chair and pushed the button to raise the ramp. "Everyone strap in. We're going to zoom out of here and go straight into the atmosphere. It'll get bumpy." I glanced around. "Where's Perdantus?"

"Already holed up somewhere," Crystal said. "He knew you would want to take off in a hurry."

I opened our comm connection to the station's network. "Our ramp is closed, Mabel. You can open the bay doors."

"Opening now," she said.

As Crystal and Jade seated themselves, Crystal looked toward the living quarters. "We have a surprise for you. When your father told his passengers that you were in trouble, two of them insisted on coming back with him."

Zoë and Echo walked onto the bridge, both dressed in camo and boots. Zoë spread her arms. "Get a load of these threads Lyric's mother gave us. We look like battle-ready soldiers. Lyric wanted to come with us, but she's still pretty weak from getting shot. Her mother grounded her. Bed rest only for at least three days."

Again I wanted to leap up and hug them, but I had to wait until I got my body back. "Thanks for coming, but you know you might be dead in less than twenty or so hours. This could be a suicide mission."

"Well, we can't let you and Crystal have all the fun." Zoë sat at the weapons' station and buckled in. "Let's hit the space highway."

"I'm going to the engine room." Echo hustled away, her voice fading as she called in singsong, "The engine room, the engine room."

Jade kissed Crystal on top of her head. "I'll check on the gliders and find a seat down there."

Oliver rose and gestured toward the first mate's chair. "Captain Julian Willis, please sit here. I'm a healer, not a pilot."

"Thank you." Papa strapped in next to me while Oliver manned the physician's station.

As soon as everyone had buckled, I looked out the front viewing window. The bay doors stood open, revealing a perfect view of Alpha

One. I took a deep breath, started the thrusters, and pushed the throttle. "Here we go."

The Nebula Nine shot out of the bay and zoomed toward the planet. Papa shifted the front window to show the view from the rear camera. He pointed toward the window. "I don't think either of us has ever seen that station from the outside."

I stared at the station, shrinking in our view. As Fairbanks had said, it wasn't a perfect sphere like the others—cone shaped from its equator downward and rounded on the top with tall buildings rising from its surface. "That's pretty amazing. I wonder how many people could live there."

"No idea." Papa switched the window to the front view. "I wouldn't want to live there. Where's the adventure in that? I would get bored."

"Same here. I'm addicted to adrenaline, I guess." I looked at my console. "Emerson, put the potential coordinates on my screen."

"Transferring now."

A map appeared, showing pulsing dots at various places on the surface. "What's the intel on these? Are any more likely than the others?"

Papa reached over to my screen and pointed. "They're color coded. Red is the most likely, then orange, then yellow, then green, then blue."

I studied the location of the red dot, out in a rural area in a range of mountains. "I know that region. It's where I cut my teeth flying a ship."

"Lots of obstacles, though," Papa said.

"The obstacles made it fun."

"Not so fun to find a place to land."

"That's true." I touched the screen. "Why is the red spot the most likely place for the device?"

"The Zeta station is not in a geosynchronous orbit, so as the planet rotates, different locations on the surface are exposed to the station at different times. Tobias found that Fairbanks sent the kill-switch disabling signal at nearly the same Alpha-One hour every day. At that time, the red spot has been the most likely to be facing the station. Our theory is that, since he was a sadistic madman, he always waited until the last hour to send the message to stop the kill switch. If he didn't, then that spot would be ready to contact the software on board the station to trigger the disintegration. We think the triggering signal is on a frequency that needs to have a direct line of sight to the target."

"Got it." I sent the map to the navigator's station. "Crystal, plot a course to the red dot. Get Emerson's help to find the fastest and most direct route without burning up in the atmosphere." A sharp jolt made me bounce in my seat. "Speaking of atmosphere, we're entering it now. Everyone hang on."

Hoping to smooth out the ride, I extended the Nine's wings and shifted to a more level flight, still within the parameters of the navigational path.

"Most direct route is set," Crystal said.

I checked the course's timing. "Seventeen minutes till landing."

"We should be out of range of the negative energy," Papa said. "Do you want to change back to your normal self for a while?"

I shook my head. "Based on the other places we've been, I think something will be transmitting the negative energy at the device's site, and I wouldn't be able to change back into Fairbanks. Besides, it hurts like crazy to transform. I can stand being the ugliest human in the universe for a little while longer."

Papa winced. "Okay. If you can endure looking like that, I can endure looking at you looking like that."

I copied his wince. "Trust me, being a man is not something I want to get used to. I'm making sure I don't eat or drink anything for as long as I can." I looked at the sensor readings on the console. The hull's exterior temperature was rising more quickly than I had expected. "It's strange that I've never piloted a ship into Alpha One's atmosphere before. Just near the ground when I was about ten, before we started most of the raids. I didn't know the air would be so dense at this altitude."

"Raise the shields," Papa said. "That will counter most of the entry effect."

I pressed the button to raise the shields.

"Shields are malfunctioning," Emerson said. "I am running a diagnostic."

Papa narrowed his eyes as he studied his console. "Probably sabotage. Someone at the station wanted to make sure we were vulnerable to attack."

"No one came on board," Oliver said. "I was here on the bridge the whole time."

"So was I," Crystal said.

I drew a mental picture of the Nine's shield schematics. Although the access panels were welded shut, a torch could open the panel to the main trunk. I could easily fix the problem, but not while we were flying. "You don't need to come on board to disable the shields. The wiring is accessible from the outside. Fossella might've sent someone to cripple us, just in case."

"You mean," Crystal said, "just in case we do exactly what we're doing?"

"Right. We'd better check the weapons. See if arming them gives us an error code."

"I'll do that," Zoë said. "First, the photon torpedoes ... nope. They're not coming online."

"They can be accessed from outside, too. Not easy, though. Only a skilled mechanic who knows the Nebula series ships could do it."

"Now the lasers." Zoë tapped her screen. "Okay. They're reporting no problems."

"Test them. Fire the lasers from all four ports."

"Port one." Zoë tapped her screen. In the front viewing window, a laser beam shot out from the right-hand port in a brief burst, sparkling as it slowly diffused in the atmosphere. Tests of the other three ports worked as well. "Looks like we're good."

"Not surprising. It's nearly impossible to disable the lasers from the outside." I heaved a loud sigh. "So we have no shields and no torpedoes. If we're attacked, we won't last long. At least the bottom panels are withstanding the entry heat."

"Interior heat is rising," Emerson said. "At the current rate of change, it will rise above human comfort levels in thirty-two seconds and above human survival levels in four minutes, eighteen seconds."

"About seven minutes till we land," Crystal said.

I looked at the digital thermometer on my console—31.6 degrees and rising. "We'll open the vents when there's enough oxygen and air pressure in the atmosphere. I've done it before. We should be fine."

"We could take a vertical dive," Papa said. "That will reduce the hull's exposure to the atmosphere and get us into breathable air faster."

"True, but doing that might be vomit inducing. Gravity's already kicked in. At least one of our crew is susceptible to upchucking."

"Better than dying." Crystal snatched a paper bag from under her console. "I've been saving this for just such an occasion."

"All right. Everyone hang on." I pushed the Nine into a vertical tilt. My body pressed hard against the straps. As we plunged, I watched the oxygen level and air pressure outside. The interior temperature rose to 43 degrees, now uncomfortably hot.

"Warning," Emerson said. "I have detected a Nebula series ship near the planet's surface. It is on a course that will intercept the Nebula Nine in approximately two-point-four minutes."

"Someone got wind of our escape." Now that the atmosphere was at the proper levels, I opened the vents. Cool air rushed in, instantly dropping the temperature. "All right, whoever's chasing us, you're on my home planet now. One terrifying gauntlet coming up." I slowly leveled out. Now less than two kilometers from the surface, I pushed the throttle and zoomed toward a mountain range. "Let's see how this captain likes Suicide Ravine."

"Suicide?" Crystal repeated. "I already puked once, and my bag's dripping. Don't make me puke again."

"Like you said, better than dying." In the front viewing window, the low hills rose into higher ones, then into mountains. When I spotted the pass and the serpentine river leading out of it, I descended to about twenty meters from the ground and made a beeline for it.

"The pursuing ship has armed its torpedoes," Emerson said.

"They'll try to take us out before we can get to the ravine."

Papa pointed at his screen. "Two torpedoes are on their way."

"At our speed, I think we can get to the ravine before the torpedoes catch up with us."

"Negative," Emerson said. "The torpedoes will strike in twelve seconds. It will take fourteen seconds to reach the outer border of the ravine."

"Then we'll go faster." I pushed the throttle further, making the Nine bounce like a wild bronco as I clutched the yoke tightly. "Hang on, everyone."

"You will now reach the ravine one second ahead of the torpedoes," Emerson said.

Papa touched my arm. "How are you going to negotiate the ravine at this speed?"

"With difficulty." A bump forced a grunt from my gut. "Lots of difficulty."

"And more puking," Crystal said.

"If I can't steer us around those bends, puking will be the least of our problems." The moment we entered the ravine between two mountains, I pulled up hard to dodge them, knowing the torpedoes wouldn't be able to miss them.

"The torpedoes have impacted on a mountainside," Emerson said.

I shut off our rear thrusters and turned on the front ones, making us decelerate so quickly, it felt like we had flown into a wall of mud.

"The other ship has broken off its pursuit," Emerson said.

"Good." I angled out of the ravine, then flew down again over a less dangerous plateau. "Let's find a place to land."

Papa touched his console screen. "Here looks good. It's only one-point-two kilometers from the red dot. An easy walk."

"Yeah. Not bad, but will the Nine still be there after we leave her? That ship's bound to return. Maybe it's calling for reinforcements to come and search for us."

"Another ship is approaching," Emerson said. "She is hailing us on a private frequency."

"Maybe the Dragon?" I tapped on the control that opened the channel. "Who's calling, please?"

Jillian's voice came through the ceiling speakers. "Only the ace pilot who chased away the Nebula ship that was about to blast you out of the sky. Apparently, it didn't like having its entire tail section shot off by a torpedo. It crashed a few kilometers from here, and I used a laser blast to take out its communications antenna. I think we're safe for a while."

"Perfect. Thanks, Aunt Jillian."

"Megan, you sound terrible. What deadly disease did you catch?"

"Fairbanks disease. I look and sound like him. Don't go into shock when you see me."

"Ewww! Thanks for the warning."

"Yeah, I'm avoiding all mirrors. Anyway, we found a place to land that's big enough for both ships. Want to join us there?"

"I thought you'd never ask. Lead the way."

"We'll keep the comm channel open. See you in a minute." Now that the danger had passed, I decelerated further and eased toward the ground. "Looks like about one minute to landing. Emerson, do you have a weather forecast for the area?"

"Affirmative. It is autumn in this region, and since we will be landing at a high elevation, temperatures are expected to drop, with a high of ten degrees. The low tonight is expected to be five degrees. Currently, it is seven minutes before noon. Thunderstorms are likely after about four p.m., which will lead to much colder temperatures tomorrow."

"So we'll probably have four hours of good weather. We need to get in and get out." I flew the Nine to the spot that Papa had pointed out, a grassy field on the flat top of a mountain. A few seconds after we landed, the Astral Dragon settled in front of us, her nose barely far enough away from ours to allow the front ramps to open.

I touched the ramp icon, unbuckled, and looked back at Zoë, Crystal, and Oliver. Both Oliver and Crystal seemed paler than usual, while Zoë, her shoulders slumped, appeared to be exhausted.

"Sorry about how rough it was," I said.

Crystal bit off a chunk of a chocolate muffin. "No worries," she said, talking with her mouth full. "I stashed this delicious muffin in my console. I have to refill after puking my guts out. Otherwise, I'm fine."

"Okay. Let's go." I rose from my seat. "How're things down in the engine room, Echo?"

Her voice came through my earbud. "Fine. Fine. Well, not so fine. I'm kind of dizzy. Actually, very dizzy. But I'm getting better now. I'm on my way to the bridge."

"And the glider bay, Jade?" I asked.

"Besides one of the gliders breaking its mooring lock and sliding against the wall, it's all good. I assume you want all of the gliders deployed, right?"

"And the rovers."

"No rovers," Jade said. "We left them on Ninety-five."

"Blazes! I forgot about that. So we're a bit pinched. What do you have in your buggy, Aunt Jillian?

"Only one glider," she said, "but we have three rovers. I'll have them out there as soon as I can. I'm only one woman, you know."

Crystal eased off her seat, still pale. "I'll help her."

"Sounds good." I looked at my father as he stood next to his console. "Shall we?"

He blinked, as if distracted. "Yeah. Sure."

"Is something wrong?"

"Not really. It just feels like we're slow walking. If this isn't the right spot for the device, we'll have to load the vehicles back into the ships and fly to the next one. There's no way we have time to check every possible location. Better if you and me and maybe Jillian run ahead, check for the device, and run back if it's not there. Stay in touch with earbuds."

"Good thinking. Emerson, open the comms throughout the ship and to all earbuds."

"All comms are now open."

"Listen everyone. Don't get the gliders and rovers out. My father, Aunt Jillian, and I are going. Just the three of us. Listen through your earbuds, and we'll let you know if we need help."

"I'm going with you," Crystal said. "Like I mentioned before, I'm not used to that keister, but I'm staying on your six."

"I should go, too," Oliver said. "I have the bag of Fairbanks body parts. Not that you can't carry it, but ... well ... it's the only excuse I have for coming with you. Oh, and I'm a healer. You might need me."

Perdantus flew to Oliver's shoulder. "And I, as well. Normally, I would ride on your shoulder, Megan, but you are ... shall I say ... far too repulsive at the moment. You understand."

"All right, so nearly everyone's going, but we'll be moving fast. No stopping to puke, Crystal. The five of us will meet in front of the ships. On the double. Zoë can fly one of the ships if necessary."

I jogged down the ramp on aching legs. The admiral's elderly limbs wouldn't move as fast as I wanted them to. Although I couldn't feel any negative energy here, that didn't mean I wouldn't feel it where the device might be. Still, if I were to transform back into myself, I could always halt the moment I felt the energy, retreat a bit, and transform into Fairbanks again. That made a lot more sense.

Papa hustled down the ramp and joined me, looking at a computer pad on his palm. "This unit will pinpoint where we need to go."

"Sounds good. And we can go faster if I have my body." I closed my eyes and concentrated. As before, I felt myself shrink back to normal, less painful than stretching, and the process seemed quicker than ever. When I opened my eyes, I smiled at Papa. "Better?"

"Much." He pulled me into a tight hug. "I've been dying to do this."

I pressed my cheek against his chest. "Same here."

When we drew apart, Jillian, Crystal, Oliver, and Perdantus joined us, Jillian carrying a large box in both arms. She set the box down and mussed my hair. "Good to have Mophead back."

I smiled. "It's good to be back."

She nodded toward the box. "Belts with holstered laser blasters. If you don't already have one, grab one."

Crystal, Oliver, and I each hurriedly withdrew a belt out and put it on. Papa and Jillian were already wearing theirs. When we finished, Papa led the way at a quick trot into a wooded area. "Everyone, on my six."

With Perdantus flying overhead, I jogged behind Papa, with Oliver on one side and Jillian on the other, while Crystal trailed me at the same pace. Even without seeing her, I could read Crystal's thoughts as if she were shouting them, probably on purpose. *Your six has improved. It was a negative six. Now it's back to a positive six.*

I looked back at her grinning face. "You're so funny."

She tossed another thought my way. *I thought so.*

We followed my father around the widely separated trees, most with low limbs and leaves of orange and red that had also scattered across the ground. Along the way, I tested my senses, trying to detect any sign of the negative energy, but so far, I felt nothing unusual.

After a few minutes, Papa stopped and looked at the computer pad. "This is the spot. At least it's somewhere close. The locator could be off by a few meters."

I scanned the area, again checking for the negative energy. With each passing moment, a sense of dread grew. The negative energy was definitely coming from somewhere. "It's here."

"Yep," Crystal said. "I feel it."

Oliver nodded. "Same."

Perdantus flew to a treetop, calling, "I will watch for trouble."

Papa sidled close to me and whispered, "Is it too late to change back into Fairbanks?"

"Let me check." I closed my eyes, focused on my mental image of Fairbanks, and tried to transform, but I could tell immediately that it wasn't going to work. "Yeah, it's too late."

Crystal squinted at the ground, tapping it with a foot. "What's this?" She swept leaves away from a concrete slab.

Papa joined her and helped her sweep more leaves until they had uncovered a concrete circle about four meters in diameter. "This might be exactly what we're looking for."

Jillian pointed upward. "I see something in a tree. Looks like an antenna. Must be wireless. I don't see a cable."

"Probably transmits the negative energy," Papa said. "Not an antenna for the kill switch. At least I hope Fairbanks wouldn't count on a tree to hold the fate of the world in its branches."

Perdantus flew to the antenna and looked it over. "It has a box attached with a power switch. Should I turn it off?"

Jillian strode toward the tree. "We have to be sure it's what we think it is. I can climb up there."

"Let me," Oliver said as he followed her. "I'll be able to tell if it's sending the negative energy. If it is, I'll feel it more the closer I get."

"Good point." She set her hands in a cradle near the ground. "I'll give you a boost to the lowest limb."

Oliver set his bag down. "That has the admiral's biometric stuff in it." He stepped on her hands, rode her lift to the limb, and climbed on, then scrambled up the tree branch by branch. At his rate, he would probably get to the antenna in a couple of minutes.

Jillian returned to where we had gathered around the concrete. The ground began trembling. A loud cracking noise split the air. The circular slab began rising slowly out of the ground, revealing a metallic cylinder.

Papa drew his blaster and waved at me. "Get out of range of the signal. We might need you to be Fairbanks."

As I backed away, Jillian and Crystal pulled their blasters and aimed them at the cylinder. "I'll be listening with my earbud," I said. "Talk loud enough for me to hear you." I turned and hustled away. After only about fifty meters, the sense of dread faded.

I stopped at a big tree and hid behind its wide trunk, peaking around it. The cylinder continued to rise. When it grew to a height about twice as tall as my father, it stopped. Lights blinked at the top of the cylinder and rotated, like a spinning jeweled crown.

"I don't like the looks of this," Papa said as he backed away and gestured for the others to do the same.

Red laser beams shot out from the crown, and the spinning action made the beams sweep across the ground, striking Papa, Jillian, and Crystal. All three stiffened, as if frozen, standing like statues.

I gasped. "Oliver," I whispered, "did you see that?"

"Yeah." His voice sounded really weak. "I don't think they're dead, though. Just paralyzed."

I swallowed hard. "Are you almost there?"

"Just another few seconds." He gasped for a breath. "The branches … aren't as sturdy … up here. I have to … climb slower."

"Okay. I'm going to try to change to Fairbanks." I closed my eyes and once again attempted the transformation process, but I couldn't do it.

When I opened my eyes, a door slid open on the cylinder. A man stepped out and looked around, his hands on his hips. "Well, what have we here?" he said, his voice barely audible. He walked to Papa and wrenched his gun away, then walked toward Jillian.

Perdantus's chirping came through my earbud. "Oliver is not able to continue climbing, likely overcome by the negative energy. He is in a precarious position and might soon fall from the limb he's clutching. I fear that he is in great danger."

"Since it is obvious that the antenna is transmitting the negative energy," Perdantus said, "I am going to shut it off."

From where I stood, I could see Oliver lying face down on a thin branch, both arms loosely wrapped around it near the trunk as the branch swayed under his weight. Perdantus fluttered from him up to the antenna and pecked at the box attached to the antenna.

A moment later, Oliver perked up and climbed to a sitting position on the branch. "Perdantus did it. The bad feeling's going away."

"All right," I said. "I'll try to change to Fairbanks. Stay up there for now." I closed my eyes once more. The transformation came easily, though still with some pain.

When I opened my eyes again, the man had already taken Jillian's gun. Both hers and Papa's lay on the ground at his feet. Now he had a hand on Crystal's gun, tugging on it with more difficulty. Finally, he jerked it free. "You're a stubborn one, aren't you?"

After taking a deep breath to steel my nerves, I strode toward the man, trying my best to take on a formal, military air. "Why did you paralyze my crew?"

"Admiral Fairbanks!" The man dropped Crystal's gun, stood at attention, and saluted. "I didn't expect to see you here."

Not bothering to return the salute, I halted in front of him and read the name stitched into his shirt—P. Wolfe. The stripe on his shoulder gave away his rank as ensign. "Really, Ensign Wolfe? Who else knows about this location?"

Wolfe lowered his arm. "No one, sir. At least not that I know of."

"Then you should investigate who your visitors are before you paralyze them. They are bound to be associated with me in some way."

"I apologize, sir. The effects will wear off in about half an hour. They'll be fine."

I let out a harrumph. "That will have to do."

"May I ask why you are here?"

I decided to go for broke. "I have made a deal with the Alliance counsel that will ensure an excellent retirement for me and a bountiful life for all of my closest confidantes, including you. My part is simple. All I have to do is disable the switch."

He drew his head back. "Really? Won't that make you vulnerable to assassins?"

"Perhaps, but I have enough money to buy an entire planet along with all the guards I need to live a peaceful existence for the rest of my days, also to reward you handsomely for all the lonely hours you have spent here to watch over the switch."

Wolfe smiled. "Thank you, sir. Thank you." A thought drifted in from his mind. *I've been here only two weeks, idiot. You're just like all the other higher-ups. A big phony.*

I cleared my throat. "I realize, of course, that you've been here only a couple of weeks, but I still appreciate your service." I folded my hands behind my back. "Now, it's been a while since I have been here, Wolfe. Would you kindly walk me through the process and jog my memory?"

"Of course." Wolfe smiled in an odd way and spread an arm toward the door in the cylinder. "There's plenty of room for both of us inside."

His expression prompted me to try to read his mind again, but now nothing was coming through. A shift from easy mind reading to impossible raised a mental alarm. What was this man up to?

At that moment, it occurred to me that I didn't have the admiral's thumbs. They were still in Oliver's bag near the tree. I glanced toward it for a split second. Oliver had just jumped down from the lowest limb and picked up the bag.

"Is there a problem?" Wolfe asked. "You're hesitating."

"You're the guardian of this station, not me." I spread an arm of my own. "After you."

When Wolfe walked in, Perdantus flew to my shoulder, dropped a severed thumb into my palm, and flew away. Now not much more than skin and a bone with some dried-out flesh around it, the thumb barely bled at all. I pushed it into my pocket. In spite of my concerns, I had to finish the job. With my powers restored, I could handle the likes of Ensign Wolfe.

I walked in behind him. A computer console stood waist high, its back curved against the cylinder's far wall, angled for easy access to all of the controls. A fluorescent lamp on the ceiling provided plenty of light. Whether this place was powered by solar panels or a generator somewhere, I couldn't tell. It was definitely too remote for a traditional power source. Because of how critical it was to the survival of the planet, it probably had plenty of battery backup.

Wolfe stood sideways in front of the console controls and pointed at a scanning pad on the surface. "Just press your thumb there to get the highest security clearance."

My lie detector alarm stayed quiet, and I was still unable to read his mind. Either way, my own thumb probably wouldn't work. Or would it? Maybe I could use the failure to make up an excuse to get him to leave. Or I could just use my powers to throw him out.

I pressed my thumb on the pad. A message flashed on a screen embedded in the center of the console—Print Recognized. Then my photo appeared, a photo of my real self.

I stepped back and tried to sound authentic. "What is the meaning of this outrage?"

Wolfe flipped a switch on the console. A purple ceiling light turned on. The horrible feeling came over me, worse than ever. "It reads DNA as well as prints," Wolfe said calmly, "It knows who you really are. The pirate, Megan Willis."

I grabbed his arm and tried to reach his heart with my mind, but it didn't work. My powers were gone.

Wolfe wrapped his hands around my throat and squeezed, hard enough to cut off most of my air flow. "Admiral Fairbanks warned me about you, and I was ready. First, I tested your mind reading and fed you a lie about me being here two weeks. Worked like a charm. The admiral said you probably wouldn't be able to detect a lie I told in a thought, and he was right."

I forced in a strangled breath. "He's … dead …"

He squeezed harder, cutting off all of my air. "You're lying. This station received his signal less than twenty-four hours ago."

I clawed at his eyes, scratching his forehead and cheeks. Then, summoning all of my strength, I pushed my knee into his groin, but I couldn't thrust hard enough. He grunted but nothing more.

Oliver leaped into the cylinder, grabbed Wolfe's wrist, and tried to wrench me free. Wolfe let me go with one hand and punched Oliver in the face. He backpedaled out of the cylinder in a dazed stagger, and the thump of his fall reached my ears. One second later, Perdantus flew in and scratched at Wolfe's eyes, screeching like a crazed bat.

Wolfe swatted him with a hard backhand that sent him tumbling through the air outside. Wolfe regripped me with both hands. "Now that your friends can no longer help you, you're going to die."

My vision darkened. The now-familiar feeling of passing out came upon me, but this episode wouldn't end in a short blackout. I wouldn't wake up at all.

Wolfe gasped and let me go. I dropped to my knees and sucked in shallow breaths through my aching throat. I had no idea why he released me. My oxygen-starved brain couldn't focus on anything but trying to survive.

Wolfe trembled as he collapsed to his knees. "What's happening?"

I peeked outside. Zoë stood about a dozen paces away, while Echo knelt next to Oliver. Zoë held her fist out toward us, likely compressing Wolfe's heart. I lunged for the negative energy switch on the console and flipped it off, dousing the purple light. As I continued sucking in breaths, I looked outside again. Echo still knelt next to Oliver, a hand on his head. "You saved her, Zoë! You saved her!"

"Yep," Zoë said. "Good thing you talked us into checking on them."

With my own powers returning, I grabbed Wolfe by the collar, dragged him outside, and threw him headlong. He slid across the ground a couple of meters. When he stopped, he writhed in a curl and moaned for a moment before lying deathly still.

I waved at Zoë. "Let him go, but be ready to grab him again."

She lowered her hand and stood next to him. Wanting my younger, faster body back, I quickly reverted to my normal form, then hurried over to Oliver and knelt across from Echo. For the first time, I noticed Perdantus lying on Oliver's chest. "How are they?"

"Alive," Echo said. "Both are alive. Unconscious, though. Definitely unconscious."

I nodded toward the cylinder. "Check out the technology in there. First, see if you can find a way to counter the paralysis ray he used on Papa, Jillian, and Crystal." I dug into my pocket, fished out the thumb, and gave it to her. "Then have a look at the system to see what we need to do to disable the kill switch."

"Okay. Okay." Cringing, she took the thumb and ran into the cylinder.

I laid a hand on Perdantus and peered past his feathers and skin. He seemed to have no broken bones or internal bleeding, and his heart pumped strongly. He was probably just stunned. I moved my hand to Oliver's forehead. Inside, I found a pool of blood. That couldn't be good.

I focused on the wound and sealed it, but did I repair it in time? Was there any brain damage I couldn't see?

Perdantus chirped from Oliver's chest, now standing with a wobble. "Is he all right?"

"I'm not sure." I kept my hand on his forehead. "I'll keep pouring energy into him to see if that helps."

The beams from the cylinder's crown flashed on and spun again, this time sending white light instead of red. When the light swept across Papa, Jillian, and Crystal, they dropped to their knees and shook their heads, apparently trying to cast off the paralysis effects.

"Uh-oh," Echo said from within the cylinder. "This is not good, not good at all."

I looked at her through the open door. "What's wrong?"

She stepped out. "The admiral's thumb got me past the first hurdle, but now it's asking for a retinal scan. The screen says the kill switch will activate in one minute if we don't pass this challenge. I guess if we don't pass, it will know we're intruders."

"And disintegrating the planet will kill the intruders. I wonder if I should switch back to his form and try to use those eyes." I shook my head at my own idea. "But I don't think that'll work. It didn't for the thumbprint."

"And," Echo said, "we have only one shot at this. Just one shot. And maybe about thirty seconds to go."

Oliver murmured something I couldn't understand.

"Oliver?" I leaned over, setting my ear close to his lips. "Say it again."

He breathed something that sounded like words, but I couldn't make them out. I drew back and looked at his closed eyes. "Say it in your mind, as loud as you can."

As I mentally drilled into his brain, words flowed, weak but understandable. *Check the bag.*

"Check the bag?" I repeated out loud.

"The bag!" Crystal shouted, pointing. "The admiral's bio stuff."

I leaped up, ran to the bag, and opened it. An eyeball lay inside along with a tuft of hair. I shouted as I hustled with it toward Echo. "I've got a retina! How much time left?"

She ducked inside. "Nine seconds! Nine seconds!"

I ran in and snatched the eyeball from the bag. "Where do I put it?"

She pointed at a flashing light in a recess on the wall. "There. Right there."

I held the eyeball in front of the light. Something on the console beeped. "Is that good?"

Echo looked at the console screen. "Yes. Yes. The system accepted the retina. Now I'm watching for the next step. There's always a next step."

While she watched, I looked outside. Jade climbed out of her two-person glider and handed a coil of rope to Jillian, probably because Jillian called her through an earbud and asked for it. Papa walked on stiff legs from person to person, checking on them while Jillian tied Wolfe's wrists together with the rope as he lay in a motionless curl.

Jade and Papa lifted Oliver into the glider's passenger seat. Worry for him sent heat into my ears, but since he was able to communicate with his thoughts, maybe his brain wasn't damaged too badly.

"Did you frisk Wolfe?" I asked Jillian.

Jillian rolled her eyes. "Of course, Mophead. What kind of idiot do you think I am?"

"The kind of idiot who'll frisk him as soon as I look away."

She sighed. "You're right. Can't fool a lie detector. I'll do it now." She patted him until she reached his midsection. From a back pocket, she pulled out a wallet. She opened it, revealing several notes of currency. "That's not a weapon." She slid it back into his pocket.

"Okay, okay," Echo said, "here's a diagram that shows all of the Zeta spheres and how the kill switch is connected to them."

I turned and looked at the console. It showed six orbs with one at the center and a line connecting it to each of the other orbs.

Echo pointed. "That's the Alpha One station in the middle. When the kill switch activates, it waits for one hour before sending a signal to the Zeta orbiting Zeta Four, and that station's kill switch activates by moving the disintegrating guns into position. That takes about five minutes. Then the guns start zapping Zeta Four. The station rotates, allowing other guns to shoot while the first ones recharge. As the disintegration spreads across the planet, the guns aim at portions that remain. According to the documentation, the disintegration should take about fifteen minutes."

I imagined the process—guns firing laser beams that shifted as they ate away the planet, exactly as Tobias theorized. "Okay, so what happens after Zeta Four gets destroyed?"

"Not after, but during Zeta Four's destruction, Epsilon kicks in. First—"

"Wait." I shook my head. "Sorry I asked you to go on. This is going to take too long. I don't need the blow by blow if you'll just disable the switch. Can you do that?"

She pointed at a skull-and-crossbones icon. "That might be it, but I'm worried. Really worried."

"Why?"

"The skull might mean tapping that button is deadly to the kill switch, but it might mean that it activates the kill switch immediately. That would be bad, really bad."

"I agree. Too dangerous to try it. But Fairbanks seemed to be saying there's a way to disable the switch. It has to be somewhere."

"Maybe, but I don't see it on the screen or in the documentation. I don't see it at all."

"Then that button must be the way to deactivate the switch. It activates on its own when Fairbanks dies, so it doesn't need a button to do it."

"You're probably right. Definitely probably right. But do you want to be the one to try it?"

"No, but if we don't, we *know* it'll be activated in a few hours. And, speaking of hours, does the documentation say why it delays sending a signal to the Zeta station in the Zeta system for one hour?"

"It says that those in Fairbanks's ..." Echo drew quotation marks in the air. "Inner circle get a signal that the switch has been activated, and it gives them an hour to scramble to evacuate whatever planet they might be on."

"So his friends and family can scram, but they couldn't evacuate an entire planet in an hour."

Echo shook her head hard. "Impossible. Absolutely impossible."

"Let me get this straight." I nodded toward the skull icon. "If we try that button, and it activates the switch, we would have one hour till the zapping starts."

"Exactly. Exactly."

I sighed. "All right. Go on with the explanation. I need to know everything."

"Sure. Sure. Like I said, while the Zeta system's Zeta station is destroying Zeta Four... we'll call that station the Zeta Zeta ... Epsilon Zeta starts the process one minute after Zeta Zeta starts by moving the Epsilon guns into position."

"Automatically? So it doesn't need to hear again from any other station?"

"Right. Then while the Epsilon Zeta is slaughtering billions on Epsilon Three, Delta Zeta starts moving its guns, and so on in reverse alphabetical order, or in beta-alphacal order, I guess."

"Does it say why they don't all start at once?" I asked. "Why is there a delay between them?"

"The delay is a failsafe in case there's a glitch in communications. If the kill switch activates, the guard here, as a member of the inner circle, is supposed to evacuate to the Alpha Zeta. From there, he would zap himself in a glider to the Zeta Zeta first and verify that the guns have started moving. If they haven't, he would activate the switch manually. Then, he would use one of the guns to zap himself to the Epsilon Zeta to do the same thing, and he can do that because he would have a controller that moves the gun in his bay to where it needs to be to zap his glider. Then he would move on to the other stations until he arrived at the Alpha Zeta. Without the delay, it would be impossible to go to all the Zetas."

"Right. And once he returned to the Alpha Zeta, he would probably board a star cruiser to take him to safety. Since the Zetas themselves aren't in danger, he could wait for someone to pick him up, or maybe one will already be there for him to hitch a ride on."

"True. True." Echo narrowed her eyes. "Why did you want to know about the delays? Are you plotting something?"

"Maybe. It's helpful to know that it's possible to go from station to station while the switch is active."

Echo winced. "Possible, yeah. But that ensign had the worst job in the universe. Making sure billions of innocent people die. He must be a monster, a real monster."

"He felt like a monster while he was choking me." I imagined the process of zapping from one Zeta to another, using the five-minute delay to dash around the station to do whatever needed to be done before leaving in a rush. "Stay here and keep looking for what that icon means while I check on something."

"I will. I will."

I walked out and looked around. The glider was gone, and so were Oliver, Jillian, and Zoë. Papa, Crystal, and Jade remained, facing me from about five meters away. Wolfe still lay motionless on the ground. Jillian would probably return to pick him up soon.

Crystal crossed her arms. "About time you came out, girl. The clock is ticking down toward mass murder."

"I know." I strode straight to Papa and spoke in a no-nonsense tone. "When Mabel mentioned possibly blowing up the Alpha Zeta station with a nuclear bomb, you mentioned that you experimented with making your own nukes."

He nodded. "That's right."

"How many did you make?"

"Ten."

"Did you ever test any of them?"

"Yes. On an isolated asteroid about the size of … well, one of the Zeta stations."

"And what was the result?"

"Total destruction. But, like I told Mabel, I abandoned the project because they leaked radiation. Even though we kept them in lead-lined boxes, anyone who set them in place and activated them would get contaminated and likely die. At least that's what happened to the ensign who volunteered to place the bomb on the asteroid."

"What if you were to use an unmanned drone?"

"I thought of that, but the bombs I had weren't remote controlled. Someone had to set a detonation timer on them manually, giving the person enough time to get far enough away before the explosion. I was working on a remote when I got drummed out of the Alliance. That's when I turned against them and hid the bombs. I couldn't figure out how to destroy them without getting radiated myself, so I just kept them in their lead boxes."

"Where are they now?"

At this point, his aspect changed to a fatherly frown. As usual, he could read my mind without Starborn powers. "Are you seriously thinking about using the bombs to blow up the Zeta stations? That would be suicide."

"Not necessarily. I'm a self-healer."

"True, but …" He paused for a moment before shaking his head. "I don't know how to finish that. But can you heal your own radiation poisoning? It's not like a broken bone or a bleeding artery. It eats you at the cellular level and causes horrific cancers."

"To save billions of people, I'm willing to risk it."

"Of course you are." He let out a sigh and patted my shoulder. "I'm not surprised in the slightest."

"Then tell me where the bombs are. We have no time to lose."

"But what about disabling the kill switch? That's why we came here. Couldn't you find how to do it?"

"Let me show you." I led him into the cylinder and gave him a quick explanation of what Echo had found and how the skull button could be a trigger instead of a disabling switch. I also explained the built-in delays that would give me time to destroy every station. All the while, Echo scrolled the console screen through hundreds of lines of what looked like documentation as she searched for an answer to the skull-button mystery.

"So," Papa said as he stroked his chin, "if you push this button and it activates the kill-switch, you'll have one hour to get the bombs to the Alpha Zeta station and then to the Zeta Zeta station to start the bombing process. And if you get there early, you can take more than five minutes between stations."

"Trust me, I'm getting out of there a lot quicker than five minutes. I don't want to hang around those bombs."

"Good point. And transporting the bombs to the Alpha station in under an hour is cutting it real close."

I nodded toward the console. "If that button doesn't disable the kill switch, you'll tell me where the bombs are?"

"No. I'll go there myself and do it all, including taking them to the stations. I can't let you take that risk."

Heat burned through my cheeks, but I kept my tone in check, firm but respectful. "Papa, I've been taking deadly risks since I was ten, risks that you told me to take. You trained me to face fear with courage, and I have done that time after time after time. I rescued enslaved kids on multiple planets, I got stung by a deadly bramble bee, I started a refuge colony in the midst of erupting volcanoes, I repaired a starship with a dismembered wing, I stopped Admiral Fairbanks, his evil wife, and his even more evil daughter, and I annihilated the child-slave business in every star system. And I have powers you don't have." I showed him the bracelets on my wrists. "I can run faster, jump higher, and get the job done in less than half the time you could do it, so I have a better chance of saving the planets than you do."

My heart pounding, I took in a deep breath and looked into his glistening eyes as I slid my hand into his. "And I have a better chance of surviving the radiation. If you go, you'll certainly die, and we would never be together again."

He snatched me up into his arms and held me tightly, whispering, "How can I possibly say no? You were born to do this."

After kissing me on the forehead, he set me down and brushed tears from his cheeks, emotion pitching his voice higher. "But maybe the button will disable the kill switch, right? Maybe all of this talk was just an exercise in worrying over nothing."

I shook a finger, half smiling. "But if it activates the switch, you won't change your mind. You'll let me go alone."

"After I help you load the bombs in your ship, yes, I'll let you go alone." He sighed. "I can't believe I said that out loud."

"And you told the truth. My Starborn power says so." I wrapped my arms around him in another tight hug. "Thank you for trusting in me, Papa. It's good to have your blessing."

He patted me on the back. "You deserve that and much more."

I drew away and looked at Echo. "Find anything new about the button?"

She shook her head. "Nothing. Nothing at all."

I glanced outside. Jade and Crystal sat in the two-person glider as if waiting for us to come out, Wolfe still on the ground nearby.

When I refocused on the console, I touched the screen. "Okay, remind me why we're not just destroying this outpost. If we did, would it stop the kill switch?"

"Definitely not," Echo said. "They will activate on their own."

"Okay, then ..." I reached for the icon. "Let's push the button."

I pushed the skull-and-crossbones button. An alarm blared. A red light in the ceiling flashed. The diagram of the Zeta stations reappeared on the screen with a banner at the top that said, "Destruction Switch Activated. Kill Messages Sent to Zeta Stations." A timer on the screen began counting down—59:59, 59:58, 59:57 …

My throat tightened, forcing me to swallow. "We have less than one hour."

Papa grabbed my wrist and Echo's. "Let's go!"

"Wait! Wait!" Echo pulled free and pried the console's palm-sized monitor from its mooring. "This has a timer that'll tell us when the switch starts the Zetas. Whenever it's near a Zeta station, it'll update what's going on at all of the stations. And it might be the controller that Wolfe was supposed to take with him. It's important. Very important."

"Bring it along," I said as we ran out of the cylinder. I looked around. Jillian was nowhere in sight. Breathless, I looked at Jade. "Papa and I have to hurry. The switch activated."

Jade climbed out of the glider. "You two ride in this one. Crystal and I will babysit Wolfe until Jillian returns. When you get to the ship, send another glider with Zoë. We'll need four seats." She sat next to Wolfe and waved at Crystal. "C'mon. They have planets to save."

Crystal climbed out and sat next to Jade. She looked at me. "Keep us up to date."

Wolfe thrust his lower body toward Crystal and clutched her in a scissors hold with his legs, his wrists still bound. "Everyone stay where you are, or I'll kill this girl. I have a suicide pack in my pocket that'll activate on a voice command."

"What do you want?" Papa asked as he withdrew his laser blaster.

"I want the admiral's kill switch to work. I've been listening to you traitors. I know he's dead. Now I have to make sure his glorious plan succeeds, even if it means I have to die. We'll just wait right here till it's all over."

I whispered to Papa, "He seems to be telling the truth, but Jillian checked him. All he had was a wallet."

Papa nodded. "During my pirate years, I saw miniature suicide bombs that look like a wallet. Not a huge explosion but big enough to kill him and Crystal. And Jade might be close enough to get hurt."

"I can kill him by stopping his heart, but not before he could give a voice command."

"Just shoot him!" Crystal said. "Draw one of your blasted blasters and shoot him in the head! If you don't, I'll die anyway. All of us will. It's a no-brainer."

Papa looked at me and whispered, "Crystal's right. Maybe I can drill a hole in his head that'll kill him before he can say anything. We don't have time to come up with another plan."

I took a deep breath. "You're the best shot in the family."

Papa aimed the gun. Jade lunged at Wolfe, wrestled Crystal from him, and pushed her toward us. Just as Papa pulled the trigger, Wolfe grabbed Jade and shouted, "Detonate!"

As the laser bullet flew toward them, an explosion erupted at Wolfe's back and engulfed him and Jade in flames.

Crystal screamed. I turned my head, trembling. Papa cried out, "Dear God!" He gathered Crystal and me, one in each arm, and lifted us into the glider, blocking our view of the carnage. "Echo!" he called as he straddled the glider's nose, "find a place on the back."

Echo ran to the glider, sobbing. Once she had seated herself on top of the rear section, Papa slapped the side of the glider. "Megan, fly us to the ships on the double. You don't have time to grieve."

Steeling myself, I pushed the throttle. As we zoomed through the forest, I glanced at Crystal. She stared straight ahead as if in a trance. Within only a few days, she had found her mother in a wonderful reunion, then lost her in a brutal explosion triggered by a crazed zealot. I wanted to speak words of comfort, but nothing came to mind. I had to focus on my nightmare. I would soon be putting the lives of countless people in my hands, including my own life. And I had to do it alone.

When we arrived at the ships, Jillian stood between the two ramps, her expression expectant. Oliver lay on the ground with Perdantus on his chest. "I was about to come with another glider to collect the others, but—"

"Stop talking." Papa jumped off our glider and pointed at the Astral Dragon. "Megan and I will take the Dragon. Jillian, take the Nine to the Zeta station with everyone else on board. Since the kill switch has been activated, you won't—"

"What?" Jillian said. "Already? I thought we had a few hours."

"Long story, but there's only one hour to doomsday. And Jade and Wolfe are dead. No one is left to collect."

"What? Jade's dead? How did—"

"No time to explain. Just get everyone into the Nine and fly to the Zeta station. With the kill switch activated, I don't think you'll run into any resistance. After Megan and I do something, we'll meet you there. Then I'll leave the Dragon with her at the station, and I'll need a ride on the Nine to get to safety. We'll explain everything through our comm link on the way."

"Okay, if you say so." Jillian set her hands on Crystal's shoulders. "Come with me, Honey. I can't imagine the pain you're feeling, but we'll get through it. I promise." Jillian and Echo helped Crystal climb out of the glider. Still staring blankly, Crystal moved like a mindless robot.

As Jillian led Crystal up the Nine's ramp, Jillian looked back. "Echo," she said, "watch Oliver. I'll get him in a second."

"No time to lose." Papa took the console screen from Echo and ran up the Dragon's ramp.

My whole body quaking, I called to Papa, "Hang the hurry!" I ran into the Nine, caught up with Crystal, turned her toward me, and hugged her close. "Oh, Crystal, I'm so sorry."

Her arms hung loose, not hugging me back. When I drew away, her eyes focused on mine as she scowled. "You're lying. You're not sorry. It's all your fault. Everything's your fault." She balled her fists and beat them against my chest. "Ever since I met you, I've seen nothing but death! I should've never been on your six. You just led me into horrible places. And now my mother's dead because of you." She pounded a final fist into my chest and collapsed to her knees, her head down as she bawled, "I hate you! I hate you!"

I reached to touch her, but Jillian grasped my wrist. "Not now. I'll take care of her. You have to go."

Tears dripping from my chin, I nodded, still trembling as I whispered, "Thank you."

I hurried down the ramp, knelt at Oliver's side, and slid my hand into his as Echo looked on. "Oliver ..." My voice choked worse than ever. "I have to go on a dangerous mission, and I might not survive. I just wanted you to know that you're more than a friend to me. More than a brother. When I met you at the factory, you were my lifeline. I would never have made it without you." I leaned close and kissed his forehead, then gave him a longer kiss on his cheek. "No matter what happens, I will always love you."

Thoughts poured from his mind. *I love you, too, Megan, and I always will.*

I let his hand slip from mine. A sob tried to break through, but I sniffed hard to hold it back. Perdantus flew to me and landed on my shoulder. "May I go with you, Megan?"

I strode up the Dragon's ramp. "No, Perdantus. I'm sorry. It's far too dangerous, and I need to move fast."

"I am faster than you are, and I can go places that are inaccessible to you. I have helped you out of terrible situations before, have I not?"

With Papa already in the captain's seat, I took the first mate's station. "You definitely have. More times than I can count."

"The ramp's closing," Papa said, tapping on his console screen. "Perdantus can come with us on the first leg. You can decide later if he'll go with me on the Nine or stay with you on the Dragon."

As the ramp lifted, I let out a sigh. "All right, Perdantus. I'll think about it. Find a place to hole up. If you think my piloting can get crazy, wait'll you see how my father flies."

"I will." He leaped off my shoulder and flew from the bridge.

"Sonya," I said, "kindly inform Emerson that we have Perdantus on board."

"With pleasure," Sonya said through the ceiling speakers. "We were conversing while you were out, and I think Emerson is the most—"

"I don't want to hear about it, unless you have something I can use for our mission. I'm kind of dazed right now. Sorry."

"I understand," Sonya said. "I heard the news about Jade."

"Here we go." Papa handed the outpost's console screen to me and set the engine power and lower thrusters to maximum. The Dragon shot straight up, pushing me down hard in my seat. Once we rose above the trees, he shifted to the rear thrusters and pushed the throttle. We zoomed forward, jerking me against the back of the chair.

In the front viewing window, the tops of two mountains zipped toward us. Papa veered hard to the right to miss a peak, then straightened and ascended to about five kilometers. When we leveled out, he looked at his console screen. "Weapons cache in two minutes."

I looked at the console pad Echo had grabbed, trying to get my mind off Crystal and her mother. "Forty-seven minutes till the Zeta Zeta starts disintegrating Zeta Four. I tapped on the circle representing that planet. A window opened with relevant stats. I read them loudly enough for Papa to hear. "Residents of Zeta Four. Three hundred and seven million humans, nine million Savettes, whatever they are, and six hundred thousand Olanders. I don't know what those are, either."

"It's listing the sentient species," Papa said. "I've met a couple of members of both Savettes and Olanders. Savettes are bipeds, super smart, not very communicative. Really stoic and perfectly peaceful, unless you directly insult them. Then you might get a punch in the nose, but not much more. Olanders are fun-loving quadrupeds, like land-bound otters, I guess. Not as smart as humans, but far friendlier. They seem to love everyone."

"And they would all die." I tapped on the other planets and read their stats as I added up the counts of their residents. "If I can't stop the Zeta stations, more than twelve billion sentient beings will die, and I guess trillions of non-sentient creatures will get slaughtered, too."

Papa nodded. "That about sums it up. I hope that burden doesn't overwhelm you."

"Not at all, really. With so many lives on the line, I know I have to get this done. I don't have a choice."

"You do have a choice, but I know you wouldn't take it, so there's no use talking about it."

"You mean fly the Dragon to a safe world and live for ourselves like cowardly narcissists?" I huffed. "You're right. That'll never happen."

"Of course not. I was referring to me taking your place, but you've already convinced me that you're the best option to save everyone. It'll just stab me in the heart to let you go."

I took his hand and looked into his eyes. "I know, Papa. I know. Thank you for believing in me."

"You proved yourself too many times for me not to." He drew his hand from mine. "Let's get this done."

He down-throttled and pushed the Dragon into a steep dive. After about ten seconds, he leveled off again and landed on a meadow close to a narrow stream. An old shed stood between the ship and the stream about twenty meters away.

"Update our feathered passenger." He tapped on the control to open the ramp. As it lowered, he rose and strode to a supply closet at the rear of the bridge. "We'll need a hand truck. The boxes aren't too heavy to lift, but it's easier to haul them on wheels."

I set the Zeta control screen on my ship's console and opened the comms. "Perdantus, we'll be here for a few minutes. We just have to bring the bombs on board. You might as well stay where you are."

Papa and I jogged down the ramp, Papa pulling a two-wheeled upright hand truck. When we arrived at the door of the shed, he spun the wheel on a combination lock, disengaged it, and pushed the door open, revealing a dim floor with straw scattered across it. After we stepped in, he closed the door, dimming the room. Using his foot, he swept some of the straw to the side, exposing a handle. He grasped the handle and lifted a trapdoor.

Below, several black boxes sat on a concrete floor, filling the shallow recess. Papa sat with his legs dangling in the cavity and dropped to the lower floor, his shoulders even with the upper floor. He squatted, lifted one of the boxes, and slid it close to my feet. "When we get three on the truck, haul them into the Dragon."

Engine noise drew closer, growing to a roar. We both looked up, but the roof blocked our view. "It's a Nebula series ship," I said as the noise died down. "I would know that sound anywhere."

Papa whispered, "If they spotted the Dragon and landed near it, let's hope they don't look in this shed. What's in here is more important than what's on our ship. We can call the Nine to come and pick us up if necessary."

The shed's door creaked open, revealing Crystal standing in the gap. With tear tracks on her cheeks, she held out her arms and squeaked, "Megan!"

I leaped to Crystal and wrapped my arms around her. "I'm here, Crystal. I'm here."

She held me tightly. "I'm sorry for what I said. I didn't mean—"

"Shhh, shhh. I know you didn't. I know you didn't."

After several seconds, Papa cleared his throat. "I hate to break this up ..."

"I know." I let Crystal go and brushed tears away with a sleeve. "C'mon, Crystal. You can help me."

"Of course." Crystal leaned out the door and waved. The Nine's engines started again as it took off. "Jillian's leaving me with you for now. I can go with her later."

"Sounds good."

Working together, Crystal and I pushed the lead box toward the hand truck. With two hinges on one side and a latch and combination lock on the other, it was obviously designed to be opened easily by whoever had the right code. We slid the box over the truck's protruding steel blade, then stacked the second on top of the first and the third on top of the second. Of course, I could have used my telekinetic powers to help me lift them myself, but this way Crystal could be part of the process. She needed to help.

Once we had all three on the truck, I pulled while she pushed, and we hauled it to the Dragon and up the ramp. After we unloaded them on the bridge, we hurried back to the shed with the truck. Papa slid the last of three more boxes across the floor, climbed out of the hole, and closed the trap door. Without bothering to wait for us to help, he stacked the boxes on the truck, grabbed its handle, and rushed out of the shed. "We have to hustle. The Zeta station might not be as close as I'm hoping."

We followed at the same pace, ran up the ramp behind him, and hurried to our seats. "Sonya," he called, "close us up." While the ramp lifted, he unstacked the boxes, left them near the ramp, and ran to the pilot's chair.

I checked the Zeta screen. "Twenty-six minutes to go, Papa."

"Buckle up for some heavy g-forces."

The moment we all strapped in, Papa pushed the lower thrusters to max. We shot up so fast, my teeth ached, but this time, he kept those thrusters activated, sending us higher and higher. "Sonya, do you see the Zeta station anywhere?"

"Yes, Captain Willis. It's so big, it's hard to miss. You probably could have found it yourself."

"No time for snark. Set the level to zero."

Sonya sighed. "If you insist, Captain. My snark level is now at zero."

"Plot the fastest course to the Zeta and send it to my console."

"The fastest course to the Zeta station is now on your console."

Papa altered the thrusters to send the Astral Dragon into the initial vector and pushed the throttle slowly forward. As the ship's angle moved from a vertical rise to about a sixty-degree upward angle, the g-forces shifted with the change, and the spike in forward speed pinned me to the back of my chair again.

As Crystal sat quietly at the navigator's station, looking like she was battling nausea, I watched the front viewing window. The sky grew darker and darker. Soon, a shining dot appeared, the Zeta station's metallic shell reflecting the Alpha star's rays.

Papa swiveled toward me. "Are you going to wear a pressurized suit?"

"I hadn't thought about it. I guess I should. It'll save time not having to wait for air to fill a station bay."

"Exactly. Better get a suit on. I saw the black one you used to wear during stealth operations, but I don't know if it still fits you. I modeled your new one after it, but I think that one's on the Nine."

"The old one was too big for me then. It should fit fine now." I unbuckled, rose to my feet while leaning against the g-forces as Papa continued accelerating, and hurried toward our quarters, now allowing the forces to speed me along.

When I arrived, I opened the closet door, found the suit, and hurriedly put it on over my clothes. Although snug and form-fitting, it would be good enough. Apparently Papa or maybe Echo had cleaned it and polished the metallic portions, making it shimmer in the light.

I pulled the helmet from a bracket at the back of the closet and carried it to the bridge, now trudging against the g-forces.

As I passed Crystal, she whispered, "You look great, Megan."

"Thanks."

When I sat in my seat, Papa looked me over. "When you finish this mission, you'll look fabulous when all the cameras record your victorious return."

"Knowing the media on Alpha One, they'll call me a villain for destroying the Zeta stations." I looked again at the Zeta screen. "Fourteen minutes till the Zeta Zeta activates. How long till we dock?"

Papa looked at his console. "Eight minutes, four seconds, that is if we find an open arrival bay quickly. The kill switch might've locked everything down."

"Right. Something else I hadn't thought about."

"And I forgot something." He unbuckled, rose, and nodded at my console. "You fly for a minute. No need to accelerate anymore. We'll make it on time. Decelerate according to the timing schedule Sonya programmed."

"What are you going to do?"

"Unlock the bombs so you won't have to waste time unlocking them yourself."

"Good thinking."

He walked to the edge of the ramp, crouched at a box, and spun the lock's dial. "These boxes are hermetically sealed, so they're airtight. When you open them, you'll probably hear a hiss. That's normal."

"Got it."

He opened the first lock but left the box closed, then moved to the second one. "Don't open them till the last second to minimize your exposure to radiation."

"Now *that's* something I already thought about."

"Detonating it is easy. You spin a dial to set the timer, then flip up a red cover that protects the toggle, then flip the toggle."

When Papa finished detaching the locks, he jogged back to his seat, not bothering to strap in. Jillian's voice came over the ceiling speakers. "Well, it's about time you showed up. I'm getting a visual on you. Do you see us? Emerson's flashing our docking lights."

I squinted at the viewing window. With the Zeta station as a backdrop, now filling nearly half of the screen, red lights blinked near the left edge. "Yep. We see you."

"Well, we've got a problem. The doors are all closed. Echo's trying to hack into the system to open one, but the entry channel she tried is locked down as tight as a drum."

"Yeah. We were wondering if that might happen."

"Well, it did. But she says that the console pad she gave you might be able to get us in. It has special security clearance. She'll walk you through it, and she promises to cut the echoes the best she can."

While Papa took over the piloting, I set the Zeta pad on my console and looked at the screen. "Let's do it. We have only seven minutes to go."

"Megan," Echo said through the speakers, "remember the diagram with the stations on it? There were six circles with the Alpha Zeta in the middle."

"I remember."

"You need to bring that up again. Find an icon that looks like a little numeral six. That's for the six stations."

I scanned the icons until I found the six and tapped on it. The station diagram popped up on the screen. "Got it."

"Now tap on the middle circle. I'm hoping that'll give you access to the Alpha station."

I tapped on it. Boxes with numbers and on-off switches filled the screen, though all of them were grayed out, as if inaccessible. "Okay. I have a bunch of meters and switches. Any idea which one will open a door?"

"Look for a box where you can enter a bay number, probably at the top left. We're close to bay C-Nine. Type that in, the letter and the numeral, and then the enter key at the lower right."

When I did, the other fields flashed on along with labels next to each. I read them out loud. "Okay, transport ability is on, air pressure is showing zero, lights are on, door opening is showing off. I'll turn that on now." I slid the indicator from off to on.

"You did it! You did it! Oh. Sorry for the echo. But the door's opening."

"Perfect. We'll dock there. What's the number next to it? I'll open that one for the Nine."

"It's C-eight."

"Got it." I entered the number and opened the door. "I won't have time to chat after we dock. Thanks for the help."

"You're welcome, and Godspeed, Megan. We all love you."

With my throat narrowing again, I could barely manage, "I love all of you, too."

Papa flew the Dragon into the bay and spun her bow toward the door. The moment he set her down, I reentered our bay number, closed the door, and turned on the air. "Four minutes, seven seconds till the Zeta Zeta activates. At the rate the air pressure's going up here, we should be able to open the ramp soon."

Papa jumped up and hustled to the boxes. "I'll unload one of the bombs so it'll be ready when you get back here."

"We're in," Jillian called. "Close the door and give us some air."

"On it." I entered their bay number again, closed their door, and turned on the air. "Should be good in a couple of minutes." I checked our bay again. The air pressure was now at a breathable level. Also, I didn't feel the negative energy at all. Tobias must've disabled the signal. I tapped the button to open the ramp. "Let's get this done."

When I rose, Perdantus flew in and landed on my shoulder, reminding me that I had to leave him and Crystal. "Perdantus, Crystal, listen. Lately, I've learned that I have to trust in my friends instead of just myself, and you've all been great, but this time I have to go alone and—"

"No," Crystal said, waving a hand. "Don't." She unbuckled, ran to me, and kissed my forehead. "Goodbye, Sister. … No … Not goodbye. I'll see you soon."

Perdantus flitted to Crystal's shoulder. "As will I. Go and save the galaxy, my courageous friend."

"I love you both." I hugged Crystal and rubbed Perdantus's chest feathers. "Now get your butts on the Nebula Nine and fly to safety."

"My butt is now on the move." Crystal marched down the ramp, joining Papa as he carried a bomb box out. I checked the screen again. Two minutes and six seconds till Zeta Four's doom would start, and I still had to carry a bomb out and detonate it at that station.

Papa ran back in and kissed my forehead. "I love you, and I believe in you. Now go save billions of lives. We'll be out of the bay in ten seconds." He ran down the ramp.

The moment he turned out of sight, the open ramp reminded me that my arrival bay on the Zeta Zeta wouldn't have any air. I put my helmet on, attached the gloves, and filled the suit's built-in pouches, drawing from the air in the ship. Without a tank, that would last about twenty minutes. I looked at the screen. After finding a transport button, I tapped it. A new window popped up showing a list of the other Zetas. I tapped on the Zeta Zeta and turned the system on, then grabbed the chair with my free hand.

The screen beeped and flashed a message—Bay door must be open at both stations for transport to occur. Transport will begin when the doors are open.

I groaned. Of course they had to be open. I used the controls to open the doors on the Alpha Zeta. While they slid apart, I switched to the Zeta Zeta, entered the same bay number, and opened its doors.

Soon, light flashed all around, now a familiar experience. As expected, air rushed out through the ramp opening, trying to pull me along, but my grip on the chair kept me in place. I glanced at the Zeta screen. Only sixty-three seconds left until the guns would start moving into position.

When the suction eased enough, I set the Zeta screen down and flexed my biceps to charge my legs. I ran to the boxes, picked one up, and carried it down the ramp, the Zeta's artificial gravity keeping my feet on the floor and my enhanced legs allowing me to hurry even with all the weight.

Once outside, I set the box down and opened the lid. Although it probably hissed, I couldn't hear it in the vacuum. I turned the timer to forty-five seconds, lifted the cover tab, and flipped the toggle. The timer's digital reading began counting down. I ran up the ramp, sat in my chair, and snatched the Zeta screen. Thirty seconds to this Zeta's kill-switch activation, then one minute or so after that for the Epsilon Zeta to activate. I had enough time, but only barely.

I entered my next station, the Epsilon Zeta, and turned the transport on. As before, light flashed. Again, I looked at the screen. I had one minute and twelve seconds before these guns would start moving.

After setting the screen down, with my legs still charged, I leaped up, ran to the boxes, hoisted one into both arms, and hustled down the ramp with it. Since I had to breathe rapidly to carry such a heavy weight, my air supply might run out faster than expected, but I couldn't worry about that now.

I put the box on the floor, opened the lid, and set the timer. Since the guns took five minutes to move into firing position, I didn't have to be so quick to detonate the bomb. It could explode at any time after I zapped out as long as it exploded before the guns were in place. Two minutes would work.

After plugging the number into the timer and flipping the toggle, I hustled back into the Dragon, picked up the Zeta screen, and entered my next destination, the Delta station. When I tapped on the button to transport, a message appeared— Gun is not in position. Transport will commence when the gun is in the proper position.

I sucked in a breath. Were the guns already leaving the bay? I looked at the screen. The time-to-activation number had changed to four minutes and fifty seconds, probably the time to when the guns would start firing. Echo's words about Wolfe's use of this Zeta screen flashed to mind. Supposedly, this screen could move the gun to where it needed to be to send me on to the next station.

My heart pounding like a jackhammer, I searched the screen but couldn't find anything that might control the gun. With the screen still in my grasp, I ran out to the bay floor and spotted the gun moving toward the wall. I reached a hand out, curled it into a fist to grab the gun with my mind, and pulled it back toward its normal position. It offered some resistance, but I managed to drag it back into place.

The gun swiveled and aimed at the Dragon. I leaped in with my enhanced legs, rolled past the ramp, and collided with the front of the pilot's console. The transport lights flashed. I jumped up and switched the screen to control the Delta Zeta. I had twenty seconds until the guns here would start moving.

I charged my legs and hurried through the bomb procedure. After I set the timer and toggled the detonator, I looked at the disintegration gun. It was already moving on its track toward the wall of the station, and the Zeta screen indicated four minutes and thirty seconds until planet disintegration. I was further behind than at the previous station.

As before, I mentally pulled the gun back into place and ran into the Dragon. On the screen, I entered my next destination, the Gamma Zeta, and tapped the button to transport. The console beeped and flashed a message— Gun is not in position. Transport will commence when the gun is in the proper position.

"Blazes!" The gun must've started moving again. It wouldn't stay in place on its own because the kill switch kept trying to relocate it. I ran out and repeated the pull back to the right position and again dove into the ship.

As I lay on the bridge floor, lights flashed, a signal that I was now at the Gamma station. I climbed to my feet and checked the time to gun relocation here—seventeen seconds. Now that I knew what to do about a moving gun, I didn't have to rush and lose too much air. Fortunately, Tobias had moved these guns back into place after he neutralized the attacking ships here.

After taking a deep breath, I put the console screen down, walked to the bombs, and carried one out to the bay. I set the detonator to two minutes and looked through the open doorway. Stars speckled the darkness beyond. Somewhere out there the remnants of three Zetas floated as scattered wreckage.

Or did they? I had no proof that the bombs exploded. Doubts gnawed at my mind. These were old, homemade bombs that had been left in dank storage for years. Papa never mentioned the possibility that they might not work, but it seemed to me that the possibility was real, maybe even a probability.

I glanced at the gun. It was moving toward the wall, as expected. I jogged back into the Dragon and entered my next destination, the Beta Zeta. As expected, the system told me the gun was out of position, but before going out and resetting the gun, I brought up the app window that showed all six stations and tapped on the Zeta Zeta. The screen showed the usual boxes, and a message at the top said, "Communications failed."

I breathed a sigh of relief. At least that bomb had worked. I hustled outside once more and dragged the gun back toward its firing position. With probably less than thirty seconds left before the bomb would explode, I was cutting it close.

When the gun arrived, I leaped into the ship once more, this time managing to stay on my feet. The lights flashed, sending me to the Beta station. I glanced at the Zeta screen. The guns had already started moving here, only three minutes and seven seconds to go. I had to hurry, not only because of the moving guns. With all the carrying heavy bombs and rushing around, my air supply had to be running low, but this suit lacked a usage meter to let me know for certain.

I grabbed the last bomb that we had left on the ship, carried it to the bay floor, set the timer to one minute, and flipped the detonator toggle. Now having trouble breathing, I ran up the ramp, entered the Alpha station as my next destination, hurried back out, and returned the gun to its transport position.

Another leap sent me flying into the Dragon just as the lights flashed, letting me know that I had transported to the Alpha Zeta. But with so little air left in my suit, could I detonate the final bomb? I glanced at the Zeta screen. The guns were already on the move with less than four minutes before they would attack the planet. Once again, I had to hurry. At least I didn't have to carry a bomb this time, and once I set the timer, I wouldn't have to move the gun back into place. I could rush into the Dragon and fly away at top speed, hoping that I could get out of range in time.

With the screen still in hand, I ran down the ramp and out to the bay floor. A woman in an Alliance uniform lay curled next to the box, and its lid lay open. I glanced at the bay doors. They stood completely shut. Had this woman closed it and tried to fill the bay with air but collapsed before the pressure rose enough? Maybe the door was already starting to close when I arrived.

Since I was running out of air, I had to take a risk. I detached my helmet and inhaled. Yes, there was thin air in the chamber. I set the Zeta screen on the floor, knelt next to the woman, and turned her face up, recognizing her immediately. "Mabel!" Her chest rose and fell in an even rhythm. She was alive but unconscious. Obviously, she had been exposed to the radiation. But for how long?

I glanced at the disintegration gun as it clicked along its track, then at the screen on the floor—two minutes and seven seconds until it would arrive at its outside perch where it would join the others to destroy my home planet. If I could arm the bomb, carry Mabel into the Dragon, and fly away before the blast could annihilate us, we might be able to survive.

After setting the timer for one minute, I flipped up the protective cap, and toggled the detonator switch. Although it clicked, the timer stayed at one minute. Not good. Unless it counted down, the bomb would never detonate.

I reset the toggle switch and tried again. The timer remained at one minute. I changed the timer to forty seconds and reset the toggle. Still no countdown. Once more I looked at the Zeta screen. One minute and fifteen seconds remained. Now, even if I could get the bomb to count down, I had no chance to haul Mabel to safety and zoom away from here in time, especially since I had to open the bay doors wide enough to get the Dragon out. That would take nearly a minute by itself.

As I rose to my feet, I looked for the gun. It had reached the wall where an airlock door opened to allow it to leave the bay. I couldn't let it get to the outside of the station. Although eliminating just one of the guns couldn't stop the carnage, I had to do something.

My heart thudding, I reached out, grabbed the gun with my mind and dragged it back toward its perch, straining against the usual resistance. I glanced down at the Zeta screen, barely able to read the countdown-to-death number—sixteen seconds to go. Dragging one gun was hopeless. The rest of the guns would probably be able to destroy my planet without it.

But maybe there was still a way to stop them.

I imagined where the guns had to be by now, moving into position on the exterior. I closed my eyes and spread my arms, mentally reaching out to every point around the station. I moved my arms toward my chest again and again, as if gathering floating objects into my grasp. With each gun I grabbed, pressure slowed my movements, making me strain to reach for the next one and the next one and the next one. Pain roared in my muscles. My skull pounded, threatening to crack open. Heat spiked in my chest where my locket touched my skin. The dragon's eye had to be pulsing like mad.

Something clicked near the wall. A loud hum made the floor vibrate. The guns were activating. Some might still attack Alpha One, and people would die.

I whispered, "God, help me." Then, straining with all my might, I thrust my mental arms completely around the station and swept them toward me, grabbing everything in their path. In my mind, the remaining guns broke free from their pedestals and dragged toward me. Pressure, pain, sheer agony shot through my entire body.

Metal clanked against the bay doors. Lights crashed down from the ceiling and sizzled all around. Darkness flooded the chamber. The walls groaned as if ready to implode.

Letting out a wild scream, I jerked my arms to my chest. As more crashing sounds stormed into my ears, I collapsed, and my mind melded with the darkness.

I opened my eyes. Although a slight blur veiled my vision, I could tell that I was reclining on my back surrounded by wildflowers, their red, blue, and orange hues dazzling. The aroma, sweet and smooth, smelled like … well, like home.

I bent my neck forward to look at my body. I still wore the black pressure suit that I had on while trying to destroy the Zeta stations, though the helmet was missing. Did I somehow get transported to the surface of the planet from the Alpha Zeta?

A large hand appeared above me. "Would you like to get up?"

I blinked, clearing my vision. Barnabas bent close with his arm extended toward me. "Uh … sure." I grasped his wrist and let him pull me to my feet. "How did you get here?" I quickly glanced around at the endless field of wildflowers. "And how did *I* get here?"

He chuckled. "A young woman who jumps from star system to star system is wondering how she could possibly be somewhere she didn't expect." He smiled in a kind way. "Megan, how you arrived here is not as important as understanding where you are."

"Well, it looks like Alpha One. Smells like it, too."

He nodded. "This place resembles your home on Alpha One in many ways, but it is not Alpha One."

"Is it like the place where I saw you before? Back when I was dying, and Oliver and Zoë were trying to revive me?"

"Similar. You will soon understand."

I smiled. "Okay, you're going to be mysterious."

"Yes. I need to reveal the truth slowly to keep you from being shocked." He took my hand. "Come with me."

When he pivoted, a stream came into view in the distance with tall green trees lining the shore. Three people waded in the shallows, too far away to identify, and it seemed that a screen had been draped between them and me, covering them with a blur.

As we walked toward them, Barnabas compressed my hand. "I understand that you endured quite an ordeal. Are there any lasting effects?"

I mentally checked my body. I felt no pain anywhere, as if all the lifting bombs and dragging disintegration guns had never happened. "It's strange. I feel perfectly fine."

"That's good. I'll tell you why you are pain free in a moment."

We passed the line of trees and stopped a few steps from the stream. Although the flowing water sparkled as if unveiled, the people stayed blurred. I looked at Barnabas. "What's going on here?"

"If you were to take one more step, you would walk into eternity. Beyond this veil is your forever home."

"Do you mean, like heaven?"

"Exactly like heaven."

"So I died in the Alpha-one Zeta station?"

"That answer is still pending, as it often is for you. Let me show you something before I explain." He waved a hand across the surface of the veil. The blur evaporated, making everything clear. My mother, wearing all white, waded in the water with two girls, also wearing white. They splashed each other, laughing and squealing with delight.

I cried out, "Mama!"

She stopped splashing and looked at me. A beautiful smile dressed her face as she held out her arms. "Megan!"

I took a step to run to her, but Barnabas grasped my wrist and held me back. "Not yet, Megan. Not yet."

I looked at him, desperately wanting to run to Mama. "Why not?"

"You need to know more."

Mama walked out of the stream toward me, one of the girls at each side. As they drew close, the identities of the two girls became clear—Cynda and Renalda. They stopped almost within reach and gazed at me as if in wonder.

"Hello, Megan," Mama said. "I figured out that you're not in heaven yet. Are you going to cross the veil?"

Renalda held out a hand, as if inviting me to take it. "You should, Megan. It's wonderful here. So peaceful. No whips. No bramble bees."

Cynda grinned. "And we get to watch what's going on wherever we want. And we've been watching you. It's been so exciting!"

"Oh, Megan ..." Mama's voice sounded like a lamenting song. "You've been so brave, so sacrificial, so filled with love. Maybe it's time for you to rest, take the burden of the galaxy off your shoulders. Come and join me in eternal bliss."

"I would love to, but ..." I turned toward Barnabas. "Is it my choice?"

He nodded. "In reality, you are in a desperate condition, clinging to life by a burnt thread. As during the previous similar episode, others are doing all they can to save you, but whether or not you survive is once again a matter of your will to survive."

"Did I stop the Zeta stations? Did I save the worlds?"

His brow lifted. "I suppose that's a reasonable factor in your decision making, so—"

"No." I lifted a hand. "Don't tell me. I forgot something more important." I inhaled deeply. "What happened to my father, my aunt, and my friends? Did they survive? Is there anything I can do to help them?"

"Fair questions. They all love you dearly, but, as you know, they are incredibly strong and will do fine without you, though there is one exception."

"My father."

He nodded. "Julian Willis will suffer without you. That I cannot deny."

"You have to go back," Mama said.

I swiveled toward her, blinking hard. "You don't want me to come across?"

"Oh, I do. So very much. And you would be at peace here. Still, Julian needs you. He is the strongest man I have ever met, but when it comes to his loved ones, his heart is fragile. My death is probably torturing him, though he hides the pain. I'm sure your death would devastate him, maybe send him to his grave."

I stared at her. In another time and place, I might have felt like I was being put on the spot, my emotions manipulated, but not here. Her appeal caressed my heart with pure love. "I think you're right, Mama. I have to go back. I miss you, but I'm glad to know you're okay. I guess I'll see you again someday."

"You will." She blew a kiss. "Goodbye, my sweet daughter. Please tell your father how much I love him."

"I will." I caught the kiss and pressed it on my forehead, then turned away. "Barnabas, I have to go. Now. Before I change my mind."

"Do you remember what I said the last time you nearly died?"

"I remember. I spent the last of my nine lives. It would take a miracle to save me if this happened again."

He set a hand on my shoulder. "Correct. Yet, such a miracle is possible. In order for you to make a final decision, you need to know that your health might be greatly diminished. Are you prepared for that?"

I nodded. "I know how to deal with pain. And I'm a self-healer."

Barnabas shook his head sadly. "If God grants the miracle, you will no longer be a healer, self or otherwise. It will take all of your Starborn power to bring you back from the brink of death. You will lose all of your Starborn abilities, including energizing others, though you will still be able to use your bracelets as you did before. Can you pay that price?"

I clutched my locket through my clothes. "I understand. I can pay that price to help my Papa. No question."

"Very well. Then you will be sent back." The flowers vanished. We now stood in an expanse of pure white, no ground, no walls, no sky. "This journey will take only a few seconds."

"How long will it have been since I set the bombs?"

"You'll know exactly how long quite soon."

"Okay. That's fine, but can you tell me why you showed me my mother in heaven? Since I'm going back to the living world, what difference did it make?"

"So you could see what awaits you someday. Because of your nearly unmatched sacrificial love and courage, you have been given a glimpse of your glorious forever home, a reunion in paradise to look forward to for the rest of your years. Very few have been given that blessing, and you should spread the joy of that glimpse of forever to everyone you know."

"I will." My final two words echoed in my mind. As the white faded to black, I repeated the words out loud, "I will ... I will ... I will."

A bird chirped somewhere close by. My brain translated the sound. "You will what, Megan?"

I opened my eyes. I lay in a hospital room, the lights dim and the door ajar. The bird chirped again. "Megan? Are you awake this time? Really awake?"

I turned toward the sound. Perdantus perched on the railing near the foot of the bed, staring at me. "Yes, I'm awake."

He fluttered his wings. "Well, it seems that we have been in this situation before, me watching over you when you wake up from unconsciousness."

"More than once before. Thank you for watching."

"Your father has taken the lion's share of our Megan vigil, nearly every hour of every day, though he sleeps in here part of the time. I came in only moments ago to relieve him so he could get some nourishment. Shall I go out and bring him here?

Feeling weak all over, I had to force out every word. "Not yet. Let him eat. Maybe you can tell me what's going on."

"I'm afraid I am not at liberty to tell you much. Crystal made me promise to let her tell you all the news. I will fly out and get her. She and Oliver are, you might say, camped out in the waiting room. They come in your room to see about you quite often." He flew through the door opening and disappeared.

I found the bed controls and raised the back, lifting my head and torso. With every centimeter of movement, my head pounded. When I released the button, I pushed with my legs to scoot higher. My calf muscles felt like jelly, loose and weak.

I looked at my wrists. The bracelets were gone. I felt under my hospital gown for my locket and pulled the chain, drawing it out. Although no supercharged light spilled through, the dragon's eye probably had its usual glow.

Crystal pushed the door fully open and walked in, followed by Oliver. Both smiled ear to ear, Oliver with a stethoscope hanging around his neck over a doctor's white coat and Crystal wearing a lovely mid-calf floral dress with short sleeves, pockets, and a matching fabric belt. "I've never seen you wear a dress before," I said. "Is this a special occasion?"

"It most definitely is." She kissed me on the forehead. "Megan ..." Her voice cracked. "Your Aunt Jillian had this dress made for me, and I've been putting it on every morning, hoping you would wake up that day, so you could see how pretty it is, and it would all be so special. And now …" Her voice squeaked. "And now you *are* awake. I'm so happy because you're alive, and your eyes are open, and we survived." She leaned over the bed rail and gave me a hug. I gave her one in return, but my arms felt too flaccid to make it a tight one."

When she drew back, Oliver kissed my forehead and gave me a hug, whispering, "I'm glad you're still with us."

"Where are you two living now? You're both … well … orphans, I guess."

Crystal lowered her head. "Yeah. We are. I still can't believe what I said to you when my mother—"

"Not one more word about that. That was your pain speaking. I understand."

Oliver set a hand on Crystal's shoulder. "Piper made arrangements for us, and we're waiting for our adoptions to be finalized. We're going to be together."

"Together? That's great. Who are the lucky parents?"

Crystal shook her head. "We're not telling until everything is signed and sealed. We don't want to jinx it."

"Okay. Fair enough. Let's switch to a topic I need to know about. Did I destroy all of the Zeta stations? How long was I out cold? Am I crippled for life? How is everyone else doing?"

Crystal gave Oliver a grin before looking at me again. "Okay, I've been practicing for this moment. Here goes." She took a deep breath. "Well, Sister, you sure did the job. Not only did you go nuclear on five Zeta stations and blow them to smithereens, you pulled every gun from its tracks at the Alpha Zeta and slung them into the docking bay with you. Of course, that blew holes in the walls and started sucking air out. That's when I, on your six, as usual, saw it all happen from the control room."

"You stayed behind?"

"Yep. So did Perdantus and Papa, I mean, your father. I've been calling him Papa for a while now. I hope you don't mind."

"Not at all. I'm sure he doesn't mind either."

"He doesn't. Now back to the story. We were all supposed to board the Nine, but I secretly told Jillian that I was staying. She just rolled her eyes and said, 'Of course you are.' I didn't know that Papa had already told her that he was staying. Anyway, we all hid in different places in the Alpha Zeta. When Papa and I found each other, we laughed because we both kind of knew that we both would do that. Anyway, we went to the control room and found Perdantus there. No surprise, right?"

I smiled. "No surprise at all."

"So, we were watching the bay before you showed up. I knew you would come with the Astral Dragon, and we figured we could escape with you. So, there we were watching from the control room, when the bay exit doors started closing, the Dragon appeared in the bay, and Mabel ran in to look at the bomb, fighting against the vacuum. Maybe she was trying to set the bomb off, not knowing that you were going to do that. Then she collapsed, probably from lack of oxygen or from radiation."

"Lack of oxygen," Oliver said. "Radiation poisoning is lots slower."

She nudged his ribs. "I knew that. Anyway, Papa and I put on space suits and ran down to that bay's level. When I looked through the door's window, I saw you doing your telekinetic wrestling with the guns. Since it looked like you were winning, we waited, not wanting to mess up your concentration, but when you dropped like a sock full of rocks and the guns flew in through the holes, we ran out there. Papa picked you up and started carrying you to the hall, but one of the flying guns bashed his legs and broke both of them."

I gasped. "Broke his legs?"

"Yep. But he's already off the crutches. Still limps a bit, but he should be as good as new soon. Now back to my story. When his legs broke, he made sure that you landed on the floor softly, and I was glad he got you almost to the door, because I had to drag both him and you out of there. The whole time, the vacuum from space was pulling me, making me slide back, but I finally broke free and closed the door. Then, when I looked through the window again, Mabel was gone. I guess the vacuum was strong enough to suck her into space."

"That's awful!"

"Maybe it was awful. I'm wondering if she was really trying to sabotage the bomb. I never quite figured out whose side she was on. Anyway, since you couldn't get the bomb to explode, maybe she did sabotage it. So, back to my story again. Since you saved the planet without blowing up the station, I knew I had time to call for help. I rushed back to the control room and called the Nebula Nine. They sent gliders through the holes the guns punched in the walls and rescued us. It was all pretty snazzy and exciting, but you slept through the whole thing."

"How long have I been asleep?"

"Hold on to your saddle, Sister. It's been two months and six days since you knocked yourself out with—"

I shouted, "Two months and six days!"

"Yep. A lot harder on us, though. You slept while we worried. Severe concussion, radiation sickness, and two torn rotator cuffs. Oliver was able to purge the effects of the radiation right away and heal the rotator cuffs. The rest of your damage took longer. But I needed the two months to grieve for my mother without you trying to comfort me. It gave me time to read, and not my romance novels. I got a book about idioms, like you suggested, and I memorized a bunch of them. I cried for a whole month over my mother. I'm still aching inside, but I'm not blubbering about it anymore."

"I completely understand. I cried like a baby over my mother's death."

"I remember." Crystal curled her arm around Oliver's. "Now I'm taking this incredible healer out to prepare for the celebration we've been planning. And we'll look for Papa to tell him you're awake. Won't take but a couple of minutes."

"Celebration? What celebration?"

As Crystal walked out, she replied in singsong, "You'll see, hero girl."

Now alone with Perdantus, I tapped the railing near my head. "Come closer so I can whisper. I feel so weak."

He flitted to the spot. "After two months in a coma, it's no wonder you're so weak. Just talk when you want, rest when you have to. We have time."

"That'll work."

"While you're resting, I will provide you with some news. After you tore the gun system apart on the Alpha Zeta station, Piper Altera arrived a few days later, and her husband was with her. Jillian tracked him down and rescued him, but that's another story. The last I heard, Jillian was conducting some kind of search in the Epsilon system. In any case, Piper had to travel through a wormhole since you blew up the Gamma Zeta. She immediately started work on repairing the Alpha station, but not as a transport depot—as a city. You know that it was designed to be a place to live, with hotels, restaurants, and apartments, including this hospital. Now, that dream is coming true."

"Am I in the Alpha station right now?"

Perdantus nodded. "This facility has the best medical team in the galaxy, or so I have heard. Also, the staff members are ecstatic about the work Oliver has done, including giving you treatments every day. He says you nearly died at least ten times, but not long ago, something seemed to click, and your brain started healing."

A gray-haired nurse in greens scrubs walked in, smiling. "We're all thrilled that you're awake. The news is spreading like a prairie fire. Now let me check your PEG tube and get you ready to try to walk."

While Perdantus turned his head, the nurse lifted the sheet and my gown and looked at a little valve on my stomach. "Looks good." She put the sheet and gown back in place and lowered the bed's side rail. "You can get up whenever you feel like you can but not until someone is here to help you. I'm afraid this fine bird wouldn't be able to catch you if you lost your balance."

I nodded. "Got it. No walking by myself yet."

She patted my hand. "Blessings to you, my dear."

When she left, Crystal walked in. "I couldn't find Papa, but Oliver's still looking for him. And everything's set for the celebration. I hope you're not disappointed with the number of people who could get here on short notice."

"To the Alpha Zeta? I'm not expecting anyone at all but you and Oliver and Perdantus. Oh, and is Piper here? Perdantus told me she came to Alpha One to restore the station. And Lyric? I hope she made it."

"You'll see." Crystal nodded toward the room's closet. "Get dressed. You can't make an appearance in a hospital gown. It's kind of drafty on your six, if you know what I mean. Perdantus can leave the room while I help you change clothes."

"Good." I slid my legs over the side of the bed. "I'll probably need it."

"I will find Oliver," Perdantus said as he took off and headed for the door.

Crystal helped me to my feet until I could balance myself, then led me to the closet. She opened the door and looked inside. My black spacesuit hung from a hanger on the right, cleaned and polished. Next to that hung the Astral Alliance uniform that I wore under it, the new one Papa got for me.

From the left side of the closet, Crystal pulled out a hanger with a dress that looked exactly like hers down to the finest detail.

"Why do you have two dresses like that?" I asked.

"It's not mine." She held it up to my shoulder. "Yep. It'll fit you perfectly."

I drew my head back. "What? A dress for me? I've never worn a dress in my life."

"I know." She took the dress off the hanger. "It was your mother's. Jillian said it's Papa's favorite. So I asked her to get a duplicate made for me so you and I could match at the celebration." She held it higher, showing its full length. "I thought you'd wear it for a beloved father who was here watching you day and night for more than two months. I mean, it's up to you, obviously, but if I had a father, I would wear it every day, like I've been wearing this one."

I pinched the dress's side and ran my fingers up and down the soft material. How could I say no to a request like that? "All right, but you'll have to give me a quick lesson since I've never worn one."

"Oh, that's easy. You'll get the hang of it in no time."

Crystal helped me put the dress on, cinched the belt close to my waist, and tied it in an elegant bow. The dress did fit perfectly, and it felt good, too. She turned the overhead light on and opened the closet door further. A full-length mirror attached to the inside of the door reflected my entire body. I swiveled from side to side, making the dress twirl around my legs. "It's really very pretty. I like it a lot."

"Yep. You look amazing. Papa's going to love it. And when Oliver sees you ..." She shook her head. "Never mind. I know you're not a fan of the romance stuff."

My cheeks warmed, and I managed a weak smile. "It's all right. I'm looking forward to both of them seeing me in this dress. It feels like a new me. I'm just glad to be alive."

"Speaking of a new you ..." She closed the closet door. "Do you know if you still have your Starborn powers? I have mine, and Oliver has his. After all of that body smashing you went through, I was wondering."

Recalling Barnabas's words, I shook my head. "I don't think so, but I can test it if you want."

"Sure. Try mind reading. I'll shout some thoughts at you."

As she stared at me, I looked straight into her eyes, but I couldn't hear a single word. "Nope. Nothing."

"I was thinking about porcupine ice cream."

I blinked. "You were? That's really a strange thing—"

"Actually, that was a lie. I was thinking about our amazing dresses, but you couldn't detect that I was lying, could you?"

I shook my head again. "I guess my powers really are gone."

"Not all of them. You can still energize us. The last time Oliver gave you a healing treatment, your locket lit up like a blazing red star. Your vitals improved that minute, and you woke up the next day."

"That might've been the last time I could do that."

"If so, not a big deal." She hooked my arm with hers. "We've waited long enough. It's time for the celebration. I'm going to show off this newly dressed ... um ... what's the word? I think it starts with a D."

"Debutante?"

She squinted. "Wait. That's not a real world, is it?"

"Yep. It's a Willis word. Deal with it."

"All right, debutante, let's go."

"Should I get a wheelchair?" I asked. "I'm not very steady."

"Steady enough to go where we're going." Crystal walked to the window and pulled the drapes aside, revealing a glass door that led to a balcony. When she slid the door to the side, cool air breezed in, flapping the drapes and my dress. "Right this way, Sister."

Taking careful steps, I walked out to the balcony, Crystal at my side. When I reached the railing, I looked out over a sea of people, maybe hundreds—men, women, and children, even Taurantas and Jaradians, and a few other species I didn't recognize."

When they saw me, a loud cheer erupted, shouts of "Megan!" and "Thank you!" and "We love you!"

I caught sight of Josie and Tobias near the center of the throng, both waving. Quixon stood close to the front, also waving. Heat roared into my face. My knees weakened. I had to clutch the rail to keep from falling.

Crystal curled her arm around mine and leaned her head on my shoulder. "They love you, Megan. We all do. And you deserve every bit of praise. You're the galaxy's hero."

Now crying, I sniffed hard. "I … I don't know what to say. And I definitely can't shout loudly enough to speak to them."

"They're not expecting it. Just wave. They'll love it."

I smiled and, raising my arm high, waved with as much energy as I could muster, still holding to the rail with one hand.

"Piper got them all here," Crystal said, "every slave we set free and their families, along with a few special guests, like Josie and Tobias. They live here at the Zeta station now, and as soon as word got out that you're awake, they started gathering under your window. And they hope to live here a long time, that is, if you approve."

"If *I* approve? Why would I have to approve?"

"That's another question that'll have to wait." Crystal waved her arms to quiet the crowd. When the clamor settled, she cupped her hands around her mouth and shouted, "Megan is super happy you came to show your love and appreciation. And she loves you right back. She's too weak to stay out of bed long, but she wants you to know that she'll answer all of your messages as soon as she can."

"Messages?" I asked.

She lowered her hands and looked at me. "Thousands. Tens of thousands. Emerson will help you answer them, so don't worry. And wait'll you see the gifts. Tons of gifts."

"But I don't want any—"

"Yes, you do. Don't reject their gratitude." She cupped her hands again and faced the crowd. "Food and drinks will be coming out soon, and so will the musicians." She raised a fist. "It's time to party!"

As another cheer rose from the happy crowd, Crystal guided me back into the room, closed the door, and held my hand as we walked to a recliner. "Now for the most important part. Stand here."

"Not sit?"

"Later. I promise."

I balanced myself in front of the chair. "Okay, mystery girl. I'm ready."

She grinned. "Actually, I don't think you are, but we'll see." She hurried to the door and looked out. "Did you find him?"

Oliver's voice came through. "Yep. Everyone's here."

"All right. It's show time." Crystal opened the door fully. Oliver walked in with Perdantus on his shoulder and stood at my side while Perdantus flitted to the back of the chair. Papa limped in behind him. When he saw me, he hobbled to me as fast as he could. He stood and stared at me, his mouth partially open, as if he didn't know what to do. He whispered, "You look … stunning."

I smiled and gave the dress a twirl. "I'm glad you like it."

"I mean *you*." He gathered me into his arms and held me tight. "Oh, Megan …" His voice cracked. "I'm so glad you're all right. So glad. I don't know what I'd do without you."

I hugged him as hard as I could. "Thank you for watching over me and for trying to rescue me in the docking bay."

He pulled back and brushed a tear, smiling. "Oh, you heard about that?" He glanced at Crystal. "Oh. Of course you did. And I do love the dress. You're gorgeous in it, and—"

"Plenty of time for that later." Crystal guided him to my side and pointed at the chair. "Megan, you can sit now. We have some formalities to take care of." When I sat, Crystal turned toward the door, and called, "We're ready."

Piper walked in carrying a briefcase, Lyric at her side. Lyric's smile seemed to brighten the room as Piper pulled several sheets of paper from the case.

After closing the door behind her, she set the case down and began reading the top page. "Whereas, Admiral Dwight Fairbanks promised to give the Alpha One Zeta station to Megan Willis, I, Piper Altera, as the head of the New Alliance, hereby assign the ownership deed of said station to her. I also grant her the financial assets of Admiral Fairbanks's accounts that were housed in the banks therein."

She handed Lyric the page, and Lyric brought it to me and laid it on my lap. Crystal's words returned to mind. *And they hope to live here a long time, that is, if you approve.*

I whispered, "I approve."

Piper began reading the second page. "Seeing that Oliver Tillman and Crystal Clearwater have become orphans due to the many tragic events of late, the New Alliance has found it fitting to approve their adoption, requested by them and their new family." She handed the sheet and a pen to Lyric. "Oliver and Crystal have both signed the agreement. The final signature will make the adoption complete."

Lyric grabbed a clipboard attached to the bed and gave it to Papa, along with the sheet and the pen. She pointed at the page. "Sign here."

I gasped, already crying. "Papa, you're adopting Oliver and Crystal?"

"With all my heart." He signed the page with a swirling flair. "It's done."

I pushed myself out of the chair and hugged him, then Oliver, then Crystal. Crying so hard I could barely talk, I spluttered, "Welcome to our family."

All four of us hugged and cried together. During our embrace, I glanced at Perdantus. He looked on with a forlorn expression. I reached toward him. "Get over here, you. I don't need a signed document to welcome you to our family." He flew to my shoulder as we continued hugging.

After nearly a minute, we separated. I sat in the recliner, and the others stood nearby, Perdantus again on the back of the chair. Wiping tears, I looked at Piper. "Any other wonderful surprises?"

"A few." She lifted the remaining pages. "These letters from heads of state of the other planets you saved. And also this." She turned and opened the door.

Zoë walked in, followed by Echo, Oz, and Chip. Zoë hurried to me and hugged me while the other three looked on. Then Oz spoke up. "Zoë, Piper told us not to hug her 'cause she's so weak."

Zoë pointed at me. "This girl can take it. Trust me."

"I definitely can." I pushed myself to my feet, walked to them, and hugged them all, first Oz, then Chip, then Echo. I stepped back and sighed. "It's so good to see you." I looked at Echo and smiled. "So good."

For the next hour, we chatted and laughed together, told stories of our adventures, and sometimes cried together as we remembered those we had lost. Piper arranged for food and drinks from the party outside, and we shared them together. It was definitely a great time.

Finally, everyone left except Papa, Oliver, Crystal, and Perdantus—my family, though Jillian was missing, likely on the mission Perdantus had mentioned. While they sat on the bed, I told them about my visit with Mama in heaven. I gave Papa her message, that she loves him very much. We cried once more, shedding both sad and happy tears. We knew we would see her again, and we would honor her love and courage for the rest of our days.

"Papa," I said as our crying settled, "I know we would do this all over again if we had to, but right now, I'm pretty tired."

"You can rest for a while," Crystal said. "We've got plenty of cash to live the good life. Oodles of it from Fairbanks."

"Well, I'll probably give most of it away to the families of the kids we rescued. He got it from their torture."

Crystal nodded. "True. But what would you do with yourself if you're not zipping around the galaxy, saving kids, and getting knocked out cold?"

"I don't know. Run a charity for kids, maybe? But whatever I decide to do, I just want to be with my family." I drew the locket's chain over my head and opened the clasp. The dragon's eye glowed, of course, but I already knew Papa was alive. I reached the chain toward him with the locket dangling. "I don't want this anymore. It's a reminder of being separated from you. If I'm always with you, I won't need it, and it might still be dangerous."

He extended his palm, allowing me to set the locket on it and drop the chain. He closed his fist around it and nodded. "I will destroy it. No one will ever use it against us. Oliver told me about Baranabas's departure making the gems unprotected. He already destroyed the one you gave him."

"Good." I scanned the loving faces around me. Even after so much danger, tragedy, and heartache, I knew it was all worth it. We had rescued hundreds, maybe thousands of slaves, and we had saved billions of lives. I would never regret any of the pain we suffered.

I let out a long sigh. "Thank you, family. Thank you for everything. I hope we can stay together forever."

The door banged open, and Jillian strode in. "Sorry to barge in like this, but I have news. I just returned from the Epsilon system." She looked at me. "And boy is that a long flight ever since you blew up the Zeta stations. Anyway, Mabel gave me a lead on a network of bramble bee mines."

"The same Mabel?" I asked.

"Yep. She's a sneaky one. I'll tell you later how she escaped the Alpha station destruction. Anyway, the lead panned out. I found the mines in the Epsilon system, exported there by Thorne." She set a fist on her hip and scanned us. "So what're we going to do about it?"

"What we always do." After gathering my strength, I rose from the chair, marched to the closet, and pulled my Astral Alliance uniform from the hanger. "Are we going to the Epsilon system on the Nebula Nine or the Astral Dragon?"

"The Astral Dragon," Jillian said. "Echo moved Emerson's brain into the Dragon, so now Sonya and Emerson are a team."

"Perfect." I looked at Papa, Crystal, and Oliver. "What say you?"

"Are you kidding?" Crystal got up and pulled her matching uniform from the closet. "I'm on your six to the edge of the galaxy. I just have to put this on."

Oliver raised a hand. "Same. I'm with you. A hundred percent. My uniform is in the Astral Dragon, so I'll get dressed there."

Papa set a hand on my shoulder. "Are you sure you're well enough to go?"

I nodded. "Well enough to travel. I'll be back in fighting shape soon. You'll see."

"I would be a fool to doubt your resolve." He set his other hand on Crystal's shoulder. "I'll be there to keep all of you out of trouble. We'll all be watching each other's sixes."

"Super," Jillian said. "Good thing I brought these." She tossed me my bracelets. "Catch."

I snatched them out of the air. As I put them on my wrists, I looked at Perdantus. "And what say you, my avian brother?"

Perdantus fluffed his feathers. "As you can see, I am already dressed for travel. We birds have a distinct advantage. We fly without the need of a uniform."

"Oh!" Crystal said. "Now I know what that idiom means."

"What idiom?" I asked.

"Naked as a jaybird!" She covered her eyes and peeked between her fingers. "We've been traveling all this time with a naked crew member!"

While we all laughed, Perdantus fluffed his feathers again, and his chirping tones turned playful. "And I am proud of my birthday suit, my dear family. I am proud of it."

About the Author

Bryan Davis is the author of fantasy/science-fiction novels for youth and adults, including the bestselling Dragons in Our Midst series. Other series include The Oculus Gate, Reapers, Dragons of Starlight, Tales of Starlight, Time Echoes, and Wanted: Superheroes, several of which have been bestsellers.

Bryan was born in 1958 and grew up in the eastern US. From the time he taught himself how to read before school age, through his seminary years and beyond, he has demonstrated a passion for the written word, reading and writing in many disciplines and genres, including theology, fiction, devotionals, poetry, and humor.

Bryan is a graduate of the University of Florida (BS in Industrial Engineering). In high school, he was valedictorian of his class and won various academic awards. He was also a member of the National Honor Society and voted Most Likely to Succeed. He continues to expand his writing education by teaching at relevant writing conferences and conventions.

Bryan was a computer professional for over twenty years before becoming a fulltime author in 2003. He and his wife, Susie, homeschooled their four girls and three boys, and they now work together as an author/editor team.